Suddenly there was a deep, snarling growl, like a wolf on the attack.

A dark blur moved behind the men encircling her. One by one, her tormenters were plucked up and tossed backward into the brush as though they were no more substantial than rag dolls.

Breathless and stunned, Brie stared at her rescuer. He was tall and lean, with shaggy black hair hanging over his collar. His shoulders were wide, his hips narrow, and his legs long. His coppery skin spoke of Indian blood; his eyes were the charged gray of an angry thunderhead. His face was a heart-stopping mixture of angles and planes, high cheekbones, narrow nose, full lips. He was . . . magnificent.

Ask and thou shalt receive. Awestruck, Brie gaped as everything inside her stilled. *It's him!*

She'd never seen the man before, but she knew as surely as she knew her own name that he was, quite literally, the answer to her prayers.

WARRIOR'S SONG

Janis Reams Hudson

Zebra Books
Kensington Publishing Corp.

http://www.zebrabooks.com

ZEBRA BOOKS are published by

Kensington Publishing Corp.
850 Third Avenue
New York, NY 10022

First Printing: March, 1997
10 9 8 7 6 5 4 3 2 1

Printed in the United States of America

Prologue

They were going to lose the ranch.

Despite the warmth of the August night, Brianna Flanigan shivered beneath her bedcovers. Just over three months since her parents had drowned, only another few weeks until time to sell the cattle and replenish their cash, and they weren't going to make it. They were going to lose the Rocking F.

Think! Think!, she commanded herself. *What would Da have done?*

He would fight, that's what Brian Flanigan would do. He had fought, for more than ten years, to build the Rocking F into a lasting legacy for his children. Now, as the oldest child, Brie was responsible, not only for the ranch, but for her five brothers and sisters as well. There had to be a way to keep from losing their home, their heritage.

With her fists wrapped tightly in the sheet, she pressed her knuckles to her lips and prayed. Da and Mother had taught her to stand up for the family and herself, to fight for what was hers against all comers. They had also taught her, Brian with his Catholic ways and Caroline with her Protestant beliefs, to never be ashamed to ask for help.

She needed help now. If she was going to ask, she figured she might as well go straight to the top, because she didn't think anyone else would be able to help her. *God, please send us the help we need to save the ranch. Da and Mother worked so hard all these years, don't let us lose it now, please God. Send us help. Amen.* To be safe, she unclenched the sheet and crossed herself.

At once the icy panic in her chest eased its grip. She would do what she could, and the rest would come. God helped those who helped themselves.

Taking a deep breath, Brie allowed herself to relax. Warmth eased her into sleep.

She dreamed that a man came, tall and dark, strong of body and spirit. With legs braced, he placed himself boldly between the Rocking F and the rest of the world, defending the Flanigans with strength, cunning, and wisdom.

Brie woke feeling safe and protected for the first time in months. She had prayed for help, and God had sent her the dream.

A man would come. A white knight on a charging steed. A hero sent by God to save them.

Chapter One

He figured he was less than an hour from town when he drew in his horse and pulled out his field glasses to survey the road ahead. This close to a town he was likely to meet up with other travelers. He preferred not to. He was a solitary man bent on remaining that way.

There was a birthmark in the shape of a howling wolf's head on his left shoulder blade, so they called him Wolf. Nothing else, just Wolf. But unlike the creature for whom he was named, this Wolf didn't run with a pack. He had never had a den to call his own. No mate. No cubs. He had, however, felt the cruel teeth of an iron trap on his leg.

When he'd finally won freedom from captivity, he had looked upon the world and others of his species with scorn and mistrust, for they did not see him as one of their own. Perhaps he wasn't.

To them, he wasn't a man, he was a half-breed. In his veins ran the blood of warriors. He felt the restless burning there, the urge to fight an enemy he could not find, to defend that which was not his.

He belonged neither in the white man's world, nor the **red**. He was a man without a home, a wolf without a mate. A warrior without a tribe.

He'd had another name once, a real one, but if he'd ever heard it spoken, it was too long ago for him to remember. He didn't know if it was a white or Indian name. He didn't know whether it had been his mother or his father who was Indian, nor from which tribe his parent had come. Neither did he know what had happened to them. He'd been searching for answers for seventeen of his twenty-six years. It was in a town with the unlikely name of New Hope, ironically located along the banks of a river called the Purgatoire, that he hoped to find his answers.

From the hill where he sat he spied three riders following the river below. The brand on their horses caught his attention. The Double Diamond.

He didn't have to check the folded piece of paper in his vest pocket. The Double Diamond brand belonged to the Double Diamond Ranch, which belonged to the man he was looking for.

At the sound of an approaching wagon, the Double Diamond riders down below left the trail beside the river and hid themselves from the crossroad behind a thicket of willow and cottonwood whips.

Wolf didn't need the prickling along the back of his neck to tell him trouble was brewing, but his neck prickled anyway.

Brianna Flanigan steeled herself for the ordeal of crossing the river. Faith, but it seemed she was always having to steel herself for something these days. Raising her five brothers and sisters when she herself was barely nineteen. Bartering for supplies because she didn't have cash money. Facing down the major every time he waved more cash money in front of her than a body could spend in a lifetime, offering to buy the one thing Brie would not part with—the Rocking F Ranch.

Then there was the river. Every time she rode into New Hope or returned home from there, she had to cross the river that had killed her parents last spring.

To be fair, it was usually a tame river, like today. Murky brown but trying to reflect the blue of the sky, the Purgatoire was less than a foot deep and no more than twenty feet wide at the crossing. It flowed smoothly over a sandy bed here, rushed shallowly over gravel and rock there.

But sometimes this tame, life-giving river turned into a killer. Give it an extra foot of snow melting down from the San Juans, throw in a toad-strangler of a thunderstorm across the mesas of the high plains when the river was already nearly out of its banks, and it raged and rushed, defiantly sweeping away anything and everything in its path like a hungry monster. Including, last spring, Brian and Caroline Flanigan.

Brie slowed the team for the crossing.

Next to her on the wagon seat, five-year-old Katy whimpered and buried her face in Brie's lap. "I can't look."

Brie would have stroked her sister's head, but her hands were full of reins. "You don't have to look. We'll be across in no time. The river can't hurt us when it's this shallow."

"I know." Katy nuzzled her face against Brie's thigh. The child did know it was safe to cross the river, but that didn't make her any less afraid. She knew, logically, that she wasn't likely to drown while taking a bath, either, but since her seven-year-old brother had ghoulishly explained what drowning meant, Katy had adamantly refused to allow water to even so much as trickle across her face. Face-scrubbing and hair-washing had become a genuine challenge where Katy was concerned.

"Sing me a song, Brie, so I won't think about it."

To take Katy's mind off her fear, Brie let the Irish roll thick and pure across her tongue. "A song is it you're wantin'?"

Katy giggled at the heavy brogue.

"Faith, she's laughin' a'ready and I haven't even warmed up me pipes." The giggle started with a laughing shriek this time, and Brie eased the team into the river at the shallowest crossing for miles, the spot with the lowest banks. Fortunately for her, the road from here led south directly to Jones Canyon and home.

"How's this, then?" Brie whistled a few notes of one of Katy's favorite songs as the horses pulled the wagon through the water.

Halfway across, Katy forgot her fear and sat up. "Sing it, sing it," she pleaded.

"All right, then, but you'll have to help me." Before Katy had time to realize they had yet to reach the far bank, Brie began. "Hush little baby, don't be sayin' a word. Mama's gonna buy you a pretty red bird. If that pretty red bird won't sing—"

Katy joined in. "Mama's gonna buy you a tambourine."

Smiling, they reached the opposite bank and sang the next verse together. "If that tambourine won't play, Mama's gonna buy you a silver tray."

With a hoarse caw, a crow beside the trail ahead flapped its wings and took off, its black feathers gleaming in the afternoon sun.

"Look!" Katy squealed. "We sang so bad we scared the bird."

Feigning indignation, Brie tilted her nose in the air. "What does an ol' crow know, anyway? We sang beautifully. Didn't you hear him? That was a cry of envy if ever I heard one. More likely it was the horses that scared him off."

A moment later Brie realized she was half right. Horses had scared the crow. But not her horses. From the thick stand of young willows and cottonwoods along the bank burst three riders, whooping and hollering and firing their six-guns into the air.

Brie's wagon team tried to bolt. She bit her tongue on a swear word and struggled to restrain her horses. *Damn fool cowboys,* she thought with disgust, *stinking drunk in the middle of the day.*

"Whoa, there." Swaying in the saddle, one of the riders leaned down and tried to steady the team. He overestimated his balance and fell cursing to the ground.

"Looky what we got here," another one hollered to his friends.

Struggling with the reins, Brie fought the frightened team for control. The wagon jerked and jolted, jarring a squeal out of Katy. The girl threw herself at Brie and wrapped her thin arms tight around Brie's waist. Now Brie had not only the horses to struggle with, but Katy as well. As the team began to settle, the wagon gave a hard lurch. Alarmed, Brie glanced toward the wagon bed to find the third cowboy had jumped aboard.

"Get down!" she cried. "Look what you've done! You've gone and torn open one of my flour sacks, you—" Her words ended in a shriek as she was plucked abruptly from her seat by the man still on horseback. The action broke Katy's hold on Brie. Katy screamed and fell to the ground in the scant space between the hooves of the man's horse and the front wheel of the wagon.

"Katy!" With the metallic taste of terror in her mouth, Brie clawed at the arm that held her. "Katy!"

"Well, doggone," her captor slurred. "Looky there, boys, I dropped one."

"Let me go, you bloomin' blighter!" Brie kicked and squirmed, making the horse dance sideways, thankfully away from Katy. "Katy, run!"

But Katy was too scared to run. She huddled against the wagon wheel, sobbing and crying for Brie.

Brie managed to slip from the man holding her, but there was no escape. Her captor dismounted, and the three men surrounded her, laughing, swaying drunkenly.

"Whooee, she's a hot one, ain't she?"

"I'll show you hot." Brie plowed her right fist into the

nose of the nearest cowboy, the one who'd torn open one of her sacks of flour with his spurs.

The injured man bellowed with rage and clasped his hand to his face. Blood spurted between his fingers. "By Gawd, the little hellcat busted my nose! Hold her for me, fellas. I'm gonna teach Irish Red here a lesson."

Until that instant, Brie hadn't had time to be afraid for herself. Now a shiver of panic raced down her spine. She whirled toward the wagon to grab the horsewhip but was yanked off her feet by the same iron-hewed arm that had dragged her from the wagon. She shrieked in outrage and fear.

"I got her, Harve!"

Brie kicked her captor in the shins and reached behind to claw at his face. With a yelp and a curse, he let go of her. She nearly fell, but another man grabbed her before she hit the ground. She kicked and screamed again, her breath coming harsh now, burning her throat and lungs.

"Hell, Lee, I'll show you how to hold a hellcat." But this second man couldn't hold her long before she squirmed loose again.

Brie whirled to run, intent on leading the men away from Katy, who still crouched, crying, against the wagon wheel. But everywhere Brie turned, another leering face loomed, another outstretched pair of hands groped. The men hooted with laughter and circled her, drawing closer and closer until the metallic taste of fear threatened to gag her.

Suddenly there was a deep, snarling growl, like a wolf on the attack. A dark blur moved behind the men encircling her. One by one, her tormenters were plucked up and tossed backward into the brush as though they were no more substantial than rag dolls.

Breathless and stunned, Brie stared at her rescuer. He was tall and lean, with shaggy black hair hanging over his collar. His shoulders were wide, his hips narrow, and his legs long. His coppery skin spoke of Indian blood; his eyes were the charged gray of an angry thunderhead. His face was a heart-stopping mixture of angles and planes, high cheekbones, narrow nose, full lips. He was . . . magnificent.

Ask and thou shalt receive. Awestruck, Brie gaped as everything inside her stilled. *It's him!*

She'd never seen the man before, but she knew as surely as she knew her own name that he was, quite literally, the answer to her prayers.

Then he was besieged as the three cowboys recovered from shock and jumped him all at once. Fists, curses, and grunts flew thick and fast, but it was no real contest, even at three to one. The cowboys were sloppy drunk. The dark stranger was lethal. He fought hard and dirty, using fists, boots, and elbows. He took his share of punches, but in what seemed like mere seconds, the three cowhands lay beaten and groaning. Brie had never seen anything like it.

The stranger gave the three men a look of disgust, then bent and retrieved his hat. After whacking it against his thigh twice to knock off the dust, he settled it on his head and turned to Brie. "Are you ladies all right?"

Sometime during the brief fight Katy's tears had ceased. At his use of the word "ladies" she giggled.

Somewhat dazed by all that had happened in such a short time, Brie managed to nod. "We're fine, thanks to you."

The three men began to rouse. Brie shook herself and reached for the shotgun beneath the wagon seat. When she turned back around, two of the men were on their feet and heading for her rescuer. "No half-breed bastard's gonna get the best of me, by Gawd," one muttered.

Brie pulled back both hammers on the old double-barreled shotgun and curled her finger across both triggers. "Back off."

One man's eyes bugged and his mouth fell slack. The other put his hands out as if to ward her off. "Easy, lady. We didn't mean no harm, did we, boys?"

"No harm at all, Shorty," another one slurred.

The third man staggered to his feet. "We 'uz jus' havin' a little fun, that's all."

"Fun's over," Brie announced coldly. "Get up on those Double Diamond horses and ride out. Rest assured I'll be having a little chat with the marshall about this."

"Ah, come on, honey, we—"

"You heard the lady," the stranger said coldly. "Mount up and ride."

"We're goin', we're goin'," grumbled the one called Harve.

"Well hurry up about it," Brie snapped. "This shotgun's heavy and my finger's starting to sweat. I might accidentally pull a trigger any second."

If she hadn't been so angry, and more than a little shaken, Brie might have laughed at the effect of her words. The three drunken cowboys seemed to turn stone cold sober right before her eyes. In a rush, they scrambled into their saddles and lit out across the river toward town.

The stranger who'd stopped to help watched them go. When their dust settled, he turned back to Brie. "Friends of yours?"

"Not hardly." She eased the hammers on the shotgun back to half-cocked. Propping the gun against the wagon wheel, she knelt in the dirt and helped Katy to her feet. "Are you okay? You didn't get hurt when you fell?"

Katy's lower lip trembled. "I got scared."

"Me, too," Brie said, hugging her sister. "But we're all right now, aren't we?" Brie released her and leaned back to brush the dirt from Katy's skirt and surreptitiously check for injuries.

"We're all right," Katy confirmed. A dimple winked from the chubby fold of one cheek. "The nice man helped."

"Yes." Brie stood and faced the stranger once more. "We're beholden to you, mister. I don't know—You're bleeding!"

Wolf heard her plainly enough that he brought a hand

to his throbbing cheek and felt the blood, but his mind was still trapped by hearing the little one call him a nice man. No one had ever called him nice. Probably because he wasn't. It was for damn sure that no little girl had ever smiled at him. The idea was as foreign to him as if his horse had sat up and read Scripture from the Bible.

"And your shirt's torn," the woman added. Clucking her tongue like a mother hen over a stray chick, she pulled a white handkerchief from the drawstring handbag on the wagon seat and approached him. Before he fully realized what she was about, she reached up and pressed the handkerchief to the cut on his cheek.

Wolf winced. Not so much from the pain in his cheek as from the soft, almost imperceptible, brush of her fingers on his face. If he'd ever felt anything so soft before, or so gentle, he would have remembered.

"I'm sorry," she murmured, easing the pressure on his cheek but not taking her hand away.

Wolf wasn't used to being touched, not like this. It made nerves jump around in the pit of his stomach. He didn't much like the feeling at all. In irritation, he stepped back from her.

There was a heartbeat of silence as their eyes met, his hard, defiant, hers open and inviting. Then the woman became all business, folding the handkerchief and stuffing it into the pocket of her skirt. "The bleeding's almost stopped, but you'll be coming home with us so I can clean the cut and sew up those tears in your shirt."

Wolf eyed her carefully, struggling to keep his expression blank. Funny, but he'd never had to struggle with that before. But then, he'd never seen a woman like her before, either. Her skin was as pale as cream and probably just as smooth, although he knew he'd never be finding out for himself. She might have looked like a painting, so perfect was her skin, except for the surprising dust of freckles across her cheeks and nose.

Then there was her hair, fiery red-orange, like the leaves

of certain trees in the fall. She had it pulled back and tied at the base of her neck, but pieces of it here and there had sprung free. The whole mass looked like it wanted to burst loose of the confines of the blue ribbon holding it in place. As red as flames. He wondered if it would burn his hands if he touched it, but that, too, was something he'd never be finding out.

Her eyes were the deep green of a mountain pine forest. They were looking at him now like they could see straight into his soul. Hell, she'd be wasting her time looking for his soul. He didn't have one, or so he'd been told often enough. No soul, no heart, and nothing but cold steel for nerves.

The light of battle still glowed in those green depths. Would they sparkle like that for a man? For him? Dangerous thought. Crazy thought.

Her hands, hell, all of her was as dainty as a china tea cup. She looked like a stiff wind would blow her into the next county. Yet she'd fought those men like a she-cat and hadn't done a half-bad job of it, either. She'd hefted that shotgun like she knew how to use it and was fully prepared to let loose with both barrels.

Contradictions, he thought. As delicate as a robin's egg, as tough as old boot leather. And obviously without a lick of sense. "Don't you know any better than to invite a man like me home with you?"

The woman arched her brow. "You mean a stranger who jumps into the middle of someone else's fight to save my sister and me from Lord knows what might have happened to us?" She grinned at him. "They might come back, you know. You wouldn't want all your hard work to go for nothing, would you? You probably ought to follow us home just to be sure we make it. While you're there I can tend to your cut and the tears in your shirt."

"I've had cuts and tears before."

"Not because of me you haven't." The woman turned and gave the little one a boost onto the wagon seat. "Up with you, Katy-girl. The nice man is probably hungry. We can thank him for his help by feeding him supper, don't you think?"

As the woman followed the girl up onto the seat, the little one looked up at her. "Do you think Saint Pat will like him?"

The woman gathered the reins in her small hands and threaded the traces through her fingers. She looked over her shoulder at Wolf, then smiled at the girl. "I think Saint Pat will adore him." With a snap of the reins, she urged the team to move out.

Wolf stood in the dirt beside the road and frowned. He wasn't about to follow her home like some damned puppy on a string. He was not a nice man, his cuts and tears would be just fine without her help, he didn't give a damn about supper, and no one had ever adored him in his entire life. He didn't want to be adored. He wanted to be left alone so he could go on about the business of finding his past.

What kind of woman invited a stranger home to supper? She didn't look stupid, nor did she look like a loose-moraled woman. She looked like a lady. Not that Wolf had any experience with ladies, except that they always seemed to be pulling their skirts aside, or crossing to the other side of the street, when he came near. Hadn't she heard those men call him a half-breed bastard? Didn't she realize that's exactly what he was?

She was loco, that's all there was to it. Loco, pretty as a picture, and pushy. She'd driven that wagon out as if she knew for a fact that he would follow.

With disgust, he mounted up and followed her into the mouth of the canyon ahead. Not because she'd told him to, and not because he wanted his face and shirt tended to by those gentle fingers. Not because she and the little one thought he was nice or because someone named Saint Pat might adore him. Not because she'd offered him supper. Not because the song she'd sung had struck some chord of memory that he couldn't quite pull forth. And damn sure not because those green eyes of hers tugged at something inside him that he hadn't even known existed. What that something was, he didn't know, didn't care.

He went because she was right, those three yahoos were just drunk enough to change their minds on the way to town and turn around and come back after her. From her attitude he could only assume that she had no idea what could have happened to her in the hands of men too far gone on whiskey.

Wolf shook his head, at her, at himself. He had no business getting mixed up in her troubles, but he knew himself well enough to know that he had no choice. If there was one thing in the world he could not tolerate, it was seeing a grown man use his strength against those smaller and weaker. When Wolf had heard the child scream earlier, the old scars on his back had twitched as if newly healed. Even now he had to fight to block out the past that rose up to haunt him.

Blocking the past was easier a short time later when, nearly two miles into the canyon, Wolf followed the wagon around a bend. Before him stretched a long, wide basin of rich grass where two other streams, one from the southeast, one from the southwest, joined the main stream meandering the length of the basin.

The ranch headquarters sat on a low rise at the base of a bluff. The two-story frame house looked new with its fresh white paint and dark green shutters. The covered porch across the front invited a man to sit on the swing or the rocking chair and gaze out over the land. Someone had planted cottonwoods around the house to lend shade in the summer.

There was a barn, several corrals where a few horses and cows dozed in the heat, a small adobe—probably the original homestead, Wolf guessed. Sheds, a large vegetable garden, and a small, neat apple orchard spoke of careful tending.

Someone had built something good here. Wolf had never had a home, had never even come close to having one. Never wanted one, for that matter, and wouldn't know what to do with one if he had it. He'd seen plenty of them, but none had ever tugged at him the way this place did. He didn't like the feeling.

A big red dog and two young red-headed boys bounded out of the barn. From the house came an auburn-haired girl of about twelve wiping her hands on a white apron. Wolf had never seen so much red hair in his life.

The woman pulled the wagon up before the house.

"Who's that?" The oldest boy, around nine, eyed Wolf with narrowed, hostile eyes. A territorial look if Wolf had ever seen one.

The woman set the brake on the wagon and secured the reins. "This is a friend. I've invited him to supper." She climbed down from the wagon, then helped the little one down before turning to face Wolf. "Please, won't you get down? You can water your horse there at the trough." She motioned toward the nearest corral. Just inside sat a long watering trough with a water pump at one end.

He could water his horse just as easy at the stream a quarter mile away and be on about his business. He'd done what he set out to do—he'd seen them home. There was no reason to stay. He didn't belong in a place like this. He didn't belong anywhere.

Wolf touched the brim of his hat. "Thanks just the same, ma'am, but—"

"Faith, but where are my manners?" the woman said, interrupting him. "We never even introduced ourselves. I'm Brianna Flanigan, but my friends call me Brie. This is Katy," she said, indicating the little girl whose scream had brought Wolf running to their aid. "That's Tessa on the porch. The youngest boy is Rory, and the oldest is Sullivan. We call him Sully."

"And this is Saint Pat," little Katy said, her hand buried in the long hair on the back of the big red dog's neck.

"That's short for Saint Patrick. We named him that 'cause he got rid of all the snakes, just like the real Saint Patrick did over in Ireland."

"Where's Elly?" the woman, Brianna, asked the girl on the porch.

"She's putting the dumplings in the pot."

"Run and tell her to make sure there's plenty, and while you're there set an extra place. Mr. . . ." The woman, Brianna, looked at Wolf expectantly. "What should we call you?"

He answered reluctantly. "Name's Wolf, ma'am."

She blinked—not an unusual reaction to his name— then smiled. "It's pleased we are to be meeting you, Mr. Wolf."

He nearly smiled at the Irish brogue growing in her voice. "No mister. Just Wolf."

"Well, Just Wolf, won't you get down and light a spell?" That quick, a slight Texas drawl replaced the Irish. "Elly's dumplings are guaranteed to melt in your mouth. Supper's the least we can offer after what you did for us."

"I appreciate the offer, ma'am, but—"

"Brie. My name is Brie."

Frustrated, Wolf tried again. "You don't owe me anything. I'll just be riding—"

"You said it yourself—what if those men come back?"

The lady didn't play fair. The men hadn't taken kindly to losing the fight to a half-breed, their three to his one. If they were riled enough, or got any drunker than they were, they might come back.

"What men?" Sullivan, the oldest boy, demanded.

"We ran into a little trouble on the road," Brie explained.

"Double Diamond riders, I'll bet," Sullivan said hotly.

"It's nothing to be worrying about, Sully."

"Then how come *he's* here?"

"Sullivan Adare Flanigan! Mind your tone. *He* has a name, and 'tis Wolf," Brie said, the Irish creeping into

her speech again. "And he's here because I invited him.
You'll not be makin' him feel unwelcome with yer surli-
ness."

"What happened to his face?"

"Faith, but he's not a tree stump to be talked about as
if he couldn't hear."

"There was three of 'em, Sully!" Katy's green eyes lit
with excitement. "An' they was big—"

"*Were* big," Brie corrected with a roll of her eyes.

"—and tall and mean, but Wolf whipped 'em good, he
did. I think he's our knight Brie promised."

Unease crept across Wolf's scalp. Great. She'd promised
a knight, and like a fool, *he'd* ridden in.

Sully scoffed. "He's no knight."

"No." Rory, the youngest boy, eyed Wolf. A slow smile
revealed a missing front tooth. "Who needs a knight? He's
a *warrior.*"

Wolf decided to ignore the talk. It was nothing to him.
He was nobody's knight or warrior, but if the kid wanted
to think so, he'd let him. A man didn't always like to admit
the truth, and the truth, when he got right down to it, was
that he was nothing more than a saddle bum. It suited
him fine.

With narrowed eyes, Wolf searched the area for evidence
of a man. A father, husband, older brother, anyone who
could look out for the woman and children. "You live here
alone?" he asked Brie while Katy regaled the others with
a slightly exaggerated version of what had happened.

Brie's laughter rang pure and sweet and did funny things
to his breathing. "Alone? There are six of us, Mr. Wolf.
There is no such thing as alone on the Rocking F."

"I told you," he said with a snarl. "No mister. Just Wolf."
Surely there was a man around. She and these kids couldn't
manage a ranch on their own. "Who runs things around
here?"

Brie arched a brow. "I do."

"I do!" The oldest boy, Sully, stepped forward, chest

puffed out like a banty rooster. Then he grimaced. "At least, when I'm older, I will. But I'm the man of the house now that Da's gone."

"Gone?" Wolf asked sharply.

"Dead," Brie stated quietly. "Both of our parents were killed last spring."

Wolf eyed the group before him critically. "Last spring? You expect me to believe the five of you—"

"Six counting Elly," Brie offered, her eyes flashing green defiance. "And yes, we live here alone and run this ranch. Are you staying for supper or not?"

Wolf opened his mouth to say not only no, but hell no, he wasn't about to stay, but just then little Katy turned loose of the dog and came to stand beside Wolf's horse. She reached out and put her hand on his boot. "Please stay, Mr. Wolf. Saint Pat wants you to stay."

Hell. Six kids. Living alone, trying to run a ranch. Being hassled by drunk cowboys. Damnation, what had he gotten himself into?

Supper. Only that, he assured himself. He couldn't remember the last time he'd had a real meal. If the trouble-makers hadn't shown by the time Wolf had eaten, chances were, they wouldn't come at all.

He swung down from the saddle, and the little one, Katy, clapped and squealed. "He's staying, he's staying!"

Brie breathed a sigh of relief and turned toward the wagon to start unloading the supplies she'd bought in town. She'd been afraid Wolf wouldn't stay. "Rory," she called to her youngest brother. "Rescuing damsels in distress is thirsty work. Why don't you get Mi—Wolf a nice cold dipper of water?"

"Okay." Seven-year-old Rory Flanigan flashed his snaggle-toothed grin and dashed toward the well.

"What happened to the flour?" Tessa asked, peering into the wagon bed.

"A slight mishap," Brie answered.

"The bad man busted it," Katy proclaimed solemnly.

"Leave that one in the wagon," Brie said tersely. Under her breath she added, "The major will be replacing that sack tomorrow if I have to dump what's left of it over his head."

Wolf heard her mutter and bit his tongue to keep from questioning her. How many majors could there be in the New Hope area? One. He'd checked. But he wouldn't ask about the man he'd come to find. The fewer people who knew why Wolf was here, the better. Because if United States Army Major John Palmer, Retired, turned out to be the man he sought, Wolf was going to kill him.

Chapter Two

Before Wolf's eyes, Brianna Flanigan turned into a whirlwind of activity, issuing orders with the sharp command of a drill sergeant. Red-headed children flew in all directions to unload the wagon and accomplish the other tasks she set for them.

Amid all the activity, Wolf led his horse to the corral. There he watered the animal, checked his hooves, and loosened the saddle.

While at the water pump Wolf splashed water over his face and neck and cleaned the cut on his cheek. Better to do it himself rather than let her touch him again. It was just a little cut, nothing worth fussing over. He'd done worse to himself with his straight razor.

Leaving his horse in the corral, Wolf crossed to the wagon. In addition to the broken flour sack, there were three other sacks of flour to unload, each one weighing around twenty-five pounds. He lifted two in one arm and grabbed the third with the other hand, wondering how these kids managed when no one was around. "Where do you want these?" He turned with the bags to find all six

Flanigans—including the one cooking the dumplings whom he hadn't met yet, Elly—gaping at him. Leery, Wolf stared back, wondering what the devil they were staring at. Did they not want him touching their damn flour? It wouldn't be the first time someone had been appalled that a half-breed had touched what was theirs, but Wolf hadn't expected such a reaction from these kids.

He was going soft, that was it. He should have known better than to let his guard slip and assume he would be accepted like any other man. Suddenly furious with himself, he glared at the group before him. "Something wrong?" he taunted, daring anyone to say aloud that they didn't want a dirty half-breed touching their property.

"Gallopin' goosefeathers!" The youngest boy stepped forward, eyes wide. "Even Da couldn't lift three sacks of flour at once."

The boy's words threw Wolf. They were staring at him because he could lift three sacks of flour at once? That was all?

"Rory," Brie said, finally looking around at the other children. "Everyone, time to wash up for supper. Soap and water are on the bench at the back door. Wolf, thank you. You can bring the flour into the kitchen."

Rory ignored his sister and stared at Wolf in awe. "Can you lift four?"

Once again the urge to laugh struck Wolf, and once again he strangled it. The joke was there somewhere, and when revealed, it would surely be on him. The joke was always on him. "If I have to," he told the boy in answer to his question.

"Golly!" Rory whispered in awe.

Wolf wondered if he was being unfair to suspect these kids of harboring the kind of resentment for his type, for half-breeds, that he had run into all his life.

Hell, what difference did it make what they thought? They were just a bunch of kids, and he wouldn't be hanging around longer than it took to eat the promised meal. He wouldn't even be doing that, but for a gentle touch on his face and a pair of deep green eyes.

Damn. He'd never been a fool for a woman before.

He followed Brianna Flanigan past the kids at the washstand and in through the back door into the kitchen. She directed him to set the flour sacks down beside the flour barrel in the corner.

"How are you going to lift the sacks to empty them into the barrel?" he asked.

Brie smiled. "We'll manage. I'll see to that cut on your cheek now." From a nearby shelf she took a small brown bottle in one hand and a rag in the other.

"That's not necessary," he said a little more sharply than he'd intended.

Brie pursed her lips. "Tell me something, Wolf. Why is it that a man seems to enjoy the fighting without a whimper over cuts and bruises, but pales at the thought of a little dab of medicine? It will only hurt a minute."

Wolf scowled. Did she think he minded a little pain? "It won't hurt at all," he told her gruffly. Not compared to what he'd gone through growing up.

"That's the spirit." Before he knew what she was about, she'd poured some of the contents of the bottle onto the rag and touched it to his cheek.

It stung like fire, but Wolf knew the pain was not revealed in his eyes or on his face. That was one of his earliest lessons in life—never show pain. He'd learned it well, for to show pain had been to invite more. Concealing pain was second nature to him.

"There." She capped the bottle. "We're ready for supper now. Just follow me."

Feeling awkward, Wolf followed her into a dining room, where a long table was set and laden with food. He'd eaten chicken and dumplings once in a café down in Texas, and he remembered the smell. It made his mouth water.

"You'll sit here at this end."

Wolf paused five feet away from the her, stunned. When

she had offered to feed him supper, he hadn't thought . . . he'd assumed . . . Hell, he didn't know what he'd assumed, but it had never occurred to him that he would be invited into the house to sit down and eat at the table with her family.

Wolf knew nothing of families, not really. He'd never had one. The closest he'd ever come to even being around a family was on some of the ranches where he'd worked, but none of them had ever asked him in to eat with them.

What the hell had he gotten himself into?

It felt . . . strange. And if he were honest with himself, it felt scary—but he wasn't sure he was ready to be that honest. He was twenty-six years old and had never sat down at a table to eat supper, or any other meal, with a family. It was a little like the first time he rode a horse. He'd been nine, and by the standards of the time, much older than most kids in the West when they learned to ride. But he'd gritted his teeth and hung on, and he had survived.

That's all he had to do now, hang on and survive. He didn't think he'd be gritting his teeth, what with the smell of chicken and dumplings wafting his way. But hell, who would have thought it? Wolf, eating supper with a family.

Not exactly sure what to do with all the utensils laid out beside his plate, he decided to wait and watch. The plate before him was white and spotless. He'd never eaten off anything so . . . pretty.

Suddenly terrified that he would do something wrong and make a fool of himself—after all, what did a half-breed bastard know about table manners, he thought with disgust—he kept his hands in his lap and looked around the table.

They were staring at him. Wolf's shoulders tensed. All six Flanigans were eyeing him with varying degrees of surprise, suspicion, curiosity, and delight, depending on the person doing the staring. The delight was from little Katy, seated next to him, a pile of books in her chair to make her tall enough to reach the table.

It was embarrassing having a little kid like that grinning at him all the time. And what the hell were they all staring at, he wondered defensively.

"Sully," Brianna said. "Would you say grace, please?"

Wolf froze. Christ, he thought, being deliberately irreverent. They were going to pray. Something inside him sensed an ambush. The scars on his back stung as if freshly delivered. He'd be damned if he'd sit there and take part in—

Beside him, Katy reached for his hand. Hell, how did a man say no to those damn dimples? He would have tried, but everyone was joining hands around the table, and they were all looking at him expectantly. Knowing he'd regret it, he gave her his hand.

The feel of her tiny hand in his struck a nerve beside his heart with a curious mixture of pain and yearning. To be that innocent, that trusting. That soft. Had he ever been that young?

No. He hadn't. Not ever.

Rory, on Wolf's other side, held his hand out. *Hell.* Wolf took the boy's hand. The boy flashed his snaggle-toothed grin at him.

Hell and damnation.

From the other end of the table, Sully's eyes, a lighter shade of green than Brie's, sparked with mischief. "Good bread, good meat, good God, let's eat."

"Sullivan Adare Flanigan!" Brie cried in horror. "You'll have our guest thinking we're raising a bunch of heathens."

Rory snickered, as did Tessa. Elly pursed her lips and glared disapproval at Sully, while Katy merely looked confused.

Brie took a slow, deep breath, then closed her eyes. "Dear Lord, we sincerely hope You were busy taking care of a terrible plague or pestilence somewhere else in the world just now and were too busy to hear young Master Sullivan's poor idea of a joke. And if You weren't busy, Lord, and You did hear him, we sincerely pray that You have a good sense of humor. Sully meant no offense," she added, her voice softening. "We thank You, Lord, for the grass that nourishes the cattle, and for this food before us that will nourish our bodies. We thank You for this glorious day, for our health, for our home. And we thank You for sending Wolf to help us. In the name of the Father, the Son, and the Holy Ghost, Amen."

"Amen," came the chorus from around the table.

Wolf sat for what seemed like an eternity, staring down the length of the table at Brianna Flanigan. What the hell kind of prayer was that? How dare she mention his name and her God's in the same breath? The very idea infuriated him. The damned woman had a lot to learn about God, as far as Wolf was concerned. Or a lot to learn about Wolf, but he wouldn't be around long enough for her to learn anything about him.

If God existed, Wolf could assure Brianna Flanigan that He damn sure didn't have a sense of humor.

Everyone was staring at him again. Frowning, he looked down and realized he still held Katy and Rory's hands while the others had long since let go of each other. Wolf let go of Katy and Rory as if he'd been holding burning coals.

Brie was intrigued by the stranger in their midst. The man called Wolf—"No mister. Just Wolf."—was a puzzle, and Brie had never been able to resist a puzzle. He was tall, maybe just a little over six feet, strong and leanly muscled. Certainly more than capable of taking care of himself. He could scowl fierce enough to stop a hen from laying, and his voice could be as curt and terse as any she'd ever heard.

His eyes were the key, she thought. Turbulent and gray, they could be blank one minute, cold the next, but sometimes, if she was quick enough to catch it, they appeared filled with questions over things that didn't seem curious to Brie at all. Like when Katy spoke to him. Why should that puzzle him? Her speech was clear; it wasn't as if she was difficult to understand.

Puzzles aside, she'd never seen a man handle himself as well as he'd done when coming to her and Katy's aid that afternoon. He'd taken on three men and dispatched them easily. Sure, they'd been drunk, but she'd felt their strength herself and knew that most men would not have been able to handle all three of them with Wolf's apparent ease.

His hands were broad and long-fingered, strong and sure and capable. His face . . . that strikingly handsome face had taken a battering on her behalf.

So, too, had his shirt, she reminded herself, and she'd promised to mend it. She would get to it as soon as supper was over.

"More chicken and dumplings, Wolf?" Elly held the nearly empty bowl out toward him.

No smile, no compliment, simply a nod and a gruff thank you, and Wolf took the bowl and served himself a third helping. Faith, but Brie did love to see a man with a good appetite sitting at their table again.

She missed her parents fiercely. Not a day went by that she didn't ache for the loss of the two most important people in her life. But the pain was dull now, after these many months, rather than the sharp, knifelike stabs of agony that had threatened to cripple her those first weeks after their deaths. If she hadn't been forced to see to her younger brothers and sisters, it might have taken her months to get on with her life.

Da, Mother, we all miss you still. You'd like Wolf. He seems a strange man, but a good one.

At least, Brie assumed he was a good man. Why else would he have stopped to help her and Katy?

When supper was over, Brie picked up her sewing basket and led Wolf to the front porch, where she could keep an eye on the kids doing outdoor chores, and hear the others cleaning up the kitchen inside.

"That was a fine meal, Miss Elly," Wolf said as he left the house. "I've never had finer."

Elly blushed. "Why, how nice of you to say so."

"Not nice, just the truth."

"Thank you." Elly beamed at him.

"Lookit Elly," Rory cried. "She's blushin'! Elly's blushing, Elly's blushing!"

The girl blushed harder. "I am not," she hotly denied.

"Are too! Wait'll James finds out!"

"Oh, you—"

Brie changed her mind about wanting to be able to hear the kids in the kitchen and shut the front door sharply to save Elly any more embarrassment in front of Wolf, and possibly save Wolf any discomfort from the teasing. "Don't pay them any mind," she told Wolf easily as she sat on the porch swing.

"Thank you for supper, Miss Flanigan, I—"

"Brie. I told you, my friends call me Brie."

"A woman in your position, with all these kids to look after, not to mention a ranch, you'd do best to use a little caution in who you call friend. I'm just a drifter passing through, that's all. Like I said, thanks for supper. I'll be on my way now."

"You may have so many friends that you have no need of another," Brie said tartly, "but I don't.

Wolf merely stared at her as if she were a curiosity.

"I'm sorry," she said. "That was rude of me. I'm glad you enjoyed supper. It was little enough to repay you for what you did for Katy and me this afternoon."

"I told you, I don't need to be repaid."

"Maybe not, but I have a need to do something to thank you."

"The meal was plenty. I'll just be on my way now," he said again.

"Oh, but you can't go yet! I've not mended your shirt."

"No need, ma'am. It's an old shirt. I've got another."

Brie smiled slightly. "You might as well sit down and

give me your shirt. If you don't, I'll call Katy, and she'll ask you to let her mend it." Even from where she sat she could see his shoulders tense. "I've already realized that you can't quite say no to her. Believe me, your shirt will be much better off if I mend it. Katy hasn't quite mastered the use of needle and thread yet."

Wolf stared at her another moment, then shook his head. "Never let it be said that I turned down a lady. You wanna waste your time and thread on this old shirt, I guess you can." He pulled off his shirt, revealing the top half of his faded red longjohns underneath, and handed it to her.

Brie's smile widened. "Thank you." She studied the split shoulder seam and the two rips in the front of the shirt, then cut a length of thread from her spool. She took her time selecting a needle from her case, then even more time threading the needle. She was not in a hurry to finish this chore, for that meant he would leave. She wasn't ready for him to leave.

"You're just drifting, you said?" she asked, keeping a carefully casual tone.

He leaned against the nearest porch post. "That's what I said."

"I didn't mean to sound as though I were prying," she told him quickly. "I just thought to make conversation, that's all."

"Conversation." The word came with a snort.

Undaunted, Brie smiled. "Yes, you know. That's where one person says something or asks a friendly question, and the other person responds. You've probably heard of it, maybe even engaged in it yourself once or twice. Some people call it talking."

Another long, silent stare. Then, "Most people talk too much anyway."

Brie sighed. This was getting her nowhere. Perhaps she should just come out and say what was on her mind. "Do you know anything about ranching?"

"Why?"

"Because I'm writing a book!" she exclaimed. "Faith, you're a suspicious one, aren't you? All right, let's try another question. Are you by chance looking for a job?"

"No."

"Oh." Disappointment came immediately, surprising her with its strength. Brie finished repairing the torn shoulder seam, then tied off her thread, snipped it with her scissors, and moved on to the first tear on the front of his shirt. The Lord may have sent Wolf to help her, but it looked like it was up to her to figure out how to get the man to stay.

"You lookin' to hire someone to work this place?"

Brie looked up quickly. "Someone to help out. Are you interested?"

"No."

"Oh." Brie took a deep breath. "If you're not interested in the job, you're still welcome to bed down in the barn for the night."

Wolf shook his head again. "Thanks, but I have business in town that I need to be about."

Disappointment was too mild a word for what Brie felt. Desperation was more appropriate, she thought as she looked down at the shirt in her hands. "I'll just finish this, then, so you can be on your way."

What was she going to do? She had to have help. The major's tactics were only going to become bolder, meaner. He would stop at nothing to run the Flanigans off their land. It was hard admitting that to herself, but the admission was long overdue. Supplies weren't the only reason she'd gone to town today. She'd also gone to report finding two of her calves shot. On the way home she'd been accosted by three of the major's men.

Holy Mary, Mother of God, what are we going to do?

"Is everything okay, Brie?" Tessa asked from the front door.

"Everything's fine, just fine." Brie forced a smile as she kept her eyes on the needle she was pushing through the fabric of Wolf's shirt. "If we still have some of those oatmeal cookies left, why don't you wrap some up for Wolf to take with him?"

Fifteen minutes later, with his shirt freshly mended and a half dozen oatmeal cookies in his saddlebag, the man known only as Wolf mounted up and rode out.

With the rest of her family standing around her, Brie stood on the bottom porch step and watched him go. Everything within her urged her to run after him, to bring him back. He had to stay and help them!

But he wasn't staying. He'd been her last hope. No one in town would work for a woman. She'd learned that lesson sharply during the past months. The Flanigans were, as usual, on their own.

Brie squared her shoulders. So be it. She would find a way to make the major leave them in peace. She had to. She would never surrender their land to his greedy hands. Never.

Chapter Three

The sun was setting, outlining the very tips of the San Juan Mountains far in the west, by the time Wolf crossed the Purgatoire River again and rode the twelve miles to town. The cloak of dusk softened the sharp, hard edges of New Hope, Colorado, but Wolf didn't let it fool him. He'd been in too many small dusty towns like this one in his days to think New Hope would be any different, any better, any more tolerant of a man with mixed blood than any other town he'd ridden through. New Hope would probably be even less tolerant of half-breeds than many other towns. It wasn't that many years ago that the Cheyenne controlled this area. There were still a lot of hard feelings toward Indians.

None of it concerned Wolf, however. He wasn't interested in the opinions of others. All he asked was to be left alone. Generally the look in his eyes got him that wish without too much trouble.

He rode easily down the main street until he found the livery, where he stabled his horse. With his saddlebags slung over his shoulder, he walked back three blocks to a hotel—*the* hotel—and got a room. The gold of his coin made most people overlook the color of his skin; this time was no different.

After leaving his saddlebags in his room, he went in search of a drink. After meeting up with Brianna Flanigan and her family, he could damn sure use one. He also wanted to pick up any local gossip he could about Major Palmer. A saloon was as good a place as any for hearing talk, and better than most.

From the number of men riding in by twos and threes, it appeared that every cowhand and farmer in the area had come to swell the population of New Hope in celebration of Saturday night.

New Hope might boast only one hotel, but there was no shortage of saloons. Wolf counted six within two blocks of the hotel. He bypassed a couple of the rowdier establishments—the Red Garter and the Bucket o' Blood—before finding one that, while crowded, appeared calmer.

The Branch Water Saloon near the far end of the street was, like most of its sisters, long, narrow, and smokey. Business this Saturday night was booming. Wolf eyed the patrons, searching for the three cowhands he'd tangled with that afternoon, but he didn't see them. He found a vacant spot at the bar and ordered a shot of whiskey, drank it down, and ordered another. This one he would sip while enjoying the fire in his belly kindled by the first one.

Wolf thought about sitting in on a card game—a good way to catch up on local gossip—but decided against it for tonight. He didn't know yet how these people took to half-breeds. The bartender had served him with no problem, but the three cowhands had made cracks today.

Ordinarily Wolf wouldn't give a rat's ass what anyone thought about him. He'd learned long ago to stop caring, to stop trying to make friends, stop trying to belong somewhere. Anywhere. He belonged nowhere. That's the way he liked it.

But he didn't want any trouble in New Hope until he'd

learned what he could about the major and figured out if he was the man who twenty-two years ago had sold a terrified four-year-old half-breed boy to a sick, vicious, traveling preacher who liked, among other things, to beat up on anyone smaller than himself. If the major was the one, Wolf would have to get him to talk. Who had the boy been to the major? Son? Grandson? Brother?

Wolf wanted answers, and Major Palmer was his last hope.

The investigator Wolf had hired who had come up with Palmer's name had been fairly thorough. As a captain in the Union Army, Palmer had fought in the war and come out a major. He was a widower with a widowed daughter and two grandchildren, a boy and a girl, all of whom lived on the Double Diamond.

Palmer had spent the years after the war in Denver, doing well for himself speculating in cattle, buying into the Denver Stockyards. He'd amassed a fortune. Then he'd moved his family to this southeast corner of Colorado before there'd been a New Hope. Now he owned a thriving ranch and the only bank in town.

Talk was, there'd been another bank a few years back, but when it came to mentioning what had happened to the other banker, men clammed up and darted their gazes back and forth.

Wolf sipped his second shot of whiskey and listened to the talk around him. By the time he finished his drink he'd overheard enough to know that Major Palmer was the most powerful man in the area, both feared and respected by most. In addition to the bank, he owned the livery where Wolf had stabled his horse and the hotel. It came as a small shock to hear the men around him openly talking about Palmer trying to get his hands on the Flanigans' ranch. No one seemed concerned on behalf of those six kids. The general consensus was that they would be fixed for life if they sold out to Palmer. They'd be fools to hold out much longer.

Having heard enough for one night, Wolf gave up his spot at the bar and headed for the door. The fight that afternoon was wearing on him. His cheek hurt, his ribs ached, and he was dog tired. This would be his first night to sleep in a bed in weeks and he was looking forward to it.

In an alley several blocks down from the saloon, Shorty Windholm was taking a leak against the side of the barber shop. "Sumbitch, splashed m' goddamn boots again."

Ah, hell. It wasn't the first time, and it wouldn't be the last. He was five feet ten. They didn't call him Shorty because of his height.

He finished his business and was fumbling with the front of his pants as he rounded the corner and saw the man coming out of the Branch Water. Shit if it wasn't that friggin' half-breed.

Shorty, Harve, and Lee had finished off their bottle after their encounter with the half-breed earlier in the day. On the long ride to town, they'd finished off another, too. In the process they'd managed to convince themselves that no one man—especially not a friggin' half-breed—could have bested all three of them. It couldn't have happened that way. It must have been the half-breed hassling the pretty little red-haired gal. Harve, Lee, and Shorty had rescued her and run the bastard off. That's how it must have been. Nothing else made sense to their puffed-up egos and whiskey-numbed minds.

Liking the new version much better, they told it over and over as they'd passed the bottle back and forth and meandered their way toward town. They told it so many times that they convinced themselves it must be true.

"We're goddamned heroes," Harve had declared. Lee and Shorty agreed.

Seeing the half-breed running around free didn't seem right to Shorty. Hadn't the bastard attacked a woman that very day? Why, it was Shorty's civic duty to apprehend the villain.

Lee and Harve were warming up the girls at Mabel's place at the end of the alley. Shorty would just run on down and get them. Didn't seem right leaving them out at a time like this. They were his buddies, his *compadres*. They deserved to get a share of the credit, didn't they?

Wolf was half a block from the hotel when he stepped off the raised wooden sidewalk to cross the alley. Suddenly he smelled sweat—not his own, but someone else's. And urine. The skin along the back of his neck prickled. That was all the warning he had before he was struck from behind. He was cursing himself for a fool for letting himself be taken like a damn greenhorn when pain exploded at the base of his skull and everything went black.

Sunday morning the population of New Hope swelled to even greater numbers than Saturday night as the area families came to join the townspeople for church. Not that everyone in town attended worship services. The Saturday night drunks were sleeping off their night of revelry in whatever den they'd collapsed.

Some had better excuses, or were simply more devious. The mayor, after staying out until four A.M. at a poker game with his cronies, claimed a terrible toothache. His wife didn't buy it, but she let him get away with it—again.

The marshall certainly couldn't go to church; he had a prisoner to watch. Heck, he wouldn't even be able to make it to Sunday dinner. "I know your mother will be here, and darn, honey, I sure hate to miss it, but what can I do?"

Thank God for the prisoner. The marshall's least favorite person in the world was his wife's mother.

At the First Methodist Church, Reverend Woodrow Ben-

ton was also thanking God. The congregation, having just
finished the round of opening hymns, took its seat. A
reverent hush, full and expectant, fell over the small, humble sanctuary as Woodrow carried his open Bible to the
pulpit.

He was going to make it. Not only was today's service
going to prove inspiring and uplifting—he'd worked all
week to get every word right—but he was also apparently
going to win his bet with Father Thomas down at St.
Michael's. It was obviously not the Methodists' turn to be
. . . blessed . . . with the presence of the Flanigan clan.

Brian Flanigan, God rest his papist soul, was as Irish and
as Catholic as they came. But during his misspent youth
he'd done the unthinkable and married Caroline Butler,
a Methodist girl from Alabama. Much to the dismay of
Woodrow and Father Thomas, Brian and Caroline had
brought up their children in both faiths. Each week they
alternated between the First Methodist and St. Michael's.

Heretic, Father Thomas said.

Confused lambs, thought Woodrow.

But the Flanigans, all of them, were more than comfortable with the arrangement. They had friends in both
churches. Both Father Thomas and Woodrow shook their
heads and welcomed them with open arms, each wishing
the Flanigans would choose one faith and stick with it,
each in a quandary as to which church they wanted the
rowdy Flanigan clan to choose.

Woodrow chuckled to himself as he envisioned the commotion going on at mass down the street at St. Michael's.
At this very minute the Flanigan crew was probably arriving
late and disrupting everything. The Flanigans always
arrived late, always disrupted, Lord love them. But this
time it was Father Thomas's turn. The congregation at
First Methodist this morning was quiet, reverent. Hushed.

Suddenly there was a loud thump on the other side
of the wide sanctuary doors, then the doors burst open.
Reverend Woodrow Benton's benevolent smile turned

pained as he bit back a groan. He'd just lost two bits to Father Thomas. The entire congregation turned as one at the sound of the disturbance to watch the six Flanigan children rush in breathlessly.

Naturally there were no empty spaces in the back pews. The oldest Flanigan daughter, Brianna, smiled sheepishly at the congregation and led her siblings to the front of the church and the empty seats waiting there. As they settled noisily in, Brianna looked up to the pulpit and Reverend Benton and smiled. Not the sheepish smile she gave the congregation. Not the friendly, polite smile for friends and neighbors. No, this was her brilliant smile, the one that forced irritation aside and made a person smile back and made him like doing it.

Woodrow let out a secret sigh. He'd lost his bet, but now his flock was complete. "Let us bow our heads and pray."

Brianna cast a quick glance down the pew to make certain her brothers and sisters were complying, then bowed her own head. While Reverend Benton prayed, she offered her own prayer of apology for being late yet again for church.

After the services Brie took Katy by the hand as the other children scattered to visit for a few minutes with their friends. Since school had let out last May, Sunday was the only time the Flanigans saw anyone but Flanigans, except for the infrequent trips to town during the week and the even more infrequent visits from neighbors.

The social calls from neighbors had trickled off and dried up during the past months. Since the death of Brie's parents, the major had dropped all pretense and openly let it be known that he wanted the Rocking F, and anyone helping Brie hang on to the ranch would earn his displeasure. Most of the neighbors weren't willing to take the chance of having the major misconstrue the reason for a visit, so they simply stayed away. He owned the bank, after all. He could ruin anyone he chose. Most weren't willing to cross him.

Brie didn't blame her neighbors. She didn't want the major using her as an excuse to bring trouble to others. Besides, she thought with a slight smile, she still had one very good friend that the major hadn't been able to intimidate. She waved to Letty and waited for the woman to join her and Katy for a few moments.

Letty Stockwell had been a good friend to Brie's mother, and since Caroline Flanigan's death, a good friend to Brie. Letty was in her mid-forties and Brie was only nineteen, but neither of them minded the age difference. Brie didn't know how she and the kids would have survived those first terrible days after their parents' drowning if Letty hadn't come and stayed with them. Her quiet sympathy and nononsense manner had been just what the grief-stricken children had needed.

Brie mourned the fact that she and Letty saw so little of each other, but it couldn't be helped. Letty Palmer Stockwell was the major's daughter. But Brie didn't hold that against her.

Letty was also James Stockwell's mother, Brie acknowledged with a smile as her sister Elly searched James out in the crowd beyond the church steps. Brie held on to Katy's hand as Elly joined a group of girls her own age, who were gathered quite innocently, or so they hoped everyone thought, near a group of boys surrounding James.

Tessa joined her own group of friends and so did Rory and Sully. By then Letty had broken away from her father and met Brie near the corner of the church. Not having seen each other for weeks, the two women hugged.

Letty bent down and gave Katy a hug, much to the girl's delight. "You just get prettier every time I see you, Miss Katy."

Having not a shy or humble bone in her little body, Katy grinned. "I know it."

"Katy!" Brie rolled her eyes. "You're supposed to say thank you, not 'I know it.'"

Unrepentant but obedient, Katy thanked Letty.

"And you," Letty said to Brie. "I can see for myself that you're fine. I was worried about what happened yesterday, until I saw you walk into church." Letty may have said her worry was over, but it lingered in her eyes. "You are okay, aren't you?"

One of the reasons their friendship worked so well was that the two women carried on the unspoken agreement that Letty and Caroline had shared—they did not discuss the major nor his greed for Flanigan land. Only once had the subject been broached. Last month Letty had offered to move not only herself, but her two children, also, to the Rocking F.

"You know you're more than welcome," Brie had told her, "but why would you want to come here?"

"Maybe it will stop the major from harassing you."

Brie had grimaced. "More than likely he'd just use your presence here as an excuse to have his men move in, too, and take charge."

Letty had thought about it and reluctantly agreed that Brie was right. Her father would find a way to use his family's presence at the Rocking F to his advantage.

The two women had not spoken of the major since.

Now Brie wondered what put that look of worry in Letty's eyes. "Everything's fine. Really."

"I'm so glad to hear it. And so glad our men were nearby to help."

Brie blinked. "Excuse me?"

"I know you and my father have your differences," Letty said in a rush, "but I'm so grateful to learn that it doesn't mean our hands won't help you when you need it."

"Faith, but someone's been kissin' the Blarney Stone. Just what kind of help do your men say they provided, I'd be wantin' to know."

Letty lowered her voice. "I'm sorry. I didn't think. Naturally you wouldn't want anyone to know you were attacked, but—"

"Letty, Katy and I were on our way home from town yesterday when three Double Diamond riders accosted us, pulled us from the wagon, and started shoving us around."

"*Our* men?" Letty's jaw dropped. "What are you saying?"

"I'm saying that there's no telling what might have happened if Wolf hadn't come along."

Letty's cheeks paled. "*Our* men . . . ?" Her eyes widened in horror. "You're saying *our* men attacked you?"

"I am."

"But . . ."

"The bad men tried to hurt us," Katy piped up, "but Wolf saved us. He's a nice man, isn't he, Brie?"

"Yes, honey, Wolf is a nice man."

"This Wolf," Letty said, her voice shaking, "would he happen to be a half-breed?"

Brie stiffened. "What of it?"

"Brie, he's in jail."

Brie's heart thumped in her chest. "Whatever for?"

Lines of distress etched across Letty's face. "Because three of our new hands said they came across him accosting you and Katy on the road. They said they subdued him but he got away. When they saw him in town last night they . . . they hit him over the head and dragged him to the marshall's office."

Brie stared at Letty, shock holding her still for a long moment. The thought of her tall, dark rescuer being jailed made something cold settle in the pit of Brie's stomach. She instinctively knew that, like his namesake, Wolf was meant to be free. He would hate being caged.

"Letty, I have to get him out of there."

"What are you going to do?"

Brie met her friend's troubled gaze. "Whatever I have to. He doesn't belong in jail. I'm going to get him out."

Letty stood in shock and watched Brie gather her family. A young woman and child had been attacked by the major's men, and an innocent man was in jail. Things had gone too far.

Squaring her shoulders, Letty went in search of her father. The man had to be stopped before it was too late.

Moments after leaving Letty, Brie had her brothers and sisters gathered into the wagon and ready to leave. When she turned down a side street, Sully wanted to know where they were going.

Before Brie could answer, Katy spoke up. "The bad men lied and Wolf's in jail. Brie's gonna get him out."

Brie closed her eyes and took a deep breath, waiting. After a second, no more than two, the rest of the kids erupted with cries of outrage over their new friend being jailed.

"Everyone settle down," she snapped. Pulling the wagon up in front of the marshall's office, she set the brake.

"Are we gonna bust him out?" Rory asked eagerly.

"We're not busting anyone out of jail," Elly said, disgusted. She looked sideways at Brie. "Are we?"

"Don't be ridiculous. There's been a mistake, that's all. I'm just going to talk to the marshall." After securing the reins, Brie climbed down. "I won't be long. You stay put. All of you."

Like so many of the buildings in town, the marshall's office was built of adobe. Unlike most, it stood alone, with no other buildings connected to it. Iron bars covered the small front window and the even smaller window high in the iron-bound door. Finding the door unlocked, Brie breathed a sigh of relief, knowing it meant the marshall or one of his deputies was in. She stepped inside and closed the door behind her, giving her eyes a few seconds to adjust to the dimness.

The room was small, with one desk, a small safe in one corner, a stove for heat in the winter in another, and a gunrack on the wall behind the desk. In the center of the wall opposite the front door stood another iron-bound door that led to the room containing the four cells for prisoners.

Brie had been beyond that door once last spring when her last remaining hired hand had gotten drunk and started a fight in one of the saloons. She'd fired him and left him in jail.

"Miss Flanigan." Marshall Ben Campbell rose from the chair behind his desk. He stood just under six feet, with sandy brown hair, a thick, long mustache, and deep lines radiating from his eyes. Those eyes filled with surprise and sympathy. "I didn't expect to see you here."

Just yesterday Brie had stood in this office to report finding two of her calves shot. Marshall Campbell had practically patted her on the head and told her not to worry herself over such things. He, like everyone else around, thought she had no business trying to run a ranch. He'd told her yesterday that if she sold out to the major she wouldn't have to worry about pesky little things like dead cattle. The memory fueled her anger.

"I guess you heard we caught the man who . . . bothered you yesterday."

"No," Brie said. 'What I heard was that you've jailed the man who came to our rescue."

"What are you saying?" he demanded, all indignant bluster.

"I be sayin', Marshall, that me five-year-old sister and meself were stopped on the road yesterday by a trio of the Double Diamond's foinest. Pulled from the wagon by brute force, we were. Wee Katy was thrown to the ground and could have been killed. The three were snockered. I'd not be knowin' what sort of mischief they had in mind, but 'twas fortunate indeed for Katy and meself when Wolf showed up and sent the blighters packin'.''

"Now, Miss Flanigan, I know you've got your differences with the major, but accusing his men of—"

"I wasn't accusing them of anything, until they decided

to lie and lay blame for their own actions onto an innocent man.''

''Miss Flanigan—''

''I'm the one who was attacked. Don't you think I know the difference between my attackers and my rescuer? Are you calling me a liar, then, Marshall?''

''Now, just calm down,'' the marshall said.

Brie ground her back teeth together and swallowed the brogue with effort. ''You told me to calm down yesterday when I reported my cattle are being shot. I am calm, Marshall. But I promise you, I won't be much longer if you don't let that man out of jail.''

''Now hold on, there. I don't let a man out of jail just because some girl comes in here and tells me to. I never said I had him in jail, anyway,'' he added, looking uncomfortable, as if his longjohns were riding up a little too high.

''Do you have him in jail?''

''I got a man back there, all right. Might be the one you're talking about, might not. Might just be a vagrant found drunk in an alley.''

''Might?''

Marshall Campbell shuffled his feet and looked away.

''*Might* I see this prisoner, Marshall?''

''I don't see any need for that.'' Campbell was starting to sweat. Word had come from Jennings, the major's right-hand man, to keep the half-breed locked up until Jennings came for him.

''Well,'' the Flanigan girl said, ''maybe I can give you a reason to let me see him.''

Campbell was leery. From what he'd heard, the girl was every bit the wild, fiery-tempered Irishman—or woman— that her old man had been. Damn shame about Brian Flanigan and his missus drowning that way.

''Marshall, if you don't let me see your prisoner, I'm going to step outside and call in all five of my brothers and sisters and tell them that you've arrested the man who rescued Katy and me yesterday. And then, Marshall, I'm going to send for your wife. And her mother.''

Campbell fought down a shudder. Caroline Flanigan had been one of his wife's best friends. Ben and Mavis had never been blessed with children of their own, so Mavis set fierce store by all the little Flanigan hooligans. He'd be eating cold beans for a month and his bed would be even colder if she thought her husband the marshall had anything to do with making those kids unhappy.

And Maureen—The shudder broke loose and raced down Ben's spine. His wife's mother had been born to make his life miserable. She positively doted on children, never letting him forget for a minute that her Mavis was still childless after all these years.

Maureen wasn't blind to Palmer's attempts to run the Flanigans out, either. For that alone, she hated Major Palmer like the South hated Yankee carpetbaggers. If she sniffed any hint of Palmer's involvement, not to mention Ben's, in making those six Flanigan kids unhappy . . . *Gawd, she'd castrate me, and that's a fact.*

Caught between the major's demands and the equally fearsome possibilities from his wife and mother-in-law, Marshall Ben Campbell reached for the key to the cell. Palmer was a good mile or more out of town on his way home from church by now. Mavis and Maureen were only two blocks away.

Wolf lay on the hard cot in his cell, scarcely aware of the voices in the outer office. Memories, like the sharp fangs of his namesake, gnawed at the edges of his mind. He was grateful the other three cells were empty and silent. It took his total concentration, and his hat over his face so he couldn't see or smell the bars of his cell, to keep the fangs at bay.

Iron bars had a particular smell. Like the iron links of a chain. Or an iron shackle.

Stop it.

If he let the memories in, he feared his mind, his sanity, would be ripped to shreds and he would, quite literally, go mad.

This wasn't the first time he'd been tested by being jailed. He'd seen the inside of a few other cells since breaking free and taking off on his own at the age of nine. But it wasn't those cells that haunted him. It wasn't jail cells that he hid from in his mind by pretending he was free and standing on a wide open plain with the wind in his hair and a sky overhead so blue it hurt his eyes.

It was the other. The wagon, with its barred windows, its doors that locked from the outside, completely sealing him in. The suffocating heat, the freezing cold. The dark. And the terror that had eaten at his young soul, ravaging him like the very fangs he now fought to hold at bay. After the dark would come the light, the unlocking and opening of the door, but not to freedom. The true horror started then, as it had every day from the time he was four years old until he reached nine and escaped.

"Wolf?"

Wolf ground his teeth against voicing a curse. Maybe the fangs were tearing through the outer layers of his defense. Now he was hearing *her,* Brianna Flanigan.

"Wolf?"

The voice slid over him, smooth and warm, offering a comfort and ease more real than any he'd ever known. But it wasn't real, only his imagination. For him there would be no comfort or ease. There was only the search for the truth. And maybe, if he was lucky, the chance for revenge.

"Hey, 'breed!" The marshall's gravelly voice echoed through the cell.

"Marshall!" cried her voice again.

"Wake up in there," hollered the marshall. "The lady's talking to you."

"Wolf," she said again. "It's me, Brie. Brianna Flanigan."

Beneath the cover of his hat, Wolf blinked his eyes open. Be damned, he hadn't imagined her voice after all. What the hell was she doing here? Come to gawk at the half-breed now that he was caged and harmless?

With a silent curse, he acknowledged the unfairness of his thoughts. She wasn't like other people. She'd been nice to him, had taken him home with her and seated him at the table with her family and fed him. She'd tended his cut, sewn up his shirt, and offered him a job.

She must have been out of her mind.

Schooling his expression to bland disinterest, Wolf slowly lifted the hat from his face and sat up on the cot. That same hot tightness that had struck him yesterday hit again at the sight of her. The shaded light in the cell room muted the fieriness of her hair. Her skin looked paler, her freckles more prominent. Lust, hot, blatant, and inappropriate as hell doubled up its fist and struck him. Hard.

He'd wanted women before, but not like this. This was different somehow, reached deeper into him, involving more than merely the want of flesh for flesh. In her eyes he read other promises. He read home and hearth and family, things Wolf had never known, would never know.

And he saw distress. For him? Seeing the distress on her face threatened his control. "What the hell are you doing here?" It unmanned him to have her see him locked up like a criminal, or a wild animal put on display, but he knew his feelings didn't show on his face. He was damned good at hiding his feelings. It didn't take more than a couple of broken ribs for a boy to learn that particular talent.

Brie stared at him, appalled at the lifelessness in his eyes. "Let him out, Marshall," she whispered. "Let him out now. He's not one of the men who attacked us, he's the man who came to our rescue. And he's not a vagrant, either."

"Well, now, Miss Flanigan, like I said—"

"Yesterday I offered him a job. I was hoping he'd be able to start this afternoon."

The disillusionment that crept beneath Wolf's guard surprised him with its intensity. Brianna Flanigan wasn't so different from other women after all. He didn't know what game she was playing, but they both knew damn well that he'd turned down her offer of a job.

Women were such good game players. She was trying to manipulate him. He could either back up her story and get out of jail, and end up having to work for her if he planned to stay in the area long enough to find out about Palmer, or he could call her a liar and rot where he was until the marshall decided to let him out.

Wolf arched a brow at her in mock salute. Without telling a literal lie, she had him, and she knew it. She *had* offered him a job. She hadn't lied and told the marshall that he'd accepted, only that she'd wanted him to start work today. Clever girl.

"How about it, mister?" the marshall demanded. "Are you working for the Rocking F?"

Wolf sighed quietly. "Not from in here, I'm not." He guessed it couldn't hurt to go along with her, maybe help her out for a few days. But no more than that. He had business to take care of.

With a growl of frustration, Marshall Campbell unlocked the cell. Hell, Palmer would have his ass for this, Campbell knew. Not just for going against Jennings's instructions, but for inadvertently lending aid, so to speak, to the Flanigans.

What the hell. The old bastard's had things his way too damn long. And he ain't near as mean as Maureen. Especially if he threw Mavis into the mix. Besides, Marshall Ben Campbell didn't much like being lied to, most particularly when the lie had him arresting an innocent man.

Admitting to himself that releasing the half-breed could very well cost him his job, Campbell sighed philosophically. He was getting too damn old to be marshall of a rowdy young town like New Hope anyhow. If the major got him fired, maybe he'd finally open up that little gun shop he'd been dreaming of for years.

By the time the wagon full of Flanigans left town, their tall, taciturn companion on horseback had uttered a total of three sentences. "Yes," when Katy asked him if he was going home with them; "I have to get my horse," when Brie asked where he was going; and, wonder of wonders, all on his own he'd offered, "I need to stop at the hotel and pick up my things."

For the entire rest of the trip home, he spoke not another word. Anger fairly radiated from him in waves. Brie could practically see it, like heat rising from the desert floor.

She couldn't blame him, really. No man wanted to be rescued from jail by a woman. No man would like being coerced into taking a job he didn't want, a job he had already refused. But Brie couldn't afford to let her conscience bother her. If she didn't find someone to help her resist the major's increasingly ugly tactics, she would have no choice but to move the children to the safety of town.

Such a move smacked too much of defeat for Brie's comfort. Her father had intended that his ranch be passed down to his children. For Brie, holding on to the ranch was nothing less than a sacred trust. One she refused to abandon. If she had to force a man to help her, so be it.

She'd prayed for help, and Wolf had appeared. There was no way she was going to let him hold out on her and God both.

Chapter Four

All the way from town Wolf rode several paces behind the wagon, and off to the side to avoid the dust. As the wagon pulled into the yard, the big red dog scrambled from beneath the front porch and stirred up his own dust cloud with his tail.

Brie pulled the wagon to a halt and climbed down while Wolf dismounted at the corral across the yard. The two boys, he noted, quickly took charge of unhitching the team while the three younger girls went into the house.

Wolf had been trying all the way from town to figure out what the hell was going on. Not with Brianna Flanigan. He understood her motives just fine. She needed a hired hand and no one would work for her because of the major. Or because she was a woman. Wolf appeared to be her last choice. No surprise there. He'd been somebody's last choice more than once. Brie deliberately put him on the spot with the marshall, leaving Wolf no polite way out but to go along with her.

What he couldn't figure out was when the hell he'd

become so damn polite. Why had he meekly gone along with her story?

That was easy enough—to get his ass out of jail. But once out, why had he collected his horse and his gear and followed her all the way back to her ranch like a trained dog?

"I can't make you stay."

Her voice poured over him like cool water on a hot day. Wolf turned from staring blankly into the empty corral to find Brianna—Brie—standing next to him and squarely meeting his gaze.

"That's right," he told her. "You can't." But he owed her for getting him out of jail. No telling how long that marshall had been prepared to hold him.

"I can pay room and board and fifty a month."

"Foreman's wages?"

"That's what I need, a foreman."

"The pay is decent, but I told you I wasn't looking for a job. Name me one good reason why I shouldn't just mount up and ride out."

"Because we need you."

Wolf shook his head. "So you need a little help around here. You don't know anything about me. For all you know, I'll rob you blind."

The slight angling of her chin spoke of defiance, determination. "What are you going to do, stuff a few laying hens into your saddlebags? Or maybe you're thinking of making off with some of our cattle. That's about all there is to steal around here. Besides, you don't look like a thief to me."

No one in his life had ever looked at Wolf with so much trust before, or so much hope. The trust and hope in her eyes humbled him in a way he'd never been humbled. He didn't know why he was arguing with her. She'd helped him out of a tight spot, and now he would help her.

He took off his hat and ran the fingers of one hand

through his hair. "Just exactly what kind of help do you need?"

He'd expected to see relief cross her face that he'd asked. Instead, for the first time, he read unease on those delicate features.

"Why don't you unsaddle your horse, then come over to the porch. We'll talk about it over a glass of buttermilk."

Buttermilk? Wolf bit back a laugh. Hell, he'd struck deals over beer, whiskey, tequila, pure homebrewed lightning, and a few other things that he wouldn't care to name. But *buttermilk?*

Then he lost all urge to laugh. Her offer merely pointed out the vast difference between Brianna Flanigan and the man known only as Wolf. Buttermilk was part of her life. So was trust, and hope, and the innocence shining in her eyes. Wolf had never experienced any of those things. Never. At least, not since the age of four. If he'd known them before then, they were lost to him by the passage of time and the horror of the years that followed.

He noticed Brie eyeing him and realized he was scowling at her. "Maybe you'd prefer apple cider?" she offered.

Wolf shook his head. "Either one. I'll take care of my horse, then we'll talk."

Brie nodded and walked away, guilt eating at her. Guilt, doubt, and fear. He wasn't likely to stay if she told him the truth of their situation, yet staying would put him in danger. She had no choice but to be honest. The idea of asking a man who had helped her to put himself in danger for her, much worse danger this time, made her hands shake.

But she would ask, because she had no choice.

She went into the house and lifted the trap door in the kitchen floor. Cider, then, since the mention of buttermilk had drawn his eyebrows together in a deep frown.

Climbing back up the ladder with the jug, she pictured the well-used six-gun on Wolf's hip. When she climbed out of the small cellar and let down the door, her hand trembled just the slightest bit. Was she hiring a gunman?

With a quick, silent prayer for forgiveness, she crossed herself and swore she wouldn't think of Wolf that way. She was hiring help. That was all. And maybe . . . protection.

Elly handed Brie two tin cups. "Is he going to stay?"

With the cups in one hand and the jug in the other, Brie headed for the front porch. "I hope so."

Wolf was crossing the yard toward her as she poured the cider, trying not to spill it. Damn the trembling. "I hope you like it. We make it ourselves from our own apples."

Wolf took the offered cup. He looked into it, then at Brie. "Are you afraid of me, Miss Flanigan?"

Startled, Brie blinked. "Of course not."

"You're trembling."

A flush heated her cheeks. "How kind of you to point it out."

"I'm not a kind man."

"You are when you want to be. It was kind of you to help Katy and me yesterday."

"Why am I here, Miss Flanigan?"

"Brie. My name is Brie. And I'm not entirely sure why you're here."

"You'd rather I'd told the marshall the truth? That I'd already turned down your job?"

"You could have." She finished pouring cider for herself and set the jug on the porch. "Or you could have ridden off on your own as soon as we left town."

Wolf had been wondering why he hadn't done just that. It would have been easy. For him, it would have been smart. But damn his hide, six kids couldn't run a ranch.

"We need help, Wolf."

"You need more than that. What is it you think one man can do?"

Brie's heart raced like a runaway stallion. To stall, she took a sip of cider. Looking out across the valley at the thick grass that would feed Rocking F cattle over the winter—if she managed to hang on to the ranch that long—Brie gathered her courage. "I . . . someone is shooting my cattle."

Wolf's gaze sharpened.

"Two days ago I found two calves shot through the head. That's why I went to town yesterday, to tell the marshall."

"What's he going to do about it?"

"Nothing."

"Why?"

"Because we both know who's doing it. I have to be honest with you, Wolf. There's a man, Major Palmer. His ranch, the Double Diamond, is south of the valley, farther upstream beyond the next canyon."

"Those were his men yesterday?"

"Yes. I thought I knew all of his men, by sight at least. These must be new hands."

"You think this Palmer shot your calves?"

"Not personally, but I believe he had it done."

"You think he set those men on you yesterday?"

Brie paused. "I don't know. I know he wants this ranch, but I never thought he'd go so far as to . . ."

"Why does he want your ranch?"

She shook her head and drew in a deep breath. "Because he's greedy. He runs too many head in his valley and up on the east mesa. Every year he gets more and more sagebrush and less and less grass. Da was always careful not to overgraze the grass, so ours is in good shape on the west mesa and in the valley. Then there's the water. There's no water up on the east mesa. The major has the stream, of course, and the creeks that feed it, but most of his creeks go dry by midmorning and don't run again until nightfall."

"I've heard of that."

"Two of our feeder creeks here in the valley do the same, but we've got three more that run all year, except during the worst droughts or when they're frozen. And we have two springs up on the west mesa."

"So he wants your grass and your water."

"He wants to own everything. He's an ordinary rancher who fancies himself a cattle baron, or so Da thought."

Wolf absently touched a hand to the knot on the back of his head.

"Then there's the coal," she muttered.

Wolf's eyes narrowed. Slowly he lowered his hand. "The what?"

Brie shrugged. "It's not enough to make anybody rich, but it's enough for the Rocking F's needs for the foreseeable future."

"Coal."

"Yes, you know, that black stuff you dig out of the hillside that burns in your stove instead of the wood we obviously don't have."

"You have coal."

Exasperated, Brie frowned. "We have coal. I said so, didn't I?"

"And this major knows you have coal."

"He knows we have coal."

"I'm no coal miner."

"I don't expect you to be. The coal is only for heating the house, and cooking. It's the ranch I'm hiring you to run."

"Where is this coal mine?"

Brie pointed toward the southwest. "About two miles, there."

Wolf squinted and stared, but the distance was too far. Jesus. Coal. In a country with so few trees, a man couldn't heat his house through a single winter. Men had been known to kill for less. "What is it you expect me to do?"

"Help us keep our herd, our ranch. Help me find men who'll work for us. If you could just stay through the fall branding," she added in a rush, "and help us get our herd to market . . ."

Sully sauntered up just then, thumbs hooked behind his suspenders, a piece of straw sticking out of his mouth, obviously trying to look adult and nonchalant. He eyed Wolf up and down. "So, you stayin'?"

Wolf didn't have to remind himself to step carefully where the boy was concerned. Sully's vulnerability showed in his eyes. He was a boy who wanted to be, thought he had to be, a man. "I'm thinking about it," Wolf said. "Do you think I should?"

Sully flushed with pleasure and importance at being asked. Then, unsure, he looked to Brie.

If she hadn't thought it would send Wolf running, she would have kissed the man for not summarily dismissing Sully, the way most men would have. She'd been right. Wolf was a kind man. Rather than answer Sully's inquiring look, she raised a brow, silently asking for his opinion.

"Will you help us with the cattle?" Sully asked the dark man who towered over him.

"Well, I don't know a thing about apples," Wolf said, nodding toward the orchard, "except how to eat 'em, and I'm no good with a garden. I guess cattle's about all I know."

Sully glanced at Brie again. This time she gave him a slight nod of encouragement.

"She talk money with you?" Sully asked, his eyes narrowed.

"She did."

"She tell you we don't have any money, won't have any until we sell our cattle this fall?"

Flushing bright red—she hadn't gotten around to mentioning that he wouldn't get the money she'd offered until fall—Brie looked quickly away.

Wolf eyed her and gnawed on the inside of his cheek. "Well, now, no, she didn't actually mention that."

"I . . . was just getting ready to," she offered in a weak voice.

"Uh oh," Sully said.

Wolf used his thumb and forefinger to pull down the corners of his mouth. It was either that, or burst out laughing, and Wolf was not a laughing man. "Fall, huh?" He didn't think he'd ever met a woman with more audacity, more sheer nerve than Brianna Flanigan. She knew what she wanted and she wasn't about to let a little thing like lack of money get in her way. And for some reason beyond his understanding, she wanted him. "I guess I can live with that."

Brie's eyes slid closed for a moment, then she looked at him with such gratitude that it shook him.

The boy studied him another moment, then stuck out his hand. "Well, I guess you're hired then. Welcome to the Rocking F."

Brie's lips twitched, but Wolf wasn't tempted to smile at Sully's manly act. Wolf understood the fragile pride of a nine-year-old boy and was not tempted to smile at all. Solemnly he shook hands with Sullivan Adare Flanigan.

Sully beamed with pride and importance. After the handshake, he turned and dashed toward the barn, all young boy again. "Rory, he's stayin'! He's stayin'!"

Brie chuckled. To Wolf she said, "Thank you, Wolf."

"Don't thank me yet. I haven't done anything."

"Oh, but you have. You treated Sully with dignity instead of laughing at him. You agreed to stay and help us."

"For a price."

"A price you won't get until we sell the cattle."

"About that," Wolf said. He paused a moment, wondering where the sudden thought had come from. But deep inside, he knew. "Would you be interested in paying me in cattle instead of money?"

Surprised, Brie thought a moment, then smiled. "I think we can work something out."

Wolf nodded, wondering if he was being a fool. But he'd never had a home. It was time he built something, if for no other reason than to prove to himself that he could. He wanted a ranch of his own. When his business with Palmer was done, there would be nothing to stop him from finding a place of his own with green grass and free-flowing water. A place like this one, he thought, looking around.

Nothing to stop you but a hangman's noose.

Wolf shook the thought away. He was too smart for that. He wasn't a cold-blooded killer. He'd have to find another way to do what he'd come for, because he didn't intend to die for it. But one way or another, if Palmer turned out to be the man he was looking for, Wolf would see the bastard dead.

Brie wondered at the grim look that crossed Wolf's face. She'd thought her agreement to pay him in cattle would have pleased him. A dozen questions crossed her mind, but Wolf's expression cleared and he finished his apple cider.

She finished hers and offered him more.

"No, thanks. I've accepted your terms and we've agreed on my pay, but there's more."

"More?"

"You're hiring me to be foreman. That means I run things. I don't come to you for permission. I'm in charge."

The hard look in his eyes sent a shiver down Brie's spine. She steeled herself against it. "When it comes to the day-to-day running of the ranch, looking after the stock, hiring men, you're in charge. But you aren't being hired to make major decisions that affect me and my family, about how we live, what we do. I don't intend to tell you what to do, but I expect you to tell me what you're doing, and to talk to me about anything that affects my family."

"And if we disagree, I suppose you're going to remind me you're the boss."

"Maybe. I'm sure we'll disagree now and then, but I hope we'll be able to talk things out sensibly." Brie didn't want the conversation to go any further for fear Wolf would change his mind about working for her. She wasn't prepared to tell him he could do whatever he wanted, yet she didn't want him to leave. To distract him, she took the empty cup from his hand. "If you'll get your gear I'll show you to the bunkhouse."

"That can wait. I'd rather ride out and take a look around. Get the lay of the land."

Brie hesitated, then nodded. "I'll go change, then. I'll be ready to ride in fifteen minutes."

Wolf shook his head in amazement. "Lady, don't you have an ounce of caution in you?"

Brie narrowed her eyes. "You're the one who needs the caution. If you don't start calling me by my name I'm going to dump the rest of this jug of cider over your head."

Wolf ignored her attempt at a threat. "You don't know me, you don't know anything about me. You've just hired a total stranger to be your foreman. A stranger you found in jail. Isn't that bad enough without wanting to ride out alone with me?"

She cocked her head and almost smiled. "Are you saying I shouldn't trust you?"

"You shouldn't trust anybody this easily."

"I'm sorry to disappoint you, but I do trust you. I happen to be an excellent judge of character, and I usually trust just about everyone until I have reason not to. I also happen to be the one who hired you. I'll be ready to ride in fifteen minutes," she repeated.

"There's no need for you to go. I'm just going to take a look at the grass up the valley."

"I'd like to show you where I found the dead calves two days ago."

"Just tell me the general area. I'll find it."

"You can do that? How?"

"Experience."

Brie cocked her head. "You really don't want me to go with you, do you?"

"No, ma'am," he admitted. "I'd rather take my own impressions this first time."

Brie knew she shouldn't be feeling such keen disappointment at his not wanting her along, but she wouldn't argue

with him nor force her company on him. She was too glad
he'd agreed to work for her to chance pushing him just
yet. "If you make it to the far end of the valley, the small
adobe there is our line shack."

"You own the whole valley outright?"

She gave him a small smile. "Not exactly. We own both
ends outright."

"Which keeps everybody else out of the middle."

"That's right."

Wolf set his cup on the porch railing and tugged on the
brim of his hat. "Don't look for me back before sundown."

"If you'll wait about an hour, dinner will be ready."

"No use wasting daylight. I'll manage, but thanks for
the offer."

"I'll put a plate aside for you. Just come to the house
when you get back."

Wolf nodded again, thanked her, and walked away.

Brie watched him go, then picked up his cup and went
inside. As she turned to close the door behind her, she
thought there was something in his walk, in the set of his
shoulders, the sureness of his stride, that set Wolf apart
from other men she had known. He seemed so . . . solid.
So self-assured, confident. And solitary. There was an
aloneness about him that created an ache in Brie's chest.

Questions assailed her. Who was he? Where was he from?
What was he doing in this sparsely populated corner of
Colorado? Did he have family somewhere waiting for him?
Friends? A sweetheart? Somehow, she didn't think so. He
appeared a man apart. Alone. A private man. Was he
lonely?

How could he not be? Brie had never been without
her family. She couldn't imagine being as alone as Wolf
appeared to be.

"What are you looking at?"

Brie whirled in surprise to find Tessa peering over her
shoulder. "Nothing," she answered, wondering why she
was breathless.

Through the doorway Tessa saw Wolf. Her gaze traveled back to Brie. Slowly, her eyes widened. "Oh, my word."

"What?" Brie asked. "You look like you've just swallowed a worm."

"Brie, we don't know anything about him."

"What are you talking about?"

"Wolf." Tessa gripped Brie's hand tightly. "You only met him yesterday."

"I know that."

"But . . . you were looking at him just now the same way Elly looks at James, and everybody knows she's been in love with him her whole life."

For a long moment Brie could do no more than gape at her middle sister. It was . . . it was . . . "That's the most ridiculous thing I've ever heard."

"It is not. Everybody knows Elly loves James."

"Not Elly, you ninny. You said that I . . . Well, it's just ridiculous, that's all."

"I know what I saw."

"You don't either. Why, I only met the man yesterday."

Tessa rolled her eyes. "Which is why it's ridiculous for you to look at him the way you were just now."

"Of course it's ridiculous! I wasn't looking at him in any particular way at all."

"If you say so," Tessa said with a smirk.

As Wolf rode away from the ranch headquarters, he shook his head. *Come to the house when you're hungry.* He couldn't remember a time in his life when he wasn't hungry—for something. A home, family, warmth, food, safety. Those hungers were so constant that he barely acknowledged them anymore.

His saddle was his home, his horse his family. For years now he'd had no trouble providing his own warmth and food. He made his own safety by whatever means necessary. He no longer felt threatened, he acknowledged as he crossed the stream and walked his horse toward the south end of the valley. Except occasionally, like earlier in the jail, threatened by his own past. Or like when a five-year-old girl held his hand at the supper table. Or when Brianna Flanigan looked at him with green eyes filled with trust and faith. That threatened him. Threatened the hell out of him.

Threatened him to the point where he refused to think about it. Instead, he studied the grass. Grama mostly, a foot or more tall, with a good mix of shorter buffalo grass. Both were good feed for stock. Both grew thick, meaning the valley hadn't been overgrazed. The dozen or so horses running loose wore the Rocking F brand.

He saw the small adobe at the far end of the valley long before he reached it, but only through his binoculars. If Brie hadn't told him it was there he probably wouldn't have noticed it until he was right on it, so well did it blend with the rocks and scrub and grass around it.

Cattle stood belly-deep in grass around the adobe. They'd long since lost their winter leanness and were fattening up nicely. Brie should be able to get a good price for them if she—or he, he reminded himself—timed the drive to market just right.

He checked hindquarters to make sure no stock had been missed in the spring branding. He almost wished he hadn't. The Double Diamond brand rode on each cow and calf. There wasn't a Rocking F cow in sight.

"Come on, boy." He nudged his horse into a ground-eating lope. "Let's see where they came from." He rode to the south end of the valley where the land rose sharply on either side of the stream and formed a deep canyon barely two hundred yards wide. He studied the ground beside the stream. Cattle had come through there recently, all right. Trouble was, they hadn't come through on their own.

"Well, hell."

Chapter Five

Brie stood on the porch and watched as late evening shadows lengthened and stretched into dusk across the valley. Wolf hadn't returned and she was getting worried. He'd said he had business in the area. Had he changed his mind about working for her and ridden off to take care of his own concerns?

She shook her head in frustration. He wouldn't do that, wouldn't just ride off after agreeing to work for her. Not without telling her. He wasn't that kind of man.

Brie's pulse pounded hard. Maybe he was hurt. Maybe he'd run into some type of trouble down the valley and couldn't get home. Maybe he'd run into those three Double Diamond hands he'd sent packing yesterday.

"I'm being foolish," she muttered to herself. Wolf was a grown man, more than capable of taking care of himself.

Elly and Tessa had cooked dinner that afternoon when they'd come home from town. All the kids had asked why Wolf wasn't there. Katy had pouted over his absence. Because Elly and Tessa did virtually all of the cooking these days, Brie took over the cleaning up whenever ranch business permitted. Today, it had permitted.

After washing the dishes and cleaning the kitchen, Brie had used Wolf's absence to attack the dust and dirt that had collected in the bunkhouse since the last of their hands had left more than two months earlier.

Brian Flanigan had built the small adobe for his family when he'd first moved them from Texas to Colorado back in '76, eleven years ago. Its two rooms were cool in summer and warm in winter. During the summer, the wooden lean-to on the east side served as the kitchen. When there were enough hands to warrant their own cook, that is.

With the dust and dirt gone, the adobe was once again clean and neat, but there was no disguising its purpose. The front room was intended for the foreman or the top hand, and contained a narrow bed, three old wooden chairs, a small scarred table, and a few pegs on the wall. Four bunk beds for the rest of the hands took up the space in the back room.

After cleaning the bunkhouse, Brie had pulled weeds in the garden until the light began to fail. She had washed and changed into clean clothes, but was now too restless to set her mind to other chores. Where was Wolf? Why wasn't he back yet?

There was no need to look for trouble, she told herself again. Maybe his horse had thrown a shoe and Wolf was walking back. Surely he would show up any moment.

Still, she rubbed her arms to chase away an inner chill. Maybe she should go for a ride. Not to look for him, she assured herself, but to ease her sense of restlessness. She took one step down from the porch on her way to the barn when she spotted him crossing the stream about a half mile away in the growing darkness. Relief weakened her knees. Leaning back against the porch post served both to prop her up and to give her the appearance of casualness. She couldn't bring herself to turn her back and go in the house, but neither did she want him to think she'd been anxiously awaiting his return.

She stayed there against the porch post until he rode into the yard. With two fingers to the brim of his hat, he acknowledged her presence.

"Your supper is ready whenever you are," she called. Fearing that he would say he didn't want supper, Brie turned and went into the house. The desire to see him, talk to him, be in the same room with him, was strong, and Brie felt no need to question it or fight it.

In the kitchen she checked the plate of food she'd left on the back of the stove and was satisfied that it was still warm. Full darkness had fallen outside before Wolf's footsteps sounded on the back porch. A moment later, water splashed as he made use of the water, soap, and towel she'd left on the washstand for him.

Earlier, while she'd waited for sight of him, and then when she'd seen him nearing the house, her heart had raced. Now a calmness settled over her and she was grateful for it. As he stepped through the back door, she lifted the plate from the stove with steady hands.

She offered him a smile. "Take a seat." Her hands may have been steady, but her voice sounded breathless. She placed the plate before him on the small kitchen table, then turned back to the stove and poured him a cup of coffee. "If it's not hot enough, I can stoke up the fire."

"It's fine," Wolf said, scooting his chair up to the table.

So as not to stare at him while he ate, Brie busied herself wiping down the already clean work table next to the stove. She cast surreptitious glances his way. His features were so . . . compelling. Angles and planes, dips and hollows. His face intrigued her like none other. His pale gray eyes held secrets she yearned to delve into. Who was he? Where had he come from? Where would he go when he left the Rocking F?

He would leave, Brie knew. Probably the minute the cattle were sold at market, if not sooner.

She'd only met him yesterday. He was a stranger. How could the thought of his leaving create such an ache in her chest? With her back to him, she tried to concentrate on rubbing off a speck of dried apple pie filling. "You were gone a long time," she blurted.

The scrape of a fork across the plate halted abruptly, then resumed. The sounds of a man enjoying his dinner were all that was heard.

Brie finally stopped wiping and turned toward him. "Was everything all right?"

The man at the table met her gaze and held it while taking a long drink of coffee. Slowly he set the cup down. "No."

"No?" Brie pulled a chair out and sat across from him. "What happened? Are you all right? Were you hurt?"

"Whoa," he said, holding up one hand. "Everything's fine."

"But you said—"

"You're my boss, Miss Flanigan, not my mother."

Brie straightened her backbone and blinked. "I beg your pardon?"

"Your concern is . . . nice, but unnecessary."

"I was concerned about your welfare, that's all. It occurred to me that if something happened to you, I wouldn't know who to notify," she said stiffly.

"I've been taking care of myself all my life. I don't need you worrying about me."

Brie took a slow breath and let it out. "Does that mean you're not going to tell me if you have family or friends who might care what happens to you?"

The skin around his eyes twitched. "No."

No, he wasn't going to tell her? Or no, he had no family or friends? Brie wanted to ask, but the look in his eyes, a flash of pain covered swiftly by an impenetrable shield of blankness, forestalled her. "All right," she offered, "I won't worry about you. But when I asked if everything was all right, you said no. I'd appreciate an explanation."

While he resumed eating, Wolf explained. "I found twenty head of Double Diamond cattle at the south end of your valley."

"That's strange."

"It never happened before?"

"No, never. The canyon that separates our valley from the Double Diamond is rocky, narrow, and more than five miles long."

"Close to six by my reckoning."

"There's no grass in the canyon to speak of, so neither our cattle nor the major's are in the habit of entering it."

"They didn't do it on their own this time, they had help."

"What kind of help? Do you mean . . . someone . . ."

"Someone—three riders, to be exact—herded the Double Diamond cattle up the canyon and into your valley."

The major, again. Brie squared her jaw. "He's going too far this time, trying to take over our grass. Tomorrow I'll help you round them up and herd them right back where they belong—right up to Major Palmer's front porch."

"I took the cattle home. Tomorrow we take the wagon into town and pick up fencing supplies."

Brie sucked in a sharp breath. "You mean to fence off the south end of the valley?"

"That's exactly what I mean to do."

"'Tis a bold step, it is."

Wolf smiled slightly. "'Tis, aye," he answered, mimicking the brogue that she'd scarcely noticed had crept into her voice. "Is there any legitimate reason to allow your neighbor to come up that canyon?"

"No," Brie said slowly while her mind raced. "There's no road for a wagon, no room for one."

"He can get to and from town without coming through this valley?"

"He always has."

"Then there's no reason not to fence. You won't be hurting him, you'll just be keeping him from doing something he has no right to do in the first place. Get used to it, Miss Flanigan. Fences are the way of the future. Open range will disappear before long."

Try as she might, Brie could find no fault with Wolf's logic. She'd heard her father talking about the coming of the end of the free range. Especially since the winter before last, when so many cattle had drifted before the worst blizzards in memory and had frozen or starved to death.

But . . . fencing? The idea seemed radical. But practical. Fence in the pastures, her da had said. Plant hay for winter feed, put up windmills to draw water from the earth. Manage the cattle breeding and feeding with a purpose rather than just let it happen.

But all of that was still in the future. All Wolf meant to do now was fence the end of the valley to keep the major from running his cattle on Rocking F grass. "I think it's what Da would have done," she murmured.

"Can you afford the supplies?"

"If Mr. Winslow will give me the credit. If you'll give me a list of what we need, I'll find out tomorrow."

A look of caution crossed Wolf's face.

"What?" she asked.

He looked down at the table for a long moment before answering. "After what happened to you yesterday on the way home from town, I don't think it's a good idea for you to travel alone."

Brie bit her tongue on the response that rose, that she'd been taking herself to town and back for years. Now was no time to be stubborn. She wasn't afraid to go alone, but if something happened to her, who would look after the ranch and her brothers and sisters? Elly, as the second oldest, was already doing more than her fair share to keep things going. She wouldn't be able to take on Brie's work, too, and at seventeen, she shouldn't have to.

Brie gave Wolf a wry smile. "I can't say I like the idea of needing a guard, but I guess you'll have to go with me."

The look of caution remained on Wolf's face.

"What now?" she asked.

His chest heaved on a deep breath, and his frown creased his forehead. "It's not going to look good, you and me riding into town together. There's likely to be talk."

"Talk? About what?"

"You can't be that naive."

Brie blinked. "You mean talk about . . . you and me?"

"I mean talk, ugly talk, about a white woman taking up with a half-breed."

"Oh, good grief. If the people in town don't have anything better to do than make up stories, to heck with them. Unless," she added with a quirk of her lips, "you're worried about your reputation."

"It's your reputation you need to worry about," he snapped.

"You let me handle my reputation. You handle the ranch."

The sky was just turning gray the next morning when Wolf was awakened by the snort and bawl of angry cattle. *What the devil?* He leaped from the bed, tugged on his pants, and dashed out the door of the bunkhouse.

A lantern was lit and hanging from a nail on the outside of the barn, casting a portion of the corral in light. Barefooted, Wolf skidded to a halt at the fence and rubbed his eyes, not sure he believed what they were telling him.

Two range cows occupied the corral. Wolf had meant to ask why the day before but hadn't gotten around to it. It was just as well, because he wouldn't have believed the truth if Brie had told him.

The noise was over now, except for a few grunts and snorts from the cows. That was about all they were capable of, because Brianna Flanigan had each of them snubbed to a corral post with a rope around their necks and snouts. She had tied the hind legs of each animal together, and was presently perched on a three-legged milking stool beside one cow, her forehead pressed against the cow's side, while she milked the unhappy bovine.

Wolf shook his head in wonder. He didn't have to ask why she was going to so much trouble. The two cows must be the ones whose calves had been killed the other day. His hat was off to Brie for realizing their udders would be full to bursting if somebody didn't give them a hand.

Not that the cows were grateful for the help. Far from it. He'd had to milk a wild cow or two in his day and had to admit Brie had done everything he would have. But it didn't sit right with him that a little bit of a thing like her had to rope and tie cows before the sun was even up. "Need any help?"

With her head pressed against the warm cow and her hands working without thought to ease the cow and fill the bucket, Brie was half asleep—which wasn't a smart state to be in around these ornery cows. Wolf's voice startled her into jerking upright and whipping her head around. "Oh!"

The simple word was all she could manage. He was a lighter shadow standing in the darkness, tall, broad-shouldered. A solid presence in a morning not yet real. And he was half naked. Standing at the edge of the light the way he was, his bronze, hairless chest gleamed, intrigued. The sight, the yearning to touch that smooth flesh, made her pulse race and her mouth dry out. She'd thought it before, two days ago when he'd ridden to her rescue; he was . . . magnificent.

Wolf couldn't see the look in her eyes, but he could feel her gaze as if she were stroking him. From neck to navel and back again. The sensation sent blood rushing to his loins. Before he could embarrass them both, he stepped back into the shadows. He wanted to turn toward the bunkhouse, but he couldn't stand the thought of her heated look turning to horror at the sight of his back. "Sorry," he muttered. "Didn't mean to startle you."

Even though she was already looking at him, his voice

must have had some effect. She squeezed the teat in her hand and squirted herself in the face. A bark of laughter escaped him before he could choke it back.

While her eyes were closed, he took the opportunity to escape into the bunkhouse. Jesus, how could one woman take him from fear to arousal to laughter in the span of thirty seconds? How could she do it at all?

He didn't like it.

By the time breakfast was over and Brie was ready to go to town, Wolf had the team hitched and was waiting for her. "What do you want to do with that?" He nodded to the torn sack of flour still in the back of the wagon.

"Leave it," she said. "We'll put a tarp over it so the flour won't blow away. I'll exchange it for a new bag in town."

"Wolf!" Rory bounded out the front door and dashed across the yard. "Wolf, make her buy some licorice while you're in town."

Wolf paused in the act of covering the torn flour sack. "Licorice?"

"Yeah. She won't ever get us any licorice. Just 'cuz she don't like it—"

"She doesn't like it," Brie corrected.

"That's what I said." Rory stuck out his lower lip. "We never get licorice anymore."

Brie looked away quickly to avoid the laughing question in Wolf's eyes. She had pretty much gotten over the embarrassment of having him witness her squirting herself in the face with hot milk. After all, no one ever died from embarrassment. Did they?

At least she'd made him laugh. She'd begun to wonder if he was capable of anything so frivolous. Now she knew. All she had to do was make a fool of herself, she thought with chagrin.

He was close to laughing again, but whether at Rory's

plea for licorice or at her past refusal to buy it, she didn't know. She was sorry to deprive the kids of their favorite treat, but a penny was a penny, and she wouldn't spend a single one that she didn't have to. Let Wolf laugh if he wanted. He had a wonderful laugh.

A moment later he wasn't laughing as he urged the wagon team out onto the road toward town. He hadn't been laughing at breakfast when he'd looked at her down the length of the table and said, "It'd be a real good idea if everyone stuck close to the house and kept a close eye on each other while we're gone." He was taking the possible threat to them seriously. He was being protective of them. It seemed to come natural to him, his protectiveness. It made her wonder.

"Wolf?"

His response was a low grunt.

"Wolf, I don't mean to pry, but . . ."

"But you're going to," he said with a resigned air.

Undeterred, Brie chuckled. "Well, yes, I guess I am. I just wondered what you meant last night when I asked about your family and friends."

"I meant what I said."

"But all you said was no. Was that no, you didn't want them contacted if anything happened to you, or no, you don't have any family or friends?"

"If you keep talking about something happening to me, you're going to make me think I need to watch my back around you."

"See? I knew you had a sense of humor."

"What made you think I didn't?"

"Because until this morning, I'd not heard you laugh."

"Until this morning there hasn't been a whole lot to laugh about around here."

"Oh, I disagree." Brie smiled and looked out across the land opening up before them at the mouth of the canyon. "There's always something to smile or laugh about. Sometimes you just have to look for it. Life should be full of smiles and laughter. For instance, I could laugh right now at how well you've avoided answering my question. Did you mean you have no family, or that you just don't want me asking questions?"

"You're gonna worry this to death, aren't you? Like a dog with a fresh bone."

She smiled brightly and peered up at him. "Of course I am, so you might as well give in and answer me."

"No."

"Well! There's no need to be rude. A simple 'I'd rather not answer' would have sufficed."

"I meant, no, I don't have any family."

His words stilled her. Logically, Brie knew that there were people without families, people utterly alone in the world. Marshall Campbell had only the family he'd gained through marriage. Father Thomas had no living relatives. Wolf certainly had the look of a loner about him, but Brie couldn't imagine what it must be like having no family. "None at all?"

He shot her a glare. "I said no, didn't I?"

Saddened by the confirmation that Wolf was alone in the world, Brie placed a hand on his arm. Beneath her fingers he flinched, then stilled, his gaze glued to the horses' rumps. "You're not alone anymore, Wolf. You have us now. We're your family."

Wolf's jaw flexed. "I'm your foreman, Miss Flanigan. You hired me. You didn't adopt me."

"Well, now," she said softly as she let her hand fall from his arm. A slight brogue slipped into her voice. "Maybe we didn't adopt you, Just Wolf. But then again, I'm thinkin' maybe we did."

Chapter Six

If Wolf had hoped he and Brie could slip into town, load up fencing supplies, and slip out again without much notice, his hope was in vain. He was decidedly uneasy with the way Brie called greetings to friends, the way her friends eyed him on the seat next to her. He'd never driven a woman around in a wagon before, had intentionally never made himself so visible.

The general store sat on a corner, where the road through town crossed a side street. Wolf turned into the side street and parked the wagon beside the building. He set the brake, secured the reins, then climbed down. If Brie Flanigan had any sense, she would understand that people—white people—didn't cotton to seeing a white woman being touched by a half-breed, no matter how innocent the touch might be. If she had any sense, she'd climb down from the wagon on her own without his help.

She didn't have any sense. She sat there expectantly, waiting for him to play the gentleman. Wolf stood on the opposite side of the wagon and met her gaze.

"Wolf?"

"I'm not being deliberately rude or stupid, but you really don't want me to come around this wagon and help you down."

"Funny, but I thought that's exactly what I wanted. I would appreciate it."

"There are people watching."

She glanced back toward the street. Two women stood on one corner, three men on the other. All were staring at them. "So there are," Brie said. "They're probably wondering why you're not helping me down."

"They're more likely wondering why you would let me near you."

She tilted her head and studied him through narrowed eyes. "Does that get heavy?"

"Does what get heavy?"

"That chip on your shoulder."

If he were a praying man, Wolf would have prayed for patience just then. "I don't have a chip on my shoulder."

"You certainly do. It says *half-breed* all across the front of it in big, bold letters. Assuming, of course, that that's what you're talking about. That a white woman shouldn't let a half-breed near her."

"That's the way most people think."

"I'm not most people. Are you going to help me down, or are we going to stay here all day? I doubt Mr. Winslow will let a man he's never met before charge fencing materials to the Rocking F, so we can't get what we came for if I stay in the wagon."

By then three more people had joined the others on the two nearest corners. Hellfire and damnation, what in the Sam Hill had made him take her damn job in the first place? She wasn't going to be sensible. Damn woman didn't have an ounce of sense. He stomped around the back of the wagon, tipping his hat politely to the women there on the corner, nodding to the men, and walked up to where Brie sat waiting.

"Why thank you, Wolf, how thoughtful." She took the

hand he grudgingly offered and climbed down. She was small and dainty, but even through his heavy leather glove he could feel the strength in her small hand. The minute both her feet were on the ground he dropped her hand and stepped back.

"Thank you." The smile she gave him was warm enough and bright enough to shame the sun. But mischief danced in her eyes.

Contradictions. The woman was one contradiction after another. So smart about some things it was scarey, dumber than dirt about others.

With effort, Brie kept the smile on her face and walked to the corner. For her life she wouldn't admit that Wolf was right, that some of the people she'd known—thought she'd known—for years were already looking at her strangely, and she'd been in town with Wolf fewer than five minutes. There was nothing for her to do but brazen it out. She wasn't going to give anyone a chance to insult her or Wolf.

"Hello, Mrs. Ward, Mrs. Potter, it's so nice to see you." She smiled and nodded, then greeted the others while Wolf hung back several yards. She wasn't having any of that. "I don't believe any of you have met the Rocking F's new foreman. I can't tell you how glad we are to have him running things out at the ranch for us. Wolf," she said, turning to him, "these are some of our neighbors. Mrs. Ward runs the bakery down the street. When the smell of her baking wafts out of her ovens, I've actually seen grown men get into fistfights over who gets to buy the first loaf. Mrs. Potter operates the boarding house a few doors down from the bakery. And these gentlemen are Mr. Haskell, Mr. Devlin, and Mr. Kennedy. They each have a ranch in the area, so I'm sure you'll be running into them from time to time."

As she conducted the introductions, Brie looked each of the townspeople directly in the eye and smiled as if she had no idea what they might be thinking, as if Wolf had been wrong about them.

Wolf tipped his hat again. "Ladies."

The ladies acknowledged with barely polite nods. Frown lines appeared on their brows and their mouths suddenly looked like they'd been sucking on lemons.

Brie ignored their subtle disapproval and held her breath as, with a carefully blank expression, Wolf turned to Mr. Haskell and extended a hand. "Pleased to meet you."

If Mr. Haskell's handshake appeared reluctant, at least it was there. If his expression appeared a shade on the skeptical side, Brie pretended not to notice. Neither he nor either of the other two men, nor any of the men in the area had been willing to help the Flanigans since the drowning. Brie didn't particularly care what any of them thought.

"Foreman, huh?" Mr. Haskell said, shaking Wolf's hand.

"That's right," Wolf answered.

"Well." Brie could almost hear Mr. Haskell's thoughts. If the Rocking F had a foreman, Haskell and the others no longer needed to feel guilty about those poor Flanigan orphans out there all alone with no one to help them. The words practically danced across Haskell's face as his smile grew. "Well, isn't that fine?" he asked of his companions.

The three men looked at each other a minute, then Kennedy and Devlin both smiled.

"Fine, indeed." Devlin extended his hand to Wolf and pumped it enthusiastically.

Next came Kennedy. "Foreman of the Rocking F. Well, welcome to New Hope, Mr. Wolf."

As Wolf shook hands, he eyed the men carefully. Brie could feel his doubt and mistrust. "No mister," he said. "Just Wolf."

Brie's cheeks were starting to ache from forcing a smile. "You were all obviously on your way somewhere," she told the men and women. "We have business with Mr. Winslow, so we won't keep you. It was nice seeing you." Without waiting, she turned aside and walked the few feet of board-walk to the door of the general store. This time Wolf didn't hang back; he was right on her heels. When she glanced at him over her shoulder as he opened the door for her, he glared at her with narrowed eyes. She merely smiled and stepped into Winslow's Mercantile.

Just inside the door Brie paused, as she always did upon entering, and savored the smells. Vinegar from the pickle barrel in the corner. New leather from the tack, boots, and work gloves along the wall. The starchy smell from the bolts of new calico and gingham on the table in the back. Dozens of other smells, too, mingled and mixed until Brie couldn't separate them, but she savored them.

Three other customers were looking over the merchan-dise. Brie recognized one as a Double Diamond hand.

Behind her the bell over the door jingled as Wolf fol-lowed her in and closed the door. He took off his hat and held it against his thigh.

The brown curtain that separated the store from the storeroom and living quarters in the back of the building wavered and Horace Winslow stepped through. "Miss Brie, howdy." His smile was as bright as his shiny bald head. "You were just in two days ago. Forget something, did you? I know, Miss Katy made you come back for licorice."

Brie laughed and glanced at Wolf, then back at Mr. Winslow. "It was Rory this time, but I didn't make any promises."

When she introduced Wolf, Winslow's reaction was simi-lar to that of the other men, cautiously shaking hands and forcing a smile. "Rocking F Foreman. Well, I'll be."

"And as such," Brie told Winslow, "he'll need to buy supplies on the Rocking F account from time to time. I wanted to let you know in advance so there won't be any question."

Winslow frowned and shuffled his feet. "Are you sure,

Miss Brie? I know you're trying to be careful with your spending. Way I hear it, this fella, no offense, mister, but he's new around here. A stranger. No tellin'—"

"I'll be thankin' ya for your concern," Brie interrupted, her temper moving from steaming to slow boil. "But Wolf isn't a stranger. 'Tis our foreman, he be." Her eyes narrowed and her smile turned brittle. "I'll be thankin' ya, too, for questioning my judgement and Wolf's honesty, and for discussing me financial situation in such a public manner as this. I can't be tellin' ya how much that pleases me."

"Now, Miss Brie, I'm only tryin' to look out for you and your family, what with your poor parents drownin' and leavin' you out there all alone."

"Faith, and I'm sure you are, Mr. Winslow. We've come for fencing supplies. Wolf?" She turned to her foreman. "Do you see what we'll be needin'?"

Wolf's eyes were narrowed and hard as he took in not so much the merchandise, but the other people in the store. "No."

"Fencing supplies are out back," Winslow offered with a wave toward the curtain where he'd entered. His brow furrowed. "What are you gonna fence?"

Brie saw the unease in his eyes and knew the reason. There had been trouble over fences north of town. Some people fenced land that didn't belong to them. Some fenced neighbors away from shared water. Every cowhand in the state, it seemed, carried wire cutters in his saddlebags these days. Just in case. And extra ammunition, for when the shooting started. Mr. Winslow had reason to be concerned. But not about her.

Then, too, her temper was still smoldering over his earlier comments. "Out back?" she asked, deliberately ignoring his question. "Would you be showin' us, Mr. Winslow?"

The man flushed and huffed, then nodded. "Follow me."

As they followed him through the curtain and out the

rear door, Brie glanced back and saw the Double Diamond hand rush out the front. The other two customers, whom she recognized as hands from other ranches but whose names she didn't know, had their heads together and were talking in low tones.

The word would be all over the country by noon that Brie Flanigan had hired a half-breed foreman, and that the Rocking F was buying fence.

Wolf looked over the rolls of wire arranged on a work table outside the back door of the mercantile and selected a specific type. Brie couldn't tell the difference between the fence rolls; they all looked painfully sharp and lethal to her. When he told Winslow how much wire he wanted, Winslow obviously realized they weren't fencing in half the prairie and looked relieved.

It seemed Mr. Winslow was in the mood to patronize her, for after Wolf selected the desired amount of wire, a pair of wire cutters, and a few other items Brie wasn't sure of the use of, Mr. Winslow gave her a pitying smile. "Your new foreman has made excellent selections, Miss Flanigan. Perhaps too excellent. The cost . . . well, I feel obliged to tell you that this will extend your credit to the limit."

Brie blanched. The sale of her cattle was still weeks away. She didn't have enough supplies to last until then. Without credit, how were they to get more flour, salt, sugar? How was she to afford new clothes and boots for the boys— boys grew so terribly fast. As did girls. Everyone but Brie had outgrown last year's clothes and footwear. So many expenses still to come. So long to wait for the money to pay her bills.

But Wolf said they needed the wire, and she certainly had no intention of allowing Double Diamond cattle to graze her winter pasture down to the ground in the valley, forcing her cattle to spend the winter up on the mesa. Was she to be forced, then, to choose between her cattle, which meant the future of the ranch, and food and clothes for her brothers and sisters?

Wolf's quiet voice intruded into her fearful thoughts. "Just how much are you charging for the wire?"

"Barbed wire is expensive, young fella."

"How expensive?" Wolf asked quietly.

"Why, it's twenty cents a pound."

One corner of Wolf's mouth stretched. He gave Brie a look, then settled his hat squarely on his head. "I don't think so."

Winslow puffed out his chest. "You have a problem with that, 'breed?"

Brie's stomach tightened. She'd never heard anyone speak so rudely to another person. Despite her money worries, she was just about to give Mr. Winslow a piece of her mind and the sharp side of her tongue when Wolf spoke again, even more quietly than before.

"No problem at all, white man. It's your store. You charge what you want. But the Rocking F won't be paying twenty cents a pound for wire. It'll be worth the trip to buy it in Las Animas. When I came through there a few days ago a pound of that same wire was going for four cents."

"Four cents! Why, I paid more than that for it myself," Winslow protested.

Wolf turned to Brie. "If we start out now, we can probably make it back to the ranch by dark."

Brie swallowed. They would have to run the team into the ground to go all the way to Las Animas on the banks of the Arkansas and be home by dark. "All right."

"Fifteen cents," Winslow offered quickly. "I won't make a profit, but it would be a shame for you to have to travel all that way. Fifteen cents a pound. It's a fair price."

Wolf turned back to him with a shake of his head. "I'm not doubting your word about it being fair, but Miss Flanigan won't be paying it." Wolf turned back and gestured Brie toward the door.

"Twelve cents."

"You ready, Miss Flanigan?" Wolf asked solemnly.

"They're not likely to extend credit to the Rocking F up in Los Alamos," Winslow said quickly. "How will you pay for it?"

Brie arched an eyebrow in a perfect imitation of her mother whenever someone said or did something she'd considered *untoward*. "That, sir, is none of your concern."

Winslow flushed. "I'm just thinking of your welfare, Miss Brie. I'd hate to see you travel all that way, only to come home empty handed."

Her second brow arched up to join its mate. "Do you hate the idea enough to lower your price, Mr. Winslow?" At her words, she sensed Wolf's approval. Something warm unfolded within her.

"Now, Miss Brie, you just don't understand about commerce. 'Course it's not your fault, being a female and all."

"Sure, and if you mean I don't be understandin' how the same wire can sell for so much higher here than at Las Animas, then you be right, sir."

Wolf touched the small of her back with his hand. "Are you ready to leave?"

"Ten cents," Winslow offered, seeing the sale slip away.

"Five," Wolf said, "or we leave."

"Seven. That's as absolutely, positively low as I can go."

Brie glanced at Wolf, then at Mr. Winslow. "Seven, and you take back a sack of flour torn up by a Double Diamond hand and charge the replacement to the Double D."

"Charge Rocking F flour to the Double Diamond? Why, I can't do that."

Brie tugged at the edge of first one glove, then the other, as if making sure they were on securely. "That's my final offer, Mr. Winslow. Take it or leave it. Seven cents a pound, which is still too high, in my estimation, and a sack of flour. Do we have a deal?"

"You'll beggar me!"

One corner of Wolf's mouth curved in a travesty of a smile. "Seven, a bag of flour, and I won't ride up and down the street announcing that you're trying to take the very food from the mouths of orphans.''

Brie pressed her fingers to her mouth and coughed to cover the sudden inappropriate laughter that threatened. Mr. Winslow's cheeks quivered and turned red. ''Why, how dare you threaten such a thing, you lowdown, dirty, stinking—''

''Come on, Wolf.'' Brie lost all urge to laugh. ''The price in Las Animas was dropping by the day. I'm sure it's down to two cents a pound by now.'' She turned toward the door; Wolf turned with her.

''Wait! All right, all right. Seven cents a pound.''

''And a sack of flour.''

Winslow winced, then heaved a gusty sigh. ''And a sack of flour.''

Brie glanced at Wolf, then pursed her lips and gave Mr. Winslow a brisk nod.

''In that case,'' Wolf said, ''toss in three sticks of that dynamite in case I have to get rid of any boulders in the fence line.''

When she stepped back into the store a moment later, elation filled her and laughter threatened. She managed to hold it to a grin. The grin broadened a moment later when Wolf stopped at the counter and withdrew a handful of licorice sticks from the jar there. ''Add these to the bill,'' he told Mr. Winslow.

After their purchases were loaded in the wagon and the torn sack of flour had been replaced, Brie followed Wolf back into the store. He pulled a piece of paper from his pocket and asked to borrow a pencil from the storekeeper. Curious, Brie watched and waited. When he finished, Wolf posted the note on the notice board beside the door. She stepped up to read it.

> *ROCKING F HIRING RIDERS.*
> *SEE FOREMAN.*

Excitement rushed through Brie's chest. Most men wouldn't work for a woman. With Wolf's notice, maybe . . .

Boot steps thudded on the wooden floor, accompanied by the jingle of spurs, as someone neared Brie and Wolf from behind. A gloved hand reached over Brie's shoulder and tore down Wolf's note.

Wolf turned slowly, but Brie whirled, laughter and excitement replaced by outrage, and glared at Hank Jennings, foreman of the Double Diamond. She tossed her head and gave a dainty sniff. "Are you applying for a job riding for the Rocking F, Mr. Jennings?"

Jennings laughed as he wadded up the note and threw it aside. "That's real funny, Miss Brie. Real funny. No, I'm not riding for the Rocking F, and neither is anybody else from around here." He gave a slow, confident look around at the half-dozen men who'd entered while Brie and Wolf had been out back. "No ma'am, nobody from around here will be working for the Rocking F. If they know what's good for them."

"How dare you!" Brie cried.

Jennings ignored her and eyed Wolf. He stared so long and hard that Brie forgot about the note wadded up on the floor. What little she knew of Wolf told her he was not a complacent man, not a man to take Jennings's look as anything other than the insult it was meant to be.

"This the half-breed that talked his way out of jail?" Jennings taunted with a sneer.

"What a despicable thing to say! 'Twas your men," Brie said heatedly, her voice ladened with a heavy brogue, "who set upon Katy and me. 'Twas Wolf who saved us from a mauling or worse at the hands of those brutes you hired."

"So now you've got the redskinned bastard living out at the ranch with you," Jennings taunted. "Fine example you're setting for those kids, letting them watch this Injun crawl under your skirts. Your mama would be turning over in her grave if she knew."

A red haze of rage blurred Brie's vision. As she stood

between Jennings and Wolf, Wolf tried to push her aside. She knew what he would do, had seen the way he'd dealt with the three men who had attacked her and Katy. He would get in a fight right here in the store, not for the slurs against himself, but for the way Jennings spoke to her.

But it wasn't his fight, not this time. There was too much Irish in her blood to allow her to stand by and let someone else fight her battles. "That may be, ya bloody blighter," she told Jennings. "But I take after me da, and he'd be cleanin' your clock." With both fists raised, she bounced around before him like a pugilist on springs.

She didn't plan it, not really. Didn't know she was going to do it, and an instant later, didn't realize she had done it. But suddenly she feinted with her left and jabbed with her right. Numbing pain shot from her gloved knuckles all the way to her shoulder. It took a stunned moment for the correlation between the pain in her hand, Jennings's bellow of rage, and the blood gushing from his nose to make sense in her mind.

Jesus, Mary, and Joseph! I hit him!

"Whoo-whee!" cried a man who'd been sorting through the tinned goods on a shelf.

"By gawd," someone else muttered, "she done went and punched him!"

Wolf felt his blood heat. The word that left his mouth was low and vicious. Damn fool woman. She had more temper than brains. Not that Jennings hadn't deserved a good pop in the nose. Wolf had moved to deliver the blow himself, but Brie had gotten in the way. Now Jennings growled and raised his fist.

With a snarl, Wolf yanked Brie aside, out of the man's reach. "Touch her and die, Jennings."

"Go ahead," Brie taunted, dancing back between Wolf and Jennings. "Come on, ya bleedin' coward, I dare ya."

Jennings lunged, but two men grabbed him from behind

to keep him from hitting her. Their actions saved his life, for Wolf's threat had not been idle.

Unconcerned that her opponent was temporarily unable to fight back, Brie advanced on him, ready to swing again. Wolf wrapped both his arms around her, trapping her arms against her sides, and whirled her away. "That's enough," he hissed in her ear.

"'Tis not enough!" Brie worked her way loose from Wolf's hold and spun back toward Jennings. He was still held from behind by the two men. As he snarled and struggled to free himself, Brie jabbed a finger into his chest. "I'll be thankin' ya to keep your filthy words to yourself, Hank Jennings. And while you're at it, you can keep your cattle off my grass and your men off my land."

Wolf reached for her again, but she batted his hands away and gave Jennings another jab in the chest. "The next Double Diamond beef I find on the Rocking F is going to end up on my supper table."

Wolf managed to get his arms around her and haul her back again. She struggled and kicked, accidentally connecting with Jennings's shin. The man cursed and heaved to get loose.

"And the next Double Diamond rider that comes on my land or gets anywhere near me or mine," Brie said heatedly, "will get a load of buckshot for his trouble."

Someone opened the door beside Wolf and he hauled a kicking and hissing Brie outside.

"And for your information," she shouted back at Jennings, "Wolf is a gentleman!"

"Enough!" Wolf roared in her ear. "You made your point." He hauled her around the side of the building and tossed her unceremoniously onto the wagon seat. With fire in her eyes, she started to climb down. Wolf pushed her back none too gently. "Stay!"

Brie fell back onto the seat with a huff. Wolf held her there until the blaze of fury left her eyes. "Don't move from that seat. I'll be right back."

"You're not going in there—"

"Sit down and keep quiet," he snapped. "You've caused enough trouble for one day."

"Me! It was him—"

"Quiet! I'm going back in that store to repost my notice, and you're going to sit here and wait for me." Wolf stomped off, swearing under his breath. At the corner of the building he looked back and with a sharp glare, stopped Brie from climbing down from the wagon.

When he pushed open the door to the store a moment later, Jennings, with his bandanna pressed to his bleeding nose, was reaching for the door handle from the inside. The door whacked him in the face.

Jennings staggered back, a hand to his forehead and the mark left by the door. "Goddamn! You stinking half-breed."

Ignoring him, Wolf walked to the counter. "Got a piece of paper I can use to rewrite my notice?" he asked Winslow.

Winslow looked to Jennings as if for permission.

"If he's in charge," Wolf said of Jennings, "maybe it's him I should be asking."

Winslow flushed. "I run my own store, make my own decisions, young fella," he said gruffly. "Here's your dang paper, and here's a pencil to write with."

Wolf thanked him, wrote out his notice again and posted it where the other had been.

With a low curse, Jennings reached for it. Wolf grabbed the man's hand and stopped him. "I wouldn't do that, if I were you."

"You're new here," Jennings said coldly, "so you maybe don't realize who you're talking to. I'm the foreman of the Double Diamond, and nobody tells me what I can and can't do."

"That's fine," Wolf allowed. "But if that notice isn't right there the next time I come to town, I'll know who took it down. And if I hear of you ever talking dirty about Miss Flanigan again, I'll come looking for you."

Jennings looked him up and down, then snorted. "You and what army, half-breed?"

Wolf taunted him with a smile. "If a girl half your size can do that much damage—" He waved toward the blood still seeping from the man's nose. "—I don't think I'll be needing an army."

"I'll kill you for that."

"Not in here!" Winslow bellowed.

"To hell with you," Jennings snarled back. He went for his gun.

Wolf was much faster. By the time Jennings had his gun halfway out of his holster, the barrel of Wolf's .45 was pressed to the underside of Jennings's jaw. "Think real hard, Jennings, before you pull a gun on me."

Jennings's eyes widened. His Adam's apple rose, then fell. Slowly, carefully, he eased his pistol back into the holster and held his hand out to his side. "No need to get all riled over a little misunderstanding, mister."

Wolf lowered his .45 and holstered it. "Glad you agree." With a tug to the brim of his hat, he stepped around Jennings. At the door, he turned back. "By the way, don't bother running any more Double Diamond cattle up the canyon and onto Rocking F grass. We're stringing fence across the end of the valley."

When Wolf stepped out the door, his last sight was of Jennings's face turning beet red in fury.

Wolf slammed the door. Son of a bitch. Before this was over, he'd probably have to kill Jennings.

Brie sat beside Wolf on the wagon seat and fumed over his high-handed treatment of her, as well as the ticcing muscle in his jaw. "'Twas my character and morals dragged through the dirt, not yours. I don't see what it is you have to be mad about."

The muscle along his jaw flexed. "Mad? Hell, Irish, I'm not mad. I'm goddamn good and pissed off. If I'd known

I was going to have to kill a man, I'd have thought twice about taking this job."

Brie's anger drained away as abruptly as did the blood from her head. Something like terror replaced both the emotion and the blood. "Kill? You . . . you didn't . . . What are you talking about?"

Wolf shot her a terse look. "Jennings."

Brie gaped. "You . . . you didn't . . . Wolf!"

"No, I didn't kill him. Yet. But he's going to make it damn near impossible not to."

"You . . . you'd kill a man for . . . for talking dirty?"

"Great." Wolf rolled his eyes in disgust. "Now she thinks I'm stupid. No, I wouldn't kill a man for talking dirty. You obviously don't know much about men."

"Right now I don't think I know much about anything, least of all whatever it is you're talking about."

"Irish, a man who'll say things in public to a woman, things like Jennings said to you, is a man to watch out for. There aren't enough good women to go around out here in the middle of nowhere to be insulting them like that."

"You won't get an argument from me, but what happened back in town isn't worth killing over."

"Not the words, no. But you humiliated him in public. Jennings seems to think real highly of himself. A man like that doesn't take to being humiliated, especially not in front of other men, and not by a little slip of a girl. Then, too," he muttered, "I didn't help much either. He's been laughed at by other men now. He won't stand for it, Brie. The Chinese call it losing face. Jennings has lost face, and he's got to get it back."

Brie scoffed and turned her face into the wind. "What's he going to do, attack me and the kids? That's not likely to help him get his face back."

"No, it's not. But he'll be too mad to think straight. Or maybe he'll get sneaky about it, waiting until you or one of the kids is off somewhere alone." Wolf glanced at her and something twisted inside his chest. The breeze stirred by their passing teased the bright red curls that had worked their way from beneath her bonnet. The thought of anything happening to her was startlingly hard to bear. Something about her stirred his protective instincts.

Those instincts had always been particularly strong. He'd always been driven to do what he could when someone weaker was being threatened by someone stronger. But it had never felt like this before. He'd never felt so totally compelled. She wasn't just someone weaker than the threat before her. She was Brianna. And she needed him.

Once again, as it had a few days ago when he'd first seen her, that alien sense came over him. It felt like . . . belonging. He had the brief flash of belief that with this woman, he'd finally found a home.

Stupid. And pointless. There was no home for the man known only as Wolf. Never had been, never would be. But he would not fight his protective instincts. He would do what could be done for Brie and her family. "I don't want anyone going anywhere alone from here on out. Everyone stays close to the house and barn, and all of you have to let someone else know where you're going at all times. There's going to be trouble, Brie. Bad trouble. I can taste it."

"There's always trouble in one form or another." Brie touched a hand to his arm and spoke softly and with confidence. "God will watch out for us."

Wolf snorted. "Irish, if there is a God, he wouldn't spit on me if I was on fire."

Genuinely shocked by his words and his derisive tone, Brie stared at Wolf's profile.

"If you're counting on me for help," he said darkly, "you'd better forget about any divine intervention."

Chapter Seven

Wolf couldn't guess how long Jennings would wait before striking, so for the next couple of days he stuck close to the house. There was plenty of work to keep him busy. He greased the big wooden hubs on the wagon and replaced a worn strap on one harness. He reset two poles in one of the corrals.

One of those wild cows Brie milked every morning had managed to cut her left foreleg. To keep out the screw-worms and blowfly eggs, Wolf daubed the cut with a noxious mixture of carbolic acid and axle grease.

From the time Wolf had begun to work on the list of chores he had set for himself, something odd had happened to his shadow. It had developed companions. Everywhere his shadow stretched, two shorter ones bobbed along on either side. Rory and Sully dogged his every step. Their presence took some getting used to for a man used to being alone. So did their questions. He'd never heard so many questions in his life.

"How come you're doing that?" That, being greasing the hubs on the wagon.

"So the wheels won't wear out too fast and start to squeal."

"You mean like a pig?" An even shorter shadow had joined the three "men." "We had a pig once," Katy announced. "It squealed."

"No, dummy," Rory answered in disgust. "He don't mean like a pig. Girls are so *dumb.*"

"I am not dumb!" Katy did a credible imitation of Brie as she'd looked in the mercantile the day before by doubling up her fists and waving them beneath her brother's nose. "Take it back, Rory."

"Dumb, dumb dumb. I will not take it back. Girls are— *oomph.*" His breath left him in a grunt as Katy's tiny fist plowed into his belly.

Sully rolled his eyes. "Kids," he said with disgust from his much older vantage point.

Rory's eyes narrowed at his little sister in murderous threat.

"Uh . . ." Wolf began. But he didn't have the slightest idea what to say to little kids to stop a fight. At any rate, he realized a moment later, it would have been a waste of breath.

"I'll get you for that," Rory threatened.

"Get you, get you," Katy sang. Then she stuck out her tongue and the race was on. Rory lunged, Katy squealed, either like a worn wagon wheel or the aforementioned pig, Wolf wasn't sure, but the sound trailed over her shoulder as she turned and ran.

Rory was after her like a shot. But instead of screaming for help, Katy was shrieking with laughter. Wolf relaxed, realizing this was an old game between the two. The concept of siblings combining anger and fun wasn't totally foreign to him; he'd heard stories around campfires for years. But he'd never been privy to a closeup look at the inner workings of a family. He stared, fascinated, his heart thumping hard in his chest and a sense of yearning swelling in his throat.

"Whatsa matter, Wolf?"

Wolf tore his gaze from the pair of children, both now giggling and rolling in the dirt like two pups. "Huh?" He looked up from where he squatted beside the wagon to find Sully staring at him, red head cocked to one side and a frown line forming between his green eyes. Not the same brilliant pine green as Brie's, not the that vibrant, compelling green that a man could fall into and drown in, but lighter, with a touch of gray. "Did you say something?"

"Is something wrong? You looked kinda funny there for a minute, like Saint Pat looks when the mama cat won't let him play with her kittens."

Wolf flushed, then laughed at himself. Sully had hit the nail square on the head. Wolf would have likened the feeling that had run through him as being akin to a boy with his nose pressed to the glass window of a store, looking in at the candy in the jar on the counter and knowing it would be forever out of his reach, but dogs and kittens was close enough.

"Naw," he told Sully as he dabbed the last load of grease on the hub before him. "Nothing's wrong." Nothing but a fool wishing for the moon. What the hell would a man do with the moon if he had it?

Finished with the wagon, Wolf, with Sully's help, stored the grease back in the shed where it belonged, washed up at the pump, then started resetting two more loose poles on the corral for the wagon horses. Much the worse for wear, Katy and Rory dashed over to watch. Their disagreement was apparently over.

By the time the poles were reset, Tessa stuck her head out the back door of the house and called everyone to supper.

Wolf would have avoided the event if he could, but Sully stuck to his side, and for the life of him, Wolf couldn't think of an excuse good enough to avoid sitting down to supper with the Flanigans without appearing rude.

If he wasn't concerned about what Jennings might do,

Wolf would have spent the day up on the mesa checking the cattle. He still needed to do that, but not yet. He wasn't comfortable leaving Brie and the kids alone.

He could find another chore that would keep him close, but away from supper, but an afternoon thunderstorm was rolling in from the mountains. He might be able to find work that needed doing in the barn, but he'd already done everything that really needed doing.

So he would join them for supper, would sit at the head of the table—it wasn't lost on him that that was the place they had given him. It was that, as much as the mere oddity of joining a family for dinner that made him feel as though he were trespassing. Then there was the ambiguity of prayer time. Holding a child's hand in each of his felt so good it scared the hell out of him; feigning respect for a God who had long since abandoned a scared little boy called Wolf was enough to make him want to swear.

Even that was nothing compared to what happened inside his chest when he happened to look down the length of the table, past the plates and bowls and platters filled with the best food he'd ever eaten, and run smack into the mountain-pine green of Irish eyes. If he didn't know better, he could have been fooled into thinking that sitting at that table was right where he belonged.

He hated sitting down at that damn table.

The next day Wolf charred the ends of the fence posts he would use to string the barbed wire so the posts wouldn't rot in the ground. The day following, as soon as he could get away from the breakfast table, he loaded the posts and wire into the back of the wagon and hitched up the team. He was carrying his rifle and extra ammunition from the bunkhouse when Brie joined him.

In the early morning light, the fire in her hair was muted and her pale skin looked like a smooth pearl he'd seen once. Her lips parted in a smile and made him want to taste them, feel them pressed against his own.

He wouldn't call himself a fool for the wish. She was a beautiful woman. She probably had this effect on nearly every man who saw her. The most intriguing thing was, he didn't think she knew it. Innocence shown from those bright green eyes. He told himself that the curiosity and interest that mingled with the innocence was only a trick of the morning light.

He forced himself to look away from her eyes, and that's when he realized she was dressed differently than he'd ever seen her. Instead of gingham or calico, with a bonnet holding most of her hair up and away from sight, she wore a dark corduroy skirt, a plain blue man's shirt, sturdy boots, and a black, low crowned hat, the chin strap dangling to her collarbone. In the crook of one arm she carried a wicker basket. "Going somewhere?" he asked.

"With you."

It was the last thing he'd expected her to say. "Why?"

"You're going to start putting up the fence, aren't you?"

Warily, he nodded once.

"I want to help."

Wolf stuck his tongue against his cheek. "Fine. You can dig the post holes. I've already loaded the pick axe."

She gave him a carefree shrug and smile. "I don't know how good I'll be at it, but I'll give it my best."

"I was joking. You can't dig post holes."

"You're probably right, but I can help string wire."

Wolf glanced down at her bare, slender hands and fought a shudder. The thought of them cut and torn by the sharp barbs on the wire nearly made him ill. They looked too soft for hard work, yet he knew she worked hard. What would it feel like to have her pale hands touch his dark skin? The touch he only imagined sent heat and blood rushing to his loins and a curse rushing to his lips. "You should stay home and keep a sharp eye out for trouble."

"Elly will do that. She **can** keep an eye out and make sure everyone's safe."

"What about your safety?"

"You'll see to that. And I'll see to yours."

He paused in the act of stowing his rifle within easy reach beneath the seat. "You'll what?"

"You can't watch the hills, much less your back, while you're digging post holes and stringing wire."

"Thanks for the concern, but I'll be fine."

"You're probably right, but I won't be. If I stay home, I'll just fret and worry all day, wondering if you're okay."

Wolf frowned. "Are you in the habit of doing that? Worrying about people?"

"Outside the family, you mean? No. This is a first for me, but I can't seem to help it. I guess you'll just have to humor me." With no further word and no knowledge of the panic her words stirred in Wolf, she handed Wolf the basket, then lifted her foot to a spoke on the wheel and climbed on board.

In a daze, Wolf stuck the basket behind the seat and climbed up and joined his employer. It was a good thing it didn't take much concentration to thread the traces through his gloved fingers and urge the team out of the yard, because he'd have been in trouble. His mind was still stuck on Brie's artless confession that she would worry about him if he went alone to the other end of the valley.

No one, as far as he knew, had ever worried about him in his entire life. Oh, Lazarus had worried—but not about Wolf's safety. No, the bastard had worried only that Wolf might escape.

Brie gripped the edge of the seat, hoping Wolf would believe she was merely holding on. She didn't want him to realize her hands were shaking. They shook in relief; he wouldn't understand that. She barely did herself.

When she'd realized during breakfast that Wolf

intended to ride alone to the end of the valley today to start putting up the fence, all she'd been able to see was the look of rage in Hank Jennings's eyes. Wolf was right; she should never have hit the man. Now he was likely to take his anger at her out on those around her who were the easiest to get to. The most logical choice would be to take it out on Wolf. The best opportunity would be when Wolf was out riding alone, or distracted by putting up a fence. Brie couldn't let him go alone. Someone had to watch. Someone had to give warning if the need arose.

They drove upstream to the south end of the valley, beyond the small adobe line shack that belonged to the Rocking F, and on to the mouth of the long, narrow canyon that separated—or linked, depending on one's point of view—the Rocking F and the Double Diamond.

Neither Brie nor Wolf spoke during the entire trip. Wolf was a quiet man by nature. Brie, normally outgoing and talkative, held her tongue, knowing that Wolf would have preferred she stay home with the others. The creaking of the wagon and the jingle of harnesses were the only sounds as Brie lifted her face to the breeze. She was more than comfortable with the silence between her and Wolf, and the comfort surprised her. She usually preferred lively conversation to silence. But with Wolf, everything seemed different. He was so strong and solid beside her, conversation seemed unnecessary.

Wolf turned the team away from the rutted wheel tracks they'd been following and pulled to a halt at the east side of the canyon mouth. This, then, would be the place where the fence began. He climbed down and started unhitching the team; Brie jumped down and helped him unharness the horses and turn them out to graze.

Still silent, Wolf began unloading materials and tools from the wagon. Intent on helping, Brie reached for the pick axe.

"I was only kidding about you digging the holes," Wolf told her.

Brie hefted the pick from the bed of the wagon and offered Wolf a smile. "I know, but I can at least carry tools."

Wolf didn't like the idea of her hauling heavy, dirty tools. He didn't much like her being here at all; he shouldn't have let her come with him. The skin along the back of his neck was prickling, warning him of trouble in the air. She shouldn't be here. "You don't need to carry anything. Why don't you find a spot over by those rocks and rest?" *Where you'll be out of the way if trouble starts,* he added silently.

"Rest?" She laughed. "Do you think I'm so feeble that a short ride in a wagon can wear me out? I didn't come out here to rest. I came to help."

Wolf scowled. "You ever string wire before?"

"No, but I can learn."

"No need for you to learn. It'll go easier if I work alone."

"You're used to that, aren't you?"

"Used to what?"

"Working alone."

"That's a fact." At the side of the mouth to the canyon, he propped his rifle against a boulder, raised the pick in both hands, and swung at the rocky ground. The shock of hard iron meeting iron-hard ground shot up his arms to his shoulders, into his neck, and down his spine. It served him right, he thought as he swung again, harder this time. He had no business liking the way that flat-crowned hat sat her head, or the way the worn man's shirt draped her form like silk. He had no business feeling a sting of something irrational while wondering whose shirt it was. "You want a gate?"

Brie stared. The power of his swing, the way his shirt pulled taut across his shoulders, the play of muscles beneath the fabric . . . Her mouth turned dry. "A what?"

With his back to her, he swung again. Rock chips sprayed across his boots and clattered across the ground. "A gate.

Do you want a gate in the fence so you can take the canyon trail to the Double Diamond?''

"I thought the whole point of the fence was to keep them out. If I can use the gate to go to the Double Diamond, what's to stop them from using it to get to us?"

Wolf swung again. "Nothing. But better a gate a rider can ride through than having your wire cut every time you turn around. Maybe with a gate, the fence won't seem like such a hostile move to Jennings and his boss, the major."

"All right, we'll have a gate."

Wolf acknowledged her decision with a nod, then put his back into the next swing. The pick broke through the remainder of the surface rock and into the soil beneath. With a satisfied grunt, he dropped the pick and took up the hinged post-hole diggers. With all his strength, he rammed the sharp blades into the ground. They bit down about three inches and no more. He worked the handles and pulled upward, lifting out the dirt trapped between the curved blades and piling it beside the hole.

Again and again he sunk the blades of the post-hole diggers into the ground, each time biting deeper into the soil, until he decided the hole was deep enough. He turned toward the pile of posts he'd unloaded from the wagon, but Brie had beat him to it. She'd selected a post and was holding it out toward him.

"Thanks." He took the post from her hands and rammed the scorched end deep into the hole. He filled in the hole with rocks and loose dirt, then hefted a big rock to pound the post in until he was satisfied that it was secure. Afterward, he rolled two boulders, each about a foot-and-a-half across, in place to brace the post against the pull of the wire he would string.

From there, taking his rifle with him even though the distance was only a few yards, Wolf moved on and set the next post, and the next. When each hole was dug, Brie carried him a new post. These not being end posts like the first one, they didn't require boulders at their bases to hold them against the pull of the wire, as the pull would be equal from each side.

Brie watched him work tirelessly, but with effort. Sweat streamed down the sides of his face and dampened his shirt. After the third post, he paused and rolled his bandanna into a band and wrapped it around his forehead to keep sweat from dripping into his eyes as the sun rose and the day turned August-hot.

Brie stirred herself from staring—faith, but she'd never been so fascinated with a man before!—and carried the canteen to him. He stopped working long enough to take a drink, thanked her, then turned back to his task.

Brie felt useless. "Can I help?"

"No." Wolf knew his reply was terse, but he couldn't help it. The prickling along the back of his neck was growing stronger by the minute. "That hat's not enough protection. You'll burn out here in this sun. Why don't you find a patch of shade over in the rocks?"

"I'm a big girl, Wolf. I know when to get out of the sun, just like I know when to come in out of the rain."

"If you say so."

Brie refused to let his tone and manner hurt her. He hadn't wanted her to come with him today. If he was brusk, it was no one's fault but hers. She hadn't missed the way he never stepped out of reach of his rifle, nor had he taken off his holster and pistol. His gaze darted constantly in all directions, sharp and alert, like a wild, wary . . . wolf, she thought, searching for any threat. She didn't know if he really expected trouble from the Double Diamond, or if he was merely a cautious man. But his actions made her doubly glad she'd come with him. She, too, could watch.

She brought him posts when he needed them, and an occasional drink of water, and otherwise kept her silence, and kept watch.

When the sun was almost overhead, she pulled the basket from behind the wagon seat and spread their lunch in the scant shade of the wagon. Wolf stopped work long enough to eat the thick sandwiches she'd brought, then went straight back to work. Something seemed to be pushing him, or he was pushing himself for some reason. To finish as quickly as possible before trouble found them? Brie wondered, but didn't ask.

About an hour after lunch Wolf dug the hole for the last post, across the stream from where he'd begun that morning. At the stream itself, the banks were nearly vertical, dropping five feet to the water below. Wolf had set one post about two feet down each bank to keep all but the most determined cattle or men from slipping beneath the fence where the ground dropped away to the stream below. A man or animal could still travel beneath the fence, but he or it would have to do so via the middle of the stream, which was two feet deep here where the high banks confined it.

Not perfect, but it was the best that could be done, given the lay of the land. Wolf doubted that anyone would be bothered with trying to run cattle either single-file down the stream or through the gate.

They might be inclined to cut the wire, but Wolf would have to deal with that if and when it happened.

Brie was headed his way with the final post. To keep her from having to wade the stream, Wolf, as he'd done for all the posts on this side, slid down the bank, crossed the stream, and reached as she handed the post down to him.

From the corner of his eye he saw a flash, a reflection of light bouncing off metal, up on the east rim of the canyon at Brie's back. The prickling on the back of his neck suddenly felt as though a dozen hot needles were stabbing him. If that was a rifle, Brie stood in the direct line of fire.

Without thought or a second look, Wolf threw down the post Brie had just handed him. His rifle was up on the bank behind him; Brie stood just above him, effectively shielding him from whatever threat sat perched on the rim of the canyon. His heart skipped a beat. There was no decision to be made. "Get down!" He grabbed her hand and jerked her over the edge and down the bank.

Brie shrieked in surprise, then her breath left her in a whoosh as Wolf wrapped his arms around her shoulders and flattened her against the steep bank, holding her pinned there by his weight and strength.

A hot sting tore across the top of Wolfs right shoulder. A puff of dirt exploded from the opposite bank at his back.

Brie was too shocked and breathless to ask questions. She didn't have to ask. The whine of rifle fire echoed down the canyon. *Someone was shooting at them!*

Suddenly Wolf rolled away from her. She wanted to snatch him back, to hold him close and somehow protect them both. But her heart was pounding so hard in sheer terror that she couldn't move. *Damn them! Damn the major and Jennings and their men!*

There wasn't a doubt in Brie's mind that the gunman was from the Double Diamond. Somehow she had never thought it would come to shooting. *Dear God, how could things have gone so wrong?*

Her thoughts took barely a second, the same amount of time it took Wolf to lift his head and peer up over the bank. The same amount of time it took their attacker to fire another round.

"Wolf!" Brie grabbed his neck with both hands and yanked him down below the edge of the bank.

Above them, the shot fell short and hit the ground at the edge of the bank, scattering dirt and tiny chips of rock down on them.

Wolf swore sharply and shoved Brie farther down the bank so he could cover her head and protect her from the sharp bits of rock showering them.

A third bullet whined and struck the opposite bank. From the spot where it hit, it was plain to Brie that Wolf would have been struck if he'd still been peering up over the edge. She wrapped her arms around his chest and held him with all her might.

Wolf swore again, this time in frustration. At this distance his .45 would be all but useless. He needed his rifle. The rifle he'd left propped near the last hole he'd dug, twenty yards away. Twenty yards away, no cover between here and there, and no cover once he reached the rifle. Son of a bitch. A fat lot of good he'd do Brie if he got himself killed.

There was nothing for it. If the distance was too far for his .45, he'd just have to shorten the distance. He glanced downstream, away from the canyon. The streambed meandered, curving here and there, with an occasional clump of cottonwood and willow whips to shade itself. Barely enough cover, but it might work. "Stay here," he hissed at Brie, "and stay down."

Before Brie could suck in enough air to ask where he was going, he was yards downstream, running in a crouch to stay hidden from the gunman. At the first bend in the stream, Wolf was also hidden from her.

Heart thundering in her ears, Brie prayed for his safety. It never crossed her mind that Wolf was running away, that he would leave her there alone and just . . . leave. She wasn't sure exactly what he was doing, but she trusted him. With her life.

For his own safety, she had to make certain that whoever was up there on the rim didn't realize Wolf was moving. She thought about poking her head up over the bank to let the gunman see her, so he would know someone was still here, but just then another bullet plowed into the bank opposite her. She flinched at the impact and realized she wasn't quite as brave as she'd thought.

She spied Wolf's hat, laying almost in the water along with hers, where they'd fallen when Wolf had pulled her to safety. Beyond the hats, the post Wolf had jerked from her hands and tossed aside rested where it had landed, half in the water of the stream. Maybe . . .

With her back pressed flat against the bank, Brie inched her way toward the fallen post. Forgetting for an instant just how visible she would be to the man on the rim, she leaned forward to grasp the post by the end that rested on dry ground just below her feet. A bullet struck the post mere inches from her hand.

Brie shrieked and jerked back, staring in shock from the new hole in the post to the three long splinters sticking out of the outer edge of her hand. For not the first time in her life, Brianna Flanigan swore aloud. It didn't help.

"Mother, you were right," she muttered beneath her breath. "A lady should always wear gloves." If she'd had on her leather gloves, she might have been saved the present pain, and the soreness she knew would remain for days.

At the sound of the shot and Brie's shriek, it took all Wolf had to hoist himself from concealment below the bank and into the relative cover of the short stand of new young trees at the second bend in the stream. His gut urged him to race back to Brie. Was she hit? Was it bad? God *damn* the bastard shooting at her.

"Stop that!" Brie shrieked, assuring Wolf she was all right, and at the same time, making him want to laugh. "What do ya want, ya bleedin' blighter?" she cried, her voice carrying easily.

Good girl, Wolf thought. By accident or design, she was keeping the gunman's attention on her, surely making him think Wolf was still there with her. He just hoped like hell that she had enough sense to keep her head down.

Another shot rang out.

"What the devil kind of answer is that, ya bully?" she called out.

Wolf had the strongest urge to work his way back to her side and kiss that tempting Irish mouth of hers. But kisses aside, he didn't dare go back. He wouldn't be much help if he kept himself pinned down with her. He had to get up on the rim.

At the edge of the trees, he waited for another shot. The instant he heard it he sprinted for the side of the adobe shack. From there he could work his way back toward the canyon, make it up the hill and onto the mesa only yards from the gunman.

As he made it to the protection of the stout adobe, Brie, having pulled the splinters from her hand, reached again for the post at her feet, this time bending sideways and keeping her back to the bank rather than leaning forward and exposing herself.

She dragged the post back upstream, then used the toe of her boot to inch Wolf's hat up far enough so she could reach it. The way her heart pounded and her hands shook, it was a miracle she didn't drop both hat and post into the center of the stream, where they would have been washed away out of her reach.

But as she'd told Wolf a few days earlier, God must have been watching out for her. He didn't give her much help in propping Wolf's hat on the end of the post, however; it took her three tries before her violently shaking hands accomplished the task. Then she rested against the bank a moment, trying to catch her breath, before grasping the post in both hands and raising it high enough to expose Wolf's hat to the man on the rim.

It was a variation on the trick she and the kids used frequently on each other when playing hide and seek. Leave a hat, bonnet, or shoe barely showing from an otherwise good hiding place, to fool the seeker. When the one who was "it" ran forward, thinking to tag someone who obviously hadn't hidden as well as assumed, the "hider" would sneak silently from concealment to a new hiding place, one where the seeker had already looked.

This time, however, something more was called for than just leaving a personal article in plain sight. She had to *move* the article into sight. It was the movement that might convince the man on the rim that Wolf was still down here.

The instant the hat broke the top of the bank, another shot rang out and echoed down the canyon. The man had aimed low, intent on hitting more than just the hat. The bullet thudded into the top of the post as it would have the top of Wolf's head if he'd been wearing the hat. The force of the impact drew a cry from Brie's throat and sent a jarring shock wave up her arms as the post seemingly flew from her grasp. Post and hat landed in the stream. The post hit with enough force to splash water across Brie's skirt before the current took both post and hat downstream out of her reach.

That shot told Wolf the gunman was still watching the stream. At Brie's cry, Wolf once more clamped down on the powerful urge to run to her side. Did that cry mean she was hit? He was too far away now to do her any good. If she'd been hit, someone would die.

In the curve of the valley, just before it narrowed and turned into the canyon, the ground rose in a series of hills on the east side rather than a straight wall. Wolf was nearly to the top when the sound of hoofbeats carried from the direction of the gunman's location.

Wolf swore and scrambled the rest of the way, until he could see up onto the mesa. "Son of a bitch." The bastard was getting away. Wolf drew and fired, knowing it was a wasted effort. The man was moving too fast.

Down on the stream bank, Brie heard the shot and knew it hadn't come from the gunman's rifle.

Wolf! He'd made it up to the mesa!

Brie held her breath and listened with her whole body, waiting to hear the return fire from the rifle. She heard nothing but the breeze rushing through the canyon and the rippling music of water dancing over an occasional rock along the bed of the stream at her feet.

Where was Wolf? Had he shot the gunman? What was taking so long? It seemed like hours since she'd heard the pistol shot, yet she knew it had only been moments.

The sun beat down on her head and burned her face.

It glanced off the water below and stung her eyes. But it didn't appear to move at all.

Where was Wolf?

She waited . . . and waited. Until she thought she might scream. Until she couldn't wait any longer. Just as she told herself that surely it was safe to come out of hiding, surely Wolf should have been back by now, she heard the voice she'd been praying for call her name. She had never heard a sweeter sound. She desperately wanted to see him, to assure herself he was all right, she told herself. But her innate honesty forced her to admit, although only silently, that what she wanted most was the feeling of safety she always experienced in his presence.

"Wolf!" Frantic with the need to see him, she turned and scrambled up the bank until she could see over the edge.

"Brie! Answer me!"

"I'm here!" She saw him then, trotting toward her from the base of the hills that rose to the mesa top.

"Are you all right?" He skidded to a halt just before tumbling down the bank on top of her.

By the time he reached her Brie had managed to control her shaking, if not the erratic pounding of her heart. But one look into those gray eyes, still lit with the fierceness of battle and tinged with worry for her, and the trembling started all over again. She raised her arms in a silent plea.

Wolf read the fear and the need in her eyes, felt the same pounding inside him with every beat of his heart. Though his mind told him she was all right, that the crisis was over, the message somehow didn't make it to his hands. He bent down and placed them around her waist and pulled her up the bank and into his arms. "You're all right?"

Her head nodded up and down where it pressed against his chest. "Y-yes. You?"

"I'm fine."

His sheltering arms were warm and strong around her.

Brie wanted nothing more than to stand in the circle of his embrace forever. She forced herself to ask, "Is he gone?"

"Yeah, dammit, he got away. You sure you're all right?"

Brie took a deep breath to steady herself. The shaking was easing; the icy cold in the pit of her stomach was melting from his warmth. And something else was starting to stir in her blood, a new kind of warmth, a new kind of need. Unsure of what to do with such feelings, Brie braced her hands on Wolf's biceps and reluctantly pushed away from his chest. Her wobbly knees gradually steadied, and she let go of his arms.

Then she saw the blood. The ice fell back into the pit of her stomach. "You're hurt!" She stared in growing horror at the long bloody hole in the sleeve of his shirt. "Wolf! You're hit!"

Wolf glanced down at the tear in his shirt. "Just a nick."

"Let me see." Not daring to breathe until she saw for herself, Brie tore the hole in his shirt wider.

"Hey, my shirt!"

"The devil take your shirt, 'tis your arm I'm worried about." With her hands once again trembling and her mouth as dry as drought-stressed grass, she stared at the inch-long mark on his upper arm.

This was silly. She'd seen wounds before. She'd done worse to herself cooking supper. What little blood there was had long since stopped seeping from what Wolf had accurately described as a nick. A slight red mark was all that marred the bronze skin of his upper arm.

So why was her heart pounding as though trying to beat its way out of her chest? Why, now that the trouble was over, the gunman gone, the wound so very minor, did the copper taste of fear coat her tongue?

"Brie, it's nothing."

She tried to swallow but her mouth was too dry. "I know," she managed. Her eyes slid shut, and in a tiny voice she whispered, "Thank God."

Her concern touched him. Her touch burned him. Wolf

waited for her to take her hand from his arm, but she didn't. She merely stared up at him with those huge green eyes that could pull a man in and drown him. And make him be glad of it. The fire from her touch spread lower. And lower.

Clamping his jaw tight, Wolf placed his hand over hers and removed it from his arm. "Brie—" He wasn't sure what he'd been about to say—something he had no business saying, he was sure. Whatever insanity he'd been about to spout—*Brie, you're so damn beautiful,* or even worse, *you make me burn. I want you*—the words died unspoken in his throat when she flinched at the slight squeeze of his hand on hers.

He instantly eased his grip, although he hadn't been holding her tightly, and turned her hand over. The skin along the outer edge of her hand was red and inflamed, and marked by three small red holes. "What's this?"

She grimaced and pulled her hand from his. "Nothing. Just a few splinters."

"Splinters? How? What happened?"

When she told him about the fence post being shot from her grasp, he cursed, long and low and hard. He took her hand again and ran his thumb lightly over the tiny wounds, feeling for any slight sliver she might have missed. "Damn fool woman, why didn't you stay still and keep down like I told you? What the hell did you think you were doing?"

"I was trying to keep his attention on me," she said, jerking her hand free, "so he wouldn't realize you were sneaking away."

To cover his surprise, and another spurt of warmth that shot through him at her courage, he smirked. "What were you going to do, shake the post at him and tell him he was a bad boy, like you would one of your little brothers?"

Brie's mind whirled in confusion. One minute he was warm and concerned, the next, he snapped at her. Whatever his reasons, she was grateful, she decided, for she felt on more solid ground now. Snapping back at him was easier than dealing with all the other feelings she'd experienced in the past twenty minutes. So she snapped. "I was reaching for the post so I could use it to raise your hat above the bank so he'd think you were still trapped."

Wolf had opened his mouth to say something, but at her words, he snapped it shut and blinked. "You what?"

"I'm sorry about your hat, by the way."

Wolf suddenly looked as confused as Brie felt. He glanced along the ground, then down the bank to where her hat lay beside the water. Slowly his eyes narrowed and he looked back at her. "Where is my hat?"

Uh oh. Brie's father had always been particular about his hat. He'd never owned more than two, one for work and everyday wear, the other for church, weddings, and funerals, and that only because Mother had forced him to wear something other than that old, sweat-stained, beat-up hat he loved the most.

By the look on Wolf's face, he was, in regard to his hat, a great deal like her father.

"It, uh . . . well . . . it fell in the water and floated away."

"It floated away."

"That's right."

"And just how," Wolf asked quietly, "did my hat end up in the water when yours didn't?"

Brie pursed her lips. "Because I wanted the man on the rim to think you were still here. I stuck your hat on the end of the fence post and raised it up so he would think you were moving around."

"And?"

"And he . . ." All urge to snap and argue drained from Brie. If Wolf had been wearing that at the time, he would be dead now, shot through the head, as dead as the fence post she'd dropped when the bullet had struck it.

Other things also drained from Brie just then with the realization that Wolf could have been killed. It would have been her fault. If she hadn't punched Hank Jennings in the nose two days ago . . . If she hadn't hired Wolf, he would have gone about whatever business it was that brought him to the area and would probably be long gone by now. If she hadn't hired him, she doubted the major would have resorted to gun play. If she hadn't hired him ... "I've changed my mind, Wolf. You're fired."

Chapter Eight

"I'm what?"

Brie straightened her shoulders and looked him in the eye. "You're fired."

Wolf stared back, stunned. She'd been desperate to hire him, would have forced him to work for her if she could have, and now she was firing him? It didn't make sense. And it was beside the point, he realized. Whether either of them liked it or not, he couldn't leave her until this thing with the Double Diamond was settled. Hell, people were shooting now. At her. Wolf wasn't about to walk away.

"I hate to disappoint you," he told her, "but I won't quit."

"I didn't say anything about you quitting, I said you were fired."

He gave a negligent shrug. "Same difference. I'm not going."

"I'll cut off your pay."

"Ha! What pay? You weren't going to pay me until the cattle were sold anyway."

"All right, I'll pay you off right now."

"Fine, but I'm still not going."

With eyes wide and startled, she asked, "Why not?"

"Why not? Hell, woman, what kind of a man do you take me for? People are shooting at you. Do you think I can just walk away and leave you and that bunch of kids defenseless?"

"People are shooting at you, too."

"I've been shot at before, I'll be shot at again. I won't leave you here alone to lose your home."

"It's not worth—"

"Don't tell me what it's not worth. You don't know what it's like to not have a home. It's worth *everything*. Take it from someone who's never had a home. It's damn sure worth fighting for."

Brie paused, sidetracked from their argument by his comment. "You never had a home? Surely you grew up somewhere."

"I grew up the back end of a traveling preacher's wagon. Believe me, it wasn't a home. You've got something really good here, Brie, you and your family. Your father worked long and hard for it. Are you ready to just hand it over to the first man who demands it?"

"I won't have you hurt because of us. I couldn't stand that. Please, Wolf, just go."

Eyes narrowed, hands on his hips, Wolf stared at her for a long moment. Finally he shook his head. "Hell." Then he turned and walked away.

For one insane moment, Brie wanted to call him back, to tell him she hadn't meant it. She needed him!

But she bit back the words. It was better this way. She had no idea what she'd do without him to help her, no idea how to fill the hole that would be left in her life with his leaving. But she would manage, somehow, because if he stayed, she feared he would be hurt much more seriously than a nick on the shoulder.

The logic of his leaving, however, did nothing to stop the terrible ache that blossomed inside her. *Wolf! I care.*

That's why I have to send you away. Because I care what happens to you.

She watched his loose-limbed gait carry him farther and farther away with each step. His broad shoulders and tapered back were straight and strong with confidence. She started to follow, to help him hitch the team to the wagon, when she suddenly realized he wasn't heading for the horses.

Instead, he walked toward the small stack of remaining fence posts, picked one up, then started back.

"What . . . what are you doing?" she asked as he brushed past her.

"What I came out here to do," he said tersely. "I'm putting up a fence."

"But—"

He whirled on her, his eyes as fierce and dark as a thunderhead, his lips thinned to a grim line. "I can't leave! I didn't want your damn job. I didn't come here to get involved. But I'm here, I'm involved, and I'm staying until this thing between the Rocking F and the Double Diamond is settled. End of discussion."

The sun was almost down to the horizon by the time the house came in sight. The ride back from the canyon had been made in silence. The entire afternoon had in fact been remarkably devoid of conversation, considering how much Brie liked to talk. But when Wolf had adamantly refused to be fired, words had deserted her.

What could she say to him? Not only was his mind made up, but deep inside, where she tried to keep her selfishness buried, she didn't want him to leave. It was for *him* that she wanted him to leave, and he wasn't having any of it.

He had planted the last fence post with perhaps a tad more force than had been necessary, then had started stringing the barbed wire from post to post. Brie had helped when he'd allowed it, and when he wouldn't, she'd calmly picked up his rifle and stood guard, constantly searching the rim, the hills, for any sign of trouble.

Thank God the gunman hadn't come back.

Now they were almost home. On the way back they had found Wolf's hat snagged on the low-hanging limb of an old willow.

Ahead, the house came into view. Brie straightened on the seat and leaned forward for a better look.

"Looks like you've got company. Anybody you know?"

"Yes," she said slowly. "The buggy belongs to Letty Stockwell. She was my mother's best friend. Since last spring, she's been a Godsend to us."

"And the horse tied on behind?"

Brie's stomach tightened. There was no one she would rather spend an evening with that Letty Stockwell. But . . . "It belongs to her father."

Wolf wasn't sure what he heard in Brie's voice when she spoke of her friend's father. Anger? Fear? Determination? Whatever, he didn't like the sound of it coming from her lips. "Her father?" he prodded.

"Major John Palmer."

Everything inside Wolf stilled.

So. He wouldn't have to go looking for the man after all.

If this major turned out to be the one he'd been seeking, Wolf would be able to solve his own problem and Brie's. When he killed the bastard.

"Letty." Brie's smile was genuine as she climbed down from the wagon.

"Heavens," Letty exclaimed. "You look like you've had quite a day. What's happened? Are you all right?"

Ignoring the major, who stood just beyond Letty's shoulder, Brie glanced down at her filthy clothes and grimaced. "This," she said, holding out her soiled skirt as if she were preparing to curtsy, "is courtesy of one of the Double Diamond's men, I believe."

The color drained from Letty's cheeks. "One of our men?" She whipped around to face her father. "What have you done? First those three buffoons last Saturday, now this?" Without waiting for a reply, Letty turned back to Brie. "What happened?"

Behind her Brie heard Rory and Sully taking care of the wagon team; James, Letty's son, was helping them. Margery, her fifteen-year-old daughter, had been on the porch with Tessa, Elly, and Katy, when Brie and Wolf had driven in. Now all four girls stood in the yard waiting for Brie to explain what had happened.

They weren't the only ones. Letty gripped the sides of her skirt so tight, it was a wonder the fabric didn't shred from the pressure.

Then there was the major, waiting, watching, looking for all the world as if he, too, were curious as to what Brie would say. But unlike the others, his face was not marked by anxiety.

Suddenly Brie felt Wolf's presence at her back. Rather than telling the truth, which would only upset the girls and Letty, Brie met the major's stare and smiled. "Nothing serious. Just a little disagreement with one of your men, that's all. Wolf straightened him out and sent him on his way. I don't believe either of you have met our new foreman. Wolf?" She turned slightly toward him. "I'd like you to meet my dear friend Letty Stockwell. And her father, Major Palmer, of the Double Diamond."

With one part of his mind Wolf applauded Brie's tactics: smile and act like nothing serious had happened. If the major had ordered the shooting, it would drive him crazy. Hell, for that matter, Brie hadn't even mentioned putting up the new fence, yet Palmer had to know that's what they'd been doing today. Of course, after the scene in the store the other day, Jennings could have sent the man without the major knowing. Hell, the gunman could have been Jennings himself, but Wolf didn't think so. What little Wolf had seen of him, the gunman hadn't looked big enough to be Jennings.

While all this was running through part of Wolf's mind, the other part was studying Major John Palmer. This was the man Wolf had come to find. *Are you the one?* Wolf wondered. *Are you the one who tied a twenty-dollar gold piece around the neck of a four-year-old boy and tossed him to the first bastard who came along? Or maybe you picked Lazarus on purpose, because you knew what he was.*

None of what Wolf was thinking—with either part of his mind—showed on his face. He'd learned at an early age how to school his expression to blankness. It was a reflex now. He didn't have to do it deliberately, didn't have to struggle to keep his thoughts from showing like he'd had to do as a kid. Now it was automatic.

Are you the one? he thought again.

Wolf shifted his gaze to Letty Stockwell and gave her a polite tug of his hat. "Ma'am." To Palmer he gave another nod, along with the deliberate insult of not offering his hand for a shake.

Brie and Letty herded everyone to the shade of the porch. An ordinary foreman would have waited to be invited, but both for his own benefit, and for Brie's protection, Wolf wasn't about to let Major Palmer out of his sight.

"I came to talk to you," the major said to Brie. He chuckled slightly. When he smiled, he looked downright friendly. "I think Letty and the kids came along to make sure I talked nice. But the truth is, I would like to talk to you about the ranch." Unspoken, but plain on his face, was that he wanted to talk to Brie alone.

Brie smiled back and offered Letty the rocking chair, taking the straight-backed chair next to it for herself. "Please do sit down, Major. Which ranch did you come to talk about? Yours, or mine?"

Wolf bit back a bark of laughter.

The major frowned at her, then shook his head and

chuckled. "Ah, girl, you are so much like your father. No matter what I was thinking, or how serious the situation, he could always make me laugh." Palmer sat on the porch swing and patted the empty space beside him. "Come sit by me, Margery. Mr. Wolf, did you meet my granddaughter?"

Wolf tipped his hat to the girl. "Ma'am." There was a lot of her mother in her, with that pale yellow hair and the dimple in her cheek. The eyes were the same light shade of blue, but Letty's held caution, and way in the back, sadness.

The girl's eyes were filled with laughter. She gave Wolf a teasing grin, then offered him a curtsy. "Mr. Wolf."

Damned if he didn't find himself smiling back. "No mister, ma'am. Just Wolf."

"I'm pleased to meet you, Just Wolf." With a laugh and a toss of her head—Lord help him, she was flirting with him!—she spread her skirts and sat on the swing with her grandfather.

"And this is Margery's brother, James," Brie offered as a young man of about seventeen strode up from the barn. He could have been Margery's twin, so much alike were the two of them in looks.

Wolf shook hands with James, another subtle insult to the major, then removed his hat and took up a spot behind Brie's chair, directly facing Palmer.

Major John Palmer studied the half-breed carefully. Now that Wolf had taken off his hat, the major could see his eyes better. Palmer had seen a lot of things in a lot of men's eyes, things like anger, pain, laughter, hate. Much of it had been directed specifically at him. But until he looked into the gray eyes of this 'breed—steel gray, like the well-honed blade of a knife—he'd never felt as if a man could slice him with a look. Until now. Yet the eyes held no expression. None at all.

Ice trickled down Palmer's spine. What was it about those eyes?

"Major."

His daughter's voice brought Palmer's attention around to the matter at hand. Damn the girl. She only called him by his rank when she was irritated with him. It was a trick she'd learned years ago from her mother, guaranteed to put him in a foul mood. He liked the prestige of being called by his rank. But not by his own wife, God rest her soul, nor by his daughter.

"Grandad?" Margery prompted from beside him.

Now there was a darling girl who knew how to make an old grandad feel loved. Palmer smiled at his granddaughter, then turned to Brie.

"One reason I came was to offer my sincere apologies to you and young Katy for what happened to you on the road last Saturday. Marshall Campbell explained, and I want to assure you that those three men will cause you no more trouble."

"I'm glad to hear it," Brie said.

"I understand," Palmer said, looking over her shoulder at Wolf, "that we have you to thank for the safety of the two ladies."

"I just happened to be riding by. It seemed like the thing to do."

"All the same, everyone in these parts owes you a debt of gratitude, myself more than anyone. If harm had come to them from my own men . . ." He shook his head. "I would never have forgiven myself."

"Are they still working for you?" Wolf asked.

"For now." Palmer stretched one arm along the back of the swing. "But only until I can replace them."

Maybe, Wolf thought. Then again, maybe not. Palmer was just a little too smooth for Wolf's peace of mind. Reminded him of a snake-oil salesman.

"The other reason I came," Palmer said to Brie as he pulled his arm from behind his granddaughter's shoulders and braced his elbows on his knees, "was to make you another offer."

Wolf didn't have to be touching Brie to feel the tension

rise in her. It fairly radiated from her. Everyone on the porch, as a matter of fact, seemed suddenly tense.

"For the Rocking F?" Brie asked.

"Brie, no," Tessa cried.

"Hush, honey," Brie answered. "It's all right. The major knows we won't sell the ranch."

"Even before you hear my offer?" the major asked quietly.

"I'm sure it's a fair offer, Major, but the Rocking F is not for sale."

Now, Wolf thought, studying Palmer. Now the man wasn't quite so smooth. He straightened stiffly in the swing; his jaw hardened and his eyes narrowed.

"You don't seriously think you and these kids can keep this ranch running, do you?"

"Yes," Brie said calmly. "Yes I do. Especially since we have Wolf now."

"One man?" Palmer's face was turning red. "And a stranger, at that. You don't know anything about him. For all you know, he'll steal you blind."

"Funny, but he said just about the same thing when I hired him."

"You should have listened," Palmer said heatedly. "He was probably just giving you fair warning."

"Major," Letty said in a warning tone.

"Don't you *major* me," he snarled. "There's nothing between the Double Diamond and all the grass and water it needs except this one stubborn girl and a half-breed bast—"

"Watch yourself, Palmer," Wolf warned, cutting him off. "There are ladies present."

"Why, you—" Palmer rose half out of his seat.

At a sharp nod from Letty, Margery put her hand on her grandfather's arm and tugged. "Now, Grandad, remember what the doctor said about getting upset. It's bad for your heart."

Explosive rage flashed in Palmer's eyes before he closed

them and ground his teeth, allowing his granddaughter to tug him back onto the swing. "Young lady, I'll thank you not to treat me as if I have one foot in the grave."

Brie leaned forward in her chair. "Would you like some water, Major? Elly, run get the major a cup of water. He looks terribly flushed."

It took every ounce of will Major John Palmer possessed to keep from bellowing in sheer rage. When he got his hands on Letty when they got home, he was going to give her what-for. She might be staring her forty-third birthday in the face, but by God, he was still her father. She put Margery up to that crack about his heart just to humiliate him because she liked these damn Irish troublemakers.

Palmer forced himself to take a deep breath. He shouldn't have gotten mad. He'd lost his advantage now. But the trip wasn't a total waste. He'd gotten to see the half-breed first-hand.

As his gaze connected with that of the Rocking F foreman, Palmer felt another shiver of ice shoot down his spine. What was it about those eyes?

While the major sat his horse a few minutes later, impatient to leave, Letty gave Brie a hug and whispered, "I'm sorry. I tried to keep him from coming, but when I knew it was useless, I gathered up the kids and came with him, hoping . . ."

Brie hugged her friend back. "It's all right, Letty. I'm glad you came. Besides," she added with a soft chuckle, "it gave a certain young man and young woman a chance to see each other." She looked on indulgently as Elly walked James to the buggy. Even Tessa was helping give the sweethearts a private moment by keeping Margery occupied with a plea for gossip about their friends.

"They do make an excellent couple, don't they?" Pride colored Letty's voice as she watched her son smile down at Elly.

"Yes, they do." Brie felt a small pang of envy that there was no special man for her. Then she felt Wolf's presence behind her, and wondered.

"Oh, I almost forgot to tell you," Letty said. "Reverend Benton has been called away to his mother's deathbed in Missouri."

"Oh, I'm so sorry."

"Yes, but she's in her seventies. She's had a full life. At any rate, before he left town he sent for a traveling preacher to come through in a few weeks."

Brie chuckled. "Oh, boy. Do you think he'll put on a revival?"

Letty laughed and stepped down from the porch. "I'd bet on it. If I were a betting woman."

A few moments later Brie stood at the foot of the steps in the long shadows of the house and waved good-bye to Letty and her children. When they were out of sight, she turned toward the house to find Wolf staring at her with a stone-hard look in his eyes. The same flat, blank look he'd had since their argument earlier in the day. She hated that look and vowed to do something, say something, to bring life back to his eyes. "Did you hear the news? We'll have a traveling preacher in a few weeks. Who knows," she said with a smile. "Maybe it'll be the man who raised you."

If anything, Wolf's expression grew even more remote. "I doubt it," he said coldly. "When I was nine years old, I killed him."

Chapter Nine

For a long moment they stared at each other, she in shock, he in challenge. It fairly glittered in those gray eyes of his, that challenge, but Brie didn't understand it. Her mind didn't seem to want to get past the words echoing in her brain.

She felt a little as if she weren't there. She felt as if she'd been lifted by some giant, unseen hand and slammed against the base of the bluff across the stream. For a moment, breath would not come, and her vision blurred. She blinked to clear it "You . . . killed the man who raised you? A preacher?"

Wolf's jaw flexed once, but that was the only reaction she could detect. "That's right."

Brie swallowed, her mind running in circles, her heart screaming for the pain she felt in him, the pain he kept locked so deep inside that it didn't show on his face or in his eyes as anything but coldness.

She stared at him another long moment. Then, voice shaking, she asked, "When you were nine years old?"

In an instant, the blankness vanished from his eyes. Bitterness. Challenge. Self-contempt filled them. "When I was nine years old." He stepped passed her and started for the barn.

"Oh, no you don't." Brie raced after him, grabbed him by the arm and spun him around. "Don't you dare say something like that to me and walk away. Don't you dare."

"What is it you want me to say?" he demanded.

"I don't know! Maybe you could start by telling me why you said it at all."

Wolf glared at her. He'd been asking himself the same damn question from the minute he'd opened his mouth. "Because you make me crazy."

She matched him glare for glare. "Me?" she cried.

"Yeah, you, with your smiles and your big trusting eyes."

"You said what you did so I wouldn't trust you?"

That didn't make a lick of sense, even to him. But he figured it was the truth. "One of these days you're gonna trust the wrong person and get yourself hurt, Miss Flanigan."

"Are you going to hurt me, Just Wolf?"

"Going to? Hell, woman, I damn near got you killed today."

Her eyes widened. She propped her fists on her hips and gaped at him. "By all the saints! What the devil are you talking about?"

"You know what I'm talking about."

"I assume you're talking about what happened down at the canyon. What I can't figure is how any of that was your fault."

"The fence was my idea. I should never have let you go with me. I should have made you stay home."

"Ha! You could have tried."

"Tried, hell. I should have tied you to a porch post."

"You're pretty good at this."

Wolf paused. "I don't know what you're talking about."

"I'm talking about changing subjects. But that's okay, really, because I think I have my answer anyway."

"I'm sure I'm gonna regret this, but, your answer to what?"

"To what happened. You said that when you were nine years old, you killed the man who raised you."

Wolf flinched to hear the words from her mouth.

"I asked you why you said it, but what I really wanted to know, naturally, was what happened."

"And you think you've figured it all out, do you?"

"I think so. It could only have been one of three things."

"I've just told you I killed a man, and you've decided you know why."

"You could have done it because you're an evil person," she said steadily. "But you're not an evil person."

"How do you know?"

She ignored his question. "You could have done it in self defense, but I can't imagine that a nine-year-old would have to defend his very life against a man of God."

"You can't, huh?"

"No, I think his death was some sort of accident. Knowing your out-sized conscience, you probably blame yourself for something that wasn't your fault."

"You ought to be a story writer," Wolf told her in disgust. "You've got an imagination that won't quit."

"Ah, but I'm right, aren't I?"

"No, you're not right. You don't know what the hell you're talking about."

"Then why don't you explain it to me?"

As Wolf stared at her, the anger or devil or whatever it was that had made him tell her deserted him, leaving him deflated, exhausted. Looking at the innocent conviction shining in her eyes made him feel old. Someone like her could never even conceive of what that bastard had been capable of. Wolf didn't want her to know. He didn't want such foulness to touch her life, to taint her world. He couldn't do that to her.

He shook his head. "You wouldn't understand if I tried."

"Wolf—"

"Drop it, Irish."

"If you wanted me to drop it you shouldn't have brought it up in the first place!"

"You're right. I shouldn't have brought it up."

"It was an accident, wasn't it?"

"Yeah, sure. That shovel in my hands just accidently swung around and bashed the old bastard in the head. Three times."

She opened her mouth, then snapped it shut. What could she say to something like that?

"Are you happy now?" he demanded.

When all she could do was stand and stare at him, he swore beneath his breath and turned away.

Brie would have followed and demanded an explanation, but something in his voice stopped her. He sounded . . . defeated.

Wolf? Defeated? Her mind and heart protested. He was her champion! Her knight. Her warrior. The answer to her prayers. If he felt defeated, what hope was there for her and the kids?

Selfish! Oh, yes, she did feel selfish, thinking of her and the kids when Wolf . . . When Wolf what? Hurt?

In utter confusion, Brie turned from the sight of his dogged steps toward the barn and faced the house. She didn't understand why he'd told her about killing a man, didn't understand why he wouldn't explain. Didn't understand, and greatly feared, what she thought she'd heard in his voice as he'd turned away.

He had ghosts, this man called Wolf. Ghosts Brie couldn't begin to understand, but she was Irish enough to believe they existed. How was she supposed to bear the thought of the pain he must carry inside him? Past what limits could a nine-year-old boy have been pushed to cause him to take a life?

From the barn she heard Rory's laughter and Sully's chuckle. She prayed for the strength and wisdom to shelter them from whatever ugliness had so harmed Wolf. She prayed for the strength and wisdom to either help Wolf, or let him be. She prayed for the strength and wisdom not to care any more deeply for him than she already did. Not to learn to love him. For despite all his attempts, she feared Tessa had been right last week about the way Brie looked at Wolf. She feared she was falling for him, and falling hard.

Dear Lord.

"Is Wolf coming in for supper?"

At the sound of Katy's voice Brie turned from staring out the back door toward the bunkhouse. "I think not, honey."

Brie took her arms from around her own midriff, where she'd held them for the past hour since the major's leaving to try to stave off the chill. But this chill, Brie knew, was from within. Caused by Wolf's blunt declaration.

Gently Brie rubbed at a smudge of dirt on Katy's cheek.

"Ain't he hungry?"

"Isn't he hungry."

"That's what I said."

Brie had not spoken to him since he'd left her at the porch with those horrible words. She had tried to call out to him, to demand an explanation, but words had failed her.

Brie had finally worked up the nerve to follow Wolf into the barn to ask the questions screaming in her mind, but as she'd entered the wide double doors at the front, he had slipped out the back. By the time she made it through the barn to the door in the rear, Wolf was nowhere in sight. She suspected he was now in the bunkhouse, but there had been such a look of desolation in his eyes when he'd said those horrible words, that she wasn't sure she wouldn't break down and weep if she saw it again.

"Maybe I should take him some food," Katy offered, looking up hopefully at Brie.

Brie managed a smile. "I think that's an excellent idea." If anyone could wipe that grim look off Wolf's face, it was Katy.

Wolf sat on the edge of his cot, elbows on his spread knees, face buried in his hands. He'd been sitting that way for an hour or more, trying to figure out what the hell had made him say such a damn stupid thing to Brie. The answer he came up with tasted bitter on his tongue.

He hadn't planned to say anything at all when she mentioned the traveling preacher. He'd only told one other person about his past, and that was Booker, the cowboy who'd found him wandering lost in the hills and half dead from thirst. There'd never been a reason to tell anyone else. There'd been no reason to tell Brie. Except . . .

He couldn't forget the way she'd looked at him earlier in the day, after the gunman had ridden away and Wolf had pulled her into his arms. Sure, she'd been scared for herself. But most of what he'd seen in those big green eyes had been for him. Fear. Relief. Trust. Caring. Ah, God, the caring. For a half-breed bastard with no name, no home, and a past well worth forgetting.

So at the first opportunity, he'd opened his big mouth and killed whatever tender feelings she might have been harboring for him. He hadn't done it consciously, but he'd done it. It galled him to admit that it had been for the best, too. Now she wouldn't look at him with her heart in her eyes again. *That* was for the best. For her. For him.

When the knock came at the door, he flinched. Was she coming to try to fire him again? He wouldn't blame her, but he still couldn't leave her and the other kids to deal with Palmer alone.

"Wolf?"

Wolf dropped his hands from his face. Smart woman, Brie. She knew he couldn't ignore Katy. That little charmer could wrap him around her little finger with nothing more than a smile.

The knock came again. "Wolf, we brought your supper. Are you in there? Are you hungry?"

His crack to Brie about killing the preacher had let loose all the old ugly memories that were never very far from his mind. The thought of food was enough to make him choke. But that wasn't Katy's fault. He just hoped like hell that Brie wasn't with her.

Wary, he opened the door. Relief swept through him when he found Katy, Tessa, and Rory standing there instead of Brie.

"We brought your supper," Rory told him.

"It's not much," Tessa said. "Just beans and corn-bread."

"And honey," Katy added, holding up a small earthen-ware pot. "I guess you didn't hear the dinner bell, huh?"

"I guess not." Wolf stepped back to let them file through the door.

They set the food, plate, and utensils out on the small table in the corner with great care, as if the meal were being taken in a fancy dining room rather than a bunkhouse.

As they started to leave, Wolf thanked them.

They all smiled at him. "Just leave everything there when you're through. We'll clean it up tomorrow," Tessa said.

Wolf thanked them again and closed the door behind them. With dread, he turned and faced the table, wondering if he'd be able to eat.

The old nightmare came back that night. Deep in the darkness of sleep, the grave gaped open before him.

Jimmy, Jimmy! Oh, God, look at what he did to Jimmy. He's all bloody. His eyes—God, he's staring at me with dead eyes. Not even a blanket to keep the dirt off his face, much less a pine box to bury him in. Jimmy, Jimmy! You finally did it, didn't you? You said you'd be free of the bastard one day.

His shoulders ached and his hands burned from the unaccustomed task of digging the grave. His forehead throbbed where he'd fallen and hit a rock. The chains kept getting in his way and tripping him.

Bitterness and sheer terror threatened to send him to his knees. The bastard was watching him with that look in his eyes. The look that meant Wolf's waiting was over. Jimmy was gone now. No one else around but Wolf. Wolf, old enough, finally, to attract the man's attention.

By rote, he scooped another shovelful of dirt and dropped it into the grave, trying against all common sense to keep from covering Jimmy's face. But eventually, he had no choice. His stomach rolled, his vision blurred.

When the grave was filled, he stood still, his chest heaving, his heart thundering in his ears, his knees quivering in terror. The man grinned and started toward him.

Now, boy, come here.

Wolf jerked awake with a hoarse cry. Sweat soaked his skin and the bedclothes. Bile and old, old terror clogged his throat. On a burst of lingering panic, he jumped from the bed, his breath rasping in his ears.

Goddamn. The years of relative peace were over. One small woman with big green eyes to stir his yearning, one foolish, incautious remark on his part to resurrect his past, and the nightmare was back.

Wolf waited the next morning until the family was at breakfast before leaving the bunkhouse for the barn. Visions from his nightmare kept trying to surface; he kept shoving them back down. He needed his mind clear to be prepared for whatever Palmer decided to throw at Brie next.

He was saddling up to ride out when a twitch of his horse's ears alerted him that he and the animal were no longer alone in the barn. For a long moment, the only sounds were those made by the horse. A puff of warm breath snorted through large nostrils. The shuffle of a hoof. The swish of a tail.

"How long are you planning on avoiding me?" Brie said from behind Wolf.

As long as I can get away with it. Wolf forced his hands to keep moving as he raised the stirrup and hooked it over the saddle horn. "I'm not avoiding anyone."

"You didn't come to supper last night, nor breakfast this morning."

He threaded the cinch strap through the buckle. "Wasn't hungry."

She strolled around to the edge of his line of vision. He kept his eyes firmly on the task before him.

"For a man with no appetite, you sure managed to clean up the supper the kids brought you last night."

"Maybe I fed it to the dog." With the cinch pulled tight, he jabbed his knee into the horse's belly. "Quit sucking air, you windbag."

"I do hope you're talking to the horse and not me."

After giving the cinch strap a final yank and tightening it another notch, Wolf whirled on her. "What the hell do you want?"

Brie gasped at the look of torment in Wolf's eyes. Without thought, she reached out to him. "Wolf . . ."

With a low snarl, he shrugged off her touch. "What?" he bit out.

Brie let her hand drop to her side and stifled the urge to throw her arms around him and hold him close to ease the suffering etched on his face. "I . . . nothing," she said, chickening out on bringing up the subject that obviously haunted them both—his cryptic remark yesterday evening about having killed the man who raised him, when he himself had been but a boy. "Will you be gone long?"

If her heart hadn't been breaking, she might have

laughed at the almost comical look of relief that crossed his face at her question.

"Probably most of the day." He turned back to the horse and unhooked the stirrup from the saddle horn. "I want to tie some flags onto the new fence to help keep the stock from trying to walk right through it and cutting themselves to ribbons. Do you have anything I can use?"

Brie forced herself to think about his question. "Would an old white sheet do?" She'd been saving it to cut up for her next quilt.

"Yeah. When I'm through with that I'm going to ride up onto the mesa and check on the cattle. It'd be best if you and the kids stuck close to the house."

Wolf spent the day in the saddle, but that evening he made himself sit down to supper with the family. He couldn't keep avoiding them and didn't want to be accused of it again. If Brie could pretend she hadn't heard what he'd told her . . .

Damn her. Why hadn't she demanded an explanation? Why hadn't she taken her broom and swept him right off the ranch? How could she sit at the opposite end of the table and smile at him like she was genuinely glad to break bread with a murderer?

Damn fool woman.

After that night he started filling his plate and taking it outside to eat. Let her accuse him of avoiding her. It was nothing more than the truth.

But she didn't accuse him. He didn't know what she'd told the others about his absence from meals—if any of them had even asked. He told himself he didn't care.

There was plenty of work for everyone to do so he didn't have a lot of trouble keeping out of their way. He spent most of his days in the saddle. Cattle had to be moved before they grazed the grass down too low in any one area. Their cuts and gashes had to be doctored. Strays who'd wandered too far from the main herd had to be rounded up.

A steer had to be roped and pulled from a boggy spring up on the mesa, and the sucker wasn't a damn bit happy about it. The instant the steer was free he charged. Wolf had anticipated him, but still it was a close call, because he wasn't about to let the critter keep the rope. He'd loosened the noose looped over the steer's horns and, with a flip of his wrist, freed both the animal and the rope and gigged his horse. The steer gave up the chase after a couple hundred yards.

There were more chores around the place that needed handling. Wolf put them off as long as he could, logically telling himself that the cattle had to come first. But the time came when the ranch horses had to be rounded up and herded into the corrals. He had to test them so he'd know what to expect from them. He'd been riding his own horse every day, and the animal needed a rest.

The barn roof had sprung a leak and the building itself could use a good coat of paint. One of the apple trees in the small orchard had died and should be pulled out. More coal needed to be hauled in from the small mine. He still couldn't get over the fact that they had their own coal mine. In a land nearly treeless, that source of fuel was highly valuable. No wonder Palmer wanted the Flanigans gone.

Alternating one day with the cattle and one day on the other chores, Wolf started working his way down the list of things to be done. It was hard work, but satisfying. The nightmare plagued him still, but not every night. It waited and lulled him into thinking it was gone before striking again. His work kept him sane, kept the nightmares manageable.

Hell, they might as well be manageable. There wasn't anything he could do about them but go on about his business. And staying busy helped.

Avoiding Brie as much as possible helped, too. But

avoiding her altogether was impossible. She didn't take
the family to church Sunday, preferring instead to stay
home and bake. The smell of fresh, hot bread nearly convinced him to give in and stand next to St. Pat at the back
door and beg.

Monday morning Wolf came out of the barn to find Brie
stooped over the boiling wash kettle behind the house.
That achy feeling settled in his chest again, like it did every
time he got the crazy notion of a woman, maybe even a
family, of his own. Crazy. Pointless. He could never saddle
a woman with a man like him. He didn't have room in his
life for one anyway.

He'd come to this area seeking a man. He'd found the
man, but still didn't know if he was the right one or not.
Until that was settled, there was no room for anything else.

And once it was settled, there would be no point in
anything else. Killing the man he was after wouldn't change
Wolf's past, wouldn't take away the nightmares or make
him feel clean, make him feel . . . ordinary. Worthy.

No, there would be no place in his life for a woman of
his own. Or more importantly, no woman with an ounce
of self-respect would make a place in her life for a man
like Wolf.

But there wasn't a damn thing Wolf could do about the
way his gut tightened when he watched Brie's backside
wiggle as she used a long paddle to stir the clothes in the
wash pot. Her skirt draped her hips faithfully and made
him want to cup them in his hands.

The desire to put his hands on her nearly crippled him
a moment later when Brie straightened. Closing her eyes,
she placed a hand at her lower back and arched, thrusting
her shoulders back and her breasts forward. Steam from
the tub had loosened the hair around her face and left
her looking flushed, with reddened cheeks and lips. Left
her looking like she'd just been thoroughly kissed.

Wolf's mouth went dry.

Brie chose that instant to open her eyes and catch him

staring like a hungry hound drooling over a feast. She seemed tauntingly, deliberately slow in straightening, her gaze locked steadily on his. She stood there erect and proud, her look one of sudden, explosive awareness of him as a man.

And as a man, Wolf couldn't help but let his gaze roam down the length of her, over every dip and curve. Her sharp inhale drew his eyes to her breasts. He stared, helplessly trapped by their taunting shape, by his internal need to touch, to see, to taste.

As if in response to his thoughts, the tips of her breasts peaked into hard, tiny points beneath her dress and whatever else she wore underneath it.

A look. Just a single look from him and her body responded. Wolf shook with the realization. Shook, then did the only sane thing he could—he turned and fled. Brianna Flanigan wasn't for him. Or more to the point, he wasn't for her. She deserved better, far better than a man with an embittered soul and a past better left buried in an unmarked grave with a boy named Jimmy. A past that would horrify and disgust an innocent, trusting woman like Brianna Flanigan.

Brie watched him turn and walk away. She felt all tingly inside and flushed outside, and none of it had anything to do with the washtub of steaming laundry. It had everything to do with hot gray eyes that had been about to devour her.

He'd looked as if he'd wanted to touch her in places she'd never been touched before. And she'd wanted him to touch her. Wanted it desperately. Her breasts swelled and ached with a need foreign to her, yet she instinctively knew what that need was.

Wolf.

She should be embarrassed, she supposed, over the way her nipples had contracted and hardened beneath his

stare, but she wasn't. Shaken, bemused, wanting, but not
embarrassed.

Wolf.

This, then, was what it meant to want a man. The feelings
she'd been having around Wolf for days now made sense.
Her body had understood what she wanted the minute
she'd laid eyes on him, even if her mind hadn't.

The question now was, what was she going to do about
it?

It seemed, in the days that followed, that Brie wasn't
going to have the chance to do anything about her newly
discovered feelings for Wolf. The man wouldn't stand still
long enough for her to get near him.

Not that she was actively pursuing him. She couldn't
quite bring herself to do such a thing. But he continued
taking his meals alone, continued working from dawn until
dark, continued riding out every other day to check on
the cattle.

Brie had toyed with the idea of riding with him up onto
the mesa, but she feared he would say no. She thought to
offer to help him on the days he stayed at the ranch, but
Sully and Rory were usually at his side then. She didn't
want to intrude. The boys missed Da. They followed Wolf
around every chance they got, pestering him with one
question after another, getting in his way.

To his credit, Wolf didn't seem to mind the boys at all.
She'd seen his endless patience with them and was grateful.
He was the only man on the ranch. It was natural for the
boys to look up to him. Brie only hoped they wouldn't be
devastated when Wolf left.

He would leave, she knew that. She saw it in his eyes.
He would stay until their cattle were sold, then he would
be gone, on about whatever business had brought him
here in the first place.

Brie's heart stumbled at the thought of his leaving, of

never seeing him smile at the boys again, never hearing
him tease Katy, then give in to whatever the girl asked,
never hearing his deep voice complimenting Elly on her
cooking and Tessa on how clean she kept the bunkhouse.
Of knowing there were none but children to stand beside
her the next time the major came to call. Of never knowing
where Wolf was, if he was safe or happy or sad. Of never
feeling the warm security of his presence even when he
kept deliberate distance between them.

What would she do when Wolf left? What would they all
do?

Brie placed her cool iron back on the stove and picked
up a hot one.

They would manage, she told herself. They would manage somehow when Wolf left. And she would never again
know the feel of his arms around her.

Brie's mood turned uncharacteristically sullen. She
knew it but didn't seem to be able to do anything about
it. Didn't really feel like doing anything about it. Her problem, she knew, was that Wolf was only temporary in her
life, in the lives of her brothers and sisters. That hurt, and
she didn't like to hurt, so her temper drew short. Her foul
temper made her even angrier, but this anger was directed
at herself. She'd never had bad moods before.

The rest of the family didn't know what was wrong with
her; they just gave her a wide berth and tried to stay out
of her way. Except Katy, of course. Nothing daunted Katy
Flanigan.

Brie was working in the vegetable garden and had just
managed to pull up by mistake an entire potato plant that
wasn't ready to be pulled. She was biting back curses when
Katy bounded up and squatted down next to her. "What-
cha doin'?"

"Destroying the garden," Brie muttered.

"How come?"

Don't snap at her. Don't snap at her. "Because I made a mistake."

"Oh. I'm gonna ask Wolf if he'll come to supper tonight."

Brie's fingers clenched around the already wilting potato plant. She didn't want Katy to be hurt when Wolf rejected her invitation. "Sully asked him yesterday, and he didn't come."

"But that was Sully," Katy stated, as though that explained everything. She stood up and brushed off her skirt in her best grownup lady imitation. In the same vein, she strolled sedately away from the garden toward the far side of the house.

Brie frowned and glanced down at the plant in her hand. What if Katy succeeded where Sully had failed? What if Wolf came to supper tonight and all Brie could manage was a scowl, the way she'd been doing lately?

"Katy—"

But Katy had already disappeared around the house. A moment later, laughter—Katy's, Rory's, and Sully's—led Brie to hope that Katy hadn't found Wolf yet. If Brie hurried . . .

She jammed the potato plant back into the ground and hastily made certain the roots and small new potatoes were covered with soil. She'd come back in a few minutes and water it. Maybe it would survive.

Unlike Katy, Brie jumped up and slapped what dirt she could off her skirt, then darted toward the house and the sound of shrieking children.

Ahead, Sully stepped into view from the corner of the house, laughing, backing away from whoever it was that Brie couldn't see because of the house. "Don't!" He laughed and held his hands out before him as if to ward off something. "It was an accident, I swear! No! Rory—"

Intent on her own thoughts—on stopping Katy before she invited Wolf to supper—Brie paid scant attention to Sully and didn't consider at all what Rory might be up to.

The two were always up to something. She walked past
Sully and rounded the corner of the house.

"Look out!"

The warning came too late. The egg Rory threw at Sully
struck her square in the forehead.

Wolf had just finished replacing another rail in the corral
fence—broken by a horse unused to fences—when he
looked up and saw the egg fly. He held his breath. He
wanted to laugh, but didn't dare. Brie had been growling
around the place for the past couple of days like a she-
bear with a sore paw. The mood she'd been in, it seemed
highly unlikely that she would take an egg in the face
without erupting.

He didn't know what had started her surly mood, but
two days ago she'd taken a strip out of Sully's hide for
tracking mud into the house after an afternoon rain
shower. Now she'd taken a direct hit with an egg meant
for Sully. She wasn't likely to be pleased, to say the least.

For a minute, Wolf stiffened. Would Brie whip the boys?
The scars on his back twitched. It was none of his business
how she chose to deal with her brothers, but he knew he
wouldn't be able to let her whip them. People who hurt
children should be shot.

Or bashed in the head with a shovel.

Then he shook himself. This was Brie, not the preacher.
Rory and Sully, not a young boy called Wolf. Different
time. Different place. Different people in a different world.

Slowly he realized that rather than painful, shameful,
or terrifying, this situation was . . . funny.

The scene before him would be frozen in his mind for
the rest of his life. If he were an artist, he'd want to paint
it for sheer fun, and fun wasn't a normal part of Wolf's
life. But this was priceless.

Brie stood facing Rory, her arms held out from her sides,
hands flopping. She leaned forward a bit, as if she might

tumble over and add insult to injury—dirt to the mess of raw egg oozing down her face and stringing off her chin onto her dress. Her eyes were squeezed shut, her mouth gaping.

Just outside the corral, Katy squealed with laughter.

Facing Brie, Rory stood frozen in the exact position he'd been in when the egg left his hand. His throwing arm still arched forward, his eyes still lit with the mischievous intention of getting even with Sully. For Rory, too, was covered with raw egg, although he'd taken it in the chest rather than the face.

Behind Brie, Sully stood still and stared in shock, his eyes bugging, his mouth working hard to keep from laughing. And in the side window of the house, peeking out through the curtains, Elly and Tessa had their noses pressed to the glass. They were both laughing hysterically.

With slow, deliberate motions, Brie finally raised her hands and wiped her fingers across her eyes, then glared at Rory.

"Uh . . . ah, uh . . ." Rory gulped and took a step backward.

"Oh, no you don't." Brie lunged forward and wrapped an arm around his neck to hold him close to her side. Behind her, Sully turned to run, but Brie was faster. "You!" She grabbed him by the back of his shirt and yanked him to an abrupt halt, then spun him around until he, too, was locked to her side with her arm around his neck. There was murder in her eyes.

Then, with a low growl, she brought their heads together and rubbed her egg-covered face all over their faces and hair.

"Ooh, yuck!" Rory uselessly squirmed to get free.

Sully made gagging sounds between his giggles.

Sully wasn't the only one giggling by then. Brie's laughter came so hard that she shook with it. Somehow she managed to keep an arm around the neck of each boy while dragging them across the yard. "Throw eggs at me, will you?"

"It was an accident!" a laughing Rory protested.

"I didn't throw nothin'!" Sully claimed.

"Ha!" Brie dragged them through the corral gate Wolf had left open. "You started it, you monster."

The next sound was a loud splash as Brie awkwardly dumped not only her brothers, but herself as well, into the water trough. Head first.

Wolf watched it all while his throat closed, watched the three of them come up spitting, spraying, dripping, and laughing and trying to dunk each other. Watched as water soaked the front of Brie's dress, leaving her breasts with their puckered nipples perfectly outlined.

Wolf swore at himself. He didn't have any damn business noticing, wanting.

Those two young boys had no idea how lucky they were. Wolf was glad, intensely glad for them, that they had laughter and love and the freedom to just be boys. But watching them only brought home to Wolf that he didn't belong here with these people. Even with Brie's bad mood, Katy's occasional pouting, an argument now and then between Tessa and Elly, a shoving match or even a fistfight between the boys, their emotions were so clean and honest, their sheer pleasure in the fighting as well as the love, made him feel old and tired . . . and unclean.

He was so deep into his own thoughts that he didn't at first realize that Katy had lost her pleasure in the antics of her sister and brothers. She'd gone pale and stiff as a post, with her lips trembling and her eyes wide with sheer terror.

Wolf was at her side in an instant, kneeling in the dirt next to her. "Hey, Katydid, what's wrong?"

Katy squeezed her eyes shut tight. "They're gonna drown!" she cried shrilly. "They're gonna drown!"

For a moment Wolf was speechless. Then he remembered that these kids' parents had drowned last spring in the Purgatoire. Still, Katy's fear shook him. "In the water trough?" he managed. "Not a chance. Look. Come on, open your eyes and look. They're fine, I promise. Everybody's fine, Katy.''

"What's wrong?" Brie rushed to them, dripping and flinging water in her wake.

Wolf looked up at Brie from where he knelt at Katy's side and clenched his teeth. This was the closest he'd been to her since that evening on the porch when they'd watched the major and his family leave and Brie had mentioned the traveling preacher. She stood over him now with her shriveled nipples and full breasts outlined by her wet dress and it was all he could do to remember the scared little girl at his side.

Damn his hide. What was the matter with him? He'd never been obsessed by women. Why this one, who was so close, yet so far out of his reach?

"She was afraid you were going to drown," he bit out, the anger at himself coming out in his voice.

If it weren't for Katy's distress, Brie would have questioned him about his anger. Her own foul mood, which she'd been nursing for days, had miraculously vanished with the splat of the egg on her face. But now she was concerned for Katy. Poor baby!

Brie scooped her up and turned toward the house. "It's all right, sweetie, nobody's drowning. We were just playing, you know." Starting toward the back door, Brie rocked from side to side and held Katy close.

Still shaking with fear, Katy looked up at her. "I didn't get to ask Wolf to supper."

"That's okay, sweetie, we'll ask him later."

"No," Katy said with a whine. "Ask him now, Brie, ask him now."

Seeing that Katy was going to add fretting to her fear, Brie paused and looked back. Wolf was where she'd left him, squatting next to the corral fence, frowning at her. "Katy wants you to come to supper tonight."

Surprised, he stood slowly.

"Please, Wolf." Katy said it with such a pitiful whimper

that Brie mashed her lips together. The kid was playing Wolf like a fish on a line. The hook was set and she was ready to reel him in.

Well, hell, Wolf thought. He didn't want to have supper with the family, but how could he tell sweet little Katy no, especially when she was so upset? He gave a reluctant nod.

With Katy cuddled close in her arms, Brie turned away from him again and headed toward the house. As she went, he heard her sing to Katy. "If that silver tray turns brass, Mama's gonna buy you a looking glass."

If that looking glass don't shine, Mama's gonna buy you a little pink swine.

It was a moment before Wolf realized that Brie had stopped singing. The last words had whispered only through his mind.

Where had they come from? Why did that tune seem so familiar? It was the song Brie and Katy had sung the day he met them, but even then it had tugged at some long-forgotten memory.

Chapter Ten

Brie was nervous. She couldn't believe it. She was nervous about Wolf coming to supper.

"I'm telling you, it explains everything."

Brie was just about to step into the kitchen when she heard Tessa's fierce whisper. Eavesdropping, to Brie's way of thinking, was the rudest of conducts, but something in her sister's tone made her want to pause just outside the kitchen door. She resisted the urge and entered the kitchen. "What explains everything?" she asked with a smile.

"See?" Tessa said to Elly. "Look at her. Either I'm right, or she's losing her wits."

"What on earth!" Brie cried.

Elly frowned. "I'm afraid you're right," she said to Tessa. "It certainly explains the last few days."

Brie propped her hands on her hips. "Would one of you mind telling me what you're talking about?"

"We're talking about you," Tessa said darkly.

"So I gathered. What seems to be the problem?"

"Now, Brie," Elly started.

"Don't *now* Brie me." The foul mood was coming back fast. "Out with it."

"What'd I tell you?" Tessa shot Elly a look. "Laughing one minute, mad the next. Just like you when something's going on between you and James."

"Oh, Brie," Elly said, clearly dismayed. "It's true, isn't it? You're starting to care for Wolf."

The urge to deny Elly's accusation was strong, but Brie was tired of hiding from the truth. "I care for him very much." Simply saying the words was liberating. She felt as if a great weight had just been lifted from her chest.

"Are you in love with him?" Tessa's eyes were big and round and filled with concern.

Brie threw her head back and laughed. "I honestly don't know. Maybe I am. Whatever it is, it feels wonderful."

Elly pressed a hand to her cheek. "You're out of your mind. You know how much we all like him, but Brie, he's a drifter."

"I know," Brie admitted softly. "But I can't help how I feel."

"He'll leave, Brie."

"Would you be able to stop caring about James if you knew he was leaving?"

Looking infinitely sad, Elly slowly shook her head and turned back to the stove.

"Don't worry about me," Brie told her sisters. "I just plan to enjoy having him here while I can. There's no harm in that."

"You hope," Elly muttered.

Brie refused to let Elly's dire mood affect her. She'd been in her own bad mood for days and was tired of it. Admitting to herself that she cared deeply for Wolf freed something inside her. He was a half-breed drifter with no home, no family, and he'd killed a man when he was nine years old. None of that could make her care for him less. In all honesty, those things made her feelings that much stronger. If ever a man needed loving, that man was Wolf.

Not that she thought for a moment he was going to stand still and let her love him. With the notable exception of the day they were shot at while stringing the fence and Wolf had held her briefly in his arms, he did his best to keep as much distance as possible between them.

That day of the shooting, they'd grown too close for his comfort. That was probably the reason he'd told her about killing the preacher. He'd said he told her about it so she wouldn't trust so freely. Brie knew in her woman's heart that it was more than that, though. There was something more than his strong sense of right and wrong, his sense of responsibility, keeping him at the Rocking F. Maybe, just maybe, she was that something.

Dare she hope?

Of course she dared. "I'm not Brian and Caroline Flanigan's daughter for nothing," she murmured with a smile. She wouldn't call herself spoiled, exactly, but Brianna Flanigan was used to getting what she wanted. It came to her as she changed her dress and tied her hair back with a blue ribbon that what she wanted was a man named Wolf.

"Supper's ready," Tessa called from the kitchen.

Brie rushed from her room. "I'll go get Wolf, then."

"I'll get him," Katy offered. She'd forgotten all about her earlier fear. "I'll go get him, Brie."

"That's all right, sweetie." Brie patted her on the head and stepped out the back door. "I'll get him."

Wolf bent over the washbowl beside his bed and splashed water on his face and the back of his neck. Behind him the door was open to let in the cool evening breeze. As he picked up the sliver of soap beside the bowl, he told himself for the dozenth time since agreeing to have supper with the family that he was a fool. The kids were bad enough. They pulled at him in ways he'd never been pulled before. But to deliberately put himself in Brie's proximity was just plain foolishness.

He scrubbed his face and neck and had just finished rinsing off the soap when a sharp tingling rushed up his spine. A shadow spilled across the floor from the doorway behind him. A tight, feminine gasp was the only sound, save for the occasional drip of water falling from his face and hands. Wolf stiffened as dread overcame him.

"Wolf . . ." Brie's voice sounded shocked.

The dozens of scars crisscrossing his back drew taut beneath her gaze. "Get out," he snarled.

"Oh, Wolf! They *hurt* you!"

Every word, every second that he felt her eyes on him, was like a fresh wound opening up the old scars. Shame and humiliation threatened to choke him. He meant to reach for his shirt, but instead braced his hands on the small table before him. "Get out, Brie." If there really was a God, surely He would make her leave, surely He would spare Wolf this one time. Just this once.

But as always, God wasn't interested in helping Wolf. Brie didn't leave. He should have known she wouldn't. He should have known better than to pray. Fruitless, useless things, prayers.

He heard the soft rustle of fabric, light footsteps across the plank floor. His arms trembled as he stood there, unmanned by her presence. And then she did the unthinkable. She touched him. "Ah, God, Brie, don't."

But still she touched him. Not just his back. Not just his skin. She touched his scars. And in doing so, touched something he hadn't known he still possessed. She touched his soul.

Delicate fingers trembled as they traced the length of one scar after another. Wolf held his breath, not knowing whether to curse or give thanks. No one had ever touched him like this. No one. Her touch burned him like a brand. It soothed him like cool water. It nearly killed him to stand there and let her touch him, but for his life, he could not move away.

Brie fought her threatening tears and somehow man-

aged to hold them at bay. The scars were a sacrilege, not
only against the sheer beauty of his smooth bronze skin,
but against *him*, against Wolf. The cruelty it must have
taken to so torture another human was beyond her imagin-
ing. To make it worse, they were old scars. How young had
he been?

And then she knew. He'd been nine. "He did this, didn't
he?" Her voice shook with emotion. "The preacher. The
one you killed."

"It doesn't matter. It was a long time ago."

"It *does* matter," she cried fiercely. "That anyone could
do such a thing . . ." For the first time in her life, Brie
thought she understood what true hate was. "I'm *glad* you
killed him. Do you hear me? I'm glad!"

Wolf couldn't bear the pain in her voice or the pleasure
of her touch. He whirled and gripped her shoulders,
intending to push her away. The tears gathered in her eyes
stopped him. Humbled him. Horrified him. He wasn't
worth a single precious drop. She had to know that. Yet
still she would cry for him. "Don't," he whispered in a
tortured voice. "Please don't."

Brie sniffed and stepped back, blinking her tears away.
They would only embarrass him and humiliate her.

She stood with her hands lightly touching his chest,
where they'd come to rest when he had turned around.
His eyes, oh, the torment in his eyes took her breath away.
In an unconscious offer of comfort, she caressed him with
her fingers. The flesh beneath her touch was smooth and
warm, silk over steel as she detected hard muscle beneath
his skin.

No scars here, she thought, lowering her gaze from his
haggard face to his bare chest. Nothing but sleek bronze
skin over sculpted muscles. His abdomen was ridged like
a washboard. Above, two flat male nipples taunted her. As
she watched, they seemed to draw up slightly, the centers
rising to hard points.

It was a full moment before the significance of what she

saw dawned on her. He must be feeling what she felt when her body reacted the same way. Paralyzed by the realization, she slowly raised her gaze again and found his eyes squeezed shut, his head thrown back. His mouth firmed into a thin, grim line.

Maybe he wasn't feeling what she felt when her nipples hardened. That fierce, hot excitement, that tingling that settled low and deep between her legs. Maybe he didn't like what he was feeling.

Brie jerked her hands from his chest and stepped back. A scorching blush swept up her chest, neck, face. "I'm sorry. I, uh, came to tell you supper's ready." Feeling like a fool, she whirled and fled the bunkhouse.

It was several long minutes before Wolf was able to draw a decent breath. Never had a woman played on his emotions the way Brie did. Never had one driven him from one knife edge to another so quickly, so frequently. One minute she unmanned him by staring at the horror of his back, the next she humbled him by touching those hideous scars. Then before he'd been able to think straight, she'd touched his chest, stared at his nipples.

He was infinitely grateful that her gaze hadn't drifted below his belt. He was equally grateful that he hadn't given in to the need to double over at the fierce swiftness of his arousal at the feel of her soft hands on his bare chest.

Wolf rubbed his hands over his face. Brianna Flanigan was going to be the death of him, one way or another. She was making him crazy.

All through supper Wolf was on edge. If he hadn't promised Katy that he'd be there, he would have stayed away. The embarrassment that had flooded Brie's face right before she'd run from him earlier must have faded, judging by the way she was looking at him down the length of the table.

Okay, God, let's try one more time. If you're really up there, make me stop wanting her. Make her stop looking at me like she could eat me alive.

But once again, God failed the man named Wolf. Every time Brie's gaze came to rest on him, it was anything but restful. She eyed him as though she'd been on a lifelong fast and he was a feast spread out before her.

Wolf shuddered. The images that thought conjured were erotic enough to make a man moan and beg for mercy. That there might be truth to the thought—that she might really want him—had him turning away from her and trying to pay attention to what the boys were saying.

When it came to matters of the flesh, Brie looked as if she had been on a lifelong fast. If she wasn't a virgin, the Rockies weren't covered with snow in winter. The look in her eyes, though, was hotter than what any virgin should be allowed to give. And it was aimed at him. A less scrupulous man might take advantage of the invitation in those deep green depths and literally spread himself out for her pleasure.

Dammit! Another hot shudder raced down his spine. He had to quit thinking about her!

". . . go with you tomorrow?"

Realizing that Sully was asking him something, Wolf pulled himself from the fog of lust clouding his mind. "Sorry. What'd you say?"

"I wondered if it'd be okay if I ride with you tomorrow when you go to work the cattle."

Wolf sat back in his chair, forcibly steering his mind away from thoughts of Brie so he could concentrate on Sully. The boy was nine. Plenty old enough to learn about cattle. Older than most ranch-raised boys who regularly rode out with the men. "I think that's a good idea," he told Sully.

He thought then to look at Brie to see if she objected, but her smile of approval told him how she felt.

"What about me?" Rory asked.

Wolf gave the younger boy a mock glare. "How old are you?"

Rory straighten in his chair, sitting as tall as he could. "I'm seven."

Closing one eye, Wolf stared at him. "Seven, huh?"

"Yep."

Sully made a movement that looked suspiciously as though he were kicking Rory under the table; Rory responded with a slight jerk. "I mean, yes, sir," he said quickly.

Wolf resisted the urge to look down the table again to see how Brie felt about Rory riding out with him. The boy was old enough, and Wolf would be sure to stick close to home and away from the Double Diamond. He wasn't fool enough to do anything to endanger the boys. They would be at least as safe with him as they would be at home.

He gave a slow nod to Rory. "All right. If you promise to do what you're told, and if Brie says it's okay."

"Brie?" Rory asked, looking down the table anxiously.

Only then did Wolf allow himself to follow the boy's gaze.

"Are you sure you don't mind?" she asked Wolf. "The two of them together can be a handful."

"They'll behave themselves," he said. "Won't you, boys?"

"You bet!"

"We'll do just what you tell us, Wolf."

The excitement and gratitude in the boys' eyes made Wolf's throat close with unexpected emotion.

The house was all but dark, just one low-burning light in the front room downstairs, when Wolf, in what was becoming a nightly ritual for him that was oddly satisfying, made a final walk through the barn and around the corrals. He was on his way back to the bunkhouse when a sound from the front porch of the big house drew his attention.

From the deep shadows came Brie's voice. "It was kind of you to agree to take the boys tomorrow. They were so excited, it was all we could do to get them to bed."

Fearing he would regret it but unable to stop himself, Wolf crossed the yard and stood at the base of the porch steps. From the dim glow through the screen door, he could see the faint outline of her where she sat in the ladderback chair. The noise he'd heard was the sound of the dasher surging up and down in the wooden butter churn at her knees.

"They're good boys," he said quietly.

Her husky laugh went through him like fire through dry grass. "They're a couple of little hellions. I hope you don't regret your generosity."

"I'm sure I won't." There didn't seem to be much else to say on the subject. Wolf knew he should leave, but he stayed. The trill of frogs from along the banks of the stream was shrill and loud in the night silence. Wolf nodded toward the churn. "Kinda late to be doing that, isn't it?"

"I like doing it at night after everyone's in bed. It's the only time I have to myself, but I can't stand to be idle. Besides, churning helps me think."

He knew he shouldn't ask, but he couldn't stop the question. "What do you think about when you churn?"

"Tonight I've been thinking about Mother and Da."

It had been a while since Wolf's ego had been big enough to smash. He supposed he had it coming for believing she'd been sitting there in the dark thinking about him. Made him feel small. Like an ant.

"Mother used to sit out here like this at night and churn," she said, her voice thickening. "Da would sit with her. Sometimes I'd lie awake in my bed upstairs and hear them down here laughing over something. It was one of my favorite things about summer, hearing them laugh in the dark of the porch at night."

"You miss them."

"Terribly. Mother used to sit in the rocker to churn. She would tease me because I could never get the rhythm of the churning and the rocking to match." Her voice hitched slightly at the end. "I—" A quiet sob choked off her words.

Wolf's instinct was to flee. What little experience he had with a woman's tears warned him he was being manipulated. Women could turn their tears on and off at will, just to get to a man, get him to do something he didn't want to do.

But Brie was different. She wasn't like other women he'd known. Saloon girls and whores were hard and cold. The rancher's daughter he'd nearly fallen for a few years ago had used him to make another man jealous. Even the widow he'd spent the winter with when he'd been fourteen, the woman who'd taught him how to please a woman, had been manipulative.

But not Brie. She was too soft. Too open and honest. The tears in her voice ripped at something deep inside him.

"I was sitting h-here f-feeling sorry . . . for myself," she managed, "because I don't have Mother and D-Da anymore, and I f-feel so . . . s-selfish."

Wolf climbed the steps and squatted next to the butter churn, putting him at eye level with Brie. "I've never known anyone less selfish than you."

"Oh, but I am," she countered, blinking to meet his gaze.

The dim light from inside the house sparkled on the tears drifting down her cheeks. The sight made Wolf ache.

"I had them both for nineteen years," she said between sniffs. "But y-you . . . you n-never h-had . . . _anybody_." The tears came in earnest then, with audible sobs that threatened to cripple Wolf.

"Brie, don't." But she continued to cry, and it was killing him. He slipped her hands from the handle of the dasher, pushed the churn aside, and pulled her to her feet.

"Oh, Wolf, someone should have been there for you. Someone should have protected you."

"Shh, shh." That his arms should slip around her and she should lean against his chest seemed the most natural thing in the world, yet when it happened, everything inside Wolf stilled. As though he'd never held a woman before. As though he'd never smelled sunshine in a woman's hair, never felt feminine curves pressed against him. His hands threatened to shake. His knees turned the threat into reality.

"Come on, Irish," he cajoled. "I survived all right, didn't I? Don't cry. I'm not worth a single one of your tears."

"You're wrong," she said fiercely. With one trembling hand, she cupped his cheek.

Wolf had to fight the urge to turn his head slightly and bury his lips in her soft palm with its small callouses at the base of her fingers.

"To me," she whispered, looking up at him with tear-puffed lips and shining eyes, "you're worth anything."

"You don't mean that, Irish."

Brie gazed up at him and felt as if her entire life had led her toward this moment, this man. Her tears for him were not from pity for what had been done to him, but from her own pain at the thought of what he must have suffered. For his loneliness, then, and now. And maybe a little for herself, because she knew there was nothing she could do to change the horror of his past.

"Yes," she whispered to him. "I do mean it. To me, you're worth . . . anything. Everything."

Like a lone wolf drawn toward the warmth of the fire and the promise that his hunger will be eased, yet knowing the fire itself meant danger, Wolf hesitated. To move closer, to feel the warmth and feed his soul, meant exposing himself to the deadliest of chances. But her lips were so close, her scent so sweet, the promise of her so strong, that in the end all he could do was lower his mouth to hers.

A shudder, half pleasure, half fear, shook him, threatening to send him tumbling over some dark, unknown cliff. To save himself, he wrapped his arms around Brianna Flanigan and held on tight.

Her lips parted beneath the pressure of his. He tried to be gentle, tried to hold back the sudden swift stab of need, but the tiny whimper from her throat was not one of protest, but one of encouragement. With his tongue, he stroked her lips, then dipped between them.

Cream. So sweet. She'd been dipping into the churn. But there was another sweetness, darker and full of promise, that was the taste of the woman herself. *Brie.*

The need in him exploded and he took the kiss deeper, harder, taking from her everything she offered, knowing full well that she didn't understand the promises her mouth made to his, that her body, so soft and pliant and molded so closely to his that he could feel the tips of her breasts against his chest, made to his own aching body.

Darkness swirled through his mind, threatening to block out whatever sense of decency a man like him barely possessed. His breath came faster, his heart pounded more fiercely, his shaft hardened. His hips pressed blatantly against hers.

Brie felt the ridge of male flesh against her abdomen. In sheer instinct, her hips thrust back, bringing a moan from Wolf's throat. The knowledge that she had the power to make this strong man moan went straight to her head and swirled there with all the other feelings, both physical and emotional, that stormed her senses.

Fear reared its head. She'd never experienced these feelings before, and their strength was threatening. But this was Wolf. Wolf's arms holding her securely. Wolf's lips and mouth teaching hers the way to please him, while pleasing her. Wolf's body, strong and tall and male, pressed against her, heating her blood, stealing her breath.

This was Wolf. There was nothing to fear.

But for Wolf, there was fear. The fear of losing his head and taking her down to the weathered wooden floor of the porch. The fear of pressing himself into the cradle of her thighs. The fear that the animal in him would break loose and he would take the innocence Brie unknowingly offered. The fear of losing himself completely, of ruining her irrevocably. Of damning what little soul he had left for all eternity. Because the simple truth that burned through the fog of need and hunger was that a man with no name and a past filled with shame was not good enough to even be stepped on by a woman like Brianna Flanigan.

The jolting realization that his hand was easing toward her breast broke the spell weaved by her open response and his own yearnings. He tore his lips from hers. It felt as if he were tearing away his own flesh. With his hands braced on her shoulders, he stepped back until their bodies no longer touched. His hands were shaking. Good God, his hands were shaking.

She stood there in his grasp with her eyes closed, her lips parted. Lips red and swollen from the pressure of his. With every harsh breath she took, her breasts heaved, taunting him.

There was some comfort that she seemed to be having as much trouble breathing as he did. But she was inexperienced, hadn't realized where such a kiss could lead. Wolf should have known better.

But how could he have? He'd kissed women before. He'd done more than that with some. But he'd never lost his head. Not once. Not until Brie.

He dropped his hands and took another step back. "I'm sorry." His voice came out rough and raspy.

Slowly, her eyes opened, dark and heavy lidded. Mysterious. This open, trusting woman suddenly held the mystery of all that was feminine in her eyes. "I'm not sorry," she whispered.

It was that damn trust that set him off. "You sure as hell should be," he snarled. "That damn near got out of hand."

The corners of her lips curved up. Mysteriously. "Did it?"

Wolf ran the fingers of one hand through his hair. "Look at you. You're so damn innocent you don't even know when a man's on the verge of throwing you to the ground and tearing your clothes off."

The curve of her lips deepened. Her eyes flashed with heat. "Were you on the verge?"

With a low growl, Wolf spun on his heel and stepped off the porch. "Stay away from me, Brie. If you know what's good for you, just stay the hell away from me."

Chapter Eleven

Curled on her side in her bed later that night, Brie hugged herself and acknowledged that Wolf was right, she should stay away from him. He was dangerous, to her heart, her peace of mind. He was a loner. He was a drifter. In many ways, he was still a stranger. He could, probably would, break her heart.

She also acknowledged to herself that she had no intention of staying away from him. She simply couldn't. Her heart, and now her body, would not let her. She'd been drawn to him before she'd ever met him, in the dream of a man come to help them save the ranch. Upon her first sight of him she'd known he was the one, the man she'd prayed for, the man in her dream.

Now she understood that she'd known even then, somewhere deep down inside herself, that he was more. More than just a man come to save her ranch. More even than that. He was the man she would love. She felt that love blossoming inside her heart like a flower bud caressed by the sun and rain.

He wouldn't want her love. She wasn't fool enough to

believe otherwise. He wouldn't accept it, wouldn't return it, wouldn't stay. He would, quite literally, break her heart.

Even knowing that, she could not tell herself to stay away from him. She'd seen the love between her parents and known it to be the true and lasting kind that poets spoke of. That was what she wanted for herself. Her heart, however, had settled on Wolf. He would not love her back, unless by some miracle God decided to intervene on her behalf.

She would pray for that, selfishly, with all her might. But even if God decided Wolf was not for her, Brie could not back away. She would love Wolf while he was here, and pray for the strength to let him go when the time came. She would pray for wisdom, for she did not want her love to hurt Wolf. She would pray for dignity, for she did not want him to pity her.

And she would pray for a miracle. The miracle of Wolf's love.

Wolf decided not to waste his breath on another useless prayer. If God was up there, He was probably laughing his ass off at the knife edge of pain that threatened to steal Wolf's breath. The pain of his past, and his present. The pain of his hunger, his yearning for the impossible. The pain of having to walk away from all that Brie offered him. The pain of having to stay until her cattle were sold, until the major backed off from trying to take her ranch away from her.

If he couldn't leave, he could damn sure keep himself out of range of her smiles, her whispers, her tears. He did just that the next morning by slipping into the kitchen while she wasn't there. He split open four fresh biscuits, slapped a sausage patty inside each one, and carried them outside to eat.

He and the boys were about to make a clean getaway just at sunup, when Brie stepped out onto the front porch and called his name. He thought about pretending he hadn't heard her, but both boys reined in and looked back. Reluctantly, Wolf did the same.

"If the boys get to be too much trouble, or don't do what you tell them, feel free to send them home."

"Ah, Brie," Rory whined.

"Gallopin' goosefeathers," Sully said with disgust. "You'd think we were babies or somethin', Brie."

"I know you're not babies," she said with a smile. "Just be sure you don't act like babies." Then she turned her gaze toward Wolf. "I'll see you this evening."

Wolf's hand tightened on the reins, causing the horse to sidestep. What the hell had that look meant? And that tone? She sounded like . . . like she looked forward to seeing him ride in, like . . . like . . . Ah, hell. That was no friendly smile from boss to foreman. That was a woman-smile. The kind that trapped a man and brought him to his knees.

With a silent curse, Wolf turned away and headed down the valley at a trot. Rory and Sully clamored to catch up.

With a secret smile, Brie watched them go. The look of wariness on Wolf's face when she'd said she'd see him that evening shouldn't please her nearly as much as it did. She shouldn't want him to be wary. But wariness was a far cry better than the blank, distant look he used to wear. Wariness told her that she had some sort of effect on him.

The joke, however, proved to be on her as the morning progressed and she couldn't keep her mind on any of her chores for thinking of Wolf and the way he'd held her and kissed her last night.

Then again, maybe the joke was on him after all. He'd been in such a hurry to get away from her that neither he nor the boys had remembered to take anything for lunch.

Her good mood was instantly restored. Heavens, she couldn't very well let them starve, could she? Two growing boys and a hardworking man? *Someone* would have to take lunch to them.

The morning was hot up on the mesa. Wolf brushed his fingers through his hair and resettled his hat, tugging the brim down low in front to keep the sun out of his eyes. "Just hang on," he called to Rory. "The mare knows what to do."

The short-legged paint had surprised Wolf. She was more docile than a lamb—a good horse for a seven-year-old—but she had cow sense. Wolf had sent Rory after the yearling calf they'd come across. The animal had wandered off by himself and ended up at least a mile from the herd, which was spread out beyond the low rise ahead.

"He's gonna come flying right outta that saddle," Sully said with mischievous anticipation as the mare faced off with the yearling and kept the young steer from running back down the draw where they'd found him.

"Maybe," Wolf said. "Maybe not. Your brother's got about as much grit as you do."

Sully straightened in the saddle and puffed out his chest. "You think I got grit?"

Wolf smiled. "I think you got grit. Now, if you only had lunch."

Sully slumped back in the saddle. "I can't believe none of us thought to bring anything to eat. By the time we get home my stomach's gonna think my throat's been cut."

Wolf laughed. He was glad the boys had asked to come along this morning. He was enjoying himself. He found it immensely satisfying to pass on what knowledge he possessed to boys who would grow into men on this land.

"You like it here, don't you, Wolf?" Sully asked with studied casualness.

Wolf's smile slipped. There was more to the question than what he thought of the land. It touched him deep inside to realize Sully was really asking if Wolf was inclined to hang around longer than he'd originally agreed. That the boy—both boys—looked up to him was hard to escape. They missed their father, and Wolf was the first man to come along since Flanigan's death. It was natural for them to want a man to stay around a while.

But Wolf knew he wouldn't stay. He wasn't the kind of man young boys should look up to. If Brie knew his past, she wouldn't let him anywhere near her little brothers, he thought with bitter honesty.

Rather than hurt Sully's feelings or embarrass him, Wolf chose to take the question literally, a simple seeking of his opinion of the land. With a deep breath, he studied the land around him, the endless sky, the far horizon.

He'd worked cattle from Texas to Montana, from near-desert conditions to flood plains to as high up in the Rockies as cattle could find grass. Some land he liked better than others, some was easier on man and beast, but he could find no true fault with anything he'd seen.

Yet this place, with its surprising variety, could get inside a man and tug at him. There were valleys like the one where Brian Flanigan had put down roots. There were narrow canyons with pink walls. There was more water than most people thought, although hardly any trees. Then there was the mesa, dipping and rising, while fooling a man into thinking it was flat. And over it all, through canyon and valley and across the mesa as far as the eye could see . . . grass. Tall, thick grass, bending and waving before a sweet, clean wind. Good grass. Grass aplenty. Enough, if taken care of, to raise prime cattle in this one area for generations to come.

Far away on the western horizon, he spotted a low line of dark gray. The San Juans had trapped another storm. That, too, was part of the land. If the mountains didn't drain the clouds, the storm would roll down onto the plains and give them a good drenching a couple of hours before sundown. If there was enough force left to it, they might even get a rumble or two of thunder, maybe a few streaks of lightning. Then the storm would roll on, leaving everything clean and damp in its wake. The creeks that had gone dry during the day would run again that night.

"Yeah," he said softly. "It's good land, Sully. Your dad chose well. You know, in most parts of cattle country, ranchers have to move their herds to keep them from eating the grass down to the roots and ruining it. A place like this . . . hell, here you have to move the cattle around so the grass won't get too damn tall."

Sully laughed. "No foolin'?"

"No foolin'."

"But . . . do you like it?"

Wolf heard the unspoken question in Sully's voice. *Will you stay?* Another deep breath, then Wolf brought his gaze back to check on Rory. "I like it fine, Sully. Look at that. Rory's got the steer turned around and headed toward the herd. Atta boy, Rory!"

Damned if the seven-year-old didn't sit a little taller in the saddle at Wolf's shouted compliment.

Wolf nudged his horse into motion. "Let's go catch up with him before that steer changes his mind about cooperating."

Wolf and Sully took their time, not wanting Rory to think he couldn't handle the job of returning the steer to the herd. They were about a quarter of a mile behind Rory when first the steer, then Rory disappeared over the rise.

A moment later, gunfire split the late morning silence.

Sheer terror ripped through Wolf. *Rory!* He slid his rifle from the scabbard beneath his right leg. "Ride for cover," he shouted at Sully as he dug his spurs into his horse. "Now!"

Sully didn't, of course. He followed Wolf. His little brother was over that rise, where the shots came from. Sully wasn't going to turn tail and run. Rory needed him. If there was one thing Sully's da had taught him, it was that family stuck together—no matter what.

Wolf topped the rise and hauled in on the reins, making

his horse skid on its hocks down the slight incline. At the base, amid a tumble of boulders and stunted piñon, three riders sat their nervous mounts. One rider had a pistol leveled at Rory.

As terror turned Wolf's blood to ice, rage melted it and brought it to the boiling point. God damn them. God damn them to hell and back for drawing down on a seven-year-old baby!

Rory had evidently surprised a little cattle rustling operation. A half-dozen calves had been enclosed in a rope corral, their mama cows milling around the outside of the enclosure. A branding iron that was bound to sport the shape of two diamonds side by side poked out of a small fire.

Rustling, and threatening little boys.

Bastards.

Calm! Wolf ordered himself. *Stay calm.*

Reining in his rioting emotions just then was the hardest thing Wolf had ever done in his life. Killing the old bastard who'd raised him had been child's play compared to swallowing the urge to kill the three men before him. They were the same three who had attacked Brie and Katy less than two weeks ago. Shorty, Harve, and Lee. He'd made it a point to learn their names. Shorty was the one who'd ambushed him in town. Harve was the one now threatening Rory. There was no room in the country for belly-crawling scum like that.

With his hand clenched tight on the reins, Wolf schooled his expression to one of bored curiosity and approached Rory's side. A quick glance behind told him Sully had disobeyed his order. There was no time now to argue with the boy. Wolf settled for motioning him back, for all the good it would do.

He walked his horse until he nudged his way next to Rory so that the rifle across Wolf's thighs pointed toward the riders. Dropping the reins, he used one finger to nudge the brim of his hat up a notch. Rory was pale and shaking, but otherwise appeared unharmed.

Unharmed, hell. The kid'll have nightmares for years over this.

"Looky what we got here," Shorty sneered.

Grinding his teeth against the urge to raise his rifle and fire, Wolf met the gloating stares of Shorty and his friends with a sardonic smile. "Funny, I was just about to say the same thing."

"What we got is rustlers!" Rory spurted.

"Looks that way," Wolf said casually. "Yes, sir, it sure does look that way. Well, fellas," he said slowly, "you're not drunk this time, so I guess you must be lost. Rory, you and Sully head on home now and get back to your chores while I show these three fellas the way back to the Double Diamond."

"But—" Rory started, his voice breaking.

"The kid ain't goin' nowhere 'til I say he does," Shorty snarled. "And I'm the one with the gun."

"Don't worry about that gun aimed at you, son," Wolf told Rory. "These fellas might look stupid, but even they have to know that shooting a kid, especially after attacking your sisters the way they did, would have every man and woman in three states and two territories hunting them down like dogs. Why, I bet Major Palmer himself would furnish the rope to hang 'em with. Besides which, I've got my finger on the trigger of this rifle and they know it."

They hadn't known it, according to the sudden looks of shock on their faces. Wolf grinned and edged his horse between Rory and Shorty's gun. "Run on home now, boys."

"But . . ." Sully's voice trembled. "But Wolf, there's three of 'em!"

"Yeah." Wolf kept his gaze centered on Shorty. "And there's three of us. But hell, Sully, we can't sit around all day waitin' for five or six more of their men to come by and even things up. We'll not only miss lunch, but supper, too. You two go home."

"But that'll leave you facing three of them alone," Sully protested hotly.

"Yeah. I'd say that would just about even the odds, wouldn't you? Go on, now. Both of you. I'll have your word, boys, that you'll ride for home."

Sully hesitated, wondering what his da would have done. Da would have stayed and helped Wolf, that's what he'd have done. But Da was a man. Sully and Rory were just boys. Even if they stayed, what help would they be? Maybe if they rode hard and fast they could get help. Somewhere.

"C'mon, Rory, let's get out of Wolf's way."

Shaking so hard his reins were slapping his mare's neck, Rory crossed himself like the priest taught him and prayed not to get shot in the back while he turned and rode over the rise with his brother. He also prayed that he wouldn't mess in his pants.

Wolf kept his eyes on Shorty and friends, his ears tuned to the departing boys. He waited until the sounds of their leaving faded over the rise. "Now then. Suppose one of you tell me what the hell you think you're doing slapping the Double D brand on Rocking F calves. And pointing guns at little boys."

"This here is free range land," Harve taunted. "We got as much right to be here as anybody."

"Maybe I was wrong. Maybe you really are as stupid as you look."

Shorty made a jabbing motion with his pistol that had Wolf's finger tensing on the trigger of his rifle. "Watch your mouth, half-breed."

"Watch that pistol, white man."

It was a fact that inattention had gotten many a man killed. Wolf wondered belatedly if he was about to become one of them. While he'd kept his eyes on the pistol Shorty waved at him, Harve, the one farthest away, had grabbed his rope. Wolf saw the loop sail through the air, but there was no time to dodge before it dropped down neatly around his shoulders.

With a sharp curse, Wolf raised his left hand—his right held the rifle balanced across his thighs—and grabbed the rope beyond the slip knot. At the same instant when Harve pulled to tighten the rope around Wolf's shoulders, Wolf wound the rope once around his wrist and yanked with all his strength.

Both men were fast. Both were strong. Both ended up in the dirt.

"Wait! Your hat!" Tessa reached up and straightened Brie's hat. It was made of fine Milan straw faced with velvet that matched her riding habit. Contrasting beads edged the brim, and an elegant spray of velvet fruit and satin dandelions perched jauntily on the crown. "There. That's better. Now don't ride so hard you knock it cockeyed."

"Yes, ma'am." Flushed with excitement and impatience, Brie led her horse to the stump she and the girls and their mother had always used as a mounting block.

"Wait!" The screen door slapped shut behind Elly as she dashed off the porch and across the yard. "Cookies," she said breathlessly, stuffing a towel-wrapped bundle into the pouch hanging from Brie's saddle horn. "You forgot the cookies."

"Thanks." With a breathless laugh, Brie mounted and fussed with her skirt until both her boots were covered. The skirt covered most of the horse's left side. To balance her weight, thrown to one side by the sidesaddle, she carried the food pouch on the right, along with her shotgun.

A few moments later she rode out of the yard and toward the path that led up onto the western mesa. It was there, with the herd, that she would find Wolf and her brothers.

White-faced and hollow-eyed with terror, Sully and Rory raced across the mesa toward the fold in the land that led down into the valley. Sully wanted *so bad* to go back. They shouldn't have left Wolf to face those men alone.

But again the question came to him—what could two boys do but get in the way? Maybe Wolf had already managed to get free. Or maybe, Sully thought fearfully, Wolf was already dead.

He can't be dead, he can't be dead. The words pounded inside Sully's head to the rhythm of the horses' hooves thundering across the mesa. He'd already lost his mother and his da. He couldn't lose Wolf, too!

Never had Sully been so glad to see anyone in his life as he was his big sister when he and Rory crested a rise and saw Brie riding toward them.

"Brie! It's Brie!" Rory yelled.

Brie took one look at their faces and knew something terrible had happened. "Where's Wolf?"

"Back—there," Sully managed between gasping breaths. "Three men—Double Diamond."

As the boys spilled their tale, Brie swallowed. Dear God, Wolf! *Lord, keep him safe, I beg you.*

Just in case the Lord was busy, Brie pulled the shotgun from its boot. "Which way?"

"We'll show you," Sully said.

"No! Go ho—" She was too late. Both boys wheeled their sweating mounts and raced back the way they'd come. Brie clung to her sidesaddle, cradled her shotgun, and raced after them. She had no trouble overtaking them, but ordering them once more to go home proved a waste of breath.

As they neared the last rise, Rory pointed. "They were waiting for me just over the top, down in the rocks."

Brie nodded. She knew the spot. She strained to listen for any sign that Wolf and the three men were still there, but the wind was from the wrong direction and whisked away any sound there might have been.

She turned to the boys. "You two stay put. Right on this spot, and I mean it. I'll whistle if it's—" She deliberately

cut herself off. She'd started to say she'd whistle if it was
safe for them to follow her. Judging by their mulish expres-
sions, the warning would be another waste of breath. "I'll
whistle when I need you. Don't come 'til I whistle," she
warned, "or you could mess things up. If anyone other
than Wolf or me comes over that rise, you run the legs off
those horses and get home." Having no choice but to trust
them to do as they were told, she checked her shotgun
one more time, then nudged her horse forward.

Because of the way the land rose, then fell away, she
couldn't see down to the rocks until she was fully exposed
atop the rise. The scene was just as the boys had described.
The milling cows, the calves enclosed in a rope corral. The
fire, the branding iron, three Double Diamond riders. And
Wolf.

But the three men and Wolf, instead of being mounted,
were on the ground. Pummelling each other. She was a
scant dozen yards away before one of the Double D men
noticed her. He shouted a warning just as Wolf's fist connected with his chin. Another man dove at Wolf. The
third went at Wolf from behind, pistol raised, intent on
clobbering him in the back of the head.

Brie remembered the way Wolf had quickly dispatched
these same three men the day she'd met him. But they'd
been drunk at the time. They didn't look drunk now. They
looked . . . deadly. Before the third man could hit Wolf
from behind, she raised her shotgun and fired in the air.

All four men froze.

"I've got one more barrel, boys" she said calmly. "Who
wants it?"

Wolf had no trouble recognizing that voice. While he
cursed her for showing up and putting herself in danger—
not to mention interrupting his fight—he snatched his
rifle and pistol from the ground where they'd fallen during
the fight. He'd yell at her later. Right now he would take
advantage of her interruption. "Face down," he ordered
the men. "Hands behind your heads. *Now.*"

In a matter of minutes he had each of them bound hand and foot. Only then did he think he'd conquered his fear for Brie's safety, and his anger that she would jeopardize herself, enough to turn and look at her.

"What," he asked softly, coldly, "are you doing here?"

She arched her brow at his tone. "I brought lunch."

"Lunch?" His gaze rose to her hat. "Hell. Looks like you're wearing most of it."

Wolf and Brie didn't speak much on their way to the Double Diamond. As soon as it had been safe, Brie had whistled for the boys, and they had taken grim pleasure in helping Wolf drape the three rustlers across their saddles for the humiliating ride home to the neighboring ranch. Wolf had made sure the branding fire was out and had taken down the rope corral and freed the calves, stating to no one in particular he would return later and brand them himself.

Wolf had tried to send Brie home with the boys, but she had refused. "I'm not letting the major get away with this," she'd said heatedly.

"You think I can't handle it?" Wolf had snarled.

"I think you can handle it just fine," she snapped back, not at all sure why he seemed so angry with her. "But I want my shot at him myself. That was my brother these men threatened."

Wolf's jaw flexed once, twice, but finally he'd nodded. "Fair enough."

"Well, thank you for your permission," she'd bitten off.

As they came within sight of the Double Diamond head-quarters, first one person then another stopped whatever he was doing to stare. A bruised and bloodied half-breed and a young woman in an elegant riding habit, perched on a sidesaddle, trailing three Double Diamond horses, each with a Double D rider trussed up like a Christmas goose and slung belly down over their saddles. They made quite a sight. They attracted a sizeable crowd as they neared the big log house.

Brie hadn't been to the Double Diamond since last summer when she'd come with her mother to visit Letty. Before that they had come often throughout the years, as Letty and her children had frequently visited the Rocking F. Yet no matter how often Brie came, the huge log house never ceased to take her by surprise. In a virtually treeless land, it was an awesome sight, somehow more incongruous than the barn and other out buildings, which were made, like the Rocking F out buildings, of cut boards.

Wolf rode beside and slightly ahead of her. The closer they got to the house, the stiffer his shoulders looked. He was undoubtedly waiting for a bullet. Brie wasn't worried. One of the people on the front porch of the log house was Letty. As long as Letty was there, nothing would happen. Major Palmer placed great store in his daughter's opinion of him. That didn't mean he wouldn't do whatever he darn well pleased, but if he knew she wouldn't like it, he wouldn't do it in front of her.

Beside Letty stood James and the major. Jennings strutted over from the nearest corral to join them. Wolf rode directly to the hitching rail before the porch, but did not dismount. Brie pulled up beside him. She, too, stayed in the saddle.

"Brie?" Letty eyed her warily, shifting her gaze from her to Wolf, to the three horses behind them. "What's going on?"

"That's what we came to ask the major," Brie answered as kindly as she could. None of this was Letty's fault, and Brie refused to take it out on her. When she turned her gaze on the major, however, her tone turned cold. "I want to know what your men were doing putting a Double Diamond brand to Rocking F calves."

"Well, now!" Major Palmer rocked back on his heels,

looking properly shocked. "Suppose you come inside and we'll see if we can't get to the bottom of this. Somebody cut those boys loose," he called out."

"Nobody touches them," Wolf said coldly.

"Here, now," Palmer blustered. "No call to be rude."

"This isn't a social call, Major." Brie met the major's steady gaze and held it. "What are you going to do about these men?"

"Not a thing, until I find out what's going on."

"Major Palmer, I've known you most of my life, and if there's one thing I'm certain of, it's that nothing, not one single thing, is done on this ranch or by your men that you didn't order yourself, or that you didn't know about."

"Give the man a little slack, Brie," Wolf said, leaning a forearm down against his saddle horn. "Surely the major didn't order the same men who attacked you and Katy to hold a seven-year-old boy at gunpoint."

"*What?*" Brie demanded. It seemed the boys had left a little something out of their story earlier!

"No!" Letty cried.

"Now see here!" Palmer bellowed. "I never ordered any such thing!"

"We didn't mean nothing by it," Shorty yelled from his position draped across his saddle. "The kid just took us by surprise is all."

"Caught you branding our cattle, you mean," Brie retorted.

"The fact is," Wolf said to Palmer, "that these three men of yours have got to go, Major."

"Right after they're horsewhipped," Brie added, with murder in her voice.

Letty looked up at her father, her eyes blazing. "I couldn't agree more. We don't want men like that on the Double Diamond."

"No, of course we don't," Palmer agreed. "They'll be off this ranch by sundown. See to it, Hank."

Hank Jennings glared at Wolf, but gave the major a nod.

"Oh, and Jennings," Wolf added quietly. "You'll see that they have an escort all the way out of the area, and that they come nowhere near the Rocking F. Won't you."

Chapter Twelve

"Son of a bitch!" Behind the closed doors of his office in the big log house, Major John Palmer slammed his fist down on his desk. The blow rattled the glass globe of the lamp sitting on the desk corner. It was with some small satisfaction that he saw Jennings flinch at his curse. "How could those three fools have been so *stupid?*"

"I'll get rid of them, boss."

"You're goddamn right you will. You'll have them escorted south across the state line, just like that fucking half-breed said. Fooling around with the girls when they were drunk was one thing. Getting caught rustling cattle by a seven-year-old boy, and *drawing down* on him, for Christ's sake—Make sure they don't come back," he added darkly.

Reading the underlying message in his boss's eyes, Jennings nodded. Harve, Shorty, and Lee wouldn't need to worry about finding another job. They wouldn't need to worry about a damn thing but pushing up daisies, the stupid bastards. "What about the half-breed?"

Palmer closed his eyes, tilted his head back, and took a

slow, deep breath to ease the painful tightening in his chest. God, he hated Indians, and half-breeds were just as useless. Ask him, every stinking one of the redskinned bastards oughta be wiped off the face of the earth. But Letty, damn her hide . . . if she ever found out he had anything to do with anybody getting killed . . . She was just like her mother that way.

Mary, my sweet, sweet Mary. God, after more than twenty years, he still grieved for her.

Palmer sighed. Mary wouldn't have approved any more than Letty would. But nothing was going to stop him from getting rid of the Flanigans. They had better grass, more reliable water, and coal. Damn Flanigans didn't deserve any of it. The land should have been his. Would have been his, if Brian Flanigan hadn't beaten him to it by one lousy week. The Irish, as far as Palmer was concerned, weren't but a step or two above Indians. Why didn't they stick to potato farming?

"Boss? The half-breed?"

"I'll give it some thought."

Jennings opened the door to leave, and Letty rushed in.

The major stifled a groan. She was going to nag him, he knew it. She might be his own beloved daughter, but by God, she'd turned into a nag over the years. She needed a man in her life. That'd keep her occupied and keep her pretty little nose out of *his* business.

Palmer pasted a smile on his face for her benefit. "What is it, honey?" As if he couldn't read the anger on her face.

"I was going to demand an explanation about what's going on around here, but your color doesn't look so good."

Palmer ground his teeth. If there was anything he hated worse than her questioning him and nagging him about the Flanigans, it was her nagging him about his health. "I'm fine, Letty."

"You don't look fine. We'll talk after you've rested."

The swish of her skirt and petticoats as she turned to

go grated along his nerves. She meant it, too. When she thought he felt better, she'd be all over him like flies on shit about what happened today.

Damn those Flanigans. Why wouldn't they just give up and sell out?

Wolf and Brie rode toward home side by side, but as far as Brie could tell, they might has well have been miles apart. The angry dark clouds rolling in from the mountains didn't have anything on the man beside her. They'd be lucky to make it home without getting drenched, but she was determined to get to the bottom of whatever storm bedeviled Wolf long before the rain reached them.

"You want to tell me what's eating you?" she asked.

He took so long in answering that she thought he wasn't going to do anything other than flex that hard muscle in his jaw. When he finally spoke, his voice stung like a lash. "You and those damn brothers of yours are what's eating me."

"What did we do?" she cried.

"You damn near got yourselves killed, all three of you, that's what you did."

"What did you expect me to do when the boys told me you were outnumbered three to one? Turn around and ride for home?"

"*Yes*. That's exactly what you should have done. You've got no business putting yourself in danger like that. That's what you hired me to do."

"I hired you to run the ranch, not get your head bashed in."

"I didn't get my head bashed in."

"You were about to."

"I was not."

"One of those men was ready to clobber you on the back of the head when I fired the shotgun."

Wolf opened his mouth to retort, then snapped it shut.

"Okay," he said a minute later. "Maybe I shouldn't have yelled at you. But I didn't need help from a woman with fruit on her head."

"Ah, I see."

"Good. I'm glad."

"I see that what you're really angry about is that I interrupted your fun."

Wolf gave her a startled look.

"Oh, aye." The brogue rolled effortlessly across her tongue. "I know all about men and their love of fighting. Me da was a full-blooded Irishman, ya know. Nobody loves fighting better than the Irish. Da would rather have been beaten to a bloody pulp than have somebody step in and help him. Irishmen can be so thickheaded," she added with disgust. "I'll have to add half-breed foremen to the list."

She peered sideways at Wolf to see if he smiled at her quip.

No smile. No turning his gaze toward hers. Just the bunching of that hard muscle in his jaw as he stared straight ahead.

"You scared me," he admitted, "riding into the middle of a fight like that. One of them could have shot you."

"You scared me, taking on three men that way."

"I didn't see as how I had much of a choice."

"No, you didn't. Because you were protecting Rory and Sully." A shiver of belated reaction raced down Brie's spine. "I can't believe they didn't tell me about one of the men pointing a gun at Rory."

After a slight pause, Wolf glanced at her. "Rory didn't tell you how he rode up over that rise and straight into the barrel of Shorty's gun?"

"No." Her hands tightened on the reins. "No, he didn't."

"What *did* he tell you to send you racing over the hill like that, waving a shotgun in the air, acting like some avenging angel come to earth?"

"Are you making fun of me?"

"No, I'm trying to figure out what put the fire of battle I saw in those green eyes when you held your shotgun on those three. What did the boys say to make you forget all good sense and ride into the thick of trouble that way?"

"They *said*," she answered tightly, "that you needed help."

Wolf already had his mouth open to rake her over the coals again for her foolishness when her words registered. For him? She'd ridden into trouble for him? No one—*no one*—had ever put himself in danger for Wolf. No one. Not ever. No one but the woman beside him, perched on her sidesaddle as though she were out for a Sunday ride in the park, like he'd heard the ladies in London took. No one but Brie, who had two brothers, three sisters, and a ranch to look after. Jesus, God, what if she'd been hurt— or worse—helping *him?*

A deep shudder of emotion tore through him.

They rode on in silence until Brie remembered the lunch she'd brought with her. They stopped on the wide open plain and Wolf knew that he could either watch her struggle down from that stupid sidesaddle, or he could help her. To help her, he would have to touch her, and he wasn't sure he had any business doing that. In fact, he was positive he shouldn't get anywhere near her, but he couldn't stand by and let her break a leg, or her neck. Steeling himself against the urge to whisk her from the saddle and into his arms, he lifted her down and let go the instant her feet touched the ground.

"Thank you." Her voice sounded as breathless as he felt. When he stepped away, her hand lingered on his shoulder a moment, then slid slowly down his arm. Like a caress.

Wolf turned sharply away and untied the quilt from behind her saddle. They ate in silence, with Brie trying to catch his gaze, he purposely avoiding it. She sat on the quilt with that ridiculously long riding skirt spread out around her. Wolf took the food she offered from the bag she'd brought and walked several yards away to eat standing up.

How could he react this way to her, with this crazy pounding in his chest, and worse, much worse, this need to hold her and keep her safe, this terrible craving to taste that sweet, sweet mouth of hers again? How could she look as though she wanted him to do those things?

Sully's voice from earlier in the day drifted through his mind. *Do you like it here?* Wolf looked again across the grassland that went on forever and thought, yes, he liked it here. Too much, he thought, his gaze settling briefly on Brie. Too damn much.

"Storm's comin' in," he said, studying the dark line of thunderheads rolling toward them from the west. "Time to get a move on."

Why didn't she get mad and yell at him, he wondered as they silently packed up and got ready to leave. She'd as much as confessed that she cared enough about him to ride into unknown trouble because she thought he needed help, and he'd barely spoken to her since. Why were her hands so gentle on his shoulders when he gritted his teeth and lifted her back into the saddle? Why did her eyes, so big and green and solemn, stir a fire deep in his belly?

"Brie . . ."

Not having the slightest idea what he'd been about to say, he let his voice trail off and shook his head. "Let's get out of here."

They were nearing the trail that wound down from the mesa top to the valley floor below when the storm hit. Wolf had been riding to Brie's left in a futile attempt to block at least some of the stinging wind from her. Now he cursed himself for it, for he'd allowed her to ride too close to the edge of the bluff for his comfort. He swung wide, motioning her to follow him away from the abrupt eighty-foot drop.

His head was turned to keep her in sight. She met his gaze through the sudden downpour. In that instant, a bolt of lightning struck so close that the world turned stark white and the crash of the lightning and simultaneous earth-shaking clap of thunder momentarily deafened him.

Wolf's horse reared. Gripping tightly with his knees, Wolf hung on. From the corner of his eye he saw Brie's horse rear, too, heard it shriek in terror. And saw with horror that Brie, at a disadvantage because of her sidesaddle, was not going to be able to keep her seat. As if in slow motion, she slid from the back of her terrified horse and with a scream, disappeared over the edge of the bluff.

"Brie!" Wolf threw himself from the saddle and raced to the edge. *"Brianna!"* Where? Dear God, where was she? He strained to see to the valley floor through the pouring rain, terrified of finding her twisted, broken body at the base of the bluff.

He couldn't find her. *He couldn't find her!*

"Wolf!"

Her cry was faint and shot straight through his heart. "Brie? Brie, where are you?"

"Here! I'm here!"

He spied her then, or rather, spied the dangling length of her skirt. At the spot where she'd gone over, the face of the bluff had eroded. Wolf stood on a lip that hung out over air while the face of the bluff was gouged out beneath it. Twenty feet down, there was a sandstone ledge. Wolf's heart stopped. Brie clung to the edge of the rocky ledge by her fingertips.

"Hold on! I'm coming, Brie!"

Wolf forgot that he didn't trust God, that he'd given up all hope years ago of ever having his prayers answered. As he searched for footholds on the slick, wet face of the bluff on his way to Brie, he prayed like he'd never prayed in his life. He prayed for Brie to have the strength to hold on.

He prayed for his own strength to help her, to save her from falling to certain death. *God, please, please, please.*

The slick rock that crumbled beneath his hands and boots wasn't nearly as much of a hindrance as the shaking that racked his whole body.

"Wolf!"

"I'm coming!"

"Wolf, *hurry!*"

God, please, please, please. Give her the strength, give me the speed. And keep this damn rock from falling apart beneath us.

Chunks of rock fell away beneath his feet and hands and tumbled down the bluff, nearly sending him down with them. His prayers changed to curses long before he finally reached the shelf from which Brie hung.

His heart stopped again. She was clinging by her fingertips, with nothing but thin air beneath her, as the shelf she gripped with desperation stuck out a good five feet from the face of the bluff. If she lost her hold, there would be nothing to stop her fall but the hard wet ground far below. Too damn far below.

Wolf threw himself down on his stomach and inched his way to the edge of the rock shelf, wondering if it would hold his weight. Praying it would. *It goddamn well better,* he thought fiercely.

"Wolf!"

"I'm here." He wasn't going to be able to help her while stretched out flat on his stomach. He eased carefully to his knees, ignoring the rain that made the rock slippery beneath his hands, the rain that pounded and stung and threatened to blind him. He didn't need to see now, only needed to reach Brie and pull her to safety. *Reach Brie. Reach Brie.*

He was almost too late. Even as he knelt above her and reached for her hand, her fingers slipped on the wet sandstone. She screamed. Wolf shouted and cursed, and caught her by the wrists just as she lost her grip. "I've got you!"

Damn, she was flailing her legs around so much, he nearly lost her. "Don't kick! Hold still. I'm pulling you up. Hold on to my wrists. Brie? Hold on to my wrists!"

Through the fog of terror in her brain, Brie heard him, felt his grip on her wrists as she dangled what felt like a mile above the ground. His hold was the only thing that saved her.

"Hold on," he said. *Hold on.* She tried, only to realize she was already gripping his wrists so tight that her fingers were numb. She tried to look up, to see his face, but the pounding rain forced her eyes closed. Her arms felt as if they were being ripped from their sockets, her hands were scraped raw and bloody, her knees were bruised and skinned, she was light-headed. Her lungs fought futilely for air. The bitter taste of terror threatened to choke her. But through it all, she knew that no matter what happened, Wolf would not let her fall.

Wolf wished he could have been as sure. The angle was awkward. While pulling her up, he tried not to scrape the hide off her arms against the rock. Her weight seemed too heavy, until he realized she wore an extra yard of sopping wet corduroy in that damned riding skirt. It was a wonder, he thought, straining to lift her, that the weight of the skirt hadn't carried her straight to the ground.

Slowly, gradually, with his heart in his throat every second, Wolf pulled Brie up and over the edge. Rather than let go of her wrists, he leaned back to pull her the final few inches. Leaned back until he held her safe in his arms. Leaned back until he lay prone across the sandstone shelf, struggling for breath, holding her close against his chest, with the rain pounding down on them.

He dug his heels in against the rock and tried to push himself beneath the overhang above to get Brie out of the rain. Beneath his heels, the edge of the shelf crumbled and fell away.

With a sharp curse, and holding Brie tight against his chest, he scrambled to his feet and dashed beneath the

overhang before the whole damn shelf gave way underneath them. Gasping, he pushed Brie against the back wall
of the shelter that had just enough height to allow him to
stand.

He couldn't stop shaking. For support, he leaned against
her. God, it had been close. He'd almost lost her. *He'd
almost lost her!* For the first time in his life, Wolf whispered
a genuine prayer of thanks. Brie was safe.

He felt her struggle against him. "I ... can't ...
breathe."

Through the terror that had yet to loosen its grip in him,
Wolf realized she wasn't panting from fear or exertion, she
really couldn't breathe. It was then he realized that she
felt different beneath his hands. A corset. She was wearing
a goddamn corset, and she couldn't draw a decent breath.

"You're about to pass out," he muttered, fumbling with
her sodden jacket, wasting precious seconds before he
finally got her out of it. "Hang on," he told her. "Damn,
how—" There. Buttons down the back of her blouse.

If he'd had a sense of humor just then he would have
laughed. For days he'd dreamed of getting her out of her
clothes, and here he was, doing it, for practical, unselfish
reasons. Him? Unselfish?

What little color was left in her cheeks was starting to
fade. The buttons down the back of her blouse were so
damn tiny. Progress was slow with his big, clumsy fingers.
Fingers made clumsier by the fear that had yet to leave
him, the frustration of wanting her even though he knew
he shouldn't, and the very real alarm over her not being
able to breathe. Too damn slow. He tore the blouse open
to get at the laces compressing her rib cage.

The laces were soaked. Pulling on them only served to
tighten them. With a snarl, Wolf pulled the hunting knife
from the sheath on his belt, spun Brie around to face the
wall, and sliced through the ties of her corset. Instantly
she went limp.

"Brie!"

"Oh, thank you," she whispered. "I didn't realize . . ."

"That you couldn't breathe? Damnit, don't you ever truss yourself up like that again," he bit out, fear making his voice harsh. "And while I'm at it, that sidesaddle of yours is out."

"My saddle?" Slowly she turned to face him. "What's my saddle got to do with anything?"

"It damn near got you killed, that's what. If you'd been riding astride, you'd have had a hell of a better chance of keeping your seat."

Now that her breath was returning, Brie felt her mind clear from the fear. She saw the anger in his eyes and would have given him the argument he needed, but she saw his fear, too, the fear for her safety. From somewhere, a devil grabbed at her, and brought words from her mouth that in a saner moment she might never have uttered. "You'd like that, would you?"

"For you to keep your seat and not go sailing off the edge of the nearest bluff? Yeah," he snarled, "I'd like that."

Brie held his gaze and turned her head slowly from side to side. "I meant . . . you'd like . . . getting me astride."

Wolf nearly choked. He might have convinced himself she hadn't meant that the way it sounded, but for the sudden flare of heat in her eyes. Wary, he took a step back. "You're safer in a regular saddle. You have more control."

"Oh, I don't know," she said, her voice husky. "I didn't have a bit of control last night, but I felt safe enough."

"You weren't safe," he snarled. "You're never safe with me."

"I felt safe."

"How could you?" he nearly shouted. "I was ready to tear your clothes off!"

Her eyes widened. Her breath hitched. "You were?"

"Don't tease me, Irish. You know damn well I was almost out of control last night. I even said so."

"What—" She swallowed, then licked her lips. "What stopped you?"

"Good God! Common sense stopped me."

Brie's chin angled upward. "I don't think so. I think it was fear. I think you're afraid to admit to yourself that you care for me." She tried to take a step toward him, but the extra length on her riding skirt tangled around her feet. She stumbled straight into Wolf's arms.

He pushed her away as if her touch burned. "The skirt goes, dammit." With the knife in his hand, he knelt and sliced away at the extra yard of length on the left side of her skirt.

Brie watched his competent hands wield the knife on her skirt. His hair, in fact all of him, was soaked. She tried to reach out to touch that thick, glossy hair, but a gust of wind swept an icy sheet of rain beneath their dubious shelter and straight into her face. Shivering, she suddenly realized that without her jacket, she was twice as cold as she had been.

With the cold, everything came back to her in a rush. The bolt of lightning. Her horse rearing. Feeling herself falling, falling, falling. An icy shiver racked her from head to toe. "I was so scared," she whispered. "I was so scared, but I knew you'd come, I knew you would."

Wolf shuddered, remembering how close he'd come to being too late to grab her, too late to save her. Slowly he dropped the fabric he'd hacked from her skirt, resheathed his knife, and rose to his feet before her. Emotions surged through him, hot and dark, powerful. Fear. Relief. Anger. Hunger. The need to claim the woman he'd almost just lost, to make her his once and for all, even knowing that he shouldn't, couldn't.

He knew he wasn't thinking straight when he threaded the fingers of one hand through the wet, tangled length of her hair—so damn glad she'd lost that stupid hat in the fall—and pulled her head back. Right then he didn't care about right and wrong, about the kind of woman she was, the kind of man he wasn't. He didn't care about anything but assuring himself in the most basic way possible that she was alive and safe. Slipping his other arm around her back and clutching her tightly, he took her mouth with a ferocity that would have shocked him if he'd realized it.

Brie wasn't shocked; she was grateful. She parted her lips and met the fierceness of his kiss with a fierceness of her own. She needed this, needed him. Willingly she let the sharp edge of a need she'd never felt before replace the stark terror of moments past. He was the only solid thing in a world that had, quite literally, slipped out from beneath her feet. She clung to him and gave everything she had to the kiss, trying to show him how much she needed him.

But she needed more than his kiss, more than his hand in her hair and his arm around her. She needed all of him, every solid inch of his warmth, his strength. Needed it so much that she squirmed in his embrace, trying to get closer, closer, trying to burrow her way inside his skin.

The heat of him, his taste, his strength, all combined to make her head spin. She clung to him desperately, scarcely able to catch her breath.

Her response drove Wolf on until he had her pressed hard against the rock wall with the weight of his body. A wildness he'd never known before broke free inside him. Blood rushed from his head to his loins and that fast, he was hard and aching for her. He didn't mean to thrust his hips against her, but it happened, then it happened again. She thrust back and whimpered, but not in protest.

Groaning, gasping for breath, Wolf released her hair and cupped her breast in his eager, needy hand. She was as full and soft as he knew she would be. He wanted to see her flesh, touch it, taste it. Needed to. *Had to.*

He remembered then that her blouse was still open down the back. The hand at her back found its way beneath the sodden fabric without any help from his useless brain.

Sleek. Soft, like silk. And cold. He rubbed her flesh to warm her, but also to feed his own need to touch her. He called himself a selfish bastard, but the words drowned in the flood of needs and emotions tangling inside him.

Brie revelled in the feel of his one hand on her breast, the other on the bare skin of her back. She hadn't known . . . had never guessed that the touch of a man's hand could make the world stand still, then send it spinning out of control. The hand at her back slid beneath her blouse, then around her ribs, and settled firmly, demandingly over her other breast. This time there was nothing between her and him, no fabric to get in the way. Only his hard, calloused hand on flesh that ached for his touch. She arched into his hand, wanting more. Needing more.

Someone groaned. Maybe her, maybe him. Maybe both of them. Brie didn't know. Wolf didn't care. She was perfect. A perfect fit for his hand. When he tore his mouth from hers and kissed her cheeks, her eyes, her forehead, jaw, chin . . . each spot was perfect. Soft. Silky. *His.*

He couldn't get enough of her. He trailed his open mouth lower, down her neck. When her blouse interfered, he pushed it down and out of his way. Her collarbone felt delicate beneath his lips, her skin, as sweet as honey.

Lower. Lower. Until his parted lips felt the fullness of her breast and delved lower still. The blouse slid farther down until it was gone, blessedly gone. Cupping her bare breasts in both hands, he couldn't think of gentleness, of circling her nipple with tender kisses. He was too far gone. He latched on to one nipple with his mouth and suckled hard.

Brie cried out, in shock, in something far too strong for a pale word like pleasure. She was dying, and she didn't care. She only cared that he not ever, ever, take his hot mouth from her flesh. With every pull of his mouth came a tugging sensation that reached down into her very core. It made her hips thrust against his, made her moan, made her whimper. She didn't care. Her arms came around him and held him close, pressing his head to her breast. She wanted this never to end.

A hot throbbing centered between her legs, making her crave something she didn't fully understand. She only knew that it was Wolf she craved, Wolf who could fill the empty void inside her, Wolf, who could end this torment that she wanted never to end. When his hips thrust back, his name slipped from her lips.

The sound of it drove Wolf wild. He slid his mouth to her other breast, finding it just as sweet as the first, the nipple just as hard. He couldn't stop, couldn't let her go. Couldn't get enough of her.

Before he realized what was happening, he had knelt, sitting back on his heels, and tugged her down until her skirt was hitched to her waist and she sat straddling his hips. Through his heavy denim pants he could feel the heat of her pressed against him, calling to him, urging him to slip the buttons free on his fly and sink himself into her so deep he would never—

Good God!

With a hoarse cry, Wolf pulled his lips from her breast. Brie cried out in protest. Gasping for breath, Wolf wrapped his arms around her and pulled her flush against his chest. God, what had he nearly done?

Chapter Thirteen

Wolf didn't apologize this time, but he didn't walk away, either. He held her, and she held him, until their hearts quit racing and their breath quit rasping. Until the rain stopped and the storm rolled on. They held each other as the sun came out again, low in the western sky.

As if by some unspoken signal, they let go. Brie shivered at the loss of his warmth. She looked down at herself, astonished, a little mortified, to find her blouse and chemise down around her waist, her skirt hitched up to join it, while she straddled Wolf's hips.

At the strangled sound that came from Wolf, she jerked her head up to look at him. His head was tilted back, his eyes squeezed shut. His lips were parted as if in pain. His hands were tightly fisted at his sides.

"Brie, I . . ."

"Don't you dare apologize." Her voice shook, but she couldn't help it.

"I . . . wasn't going to." Opening his eyes, he pulled the straps of her chemise up over her shoulders, then slid her blouse up her arms. Then he closed his eyes again and rested his forehead against hers. "I wasn't going to. I'm not sorry. I should be, but I'm not."

"Thank God," she breathed.

"God?" His laugh was harsh. He helped her stand, smoothed her skirt back down around her legs, then rose and stood before her. "God was looking the other way, Irish, or He wouldn't have let me touch you. This was the work of the devil."

His words made an ache bloom in her chest. She touched a hand to his cheek and gave him a tremulous smile. " 'Oh, ye of little faith.' "

Wolf grunted and stepped back. "Me of no faith." He peered up at the sky, then at the rock wall beside their shelter. "Come on, Irish, let's see if we can find our way off this ledge."

The climb up the rocks was harder on Brie than on Wolf because of her skirt. Wolf threatened to take it off her, but she finally made her way from foothold to handhold until she stood once again on the mesa above the valley. The horses were standing there waiting for them.

Wolf held out his hands for Brie to step in so she could mount. "I meant what I said about this saddle. I'm gonna burn the damn thing the minute we get home."

Brie arranged her shortened skirt the best she could, then raised a brow at him. "So I can . . . ride astride?"

It was hard to tell whose blush was worse, Wolf's or Brie's. Wolf was appalled that he had it in him to blush. He couldn't remember the last time, if there had been a last time.

He and she may have blushed the same, but with it, Brie laughed. Wolf cursed.

It took a full hour after they got home to convince everyone that Brie was, for the most part, unharmed from her tumble down the bluff. She wouldn't even have told

the others about it, but her ruined clothes required explanation.

"Your hat," Tessa bemoaned. "I guess you lost it in the
fall."

"Some prayers do get answered," Wolf muttered.

Wolf wasn't sure how Palmer was going to react to having
had three of his men hauled home belly-down across their
horses, so he put off going back up on the mesa to brand
the calves. He stayed close to the house for the next couple
of days, wondering what the owner of the Double Diamond
would do next to try to drive the Flanigans off the Rocking
F.

He didn't have long to wait to find out, although at first
he didn't think to blame the major for the stream being
low. But with the rains coming at least every other day this
time of year, the stream that cut through the valley should
have been high, not low. Wolf decided to check it out by
riding upstream. On the chance that the rains had washed
too much debris down that would need clearing, Wolf took
the dynamite from where he'd hidden it in the bunkhouse,
out of reach of the kids, and put it in his saddlebag.

It had taken him years to be able to even touch a shovel
after he'd used one the first time, when he'd been nine.
He would use one if he had to, if there were no other
choice. Like filling in around the fence posts. But for any
serious digging that required a shovel, he would either
find another way, or avoid the job altogether. He wasn't
about to stand knee-deep in cold water and shovel rocks
and gravel and whatever out of a creek or stream.

The feeder creeks were swollen with the runoff of yesterday's rain. They ran free and easy, with nothing blocking
the flow of water, yet still the stream was low. At the south
end of the valley, Wolf used the gate he'd installed in the
new fence to let himself into the canyon beyond. At the

other end of the canyon, on Double Diamond land, he found his answer.

Palmer had dammed the stream. The bastard went to a lot of trouble, too, using brush, rocks, a couple of good-sized boulders, and trees. Whole damn trees that had to have been dragged in from at least two days away.

Bastard. Did he think Wolf would stand by and do nothing?

He pulled his binoculars from their case and checked out the valley that led to the Double Diamond headquarters. His cursory glance found no one in sight, but that didn't mean anything. There were dozens of places for a man to hide. Surely someone was out there. Surely the major wouldn't go to all this trouble and not set someone to watch the dam.

It didn't matter, though, if someone was watching. His gut told him no one would interfere. The dam was only a message, a reminder that the Flanigans weren't wanted. The next move in Palmer's game.

At any rate, even if someone was watching, Wolf couldn't let the dam stand. He rode back up the canyon and left his horse on the Rocking F side of the fence. With three sticks of dynamite, a tin of matches, and his rifle, he walked back down the length of the canyon.

The Flanigans were just sitting down to supper—without Wolf, to Brie's dismay—when a loud *boom* shook the floor beneath them and rattled the glass panes in the windows.

"What . . . ?" Brie rushed outside. The others followed.

"What was it?" Elly asked, rubbing her arms as if suddenly chilled. "An earthquake?"

Brie swallowed. "It sounded like some kind of explosion."

"I don't see anything," Tessa said.

Neither did Brie. She looked everywhere, all around, up and down the valley, and saw nothing out of the ordinary.

Nothing to account for that loud boom. Nothing to explain why she and the others felt the need to speak in whispers while the laying hens cackled in protest at the disturbance.

"It sounded like the time Da blew that boulder up with a stick of dynamite last summer," Sully offered, looking to Brie as if for confirmation.

It did, Brie thought. Except not quite as loud. Maybe because it was from further away?

"Where's Wolf?" Katy asked.

Brie shivered in the evening breeze. "I don't know."

They stood outside for several long minutes, looking around, as if expecting an explanation for the explosion—if that's what it was—to present itself.

Finally Brie turned them all toward the house. "Come on. There's nothing we can do, and our supper's getting cold."

"Is Wolf coming home soon?" Katy asked.

"Of course he is," Brie answered, praying she spoke the truth. Fighting the urge to mount up and ride out in search of him, to make sure he was all right.

Riding out would be futile. It would be dark soon and she had no idea which way Wolf had ridden, no idea if he was anywhere near whatever had split the silence of the valley.

"You did *what?*"

"I blew it up." Wolf was tired, hungry, and irritable. His arm throbbed where a chunk of debris from the explosion had hit him. He'd hoped he would be able to slip into the bunkhouse without anyone noticing he was back, but Brie had obviously been watching for him. Why that should please him, he didn't know, because he really didn't want to see her right then.

He especially didn't want to see her alone in the dimly lit barn late at night, didn't want to deal with the privacy, the intimacy. He didn't want to want her, didn't want to react like a stag in rut just because she was near. He didn't want his head and heart to fill with pictures of how she would be there to greet him every day when he came home. If she were his.

But she was there, he wanted her, and his head and heart overflowed with pictures. God was laughing at him again.

With a curse, Wolf pulled the saddle from his horse and placed it on the rack next to the tack room. His arm protested. The sleeve of his shirt was stuck to his skin, by dried blood, he suspected. He kept that arm turned away from Brie as much as possible. He wasn't in the mood for one of her lectures about being careful and not getting hurt on her behalf.

"Major Palmer dammed the stream that feeds our valley, and you used dynamite to blow up the dam?"

Why was it, Wolf wondered, that when a woman was angry, her voice rose higher in pitch with each word? "It was no big deal."

"No big *deal?*" The glass in the lantern on the peg was in danger of shattering from her shriek. "You could have been killed!"

"I wasn't killed. I wasn't even hurt." *Much.* After giving his horse a final pat for carrying him home in the dark, Wolf turned, blew out the lantern, and stomped off, leaving Brie standing in the dark barn alone. At the wide double doors, he paused and looked back. "You coming?"

The rustle of her skirt was his answer as she followed him out of the barn. Instead of stalking off to the house in a huff of righteous indignation at his treatment of her, she stopped and waited while he closed and secured the big doors. He ignored her and went straight to the bunkhouse.

Thankfully, she did not follow. He heard the back door, which led into the kitchen, open, then close behind her as she went into the house. Relief relaxed his shoulders.

His relief was short-lived. By the time he lit the lamp at his bedside, hung his gunbelt on the peg over the bed, and tugged off his boots, she was barrelling into his privacy with a plate of food in her hands.

"You ever hear of knocking?" Damn, he didn't want her in here.

"If I'd have knocked, you wouldn't have answered."

"You got that right."

She slapped the plate down on the table beyond the foot of his bed. "Here's your supper."

"What's eating you?"

She whirled on him. "What's eating me? You're what's eating me. When are you going to stop trying to get yourself killed?"

"I'm not trying to get myself killed."

"You could have fooled me," she tossed back. "Every time I turn around you're facing down one man or another, usually several at once. Now you're playing with dynamite."

"Hell," he said with a harsh laugh. "I've been playing with dynamite from the minute I laid eyes on you."

Brie could not fail to understand his meaning. It was there in gray eyes turned hot, in big, strong hands fisted at his sides. In the rigid set of his jaw. In reaction, her heart sped and her blood heated. "I don't want you hurt because of me. I never wanted that."

"I know," he said tightly before turning away from her. "Thanks for supper. I'll see you tomorrow."

"Your arm!"

Wolf swore. "It's nothing."

"It's a bloody mess," she snapped back. *"I'm fine,"* she mimicked, going from concerned to hopping mad in less time than it takes for a match to flare. *"I wasn't even hurt. The hell you weren't."*

"Hey!" He'd never heard her cuss before. And he'd never seen that precise look in her eyes before, either. The anger and fear were familiar enough. They'd twisted his gut a dozen times since he'd met her. The look of challenge was new, or at least more pronounced. A sharp

I-dare-you-to-get-in-my-way look as she came at him that told him she meant business.

"Take off your shirt," she demanded.

"Hell, darlin'," he taunted with a smirk, "I thought you'd never ask."

"Funny, mister, real funny." Because he made no move to accommodate her, she reached to tug his shirttail from his pants. With a hiss of irritation, she stopped. "The blood is dried. I'll have to soak that sleeve loose."

"What you have to do is get out of here."

"I'm not leaving until I've seen to that arm," she snapped. "What happened? Did somebody shoot at you again?" She reached for the water pitcher beside him.

"Nobody shot at me. What are you—" She raised the pitcher and poured water all over his arm. "Hey!"

"That ought to do it."

"Okay, fine." With his hands to her shoulders, he spun her around toward the door. "The sleeve will soak loose and I'll be just dandy. You can leave now." Just touching her shoulders made his blood surge.

She reached the door and slammed it shut—and locked it, from the inside, damn her hide—and turned on him. "I'm not leaving." This time her voice was soft, filled with a promise she had no business giving him.

"Brie, you don't know what you're doing."

"First, I'm going to take care of your arm."

Wolf swallowed hard. "First?"

"First."

He swallowed again. "After that?"

With her forefinger and thumb, she gave a gentle tug on his bloody, wet shirtsleeve. "After that . . . we'll see."

He didn't care for her tone at all. It sounded suspiciously similar to the one she used on the kids when they were pestering her for an answer she knew they wouldn't like. He would let her clean up his arm—so she would know first-hand that it wasn't serious, he told himself. Then he would send her packing. She might have the sound and the look of a seductive temptress, but she was too naive and inexperienced to know what she was asking for. It was up to him to pull in the reins, and he would do it. Even if it killed him.

She directed him to sit at the small eating table where she'd set his supper. He sat still and watched as she lit a second lamp and placed it on the table. She was so beautiful, so graceful when she moved. The ache in him, the need to touch and hold and savor her nearness, grew.

Brie felt him watching her. It was only with extreme effort that she kept her hands from trembling. What was she doing taunting him, challenging him? Goading him this way?

Following my heart, came the answer whispering through her mind. This was Wolf. This was the man she wanted. He hadn't hidden the fact that he wanted her too. Somehow, she was going to convince him that she was woman enough for him. With hands that were rock steady, she unfastened the three buttons on the placket of his shirt. Without touching his skin, she felt the heat and strength emanating from him. "Tell me what happened," she said quietly.

Her nearness, the softness of her voice, made Wolf forget . . . whatever it was he'd been trying to remind himself. "The stream was low." He started to pull his shirt off over his head, but she stopped him and pull it off one arm and over his head, then eased it down his injured arm.

She took one look at him and gasped.

The cut was uglier than he'd figured, but she wasn't looking at his arm. He followed her gaze to his chest, then made a dismissive gesture with one hand. "Old stuff," he said of the bruises along his ribs. "Courtesy of those three ass—uh, men from the Double Diamond. Anyway, with all the rain lately, the stream should have been high. I rode south to check it out."

It was hard to talk when she was touching him, but he

managed to tell her about finding the dam, placing the sticks of dynamite. Lighting them. Running for cover, but not quite fast enough to avoid being hit in the arm by a flying chunk of rock.

Her hands were infinitely gentle as she cleaned his wound, fussed over it, wrapped it in a bandage torn from the relatively clean tail of his shirt. "Hey, my shirt!"

"It was already ruined. I'll make you a new one."

"You . . ." No one had ever made anything for him before. Certainly no woman had ever taken needle to fabric and made him a shirt. How was he supposed to put Brie out of his mind when he left, if he wore a shirt she made for him? "No need."

"Maybe you don't need it. But maybe I need to do it. Why don't you eat?"

She needed to make him a shirt? What the hell did that mean? "I'll eat as soon as you go back to the house."

"That's okay. I'll just wait and take the empty plate with me."

"Brie." That look of determination was back in her eyes, and it worried him. "Go to bed."

"Is that an invitation?"

He forced his chair back and jumped to his feet so fast that the chair bounced off the wall behind him. "What the hell is the matter with you?"

She met his glare with a calmness that only stoked his anger. "Funny, I've been wanting to ask you the same question."

"Nothing's wrong with me," he snarled.

The way she pulled her gaze down his bare chest and back to his eyes did something funny to his lungs. They couldn't seem to find air. "I meant," she said, "that I was wondering what it is that you find wrong with me."

Wolf closed his eyes in frustration. "I don't find anything wrong with you. Nothing at all, except your damn stubbornness, and you know it."

"You could have fooled me," she said, turning abruptly and pacing away from him.

"I'm sure I'll regret this, but, what are you talking about?"

She whirled and marched the length of the room until she stood almost toe-to-toe with him. "I'm talking about this." With both hands, she grabbed his face and pulled it down to hers.

Wolf froze in shock. In pleasure. There was nothing tentative in the way she kissed him, hot and hard and open-mouthed. That bolt of lightning that spooked their horses the other day suddenly seemed weak in comparison. For a moment, he let himself take what she offered, dipping his tongue inside to meet and slide against hers. His head swam. His knees weakened. His arms, without permission from his brain, started to close around her and bring her hard against him. The small needy sound from her throat brought him to his senses.

This was Brie, for God's sake. A lady. A woman who deserved better than a half-breed saddle bum. "Dammit." He pushed her away and stepped back, chest heaving, loins throbbing. "What the hell's the matter with you?"

She gave a toss of her head, as though to shake her hair away from her shoulders, even though her hair was up in pins. "That's what I'm asking you. What is it about me that makes you keep pushing me away?"

"Ah, hell." Wolf rubbed a hand over his face in sheer frustration. "You're too damn innocent for a man like me."

She crossed her arms and narrowed her eyes. "Explain."

"Explain! That just proves my point. You don't even realize how naive you are. You don't even know what a man wants from a woman, what a kiss like the one you just gave me promises."

"Don't I?"

"No, you don't." She was making him mad again. "You think it stops there? Or maybe you want a little petting, just enough to make your blood sing. A man wants more than that."

"You think a woman doesn't?"

Shit. Now she was scaring him. "Not the way a man does. A man wants sex, hard and hot, no promises, no regrets. A woman expects hearts and flowers."

"I've got my own heart, and flowers in the flower bed. Next excuse," she demanded.

"A woman has sex, next thing you know, she thinks she's in love with the man."

She glared at him. "I'm already in love with you. Try again."

Her admission hit him like a fist to the gut. "You're . . . You can't be."

"Believe me," she said, her mouth twisted in a grimace. "It wasn't my idea. It just happened all by itself, and there's nothing either one of us can do about it."

Wolf staggered back until he felt the chair behind him. He dropped down onto it, stunned. "Brie . . . Dammit, Brie, you can't mean that."

"Well, don't look like it's the end of the world. I'm sure by the time you ride out of here after the cattle are sold I won't have any trouble getting over it. In the meantime, can we just enjoy what we have here?" The request would have been a sweet one, but she was practically bellowing at him.

Something she'd just said snagged his attention. He grabbed it and held on. "You're right, I'll be leaving soon. It's better if we don't . . . get involved . . . that way."

With her arms crossed over her chest, her hands were essentially hidden. Brie clutched them into fists, digging her nails into her palms to help avert the trembling that threatened to seize her. She was fighting for her life. She couldn't help it. "Yes, you'll leave soon. I thought . . ." This was difficult, now that her anger was ebbing and fear encroached again. "That is, I'd hoped you might be will—

interested—in maybe . . . leaving me with a few good memories, something more than the memory of this terrible wanting, this wanting and not having."

Wolf buried his face in his hands. "Don't do this to me, Brie. You're a virgin, for God's sake, and I'm a man who's been on the edge too long." He dropped his hands and looked up at her. "All I can do is hurt you. Your first time, you deserve . . . tenderness, gentleness. I'm too far gone for that. Look at me." He held out his hands, palms down. "I want you so damn much I shake with it."

"Wolf . . ." His name fell from her lips like a sigh.

"Don't look at me like that. Dammit, you're a *virgin!*"

She jerked back as if he'd slapped her. Her fisted hands came from beneath her arms and pressed against her skirt. "And if I weren't?"

"It doesn't matter. You are."

"But if I weren't," she insisted. "Would you keep trying to think up excuses not to touch me?"

He wasn't about to answer a loaded question like that.

But apparently she read something in his face that he hadn't meant to reveal. She turned and headed for the door. "Fine. If my virginity is the problem, I'll just saddle up and ride to town—*astride*—and get ride of it."

"What are you talking about? What's this business about riding into town? It's the middle of the damn night. What could you possibly need to get rid of, anyway?"

"Why, my virginity, of course. I wonder, after I've gotten rid of it, what excuse you'll come up with next."

She didn't mean it. She was bluffing. Of course she was bluffing. But the mere thought of another man laying hands on her had him across the room so fast he wasn't sure how he got there. He spun her around and pressed her back against the door before she could get it open. His grip on her shoulders was too tight, but he was too busy telling himself not to shake her until her teeth fell out to worry about anything else.

"I won't need an excuse then. I'll be in jail." His chest heaved, his lungs fighting for air.

She looked up at him with startled eyes. "Why?"

"Because," he said with a snarl, "I'd have to kill any man who touched you. You're *mine.*"

Chapter Fourteen

With a glad cry, Brie fell against his chest and wrapped her arms around his neck. "Thank God." Her lips met his as they swooped down on her.

Wolf was lost. But he tried for sanity one last time. "I don't want..." He couldn't get the words out. He'd started to say he didn't want to hurt her, but how could a man talk, let alone think straight, when a woman like Brianna Flanigan touched the tip of her tongue to his chin?

"You're not still trying to convince me you don't want me, are you?" She threaded her fingers through his hair.

Wolf shuddered. "I want you so much it scares me." He hadn't meant to say that, but there it was. He kissed her hard and fast. "Don't love me, Brie. Don't let me hurt you."

"Nothing can hurt me when you hold me."

There was nothing, then, that Wolf could do but sweep her into his arms and carry her to his bed. She deserved satin sheets, lace, candles. He would give her worn sheets, a rough blanket, and a lamp that smoked because he couldn't, wouldn't, let go of her long enough to trim the wick.

She deserved pretty words, vows of love. He was too far gone to speak.

She deserved a good man, an honorable man who would stay with her, marry her, give her babies. That man wasn't here, and whoever he was, Wolf hated him. *He* was here, and *he* was the one she wanted. With her hands and lips, with the way she molded her body against his, she told him over and over that she wanted him. Even if she didn't know precisely what she was asking for.

This time the reminder of her innocence wasn't enough to deny himself what she offered. But it was enough to allow him to slow down, to ease her onto the bed rather than throw her down and pounce on her, as the wildness in him urged him to do.

She deserved better. She wouldn't get better. She would get him.

He felt her hands on his bare back, her fingers finding and tracing his scars. "You don't have to touch them," he managed, kissing his way across her face. "I know they're ugly."

"They're part of you, and I want all there is."

A shudder ripped through him. Emotion, tangled and devastating. Awe and humility, that she could feel this way about a nameless saddle bum with a past so ugly he never spoke of it, never willingly thought about it. A half-breed bastard with nothing but trouble in his future, who would leave her, when she needed a man who would stay.

Sadness, that he didn't have more to offer her.

Anger, with himself, because sadness shouldn't be a part of what was about to happen between them.

"Wolf?"

The hesitation in her voice gave him the control he needed to slow down, to set his anger aside. To give her what he could of what she deserved. Lying beside her, he took her face gently in both hands and kissed her. He hadn't known he could be gentle. Had never guessed at the rewards, until she returned the gentleness by stroking his cheek while kissing him back. He wished he'd shaved for her.

Brie didn't care that his cheek was rough with a day's growth of whiskers. She was too glad to be in his arms to care about anything else. Being with him this way, touching him, kissing him, lying beside him on his bed, felt so right, as though it were meant to be. For her, it was.

Wolf didn't think it was right, but he was beginning to think making love to Brie was inevitable. He couldn't get enough of the taste of her, the feel of her. He needed to feel more of her, needed to see her, touch every inch of her silky skin. Raising himself up on one elbow, he reached for the buttons down the bodice of her dress. Her eyes flew open.

Wolf halted. "Do you want me to stop?"

The lamplight bathed her face in gold and gleamed in her eyes, dark green now, like a forest at dusk. "I don't want you to ever stop."

A major thread of Wolf's control snapped. His fingers fumbled on the buttons. Trembled. Damn. He'd undressed a woman or two in his life, but he'd never gotten the shakes while doing it. Finally the stubborn things came undone. He parted the calico bodice only to find white cotton beneath.

"Damn, you wear a lot of clothes," he muttered.

Brie laughed, suddenly euphoric. She'd expected that making love with Wolf would be intense, powerful, exciting. She hadn't expected laughter. Boldly, she helped him undress her, refusing to be embarrassed by her own nakedness.

Refusal wasn't necessary. The blatant appreciation in his eyes, in his hands, made embarrassment impossible.

"You're beautiful," he whispered.

Suddenly she felt beautiful. Beautiful, and wanted. And wanton, she discovered, as she roamed her hands over his skin, smooth and taut over muscles honed from hard work. Velvet over steel. His chest, his back, his arms. She gloried in the feel of him, in the slight quiver of his skin and muscles wherever she touched. But his bruises—they hurt her.

Following instinct, she pushed Wolf to his back and leaned over him, tracing the outline of first one bruise, then another, where they decorated his bronze skin with varying shades of purple and green. "Your poor ribs."

Wolf lay where she'd pushed him, holding his breath, waiting for the apparition to vanish. Pale, creamy skin, a smattering of freckles across her nose, fiery red hair held tightly to her head with pins yet springing free around her face. Hands, gentle and cool, touching his bruises, yet touching so much more. She couldn't be real.

Yet she was real enough to make his heart pound and his blood sing. She traced one long scrape to where it disappeared beneath his pants. Her delicate, dainty finger stopped his heart by drifting slowly back and forth at the spot. Wolf slowly looked up to find her staring intensely at his face.

"Make love to me, Wolf. Show me what it's like."

Another thread on his control snapped loose. Blood rushed to his loins, engorging him more than he'd thought possible. He was so hard he hurt. He couldn't take her like this. He would hurt her without meaning to. She wasn't ready.

He would make her ready. He wanted her to be as needy, as greedy, as on fire for him as he was for her. He rolled her to her back and threw one leg over hers. He pulled the pins from her hair and spread all that fiery glory out around her, buried his face in it, inhaled the scent of wildflowers, sunshine, and rainwater.

God, she went to his head quicker than whiskey.

With every ounce of willpower he possessed, he fought down his own need to bury himself inside her. Using his hands and lips and body, he taught her secrets about her own body that she'd never guessed. She was soft, yet firm. Delicate, yet strong. Her breasts were made to fit his hands. He flicked his tongue across the tip of one and was rewarded with her strangled gasp of pleasure. When he covered her nipple with his mouth and suckled, her hands clutched his head and her back arched clear off the mattress.

Ah, God, her response was going to drive him right over the edge. He'd be damned if he went without her. He skimmed a hand down her ribcage, her abdomen, to the thatch of flame red hair between her legs. And beyond.

When he touched her soft, secret folds, she stiffened, reminding him this was all new to her. Reminding him he had to stay sane, at least a little longer, to make sure she found the pleasure he himself sought. He flexed his fingers once, twice, and suckled more deeply on her breast.

With a low moan, she parted her thighs for him.

She was hot and wet. Tight. God, so damn tight. As ready for him as she would ever be. But not yet, he told himself. He wouldn't take her yet. Hurting her when he entered her the first time would be unavoidable. Hurting her and robbing her of pleasure, unforgivable. He stroked the tiny bud of nerves at the top of her slickness. Her hips jerked beneath his touch. Then, with a hoarse cry, she shattered in his arms.

He'd never known such satisfaction while holding off his own pleasure. In truth, feeling the climax take her was more pleasurable to him than many of his own climaxes.

"Again," he whispered roughly, taking his mouth from her breast. "Look at me."

Breathless, unsure of what had just happened to her but knowing that she had been in some way forever changed by the explosion of sensations that Wolf had drawn from her, Brie struggled to open her eyes.

He loomed over her, blocking out the lamplight that outlined him in gold. His face was shadowed, but she knew its lines. That she couldn't see him clearly reminded her of the first time she'd seen him, in her dream. He'd been lit from behind then, too, casting his face in shadow. She'd thought he was a knight. Now she knew. He was a warrior. Her warrior.

"Again," he said again. "Do it for me again."

She didn't at first understand what he meant. Didn't understand the fierce need she heard in his voice. Then his fingers, those clever, clever fingers, flexed against her in that place that only Wolf had touched, and she was flying again. Her mind taken over by pure sensation. A burning emptiness yawned deep inside of her, an emptiness meant to be filled by this man. Only this man.

Brie wanted to tell him what she was feeling. Wanted to ask him how to make him feel the same things. But his fingers moved again, and as before, the tension mounting inside her erupted into a firestorm of feelings centered where he touched her, radiating outward, until her vision dimmed, until all she could see were gray eyes that turned darker as she watched. Then her eyes slid closed and she could see nothing but brilliant colors bursting behind her lids. She wasn't even aware that she cried out Wolf's name.

But Wolf was. And it shook him. Another thread of his control snapped. He wondered frantically how many threads were left. While the pleasure was still on her, he shucked off his pants. When he looked at her, she was watching him, wide-eyed, still gasping for breath. Her gaze slid down to his aching arousal and nearly seared him with its intensity.

"Brie . . ."

Slowly her gaze rose to meet his. Her eyes were dark, unreadable.

She would never know what it cost him to say the words, but he had to say them. "You're still a virgin. Technically."

Incredibly, she smiled. "Technically?"

Wolf swallowed. His heart thundered. His flesh cried out to join with hers. "Last chance to stay that way, Irish."

Her eyes widened. She glanced down at his erection, then back to his face. "You . . . would stop? *Now?*"

He bunched the sheet in his clenched fists. "If you ask me to."

Instantly her eyes filled. With a choking cry, she opened her arms, parted her legs. For him. "I knew there was a reason I loved you."

Shaken, uncertain, Wolf hung back. "Brie?"

"You've sent me . . . flying. Twice. Both times, it was the most . . . incredible experience. I had no idea such a thing existed. But . . ."

"But?" He tensed to pull back farther.

Brie reached for him and pulled him down. "But it was . . . lonely. I thought . . . we were supposed to go together."

The breath Wolf had been unconsciously holding left him slowly as her meaning dawned on him. God, was there ever a woman like her? Generous. Loving. So damned responsive, with a passion so clean and pure, it was about to burn him to cinders.

"Yes," he whispered, taking her mouth with his. "Together."

Slowly, carefully, every muscle trembling with restraint, Wolf eased into her. Barely. Barely. A little more. His arms shook. Sweat beaded and ran down his back.

Brie's hands clutched at his hips. "More," came her hoarse cry.

He had his answer then, about those threads. There was only one left. At her rough plea, it snapped.

He felt the barrier of her virginity, but the resistance was slight. Still, he would have moved slowly. She wouldn't let him. Her hips rose to meet his, forcing him through farther, faster than he'd meant to go. He tried to stop. To slow down, at least.

Then her hips moved and she whispered again. "More."

He moved against her, within her, farther, deeper. Nothing had ever felt so powerful as the moment when she took all of him. Nothing in his life had prepared him for

the sheer rightness of joining with her. In filling her, some
empty part of himself was filled. He felt suddenly alive in
a way he'd never been alive before. He felt whole. And
clean. Inside and out. As if, in losing himself in her depths,
he'd been reborn.

Suddenly the fierce hunger in him eased. He was in no
hurry to relinquish the most precious gift he'd ever been
given, the gift of Brie's love. He whispered her name.
"Brianna . . ."

The rhythm of their loving was slow and strong, and
Brie was with him. Her eyes held his, and holding her gaze
seemed the most intimate experience of his life, more
intimate than the mating of their bodies.

Of its own accord, it seemed, the rhythm increased.
The fire inside him, between them, flamed higher, burned
hotter. Faster, harder, he thrust into her. The sharp bite
of her nails on his back urged him on.

Then he felt it, deep inside her, the clenching of her
inner muscles around him like a velvet fist. Her eyes widened. His lids closed as the fever took him, as she took
him, straight off the edge of the world.

The first thing Brie became aware of was Wolf's weight
pressing her into the mattress. She reveled beneath it. She
relished the feel of him still buried inside her, in the way
his lips clung to her skin where he'd buried his face in
the curve where her neck met her shoulder. She never
wanted this night, this closeness she felt with him, to end.
She wanted to wrap her arms around him and hold him
there forever. Unfortunately, she thought with a touch of
humor, she had no strength with which to raise her arms.

Without warning, tears stung her eyes. A sound that was
half sob, half laughter escaped her lips.

Shaken by the sound, Wolf raised his head.

"No, don't leave me," Brie begged him, her arms wrap-
ping tight around his shoulders.

"No. I won't leave you." Not just yet. He couldn't. With his lips, he sipped hot, salty tears from her cheeks. He thought he understood her tears. He knew he hadn't hurt her, and that she'd found her pleasure in their loving. But it had been so intense, so consuming, so unlike anything he'd ever experienced before, that he wished he could join her and find an outlet through tears for the emotions that made his chest tight.

Still, her tears tore at him.

Then he heard what he thought he'd heard a moment ago with the first sound she made—laughter. Incredible, joyous, unfettered laughter. Her body shook with it. She held him tighter and rocked from side to side, laughing.

Wolf didn't exactly feel like laughing. What had just happened between them had been too . . . intense. Too far outside the realm of what he'd always believed possible between a man and woman. But he couldn't help but smile as he raised himself up to look at her.

"Damn," he whispered, "you are some kind of woman, Brianna Flanigan."

Brie threw her head back, stretched her arms into the air, and laughed again. Her arms came down and wound themselves around his neck. "And you are some kind of man, Just Wolf. The only kind of man." Her grin faded to a soft smile that twisted something inside him. "The *only* man."

Wolf rested his forehead against hers and swallowed a moan as her words pierced him. He shifted slightly, accidentally—or was it?—pushing himself deeper inside her.

Brie's eyes flew wide. "Oh."

Wolf grinned despite the renewed surge of heat in his loins. Or perhaps because of it. "Oh?" he asked.

She shifted beneath him and raised one knee, parting her legs farther and allowing him even deeper access. *"Oh . . ."* she moaned.

The next flex of his hips was involuntary, but the one after that, after she flexed back and gasped, was deliberate.

This time he could keep his head, make it last longer. After all, the sharp edge of his need had been met. He surged inside her. Withdrew slightly. Slowly reentered. Again. And yet again. As if it were all new to him. As if he'd never known a woman before. Again and again. Gradually harder. Gradually faster. Gradually hotter, more forceful. Until the idea of control and making it last became laughable. He slammed into her over and over and she met him thrust for thrust, her other knee bending into the air. He'd never been closer to a woman. Never had one take him so deep he couldn't tell who was who and didn't care.

He wasn't sure if he took her over the edge, or if she took him. They went together, in sweet, hot fire that burned the picture of her face into his mind and heart forever.

Wolf lay there in her sheltering arms until his breath returned, his heart slowed down. He had to be crushing her. Reluctant, but knowing he had to, he withdrew from her and rolled to his side, where he pulled her into his arms.

"Is it always like that?" Brie asked him. "So . . . overwhelming?"

"It never has been before for me." He wanted the words back as soon as they left his mouth. They were the truth, but it couldn't matter. He would leave her, as he said he would.

Wouldn't he?

He had a man to find. A major. He had to know if Palmer was the one. All his life he'd vowed to find the man responsible for putting him in the hands of Reverend Gilbert Lazarus. Find him, and kill him. If it turned out to be Palmer, so much the better. He would have his vengeance, and the bastard would never bother Brie again.

But for a time tonight, Wolf had forgotten all about vengeance. Inside him was the knowledge that he could stay here on the Rocking F with Brie. They could build a life together. With no other woman had he experienced what he'd felt tonight with her. Yet he knew that with her, it would always be like it was tonight. Like she said. Overwhelming.

Her fingers traced a scar across his back. "Why did he beat you?"

Reality, swift and ugly, tore apart the dream he'd been building in his head. He could never ask a woman to share her life with a man with his past. Never.

He felt the need to put distance between himself and Brie, to keep the ugliness from touching her. He rolled onto his back, but he couldn't quite bring himself to let go of her, so he kept one arm around her and pulled her against his side.

"If you'd rather not talk about—"

"Because I tried to run away once too often."

She was quiet for a long moment. Then she whispered, "I'm sorry."

Wolf sat up and turned to sit on the side of the bed. "I don't want your pity."

He wasn't rejecting her, Brie told herself, only the pain of probing into his past. She shouldn't have brought it up. "You don't have my pity. You have my admiration, for surviving, if nothing else."

The birthmark on his left shoulder blade drew her. Shades darker than his bronze skin, it was shaped like a wolf's head, thrown back and howling. Howling in pain? she wondered. Howling at the moon?

Wolf reached to adjust the flickering flame on the lamp. Brie smiled and touched a finger to his birthmark. "Did you know that when you move a certain way, this fellow looks like he's laughing instead of howling?"

Wolf looked at her sharply over his shoulder. His eyes were wary.

"I mean it," she said with a laugh. "There he goes again."

"You and Booker," Wolf said with disgust.

"Booker?" In the weeks she'd known him, Wolf had never mentioned anyone, not a single name, except for the preacher, and he hadn't named him. There was affection under the disgust in his voice when he said the name Booker. "Who's Booker?"

With a heavy sigh, Wolf lay back down and pulled her close. "A friend."

Brie snuggled against him, relieved to have him next to her again. As if to keep him there, she splayed a hand across his chest. "You said you didn't have any friends."

Wolf peered down at her, then stared up at the ceiling. "You were wondering who to notify if something happened to me. No need to notify Booker. He'd find out eventually. Him and Charlie Jim."

Brie shifted to see his face better. "Charlie Jim? Another friend?"

Wolf shrugged. "Yeah, I guess."

"You guess?"

Another shrug. "They're not friends like Letty's your friend or her girl is Tessa's friend. We don't write letters or anything. We just run into each other now and then."

"Hmmm." She smiled at him. "How many other friends don't you have?"

Wolf smiled slightly and ran a finger down her nose. "Smart mouth. I guess if I ever had to pick a man or two to trust, Booker and Charlie Jim are the only ones I could name."

"I'm glad you have them," she said solemnly. "I'm glad there are two men you can call friend. And I'm glad I'm here with you right now like this."

Wolf was glad she was there, too, but he said it with a kiss instead of words. He'd be even more glad if he thought there was a snowball's chance in hell of any kind of future for a stubborn, green-eyed Irish lady and a no-name half-breed bastard.

Chapter Fifteen

Standing in the kitchen the next morning with Tessa and Elly, Brie wondered if the change in her from virgin to Wolf's lover was somehow visible on her face.

She had hated leaving him in the middle of the night, but she knew it wouldn't have been right to let the children find her in his bed. She'd slipped back into the house barely an hour before dawn. Sleep, she decided with a secret smile, was much overrated.

"She's doing it again," Tessa said darkly to Elly.

Maybe Brie's smile hadn't been so secret.

"Leave her alone," Elly answered quietly. "After you put the biscuits on the table, go call everyone in. And make sure Rory gets his hands clean this time."

When Tessa stepped outside a few minutes later to call everyone to breakfast, Elly turned to Brie and studied her closely. Again Brie wondered if a night in Wolf's bed somehow showed on her face.

"Do you know what you're doing?"

Brie started to deny that she knew what Elly was talking about. The look in her sister's eyes stopped her. Elly knew.

Two years younger than Brie, Elly suddenly seemed older and wiser. Brie couldn't help the question that burst from her lips. "You and James?"

Elly's smile was sad. "No. We haven't. We talked about it, but we decided to wait. He wants to go away to college. It scares me, thinking of him leaving."

"Elly, why didn't you tell me?"

Elly shook her head. "There wasn't anything you could do. Besides," she added with a rueful smile. "James and I may be the same age, but I think I'm too young to . . . you know."

"I think you are too. Heck, so am I, probably."

"But it happened anyway. Do you love him, Brie?"

"With all my heart."

"What about him?"

Brie shook her head and ignored the pain of the truth. "I don't know how he feels, but I know he's not staying."

"Brie, no! He wouldn't leave you after . . ."

"Of course he will."

"But—Even after . . . ?"

Sully, Rory, and Tessa banged through the back door, cutting off whatever answer Brie might have come up with. A few moments later, Wolf came and joined them.

Brie tried not to stare at him throughout breakfast, but it was hard to take her eyes off him. It had been less that two hours since she'd seen him, but it felt like forever as she drank him in with her eyes.

After breakfast, Wolf headed for the mesa to round up the unbranded calves. Elly caught Brie alone for a moment and gave her a teasing look. "He didn't look like a man bent on leaving to me."

Brie blushed. She'd felt his eyes on her more than once during breakfast, but each time she looked, he was talking to Katy or Sully.

"He looked like he was ready to have you for breakfast," Elly added with a giggle.

* * *

Brie sat in her mother's rocker on the front porch and tended to the mending she'd been putting off for more than a week. The afternoon was hot, but in the shade of the porch, the breeze was pleasant. From her vantage point she could keep an eye on the boys and Katy and make sure they didn't wander too far from the house. With everything that had happened lately, she wasn't taking any chances.

From above the porch roof, an upstairs bedroom window slid open. "Brie?" Tessa called softly. "You out there?"

"I'm here."

"I was up here dusting and happened to look out the window. Three riders are coming in from the north. Do you think it means trouble?"

Brie told herself to stay calm. If it was someone from the Double Diamond, they would most likely have come from the south. Wouldn't they? Still, she would take no chances. Setting her mending aside, she rose and went into the house. Tessa was just coming down the stairs.

"Go—quietly and calmly—and get the kids into the house. Does Elly know what you saw?"

Tessa nodded, eyes wide in her ashen face.

"Fine. Go get the kids. Everything will be all right. I'm sure it's nothing to worry about."

But Brie intended to make doubly sure. She took the shotgun down from the pegs over the door, checked the load, and put four more shells in the pockets of her apron before stepping back outside.

A moment after Saint Pat started barking, two men and a woman walked their horses up from the stream. Brie had never seen any of them before. That they had a woman with them eased some of her concern.

But only some. The man in the lead was the most intimidating looking man Brie had ever seen. His age was hard to determine, but there was more gray than black in his short frizzled hair. He was huge and grizzled, with three white scars lining one cheek. His skin was the color of polished mahogany, and his hands were the size of hams. His bulk appeared to be solid muscle. His eyes didn't go with the rest of him, she realized. They were soft brown, like a doe, or a cow.

Brie bit back nervous laughter. She doubted the huge man would appreciate being likened to a cow.

She didn't imagine that he had the disposition of a cow, either, unless maybe a wild Texas longhorn. There was nothing tame about this man.

Wolf, where are you?

She mentally kicked herself for the question. She'd been learning to stand on her own before he came, and she would have to stand on her own when he left. She could certainly handle three unexpected visitors.

Besides, Elly was in the upstairs window with the rifle.

The second man was white, with skin weathered to a deep tan by years of sun and wind. Deep creases radiated from his eyes and lined his cheeks. His sideburns were gray, but the rest of his hair, she saw as he removed his hat, was sandy brown. He sat as tall in the saddle as the other man, but without the massive bulk of his companion. Brie sensed that this man's strength came from his lean toughness.

The woman came next, a round, middle-aged Mexican with dark brown eyes that seemed to miss nothing.

Brie stepped off the porch and cradled the shotgun in her arms, ready to swing it around to fire if need be. "Good afternoon." She kept her tone friendly. "You folks lost?"

The black man nudged the brim of his hat up a notch. "Afternoon, ma'am." His voice was deep and smooth, with the music of exotic places shaping its tone. "This is my wife, Rosa, and my partner, Thomas. My name's Mahoney."

There was expectation in his eyes. Brie obliged him with a grin. "Mahoney?" Her brogue came deliberately this time. "Me own name be Flanigan, sir. Be I right in guessin' you be tryin' to give an entirely new meanin' to the term 'black Irish' then, Mr. Mahoney?''

Mahoney threw his head back and let out a deep, booming laugh.

"Tarnation," the other man, Mr. Thomas, muttered. "That joke's so old it oughta be buried. Knock it off, Booker, and find out if the boy's here."

Brie's heart gave a little leap. "Booker?"

"Yes, ma'am." White teeth flashed behind his huge grin. With a grand flourish, he swept his hat off and bowed at the waste. "Booker Jesus Mahoney, at your service."

Brie blinked. Good heavens, what a name! Could he be . . . "Are you . . . Wolf's Booker?"

Booker Jesus Mahoney, the son of a beautiful Mexican señorita and a former Jamaican slave who'd taken the surname of his Irish master, straightened slowly in his saddle. There was no more closed-mouthed man on earth than Wolf. That he had mentioned Booker to this woman staggered him. "He mentioned my name?"

"He said you were his friend."

"Well, well, well. Did you hear that, Charlie Jim? Our boy admitted he has a friend."

The other man looked stunned. "Maybe there's hope for him yet."

"Charlie Jim?" Brie repeated, practically quivering with excitement. "Wolf's other friend." Oh, this was better than a Christmas morning surprise. These people knew Wolf. These men were his friends. Surely he would be pleased to see them.

"He's here, then?" Booker asked her eagerly.

"Not right this minute, but he'll be back this afternoon. He's gone after some calves up on the mesa." She gestured toward the west. "Please, get down and sit here in the shade where it's cool. Tessa, Elly," she called into the house as she turned and propped the shotgun just outside the door. "We have guests. Bring out some lemonade. Boys, come see to their horses."

The three visitors seemed genuinely surprised by the sudden bustle of activity as everyone dashed to do Brie's bidding.

"The Wolf you told me about, this man who talks to no one, who thinks he's not good enough for decent people, is here with all of these children?" The woman, Rosa, stared at her husband, Booker, in disbelief.

"Cherie, must you repeat everything I tell you?'" asked Booker.

Rosa scoffed. "You think the young woman does not already know the workings of his mind? Of course she does. The truth is in her eyes."

To say that Wolf was surprised was an understatement. Shocked was more accurate.

He herded the half-dozen cow-calf pairs toward the corral and hollered for someone to open the gate before the ornery critters scattered to hell and back. He'd expected Sully or Rory to come running. Maybe even Brie.

What he got was a tall, black mountain of a man. A familiar mountain. "Jesus H. Christ."

"No, no, no. It's *Hey-soos.* Must I keep telling you? And it is not Christ, it's Mahoney. Booker Jesus Mahoney."

It was an old game between them. All they needed to round it out was—

"Hellfire, Mahoney," came the deep Missouri accent that for a moment Wolf thought was only in his head. "You know you can't teach a dumb Injun anything."

"Half-breed, *mon ami,"* Booker corrected, finishing out the old ritual. "Half-breed."

Pleasure filled Wolf at seeing his two friends. He leaned an elbow on his saddle horn and watched the cows and their calves file into the corral pretty as you please. That was Charlie Jim's doing. The wildest, meanest cow in the world would walk the line for Charles James Thomas. Wolf shook his head in disgust, remembering the trouble he'd had getting these same cattle to take the trail down off the mesa. "Some day, Charlie Jim, you're gonna have to tell me your secret with these damn cows."

Standing in the shadows of the barn, where Wolf hadn't noticed her, Brie stared in amazement. She'd never dreamed she'd ever see the man she knew as Wolf laugh at being called a half-breed. The presence of his two friends had transformed him into a smiling stranger.

A part of her was fiercely glad they'd come, allowing her to see this side of the man she loved. Another part stung—with jealousy?—that he should laugh with anyone but her. It was petty and small-minded and unfair, and she was ashamed of the feeling, but it had risen inside her before she'd been able to stop it.

"Where'd you two come from?" Wolf asked his friends.

"The front porch," Booker supplied as he closed the corral gate behind the cattle. "Sipping the sweetest glass of lemonade I've had in years, poured by the prettiest redheaded lass in three states."

"Five," Wolf corrected.

In the shadows, Brie flushed with pleasure.

"Hell," Charlie Jim said, "we ain't even told you which one. Dang place is lousy with pretty redheads."

Wolf swung down from the saddle. "Doesn't matter which one. Unless you're talking about the oldest one. Then it's ten states, at least."

Charlie Jim leaned against the corral fence and narrowed his eyes. "Damnation. He ain't so dumb after all, Booker. For an Injun."

Booker eyed Wolf seriously. "You've changed, boy."

Wolf shrugged, uncomfortable with how much he'd revealed. "So where'd you come from before the front porch?"

"Montana."

"What brings you down here?"

"We heard some fool-crazy half-breed had taken on some big mean cattle baron and was lookin' for help."

"Heard that in Montana, huh?"

"Naw. We were headed south for someplace warmer than Montana to spend the winter. Heard about what you'd tangled with when we stopped in Denver."

"Just thought you'd stop by and watch the fun, did you?"

"Thought we'd stop by and save your young ass."

"No dice." Wolf grinned. "You stay longer than two days, I'm puttin' you to work. If Brie's agreeable."

"Ah, the lovely Brianna," Booker said with a perfect brogue. "We'd be working for her then?"

Wolf knew he was about to get ribbed something awful. Most men refused to work for a woman. He gave a negligent shrug. "Those are her cattle you're charming, her corral you're standing in. Her lemonade you've been drinking."

"And her foreman who's just offered you a job," Brie announced, stepping from the shadows into the late afternoon sunlight. "Wolf's in charge of running the ranch. He's only pandering to my sense of propriety, making you think he has to ask my permission. That was his first condition when I hired him—that when it comes to running the ranch, he makes all the decisions."

Of course, she'd argued with him, she remembered, had insisted that it was, after all, *her* ranch. But she didn't want these men to think . . . to think what? That Wolf was getting soft?

He eyed her now in surprise.

"Come, gentlemen," she said, changing the subject. "Elly said supper would be ready as soon as Wolf got here. She had plenty of help," Brie added to Booker. "From Rosa."

"Rosa?" Wolf asked.

"You are not the only one who can change, my friend."

"Ain't that the truth," Charlie Jim drawled. "After fifty-some years of being turned away by every woman west of the Mississippi, our *compadre* here finally found a woman deaf, dumb, and blind to all his faults."

"You?" Wolf croaked to Booker. "You have a woman?"

"I have a wife," Booker corrected, the cheerful gleam in his eyes at odds with the solemn expression on his face.

After supper, with the women and kids lounging on the porch, the three men walked out through the early evening as if by some prearranged signal.

"So what's the story with this place?" Charlie Jim asked Wolf. "We heard the Rocking F was having trouble, but folks are pretty closed-mouthed about what kind of trouble."

"Major trouble," Wolf said, chuckling at his own pun. "The Flanigans have a greedy neighbor with his eye on their land."

"Not exactly a shortage of land around here, is there?" Charlie Jim asked.

"Not hardly," Wolf said. "But Palmer, like I said, is a greedy bastard."

"Palmer?"

"Major John Palmer, U.S. Army, Retired."

Booker paused and stared hard at Wolf through the semi-darkness. "Major? *The* major?"

They had reached the corral where they'd enclosed the cattle Wolf had brought down from the mesa. Wolf propped one boot on the bottom rail of the fence. "Don't know yet."

"Don't know?" Booker reared back, his thick gray eyebrows bunching in toward each other. "You've been here how long, and you don't know yet if he's the man you've been looking for all your life?"

Wolf shrugged. "I've been busy. I promised I'd stay here until the Rocking F cattle were sold this fall. If it turns out Palmer is the one, I won't be able to hang around once I take care of him."

And he would take care of him, Wolf vowed. If from time to time he forgot for a while why he'd come to this part of Colorado, if more often than not green eyes and soft lips were more prevalent in his mind than what he'd come here for, it didn't mean he would abandon the vow he'd made so many years ago to find the man responsible for giving him to that evil, twisted—

"You're still set on vengeance, then?" Booker asked quietly.

"Wouldn't you be?" Wolf asked coldly.

" 'Vengeance is mine; I will repay, saith the Lord.' "

Wolf snorted in disgust. "I prefer Bacon's attitude."

"Ah, yes," Booker said. " 'Revenge is a kind of wild justice.' That would appeal to you, wouldn't it?"

Charlie Jim scratched one gray sideburn. "You ever think about giving it up? Letting it go?"

Hot denial rushed to Wolf's lips, but he'd never lied to these men, so he swallowed the words. He had, in fact, thought of giving it up. But only for a moment. That moment when he lay cradled in Brie's arms and thought of . . . possibilities.

"It appears you have a good thing here," Charlie Jim offered. "That girl, the oldest one, has her heart in her eyes every time she looks at you. And you," he added with a chuckle, "look like you're just waiting for the chance to carry her off. There's worse things than settling down with a good woman, on good land, making something out of life, building something. Raising a family."

Charlie Jim was hitting a little too close for comfort to a dream Wolf refused to acknowledge. "Yeah, well, if it's so great, old man, why didn't you ever do it?"

Like Wolf a moment ago, Charles James Thomas opened his mouth to speak, then snapped it shut. There was no use scaring up old ghosts. No point in reminding anybody that even if a man was lucky enough to have the things he'd mentioned—a wife, children, a place of his own—that didn't mean it would last. It didn't mean it couldn't all go up in smoke, literally, right before a man's eyes as he was forced to watch guerillas raid his Missouri farm.

Charlie Jim pushed the old memories aside, just like he'd

been doing for more than twenty years now. He couldn't change the past, couldn't undo it. And there was no sense putting thoughts like that in the boy's head.

Charlie Jim understood young Wolf's need for vengeance. That same need had ridden his own back for fifteen years. But he'd found his demons, all of them, one by one, those men who had destroyed his life in the name of war. And they'd paid. Every goddamn one of them.

Which was why Charlie Jim knew that while revenge might do to keep a man getting out of his bedroll every morning and facing the day, once it was done, it just more or less made him sick to his stomach to realize he had become the very thing he hated.

But Charlie Jim settled for a deep chuckle. "Hell, boy, I leave that sort of thing to good-looking bucks like you and Booker."

"Speaking of which," Booker said, his white teeth gleaming in his black face, "where do we bed down?"

Wolf pointed beyond the house. "That's the bunkhouse. I guess you'll be wantin' a bed big enough for two."

"There's no guess to it, my man," Booker answered.

"I'll move my stuff out into the back room. Charlie Jim and I can take the bunks there."

"Not me," Charlie Jim protested. "I'm not about to try to get a good night's sleep right next door to them two. Why, you never heard such carryings-on as them two when they come off the trail. I'll take the barn, if it's all the same to anybody."

"Damn," Wolf said. "Look at him, Charlie Jim. I swear, I think he's blushing."

"On him, how can you tell?"

"God will get even," Booker said with feigned dignity. "And I will have the last laugh on both of you."

Wolf ended up in the empty stall next to Charlie Jim in the barn for the night. There was no way he would put himself through the hell of listening to Booker and Rosa on their first night alone together, in a bed, in weeks. The memory of the night before, when he and Brie had shared that bed, was too vivid.

He'd thought that giving in to her urgings and his need would put an end to the hunger that had gnawed him for so many days. It hadn't. His hunger for Brie was worse than ever. For now he had the taste of her skin to fuel it. The feel of her hot, slick depths welcoming his flesh. The way her green eyes turned almost black just before she came.

Damn. Just thinking about her made him hard. He gave serious thought to paying a visit to the stream for a cold swim—even if it wasn't deep enough to swim in. But he'd be damned if he'd have Charlie Jim waking up and asking what he was about. Better to suffer the unrelieved ache than put up with the ribbing.

He was glad Charlie Jim and Booker had come. The truth was, Wolf needed their help. He'd meant what he'd said to Brie just last night, that if he had to trust his life to other men, these were the only two he could name. It was good to see them. The last time had been, what, two years ago?

Wolf hadn't always been glad to see that big, black, mountain of a man. It wasn't easy to look in the eyes of the only man alive who knew about his past. The first time they'd met, in fact, just the sight of Booker had scared Wolf half to death.

Of course, Wolf had been nine at the time and had just killed a man. Booker had found Wolf wandering in the mountains, delirious from thirst, hunger, pain. Wolf had taken one look at the giant and prayed that if he couldn't have the shovel he'd left back beside the dead man's body, then please God, just open up the ground and let it swallow him. Wolf hadn't yet learned that all men were not like the Reverend Gilbert Lazarus.

Booker had taken Wolf in, nursed his bloody back, fed

him. Saved his life. Saved his sanity. Taught him, incredibly, to trust. At least to trust Booker Jesus Mahoney.

At the end of that winter in the line shack, Booker had taken Wolf down to the ranch headquarters. It was there he'd met Charlie Jim, who gave him his first job. Wolf had been a skinny nine-year-old, and had never been around cattle, never ridden a horse. Together Charlie Jim and Booker had seen to that part of his education, while he fed and groomed horses to earn his keep.

He owed them. Both of them. More than he could ever repay. He hoped like hell that having them here on the Rocking F wasn't going to put either of them in danger.

Chapter Sixteen

The Rocking F's guests had not been on hand a full twenty-four hours before Rosa had taken complete charge of the kitchen.

"You're our guest," Brie protested. "You shouldn't be in here cooking for us."

Beside her, Elly and Tessa echoed their agreement. Not, Brie thought, because either girl would miss the hot, hard work, but more because they felt as Brie did, that a guest was to be waited upon.

"Guest, bah," Rosa scoffed. "My Booker, he works for your Wolf, so I take over here. These two—" She waved a hand toward Elly and Tessa. "—they work too hard for ones so young. They should be enjoying themselves, not cooking for all these people."

No amount of arguing would shake Rosa's determination. In fact, when Brie had threatened to lock her out of the kitchen, Rosa had looked crestfallen.

The woman was an excellent cook. Inserting slivers of garlic into the roast was something Brie had never seen done before. It added a wonderful flavor to the beef.

While Rosa was cooking, the men branded the calves Wolf had brought down from the mesa, castrated them, and notched their ears.

After supper that night, everyone sat out on the front porch and listened to Booker and Charlie Jim tell funny lies about the meanest bull they'd ever seen, the tallest man, the coldest winter, the toughest bronc.

"And this'un here," Charlie Jim said, giving Wolf a friendly slug in the arm. "Why, I remember the first time he tried to bust a bronc up along the Powder River. That rascal was so mean . . ."

"Yeah?" Sully prodded, eager to hear the tale about Wolf. "What happened? Did he throw him good?"

"I'll say. Purt near threw him clean out of the corral."

"Golly!"

"Yes, sir, I never saw a man throw a horse that far before."

"Wow," Sully said. "Did he—Ah, Charlie Jim, you're joshin' us. Ain't you?"

The days settled into a comfortable rhythm. One man stayed behind every day while the other two rode out to tend the cattle. The music of Rosa's humming wafted out from the kitchen all day as she happily baked, stewed, roasted everything in sight. The boys were in heaven with one man around all day and three every evening. Katy was falling in love with Rosa. Tessa and Elly were considering nominating the Mexican woman for sainthood for getting them out of the kitchen.

There had been no further sign of trouble from the Double Diamond.

And to top it all off, Charlie Jim had come back from town one afternoon and told Brie that the following Sunday, the traveling preacher would be in town for a revival. Brie had laughed with delight. Father Thomas at St. Michael's cringed whenever a Protestant revival was held

in or near New Hope. Bless him, he found such things so
. . . undignified.

Everything was going smoothly. Everything was perfect,
as far as Brie could tell. Except for one thing. Wolf was
avoiding her. The only time they were within ten feet of
each other, there always seemed to be at least three children between them, or Booker, or Charlie Jim, or Rosa.

If it wasn't for the few times she had caught and held
Wolf's gaze, she might have been able to convince herself
that she had merely dreamed their night together. But
those few times, when her eyes had met his before he'd
had a chance to look away, told her it hadn't been a dream.
Or if it had, he'd had the same dream. Those few times,
his gray eyes had turned hot, like smoke, and ignited an
answering heat deep inside her. Her heart would pound
and her mouth would dry out, while another part of her
body turned moist with memory and need.

Remembering those looks, remembering their night
together, yet knowing she couldn't slip out to the bunkhouse again to be with him, was driving her crazy.

The morning that Wolf should have taken his turn at
staying behind while the other two rode out, Brie heard
him suggest that Booker might want to spend another day
near his wife rather than staring at the back end of a steer.

Booker agreed. Which meant Wolf would be riding out.
Brie saw him enter the barn to saddle his horse. Quickly,
before anyone could interfere, she followed.

Since the sun was already up, it took a moment for Brie's
eyes to adjust to the dimness of the barn. When she could
see clearly, she found Wolf paused in the act of reaching
for his saddle where it sat perched on the rack outside
the tack room. He was staring at her, his brow raised in
surprise.

And Wolf was surprised. With all the people suddenly
crawling around the place, he thought with chagrin, he'd

lost all hope of seeing Brie alone again for longer than
two seconds.

Alone again. The thought startled him. He wasn't comfortable admitting even to himself that he'd been hoping
to get her alone, but now he couldn't deny it. Everything
they'd shared the other night, all the emotions that had
assailed him then, came at him now like a wall of water
down a dry arroyo during a flash flood.

With the light behind her, he couldn't see her face,
but he felt the pull of her. Felt everything he was feeling
emanating from her. Slowly, as if against his will—it wasn't
against his will, but it was against his better judgment—
he turned away from the saddle and took a step toward
her. "Brie?"

Without hesitating, she crossed the straw-strewn dirt
floor of the barn, wound her arms around his neck, and
kissed him. Hard and hot and fiercely.

And there it was, that fast. The heat, the hunger, the
need. Flaming out of control, making him hard and aching. He tasted coffee, honey, and the darker sweetness
that was Brie. He smelled the sunshine, rainwater, and
wildflowers in her hair. He felt her soft firmness beneath
his hands, her breasts against his chest, her breath like a
soft kiss across his face.

Without thought or care that someone—anyone—
might walk in on them, he slid his hand up her slender
ribcage and cupped her breast, flicking his thumb across
the already hardened tip. He drank in her moan of pleasure and tried to swallow one of his own. It should scare
him, this need for her. It should terrify him. But oddly,
despite his struggle for breath and the way his pulse raced,
she gave him something he'd never had in his life. She
gave him a sense of peace.

Peace, he thought, astonished. Amidst all the driving
hunger and frantic need. Peace. And the desire to carry
her into the nearest empty stall, flip her skirt up out of

his way, and bury himself so deep inside her he'd never find his way out again.

He wondered if his fierce erection was going to allow him to even walk, much less swing up into the saddle. He pressed his lips to her chin, her cheek, and nibbled his way to her ear. "Damn," he whispered. "What are you trying to do to me?"

Instead of answering, she stretched onto her toes and pressed her parted lips to his throat. His heartbeat went a little crazy at the feel of her hot mouth on his skin. Not to mention what it did to him when her weight shifted against his groin.

With one hand on her backside, he pressed her hips harder against his. There was no way she couldn't feel what she was doing to him, even through her skirt and petticoat. One petticoat, he thought, flexing his fingers.

She let out a soft moan that made his chest puff with pride. At least he wasn't the only one being driven rapidly toward the edge.

"Brie, you're killing me."

The shiver that rippled through her told him she was as affected as he was.

"I just wanted to make sure you didn't forget me while you were gone today."

Wolf squeezed his arms around her tightly. "Not a chance, lady."

"I think . . . it backfired."

"How so?"

She raised her head and smiled at him. "I'm going to be tasting your lips and feeling your arms around me all day."

Damn. There was no choice now. He had to kiss her again. Or die. When his horse snorted and stomped, reminding Wolf where they were and that anyone could walk in on them, he ended the kiss and stepped back. His heart was pounding, his chest was heaving, and aside from his earlier idea of dragging her into the nearest stall, all he could think of doing just then was grinning. Him, grinning.

Who would have thought.

Wolf and Charlie Jim rode west of the herd looking for strays. The sun beat down with late summer fierceness across the grassland. It was nearing noon and they had yet to find a single stray. Suddenly Charlie Jim burst out laughing.

"What's so funny?" Wolf wondered if maybe the older man had been out in the sun too long.

Charlie Jim sobered, looked at him, looked away, then laughed so hard he nearly tumbled from the saddle. "You," he finally managed.

"Me what?"

"You're what's funny." With the back of one glove, Charlie Jim took a swipe at the corners of his eyes.

"Me? What'd I do?"

Charlie Jim chuckled again, looking at Wolf like he'd never seen him before. "I been tryin' to figure out what was different about you since we left the barn four hours ago. Can't believe it took me this long. Musta been somethin' mighty special in the barn before I got there."

Wolf glared at him to cover the uncomfortable flush he felt rising up his cheeks. He knew damn good and well Charlie Jim had seen Brie leave the barn. The two had passed each other in the doorway. And Charlie Jim knew that Wolf knew exactly what he was talking about.

What there was in that to set Charlie Jim off like this, Wolf couldn't see. "You been out in the sun too long?"

Sometime in the last couple of minutes, since Charlie Jim had started laughing, he and Wolf had reined their horses to a halt. Charlie Jim leaned a forearm on his saddle horn and grinned at Wolf. "When did you take up whistling?"

Wolf had no idea what the man was talking about, and said so.

"That's what was so damn different riding out with you all day. Son, I hate to tell you this—" Charlie Jim used his thumb to push his hat up a notch, just to make sure Wolf had a clear view of his possum-eating grin. "—but you been whistlin' for the better part of four hours now."

"Have you been chewing loco weed?"

That set Charlie Jim off again. "Whistling all day long, and doesn't even know it. By God, there's hope for you yet, boy. Let's go find them strays." With a wild hoot of laughter, he kicked his horse into a gallop.

Wolf started after him at a much slower pace. It was a full minute before he realized he was whistling. He burst out laughing. He'd been whistling Brie and Katy's favorite song about the pretty red bird.

It felt good. Damn good. The whistling, and the laughter. He laughed for the sheer hell of it, and he laughed at himself. As far as he could remember, he'd never laughed at himself before, not really, not with honest humor.

He'd been wrong earlier in the barn. Brie wasn't killing him. She was the reason he felt more alive these days than he'd ever felt before.

As his laughter trailed away, his smile remained. Those who knew him might have ridden by without recognizing him just then. Few men had ever seen Wolf smile. None had ever seen him . . . what? What was he feeling?

It took him a minute to figure it out, and when he did, it scared the crap out of him. He was—or had been until this moment—*happy*. It was a foreign feeling, one he'd never honestly experienced before. One he'd never trusted. He didn't trust it now, either.

It seemed more than fitting that a cloud chose that moment to block out the sun.

An hour later Wolf and Charlie Jim found seven dead steers in a small dry wash. They'd each been shot through the head.

* * *

Tension on the Rocking F wound tight. Wolf had no doubt that Palmer was responsible for the dead steers, but there was no way to prove it. The trail had lead off north toward the river, rather than south toward the Double Diamond. He gave orders for everyone to keep an eye out. If riders approached the ranch, everyone was to go inside and stay there. No more going out to greet visitors.

Brie didn't argue with his orders, although she thought it highly unlikely that the major would directly attack the house.

The week stretched out slowly. Brie longed to steal a few moments alone with Wolf, but as before, there were always too many people around. Every night after supper, they all settled out on the porch to talk about the day, plan things for tomorrow.

Saturday night, Booker waited until after the younger children were in bed to bring up a subject he knew might set off Wolf's temper. "A traveling preacher, you say?" He spoke to Brie, but watched Wolf. He knew the cub hated anything to do with men of the cloth. Seeing how much Wolf had changed since coming to the Rocking F, how easy he seemed with himself, Booker wondered if the eldest Flanigan daughter had been able to bring about a change in this, too.

Wolf remained silent and studied the toe of his boot as if fascinated by it.

"That's right," Brie said. She told them about the Methodist minister being called away. "We haven't had anyone but the Catholic priest for several weeks now."

"Ah, now don't be tellin' a Mahoney that a Flanigan isn't as Catholic as the pope himself," Booker claimed with an exaggerated brogue.

"Faith," Brie answered in kind, grinning. "I'd not be feedin' ya any such blarney, Mr. Mahoney, sir. But you see, our dear mother was a devout Methodist. The Catholics and the Methodists over the years have had the rare privilege of . . . sharing the Flanigans, shall we say."

Quiet laughter spilled out into the night.

"Raised half papist, half heretic, were you?" Booker asked.

"That's us," Brie claimed.

"Do you plan to attend the services?" Booker asked Wolf.

Wolf snorted. "Not hardly. You know better than to ask."

Booker pursed his lips and shook his head slowly from side to side. "Some things, it seems, do not change. Not to worry. Charlie Jim and I will see everyone to town safely while you keep watch here. That is what you are planning, I presume."

"You presume correctly," Wolf drawled.

"Well." Charlie Jim stretched his arms over his head and yawned. "If we're all goin' to town tomorrow, I might want to think about shinin' my boots."

"You might." Rosa smiled and nodded. "Or else the youngsters will put you to shame. Wait until you see the lovely dress Brie is wearing tomorrow. Very pretty."

"Thank you," Brie said. "I want to look especially good tomorrow." Her voice hardened. "For when I talk to the major."

Wolf's head snapped up. "When you what?" he asked quietly.

"You heard me. I'm going to talk to him about those dead steers. He's got to understand once and for all that he can't run—"

Wolf's blunt, hard voice interrupted her. "No."

"What do you mean, no?" Brie's chin jutted out. "It's past time that he—"

"I mean no. You're not going to talk to him, you're not going near him."

"Excuse me?"

"You heard me," Wolf said flatly, forcefully. "No. And

that's final." He stepped off the porch and started toward the barn.

He made it ten paces before Brie had him by the arm. She jerked hard, taking him by surprise and spinning him around. "You'll not be tellin' me what to do," she said heatedly.

"I *am* telling you what to do. You stay away from Palmer, Brie, I mean it. You're lucky I'm even letting you go to town."

"Lucky!" She shook her fist beneath his nose. "I'll show you lucky. Just because we made love doesn't mean you own me."

From the porch, Elly gasped, Rosa arched a brow, Charlie Jim hooted, and Booker sounded like he was strangling on something.

Wolf stiffened as though she'd slapped him. "You wanna take an ad out in the newspaper so a few more people will know?"

"Know what?" she cried. "That we made love? Why should I care if everybody knows?"

"Why should you care?" he bellowed. "Don't you have any idea what people will say?"

"What people?"

"Anybody! Everybody! Jesus H. Christ, Brie, I'm the last man on earth you should want people to connect you with."

Brie propped her hands on her hips and glared at him. "And why are you the last man on earth I should want people to connect me with?"

"What do you want," he shouted, "a goddamn list? I'll give you a list. How about we start with me seducing an inexperienced virgin, knowing full well I plan to walk out on her before winter? You call it making love, I call it sex, plain and simple. You wanna hear more?"

"Not particularly."

"I'm a half-breed bastard in the literal sense, for starters. The reason I'm called Wolf is because nobody knows what my real name is, not even me. I don't know who my parents were, I don't know which one of them was white and which was Indian, or from which tribe."

"If you expect any of that to matter—"

"From the time I was four years old until I was nine I was either chained, or in a cage almost every minute of almost every day."

A wave of dizziness assaulted Brie.

"I killed my first man when I was nine years old. You tell yourself it was some kind of accident if you want, but the truth is, I planned and bided my time, then I bashed the bastard's head in with a shovel. I came to Colorado looking for the man responsible for the way I was raised, and when I find the son of a bitch, I'm going to kill him, and they'll probably hang me for it. *And I won't care. That's* the kind of man you slept with."

Brie stared at him with hot tears streaking her cheeks. "Because I love him."

Again Wolf reeled as if she'd struck him.

Brie turned and started to walk away. Pausing, she looked at him over her shoulder. "Just for the record," she told him quietly, "you did not seduce me. If you'll recall, it was the other way around."

Chapter Seventeen

Brie, Rosa, and Elly shared the seat on the wagon, while Tessa, Katy, and the boys rode in the bed, with Wolf riding a few yards ahead and Booker trailing behind. Charlie Jim had volunteered to stay at the house while everyone else went to the revival in town. Wolf hadn't said, but Brie assumed the change in plans that had Charlie Jim staying behind was so that Wolf would be on hand to try to keep Brie away from the major. He could have saved himself the trouble. Brie wasn't going to let Wolf stop her.

Not that Brie was looking forward to a confrontation. Last night's argument with Wolf had been more than enough for her.

Elly had wanted to drive the team—she enjoyed it, but didn't get the opportunity often—but Brie needed something to concentrate on. She couldn't afford to let her mind wander, or she'd think of last night, or the harsh look on Wolf's face this morning and the way he refused to look at her, and she would burst into tears.

She shouldn't have any tears left to shed. She'd buried her face in her pillow and cried half the night last night.

Her eyes still felt gritty and swollen, her face stiff from the salt of her tears.

Brie had known from the beginning that Wolf was more than likely to break her heart, but she hadn't counted on that happening until he left. But last night, he'd more than broken it, he'd smashed it to pieces.

She felt as if someone had carved her heart from her chest, but she felt especially bad for Wolf. The pain of finally realizing what he thought of himself, how little he thought of himself, was devastating. The knowledge that he planned to kill a man nearly crippled her.

Dear God, watch over him, keep him safe, ease the pain in his heart.

The revival was being held at the brush arbor just beyond the west edge of town. Nearby, the town fathers—or more likely the town mothers, Wolf thought, since women were the natural nest-builders—had planted trees and grass, creating a nice little two-acre park between the edge of town and the bluff of the Purgatoire. A crowd had already gathered beneath the arbor and spilled out to the hay bales lined up to be used as extra seats. A rousing rendition of "Bringing in the Sheaves" was being sung with more enthusiasm than skill.

The song made the skin along the back of Wolf's neck crawl. He hated hymns. To him they preceded sermons, and hymns and sermons were what Lazarus had used to work himself into a frenzy. The days following a revival had been so bad that Wolf had blocked most of them from his mind and to this day couldn't remember much about them.

Maybe there was a God after all, he thought sarcastically, if those particular memories were lost.

Damn, what was he doing thinking about the past anyway? It was as dead and gone as Lazarus himself. It was just this day's activities that were stirring his memories. He had bigger problems to concentrate on than things that couldn't be changed.

Long ropes had been strung from posts to serve as hitching rails where the folks from the outlying areas could tie their teams and mounts for the day. Wolf moved to the side of the road and let the wagon pass. From the corner of his eye, he saw Brie set her shoulders and look away from him.

He wondered if the giant fist inside him would ever let go of his guts. It had been twisting them into tighter and tighter knots since Brie had announced for all the world last night that she and he had made love.

Damn her for exposing herself that way. Wolf could only be grateful that no one other than his friends and her sister had heard.

He didn't have time to think about that either. The job he'd assigned himself was that of keeping an eye on Palmer and the Double Diamond hands. Being able to recognize more of Palmer's men on sight would have been a help, but Wolf remembered the few faces he'd seen last week when he and Brie had returned those three assholes to their boss.

Booker's task for the day was to stick close to Brie and the kids and make sure nobody bothered them, and that none of the little ones wandered out of sight.

Tough duty. One Wolf would have more than welcomed, until everything between him and Brie had blown up last night.

She guided the wagon to a vacant spot along the picket line with as much skill as a professional teamster. By the time she had the brake set and the traces secured, the boys had bailed out the back of the wagon, and Booker was there to help the ladies.

Katy's turn came, and she held out her arms to Booker. When he lifted her from the wagon bed she hugged him and kissed his cheek. Leave it to Katy, Wolf thought, to make him laugh when he'd never felt less like laughing.

But watching a blush creep through that dark skin was something to laugh about.

Already standing beside Booker, Brie, too, laughed at the sheepish pleasure on the big man's face. If she had to force the laugh past the ache in her heart, she at least hoped no one noticed her laughter wasn't genuine.

As the congregation finished the last verse of "Bringing in the Sheaves" and started "Onward Christian Soldiers," Brie collected three parasols from the wagon bed and led her family and the Mahoneys to the few vacant hay bales that were left. Since they were not beneath the shady shelter of the brush arbor, she was glad she'd remembered to bring the parasols.

As soon as they were seated, Brie noticed Major Palmer, Letty, James, and Margery had seats on chairs near the center of the arbor. Elly caught James's eye. He leaned toward his mother and whispered something. While everyone was still standing for the singing, he scooted out of the row and came to sit beside Elly.

Suddenly Brie really felt like laughing. Major Palmer wouldn't dare bother any of them now. Not with his own grandson on one side and a huge, black, mountain of a man on the other.

That huge, black, mountain of a man eyed James dubiously. "Who's that?" he demanded of Brie.

Booker's voice was so loud, even though he was trying to soften it, that Brie had no trouble hearing him above the singing. She obviously wasn't the only one. Several nearby people frowned and glared. Good Christians that they were.

Brie leaned toward his ear and whispered, explaining that James was the grandson of the man causing all their trouble. Booker's bushy gray brows nearly butted ends until she explained that James was sweet on Elly.

They turned then and faced the waiting pulpit, raising their voices in song. Booker's deep bass carried easily to Wolf, some distance away. He'd found a spot of scant shade at the back of the nearest building. From there he could keep an eye on everyone coming and going.

Just then he had his eye on the Double Diamond foreman. Jennings was slowly making his way down the picket lines with no apparent purpose other than to stroke a horse's muzzle here and there.

Jennings didn't strike Wolf as the kind of man who was so fond of animals that he'd deliberately seek out their company. As the man drew closer to the Rocking F team still hitched to Brie's wagon, Wolf meandered in that direction. He was almost upon Jennings, and the man didn't seem to have noticed his approach.

Wolf thought he was wrong about not having been detected, when Jennings reached down and slipped a small knife no longer than the length of his palm from the shank of his boot. But instead of turning on Wolf, who was now barely six yards behind him, Jennings reached toward the nearest of Brie's horses in a casual gesture. To anyone who couldn't see the knife, it would look as though he was merely stroking the horse, as he'd done so many others.

Jennings moved to the second of Brie's horses, and Wolf saw then what the man had done. He'd left a neat cut in the left rein about an inch short of where it connected to the bridle. Nothing too obvious, though. The bastard had stopped less than a quarter of an inch from cutting the rein all the way through. Just enough so that maybe no one would notice. Enough to hold together for a little while. Like maybe until the team got halfway across the river and the driver, helping the horses fight the current, would pull with enough force to cause the rein to snap.

Jennings apparently wasn't satisfied with cutting only one rein. When he passed the first horse, he paused and turned back, reaching a hand up toward the right rein. That's when he spotted Wolf. The knife disappeared neatly up the sleeve of his shirt. "What the hell do you want?"

Despite the rage surging through him at what he'd caught Jennings doing, Wolf managed an outward appearance of calm. He pulled his pistol and aimed at Jennings's chest. "I thought you and I could take a little stroll."

Jennings went for his pistol.

Wolf thumbed the hammer back on his Colt. "Don't bother, unless you're anxious to die."

Jennings froze in mid-reach. His face was a mask of rage. Then slowly he relaxed and sneered. "You wouldn't shoot a man during a revival, would you? Just doesn't seem very Christian-like. I'm not bothering you any."

"Yes, you are. It bothers the hell out of me to think of those kids being halfway across the river when the reins suddenly snap. Next thing you know, the whole county will be talking about what a tragedy it was that the Flanigan children drowned in the same river that killed their parents just a few months ago. Yep, that just bothers the hell out of me."

"That would be a shame, all right." Jennings shifted his weight as if to turn and leave. "Don't see as that's got anything to do with me. See ya around, half-breed."

"Don't make the mistake of thinking I won't shoot just because there are people around."

Something in his voice must have convinced Jennings, for the man halted. "What do you want, damn you?"

"I want you to leave that knife right where you slid it—up your sleeve—and take a little walk with me over to the marshall's office. You can come peaceably, or I can shoot you and drag your body through town straight to the undertaker. Makes no difference to me."

With a tight jaw and clenched fists, Jennings glared at him. "You'll pay for this, half-breed."

"So will you. Now walk."

With a low curse, Jennings turned and started toward town. "We'll see who gets the last laugh."

"I said walk." Wolf fell into step behind him. "I didn't say anything about talking."

The dusty streets of New Hope were all but empty as Wolf followed Jennings through town to the marshall's office. They passed only three people along the way. Wolf didn't lower his gun or make any attempt to conceal what he was doing.

Mr. Peeples, the druggist, stopped and gaped. "Mr. Jennings? What's going on? Who is this man? Is . . . should I do something?"

"Yeah," Jennings snarled. "You should mind your own damn business."

The druggist's thin eyebrows rose to his hairline. He stood a moment, watching them walk past. "Well, mister," he said to Wolf. "I guess I hope you don't trip. That gun could go off. You could accidently shoot the bad manners right out of him."

Half a block from the marshall's office, two saloon girls lounged half-naked in the shade on the rickety, second-story balcony of the Red Garter. When they spied what Wolf was beginning to think constituted a parade—two men walking single file—one of the women stood and leaned over the unpainted rail. The top of her chemise gaped open, giving anyone who cared to look a view clear to her navel.

Instead of looking, Jennings hunched his shoulders and trudged on.

"Hey, are you ignoring me, Hank Jennings? You better not—Sally, look! That man's got a gun on Hank. Hey, you! What do you think you're doing? Do you know who that is? That's Hank Jennings and he's the foreman of the Double Diamond. You can't point a gun at him!"

Jennings paused and glanced up. Wolf nudged him along.

"He's one of the most important men in the county!" the woman shouted.

"He's also the one who likes to wear spurs in bed." The second woman rose and joined the first one.

"But Sally, that's Hank!"

"Yeah, but what I want to know is who the other one is. Mister," Sally shouted down at Wolf. "You get rid of ol'

Hank and come up and see me, why don't ya? You don't look like the kind of man who needs to wear spurs to bed just to make himself feel like a stud."

Wolf gave them a polite nod. "Ladies."

Jennings glanced up again with a glare. "Either one of you, or any other girls in town, bed this bastard, you'll be sorry."

Sally sagged against the rail. "I suppose you're right, Hank, honey. I've bedded you a time or two and I was sure sorry."

Marshall Ben Campbell stepped out of his office. "What's all the yell—Ah, hell." He looked at Jennings, at Wolf, at Wolf's pistol. His shoulders slumped. "What now? I was lookin' forward to a nice, quiet Sunday morning."

"Campbell," Jennings said between clenched teeth. "This son of a bitch drew a gun on me for no reason. He belongs behind bars."

"You pulled a gun on him?"

Wolf looked down at his pistol, then with his other hand, scratched his jaw. "Guess I did."

"Ah, hell. Come on inside, both of you, and let's get to the bottom of this. If I don't get to that revival, my wife is gonna skin me alive, so make it quick."

Wolf made it quick. He told Campbell of catching Jennings in the act of slicing Brie's reins, and showed him where the knife was.

Jennings's face turned beet red with fury. "He's lying. Dammit, Ben, you know me."

"Yeah. I know you." Ben Campbell looked at the little knife in his hand, turning it this way and that and watching the way the light bounced off it. "I know you'll do whatever the major tells you to do."

"As if you wouldn't," Jennings snarled.

"I'm ashamed to say that until recently, you'd be right. But I don't hold with what he's trying to do to those Flanigan kids. Get in the cell, Hank. I'll go have a look at those reins."

"Damn you!" Jennings made a leap for the door. Wolf stuck his foot out and tripped him. When Jennings fell, his head hit the leg of the cast iron stove used to heat the office in winter and coffee all year long. Jennings was out cold.

"Ah, hell," Campbell complained. "Help me drag him into the cell."

After locking Jennings up, Campbell started for the door. With his hand on the knob, he paused and eyed Wolf. "You'd better be here when I get back. If I don't find anything wrong with those reins, I don't wanna have to come lookin' for you."

"I'll be here. I don't want somebody from the Double Diamond coming in here and turning him loose while you're gone."

Campbell nodded. "Fair enough."

Jennings woke up ten minutes after the marshall left. He bellowed for the next thirty, demanding to be released, boasting about what he was going to do to Wolf when he got out of jail.

Wolf sat in one of the two chairs in front of Campbell's desk, his feet up on the desk, his back to the door leading into the cells.

"Then there's sweet little Brianna," Jennings called out. "Once you're out of the way, I'll just have to pay her a visit. When I get through with her—"

Wolf's boots hit the floor hard. "One more word, Jennings, and I'll claim I had to shoot you when you tried to escape."

"Filthy stinking half-breed."

Wolf turned his back and went to stand at the window, where he could see down the street. What was taking Campbell so long? He shouldn't have been gone more than five or ten minutes, but it was going on forty-five now. Wolf wanted to get back, so he could personally watch for more trouble. He didn't trust Palmer.

Five minutes later Wolf gave up staring out the window and returned to his seat. Jennings, thankfully, had grown quiet. Finally boot steps thudded on the wooden walkway outside the door. Wolf stood and turned.

A man Wolf had never seen before stumbled through the door, Marshall Campbell right behind him. A cloud of whiskey fumes surrounded the stranger.

"Easy, there, Sam." Campbell took the drunk by the arm and led him to the cell next to Jennings.

"'Bout damn time you got back," Jennings muttered. "Let me outa this cell, Campbell, or there'll be hell to pay."

Campbell straightened slowly from easing Sam down onto the narrow cot. He left the cell and closed the door on it without locking it. Then he turned to Jennings. "I guess while I'm figuring out what all to charge you with, I can add threatening an officer of the law to the list."

Some of the tension in Wolf's muscles eased. It sounded like Campbell believed him about Jennings. "You gonna keep him locked up?"

"I am."

"You gonna let Palmer come bail him out?"

Campbell eased down onto his chair like a man twice his age might do—slowly, carefully. "Way I figure it, can't tell what the bail oughta be until I decide what the charges are. I'll have to sleep on it a night or two before I decide."

Wolf let one corner of his mouth curve. "Sounds good enough for me."

"Wolf," Campbell said. Wolf, who was walking toward the door, turned. "You watch your step, and you watch those kids. Palmer's not gonna like this, and I can't keep Hank locked up forever. Watch your back."

Wolf gave a single sharp nod. "Will do. And Campbell? Thanks."

"Don't mention it."

Upon leaving the marshall's office, Wolf nodded to the two women still out on the balcony of the Red Garter and was back at the edge of town in less than two minutes.

The singing was over and the preaching had begun. Why was it that preachers all seemed to use the same inflections, that odd rhythm they gave to their words? Wolf hated it. This man sounded so much like Lazarus it made his skin prickle.

Son of a bitch. He'd just have to ignore the voice, the words, the inflections. The hallelujahs and amens. He made his way back to the corner of the building where he'd stood before and tried to ignore that damn voice. So deep, smooth. So much like—

Wolf froze the instant his eyes lit on the man behind the pulpit. Ice shimmied down his spine and sweat broke out across his palms. It was impossible. It couldn't be—

Lazarus!

Wolf nearly choked as the name whipped through his mind.

Even if Wolf had been deaf, the man at the pulpit would be impossible to ignore. Tall and lean, he had the sharp features of a hawk, with dark eyes that, even from this distance, could pierce a man's soul. Women had always called him beautiful, but only behind their fluttering fans. A white shirt and old fashioned frock coat made his smooth, olive skin glow, marred only by a pale scar running from his temple to his cheek.

So it's true. Gilbert Lazarus had a deal with the devil.

He should have been dead. He *had* been dead!

Now he was alive, not looking a day older than he had seventeen years ago.

Wolf tried to look away, but couldn't. Something held his gaze on that face while his heart refused to beat. He was shaking now and couldn't control it. Sweat beaded across his brow, yet he was freezing cold. His stomach churned, threatening revolt.

It was impossible. But one look into those eyes and Wolf knew it was true. Gilbert Lazarus was alive.

From across the distance of a dozen yards and seventeen years, that smooth, hypnotizing voice reached out. "Gentlemen, ye must *not* succumb to the siren's call of evil women! Do not be seduced by the harlot's base intentions. Ladies, do not be seduced for evil purposes, nor must ye seduce any man. Remember! Remember poor Adam. Remember Eve and her weakness for the serpent's words! How temptingly she offered the apple to a man who did not understand the wiles of a woman. Resist! Resist temptation! If ye find yourselves—"

The words became a loud buzz in Wolf's ears and he could no longer make them out. It didn't matter. He knew this sermon by heart. He knew why the man was so effective—he believed what he was saying, that women were evil and men should have nothing to do with them. Lazarus lived his life by those beliefs. That fierce conviction rang through in his voice and mesmerized his audience to the point that Wolf was sure half the couples in town would start sleeping in separate beds until the words faded from memory.

Wolf could not stop the terror that swamped him. He tried. He told himself he was not a scared little boy anymore. He was not vulnerable to this man. He was a man now and had nothing to fear.

Yet he stood there, locked in the sickness and terror of his past, unable to even look away from the personification of evil. Lazarus could easily justify his attitude toward men and women and seduction. The man had no need of women. Not as long as there were lost, scared little boys in the world.

Chapter Eighteen

"Be fruitful and multiply," Brie muttered under her breath, "but for heaven's sake, don't enjoy it."

Beside her, Booker covered his mouth with his hand and made a choking sound.

Once more, as she'd done about every other minute throughout the sermon, Brie craned her neck and looked for Wolf. Where had he gone? Had something happened? She wasn't at all comfortable with the smug look on the major's face earlier when he'd glanced her way.

She was about to give up again on finding Wolf among the people milling around beyond the seating area when finally she spotted him standing near the old building at the edge of town. He looked . . . odd.

Brie stared at him, and her heart started pounding. She'd been right to worry. Something was definitely wrong. His beautiful bronze skin had turned pasty and he seemed to be having trouble breathing. Quickly she closed her parasol and started to rise from the bale of hay.

Booker stopped her with a hand on her arm. "You're supposed to stay here," he whispered.

"Something's happened. I have to get to Wolf."

Booker turned his massive head and studied the man he considered the son he'd never had. The girl was right. Something was very wrong. He stared to rise, but this time it was Brie who stopped him.

"You have to stay with the kids. I'll go."

Reluctantly, Booker agreed. He had sworn to Wolf that he would stay with the family. He would keep his word. "You go. Take care of the boy."

"He's not a boy, Booker," she said softly. "But I'll take the best care of him I can."

The two shared a look and acknowledged their mutual but very different love for the man called Wolf.

A few people grumbled as Brie made her way out of the crowded seating area, but she paid them no mind. She was too intent on reaching Wolf to care what anyone thought about her disruption.

Drawing closer to Wolf, she became more alarmed. She reached his side, but he didn't even notice. It was as if he was in some sort of . . . trance. His face was damp with sweat and deathly pale. His chest rose and fell rapidly with short, choppy breaths. But all of that was nothing compared to the look in his eyes. Mixed in with pain, rage, and shock, the look of raw, consuming terror made her cry out.

"Wolf?" She touched his hand, finding it icy cold and clammy.

His lips moved. She leaned closer to hear.

"I should have known that with a name like Lazarus the bastard wouldn't stay dead. This time I'll make sure, by damn." He reached for his gun.

Brie's blood chilled. "Wolf!" She grasped his hand to keep him from drawing his pistol. "Wolf!"

He blinked and turned his head toward her, slowly, jerkily, as if the muscles had rusted. "Brie?"

Brie swallowed a cry of relief as his eyes gradually cleared. "What happened? You're so pale. What's wrong?"

Beneath his ashen skin, a flush rose. "Nothing," came his curt reply.

Brie followed his gaze to the man in white behind the pulpit. A sense of foreboding crept down her spine. "What did you mean about Lazarus not staying dead?"

Wolf's expression closed off sharply, yet still, he did not look at her. He kept staring at the preacher. "Nothing. Don't worry about it." He took a step, and started to take another.

Brie pulled on his arm and halted him. Following his gaze again, she replayed his words in her mind. With a sharp gasp, she squeezed his arm. "That's not . . . Is he . . . Wolf, is *that* the man you said you killed?"

"Let it go, Brie."

"Talk to me. Tell me what's wrong. That *is* him, isn't it." She made it a statement rather than a question.

Still without looking at her, he spoke in a lifeless voice. "Go get the kids and start home." He turned his face toward her. "Just do it, Brie. Do it now." As he spoke, his eyes changed. All those earlier emotions were still there, but Brie saw something new now that frightened her. In his eyes, she saw death. Not for her. For himself, possibly. For the man in white, most definitely. It was in his voice, too, when he added, "There's not likely to be a picnic in New Hope today."

Brie felt suddenly light-headed. "You're going to kill him," she whispered in horror.

"I'm going to kill him. *Again.*"

Oh God, she couldn't let this happen! She scrambled in her mind for a way to stop him, something, anything to say that would get through to him. But what would matter to him now? He'd called this man a monster. She herself had seen what Lazarus had done to Wolf's back. Wolf hated him so much that he'd come here looking for whoever had been responsible for him having been raised by the preacher. So much that he planned to kill that man when he found him. What would one more killing matter?

Her own thoughts gave her an idea. Frantically she clutched Wolf's arm. "Wait! Think! If you kill him, you'll never find the man who gave you to him, you'll never have a chance to kill that one. Leave this one to God."

"Oh, no. I'm not trusting God with this one," he said fiercely. "Mr. Colt will make sure the bastard doesn't get his hands on any more young boys."

"More?" Brie's eyes widened. "You mean he makes a habit of it?"

Wolf knew that she didn't know the half of Lazarus's evil, but the little she did know was bad enough. "Habit's a good enough word for it." His head snapped up. It suddenly occurred to him that Lazarus might have a boy with him here in New Hope. He remembered the drill well enough. The boy would remain silent, letting no one know he was inside the wagon.

The wagon. A sharp breath hissed in between Wolf's teeth. "Where the hell is his wagon?" He knew it wasn't nearby or he would have seen it. With a quick spin on his boot heel, he strode purposefully toward town.

Brie dogged his steps, having to take two strides for each of his. "Wolf!"

"Go home," he snarled without slowing, without looking at her. He couldn't look at her. His past was on him like a tick on a hound, sucking away everything vital inside. He couldn't let the foulness of that touch Brie. "Get the kids in the wagon and get out of town."

She didn't, of course. That was one of the things he admired most about her, her stubbornness.

"You said a wagon," she said breathlessly beside him, hurrying to keep up. "I'll help you look. What kind of wagon?"

Rather than answer, Wolf muttered under his breath. He stalked through the dusty streets of New Hope looking, searching, until finally, at the other end of town, in the alley behind the Methodist church, another piece of his past loomed before him.

Wolf's steps slowed as his heartbeat raced. Time rolled out from under his feet like a receding tide, taking the ground with it, leaving him to sink into his past.

It was the same, yet different. Bigger. Newer. Requiring two horses to pull it instead of one, Wolf noted absently, judging by the rigging. With the top and sides made of wood, the sleek Studebaker was painted black, with red lettering across the sides proudly proclaiming it the property of the Reverend Gilbert Lazarus. The small windows on the sides and back were high and barred and the door was secured with a heavy iron lock, *The better to keep you in with, my boy.*

Wolf shivered as that deep voice echoed insidiously through his mind like the hiss of a snake.

Brie saw him shudder and started to reach out to him. He was pale again, his skin a pasty gray, his lips bloodless, his eyes haunted by whatever horrible thing had gripped him. "Wolf?"

He whirled on her so quickly that she stumbled back in surprise. "Get away! I don't want you here, I don't need you here. Just—get—*away.*"

Brie trembled with the certainty that something terrible was about to happen and that she wouldn't be able to stop it. There was much more to Wolf's tragic past than the beating that had left the scars on his back, and Brie had the terrible feeling it was all rising up to choke him. She didn't know how to help him, what to say to reach through the horror she saw in his eyes.

Booker. Maybe Booker would know what to do.

Wolf never saw her leave. He had turned to stare at the wagon again. Shaking. Trembling. The sour smell of fear in his nostrils and icy sweat beading across his skin.

As a leading citizen in the county, Major Palmer smiled at his neighbors and stood in line behind Letty to shake the hand of the Reverend Gilbert Lazarus. He couldn't hear what Letty said to the man, but she must have said something, for the reverend was smiling. Then Letty moved away.

"Major Palmer." Eugenia Parkinson, in charge of the local Christian Ladies Association, stood beside the traveling preacher and beamed. "Reverend, I'd like you to meet Major Palmer. Major, Reverend Gilbert Lazarus."

"Reverend." Palmer shook hands with the man.

Something that looked like cunning sparked in Lazarus's eyes. Palmer recognized the look instantly. That, and a touch of dark amusement.

"Major Palmer, a pleasure. You look familiar, sir." The preacher smiled. "Yes, I have it now. How the years seem to fly. Denver, it was, right after the War." Lazarus softened his voice in sympathy. "You had just come home from battle in time to bury your wife."

Palmer struggled to keep the shock from his face. For a moment, his mind was blank. Then he remembered, and his chest tightened. Good God, he hadn't thought of this man in years.

It had been a long time since Palmer had felt uneasy about anything, but this man made his skin crawl.

"Let me see," Lazarus said thoughtfully. "A child. Yes, I believe I recall—"

"My daughter," Palmer rushed to say, fighting a sense of panic. The man was . . . by God, the man was threatening him! Palmer narrowed his eyes. "But she was a young woman then, not a child." *Don't mess with me, you son of a bitch. I can get you lynched right here and now.*

The two men stared steadily at each other while the crowd milled and people waited their turn to meet the preacher.

The preacher's eyes turned sly. "That's odd. I could have sworn I remembered a young child."

"You remembered wrong," Palmer said mildly, aware of their avid audience. Aware that Letty had turned back and was watching with a frown. "Good day to you, Reverend."

Lazarus watched him go. He'd seen the threat in the major's eyes and it made him want to laugh. Palmer wouldn't open his mouth. He couldn't. Not without tarring himself with the same brush.

Still, that sense of something not quite . . . safe, struck Lazarus again as he turned to greet the next citizen of New Hope. It had come on him during his sermon, but he wasn't sure what had caused it.

Then he remembered, and bit back a curse. The halfbreed. The one who'd stood away from the congregation and stared at him as if he'd seen a ghost.

Gilbert Lazarus didn't believe in premonitions, but just then, for the first time in his life, a bolt of what could only be called fear shot through him.

Half-breed.

Major.

Denver.

Suddenly everything fit together in his mind like the words to a Psalm. Or a curse.

"Excuse me, Mrs. Parkinson, but do you suppose these good citizens would permit me a few quiet moments of solitude and prayer before the picnic begins?"

Mrs. Parkinson looked into the eager faces of her friends who waited anxiously to meet the preacher. They wouldn't be pleased, but she was the one in charge of the day's events. If the good reverend needed a few moments of solitude to renew his spirit, the rest of the town would just have to wait.

She turned her smile on him. "Why, of course, Reverend Lazarus, how thoughtless of us. I'm sure you must need a respite after delivering such a stimulating sermon."

Lazarus gave her his most ingratiating smile and bent low over her hand. "Madam, God has smiled on me with your generosity."

* * *

"Booker!" Brie rushed to Booker's side and grabbed his arm. "I need your help with Wolf."

"What's happened?" the big man demanded.

"That man," she hissed, nodding toward the preacher who was just then shaking hands with Major Palmer.

"What about him?"

"That's *him,* Booker, the man who ... the man Wolf thought—" She swallowed the rest of her words and looked around quickly, fearing she would be overheard by the dozens of people milling around.

She needn't have worried about explaining further. Booker's eyes widened with shock. He whipped his head around and stared at the man dressed in white. "Son of a bitch," he muttered. He turned a fierce glare on Brie. "Are you sure?"

"Yes. You have to come with me."

Booker started to go with her, then stopped and swore. "The kids. We can't leave the kids alone."

"No, we can't." Frantic, Brie wondered what to do.

The major had finished shaking hands with the preacher and had turned to talk with neighbors. Letty waved at Brie and started toward her.

Brie rushed to meet her. "Letty, I don't have time to explain, but I need you to stay with the kids."

Letty's smile of greeting faded. "You know you don't have to ask. What's wrong? You look positively shaken."

"I don't have time to explain." She took Letty by the hand and led her to where Booker stood with the children. Quickly Brie introduced her to Rosa. "You must keep everyone together. Don't let the kids separate," she said earnestly. "Don't even let Elly go walking with James. Promise me, Letty."

"Brie, you're scaring me."

"I'm sorry. Just promise, please?"

"All right," she said uncertainly. "I promise."

Brie squeezed Letty's hand in gratitude, then grabbed Booker by the arm. "Let's hurry."

With his worn black Bible tucked casually under one arm, Lazarus pulled back the lapels of his white coat and hooked his thumbs behind his suspenders. He strolled casually away from the crowd, his head down as though paying no attention to where he was heading. His seemingly aimless saunter took him between two houses and out onto a residential street devoid of people. Quickly he dropped his pretense and strode with purpose toward the other end of town.

He approached the alley behind the Methodist church with caution. At the far corner of the church, he glanced around to make sure no one was watching, then quietly slipped behind the big rose-of-Sharon blooming at the corner of the building. There he pressed his back against the church and peered cautiously around the corner into the alley where he'd left his wagon.

There he was. The half-breed. It had to be the same one. Rage filled him. Of all the boys Lazarus had "raised," the skinny little brown-skinned bastard was the only one who'd ever gotten away. *The son of a bitch damn near killed me in the process,* he reminded himself, fingering the scar on the side of his face. Lazarus owed him for that. If it was really him.

Why was the 'breed just standing there staring at the wagon? Lazarus could tell that the lock on the door was still intact, and that puzzled him. Why would the man stand and stare and not try to break in?

As Lazarus studied the man, he realized that the half-breed was shaking badly. Lazarus smiled and started to step from concealment.

At the sound of hurried footsteps from the other side of the church, he ducked back into his hiding place.

Lazarus recognized the two people instantly. The beautiful redheaded young woman with the pale skin, followed by the giant black man she'd sat next to on the bales of hay just outside the shade of the arbor. She'd had a parasol, he remembered, and she'd left in the middle of his sermon to go to the half-breed.

Their approach now startled the half-breed. One second he was standing there trembling, his hands knotted into white fists at his sides, his back to the alley where the man and woman came from.

In less than the blink of an eye, the half-breed whipped his revolver from his holster, spun on one heel and crouched, aiming the gun at the woman's belly. Lazarus stared in admiration. He'd never seen a man move so fast, with so much grace.

"Wolf!" the woman cried.

Lazarus smiled. It *was* him. The son of a bitch even still used the same name.

Then he frowned, thinking. The 'breed could cause a great deal of trouble, especially if he got into the wagon.

At the thought, sweat broke out across Lazarus's chest.

Wolf swore viciously and lowered his revolver. His hands were shaking. "Goddammit, I could have killed you both."

Booker gave a slight bow. "I, for one, am eternally grateful that you did not." Straightening, he eyed the big black wagon. "Surely this is not the same one."

Wolf's eyes cut to Brie. "She told you?"

"That Lazarus is the man from hell? Yes."

"The man from hell." One corner of Wolf's mouth curled down. "Good title for him."

"What are you going to do?" Booker asked.

Wolf studied Brie's pale face, then looked at Booker. "Before I do anything, I want you to take her out of here. Get everyone in the wagon and take them home. And keep them there."

Brie angled her chin. "I'm not leaving without you."

Wolf glared at her. Goddammit, he didn't want her to see what he feared he'd find in the wagon. But he knew that look. She wasn't going to budge. He looked to Booker for help, but the big man merely shrugged as if to say, "What can I do?"

Booker could do plenty, Wolf thought, furious. He could pick Brie up and carry her out of here if he wanted. But Wolf recognized Booker's look, too.

Defeated, Wolf let his gaze brush Brie one last time. God, she was so lovely it almost hurt to look at her, standing there staring up at him with confusion and pain in her eyes. Pain for him. Pain that would turn to disgust the minute she understood the truth.

"So be it," he said, his voice devoid of emotion. "Don't say I didn't warn you. If there's a boy in this wagon, you're about to get a glimpse of hell." He raised his gun and aimed at the padlock on the door.

"What are you doing?" Brie demanded fiercely. "Do you want the whole town to hear and come running to investigate?"

"Not particularly," Wolf said coldly. "But neither do I plan to chew the lock in two."

Brie tsked in irritation. "Step aside." She reached beneath her hat and withdrew a long hairpin. "If you're that determined, there's a much quieter way to open a lock."

Wolf hadn't planned to look at her again because it hurt too much. But he stared anyway as she bent one end of the hairpin at an angle, then poked it into the keyhole on the lock. She had to stand on her toes and reach above her head, for the wagon bed itself was nearly three feet above the ground and the lock had purposely been placed high on the door.

Wolf dimly noticed that her hands were shaking as badly as his were. "You'll never get it open that way."

About that time, he heard a soft *click*, and the lock popped open.

Booker raised one eyebrow. "What an ... interesting talent you have, Miss Brie."

"Why, thank you, sir." She gave him a polite nod.

"You do that often?" Wolf demanded.

"Not often. Just when necessary."

Wolf glared at her, because being angry with her was a hell of a lot easier than thinking about what might be waiting on the other side of the lock she'd just picked. "Nice trick. Where'd you learn it?"

"Didn't you know?" Her smile was brittle. "Lock-picking instructions come with every girl's first set of hairpins."

Wolf grunted and shoved his revolver back into his holster. It was just as well she'd been able to pick the lock. The way his hands were shaking, he probably would have missed his shot.

"You can go now," he said without looking at her.

"I'm staying."

"Why?"

"Are you going to open the door, or not?"

"For God's sake," he said desperately, "at least stand at the end of the wagon where you can't see in."

Shaken by the desperation in his voice, Brie did as he asked.

Wolf stood for another few moments staring at the door of the wagon, taking deep breaths as he prepared to face the horror of his past. Before the fear could make him turn tail and run, like he wanted to do, he reached up and removed the lock. For another long moment, he held it in his palm and stared at it. Then, with a low snarl, he hurled it down the alley, where it landed in the dirt.

Steeling himself, he turned back toward the door and pulled it open. As expected, it was dim inside, and hotter than the fires of hell. The smell struck him first, the smell of terror, the smell of evil, the smell of bay rum. Nightmare images from Wolf's past threatened to turn him into the terrified young boy he'd been when he'd lived—no, *existed*, barely—in a wagon almost identical to this one.

It could have been the same one, except for the size. The small table in the corner, the locked trunk beneath it, the built-in bed across the back end. *The iron chain, with one end bolted to the floor.*

Bile rose in Wolf's throat as he stared at the coiled length of chain on the floor. His ankle throbbed just looking at the shackle on the free end. He braced his hands on either side of the door to combat a wave of dizziness.

He shook his head to clear it. That's when he saw the boy on the bed. Crouched in the corner and curled into as small a ball of humanity as he could make himself, the child had been all but invisible. At the sight of him, Wolf's knees almost gave out.

"It's all right," he said hoarsely. "You're safe now."

With a soft mewling whimper, the boy, who looked to be around twelve, stared at Wolf with wide terror-filled eyes.

At the startled feminine gasp from behind him, Wolf whirled. "Goddammit, I told you to stay back!"

Brie stumbled backward and would have fallen if Booker hadn't steadied her. She covered her mouth with both hands to keep back the cry that rose to her lips. The soft, soothing tone of Wolf's voice had drawn her to his shoulder to peer into the wagon. His enraged snarl at her barely fazed her. It was the sight of the bruised and battered boy on the bed in the wagon that shocked her.

"Come away, Miss Brie," Booker said quietly. "You'll only humiliate the boy."

From his tone, Brie wondered if he meant the boy on the bed, or Wolf. The sick feeling in her stomach told her that something more terrible than beating a child was going on here. Wolf's scars, his words of cages and chains came back to her. A man didn't have to chain a boy in order to beat him.

Bile rose in her throat.

Chapter Nineteen

Shaking, Brie stood beside Booker and watched Wolf climb up into the wagon.

"It's all right," came Wolf's voice softly. "I won't hurt you. I've come to take you out of here."

No answer came that Brie could hear. No cry of gratitude, no voiced objection, nothing. Wolf spoke again, his voice low and quiet, his words indistinguishable to Brie.

After several minutes, the wagon creaked, and Wolf stepped out. Behind him came a boy of around twelve. Lank brown hair hung down over his forehead to dull, colorless eyes. In between vivid, colorful bruises, his skin held the pallor of one who never ventured into the sun, and he was much too thin for a boy his size. When he climbed down at Wolf's urging she realized he was as tall as she was.

He glanced frantically, fearfully, up and down the alley.

"He's not here," Wolf said. There was no need to name the man he spoke of. "Come on. Let's get away from this place."

The boy shook with terror. "He'll kill me."

"I won't let him near you ever again. I promise. And neither will he," he added, nodding toward Booker.

The boy looked at Booker and trembled harder. His protruding Adam's apple bobbed up, then down.

"Look at him," Wolf told the boy. "He's so big he could crush Lazarus with his bare hands."

"And I believe I will do just that," came Booker's deep rumbling voice, "the minute we get this young man settled someplace safe."

The boy's wide, frightened eyes darted from Wolf to Booker. He backed away until he came up against the side of the wagon. His gaze connected with Brie's, pleading for something she didn't understand at first.

Then it dawned on her that it was the men he was so afraid of. He'd been abused by a man, so perhaps it made sense that he would fear other men, especially strangers. Her heart broke for him. He might be as tall as she, but in his eyes she saw a terrified child. Forcing a smile, she stepped forward. "Hello. My name's Brie. What's yours?"

The boy swallowed hard. "S-Stevie, ma'am."

Brie's smile came easier. "Stevie. I like that. Would you like to come with me?"

"Yes." His answer came immediately, without hesitation, without asking where she was taking him or why. His only hesitation came in leaving the security of the wagon at his back. His fear-filled gaze darted to Wolf, then Booker, then lit on Brie again.

Stepping forward, Brie held out her hand to Stevie. "Gentlemen, if you'll lead the way, Stevie and I will follow."

Wolf and Booker led the way to the marshall's office. Thinking the boy could do with a hot meal before having to face anyone else, Brie started to object. The look Wolf shot her over his shoulder stilled the words on her tongue. He was right. Lazarus had to be stopped. Putting it off even another few moments seemed unthinkable.

The boy was clearly terrified to be in Marshall Campbell's small office with three big men. He sidled up next to Brie and stood there trembling. "Are they gonna put me in jail?" he asked her.

"Oh, Stevie, no." Brie placed her arm around his shoulder.

The boy flinched and jerked away with a cry of pain.

Brie, too, nearly cried out, as a picture of Wolf's scarred back flashed through her mind. Had Stevie been beaten that severely? She prayed not, but it was obvious that a simple touch caused him physical pain.

From the cells in the back room, a man's voice bellowed. "Is that somebody come to bail me out?"

Brie's eyes widened. "Is that Hank Jennings?"

Campbell shot Wolf a curious look, then stepped over and closed the door to the cell room. "That's him. Don't pay him no mind. Now, what's this all about? Who have we got here?" He nodded toward Stevie.

"Stevie." Brie spoke softly but firmly. "Show Marshall Campbell your back."

Stevie looked at Brie, pleading with his eyes.

Brie touched a hand to a small, unbruised spot on his cheek. "It's all right," she murmured.

Across the small room, Wolf watched Brie work her magic on the boy. A deep shudder wracked him. What he wouldn't have given in that moment to feel that soft, delicate hand cup his face in comfort.

Slowly, reluctantly, the boy turned and let Brie lift the back of his shirt. Vivid, ugly bruises even worse than those on his face covered his back. Wolf breathed a sigh of relief that the skin wasn't broken. There were two thin scars, but nothing else except bruises.

Brie lowered the shirt and faced the marshall. "You have to arrest Reverend Lazarus."

"What?" Campbell's mouth fell open. "Are you saying the traveling preacher did that?"

"Tell him, Stevie," Wolf said. "Tell him all of it."

The boy stared at Wolf, and slowly the terror drained from the boy's eyes. "You know," Stevie breathed.

Wolf closed his eyes a moment, fighting the urge to run, then met the boy's gaze. "Yes. I know."

"Know what?" Campbell demanded. "Somebody wanna tell me what this is all about?"

Wolf clenched his jaw and paced to the window. "Brie, why don't you step outside?"

"And leave Stevie here with three men, when he's obviously afraid of men?"

The muscle along Wolf's jaw flexed. He stared out the window fixedly.

Booker shifted on his feet. "Perhaps I can—"

"Lazarus," Wolf said tightly, "has a . . . preference . . . for boys."

Marshall Campbell went utterly still.

It was a full moment in the dead silence that followed Wolf's words before he turned from the window and faced Brie. He watched her face as understanding dawned, followed swiftly by a look of horror that chilled him.

She knew. She finally knew the truth. There would be no more soft touches, no more kisses, no more nights like the one they'd shared. Not for him.

"Dear God," she breathed. "You mean—"

"Yes." Wolf clenched his fists at his sides. "He has no use for women, because he prefers to screw young boys."

Shock stole the color from her cheeks. Wolf watched, striving desperately for detachment, as she tried to swallow.

"Good God A'mighty," Campbell breathed. "Boy," he said softly to Stevie, "is this true?"

Mutely, with tears of shame streaming down his ashen cheeks, the boy nodded.

"Son of a—" Campbell bit off the rest.

"Wolf," Booker said quietly, "you might want to add, for the lady's benefit, that Lazarus likes them of a certain age, and that you were too young for him."

"What difference does that make?" Wolf snarled. He'd seen the horror in Brie's eyes. He'd felt it on his skin. That he had not actually suffered firsthand that final degradation made no real difference.

Stevie turned to Wolf, his eyes widened and filled with awe. "You're the one."

Warily, Wolf eyed him. "The one what?"

"The one who got away. He . . . he talks about you when he drinks."

Wolf turned on Campbell. "If you're not going to arrest him, say so now, and I'll take care of him myself."

"Looks like a miracle to me that you haven't already killed him."

"Not for lack of trying," Wolf muttered.

The door to the office flew open and Campbell's wife, Mavis, rushed in. "Oh, I'm sorry, dear, I thought you'd be ready to come to the picnic by now. It's just getting ready to start. I can introduce you to Reverend Lazarus."

Campbell plucked his hat from a peg on the wall. "I'll send Bo back to watch the office and keep an eye on the cells," he said to no one in particular. To Mavis he said, "Lead the way, hon. I'd like to meet this reverend."

Stevie backed against the wall like a hunted animal.

Campbell eyed the boy for a moment. "Mavis, I need a favor. This is Stevie. I can't answer any questions just now, but he's had a rough time of things lately, and I need you to take him to the house and get some food into him."

Mavis blinked. "Right now?"

Campbell held his wife's gaze purposefully. "Right now. Please."

"But there's plenty of food at the picnic, and young boys always enjoy picnics. Why, there'll be games—"

"Not this time," Campbell said. "What Stevie needs most right now is privacy, food, and maybe the kind touch of a woman. Will you do this for me, Mavis?"

Mavis had no idea what was going on, but Ben had never asked anything like this of her. A dozen questions begged to be voiced, but he'd already said he couldn't answer. The poor boy looked positively terrified, and she could see for herself that he needed tender care and at least a year's worth of good, solid meals under his belt. Why, he didn't even have shoes! Her heart broke.

"Mavis?" Ben asked again.

Mavis looked at Ben, then at the boy. She held out her hand and smiled. "Do you like ham, Stevie? And fresh bread? I baked four loaves just this morning."

Uncertain, Stevie glanced at Brie.

"Go with her, Stevie. Mavis will take care of you. She won't let anyone hurt you, I promise."

Hesitantly, Stevie took Mavis's hand.

"Mavis," Ben called softly as she turned to go. "Don't let . . . anyone near him. No one, you understand? Not a soul."

Lazarus was gone.

He'd been seen strolling casually away from the congregation for a private moment of prayer shortly after his sermon. He hadn't been seen since. His team of horses was still at the livery, his wagon and everything in it still in the alley behind the Methodist church. But the man himself was nowhere to be found.

The town was abuzz with gossip.

"Somebody kidnapped him."

"He ran off with a woman. I said he was too handsome for his own good. Didn't I say that, Mabel? Count the women. Who's missing?"

"Could he have fallen in the river?"

Marshall Campbell organized search parties. Citizens gathered and searched every building in town. Riders followed the river downstream for five miles. Not a sign of the man was found.

From his position in the bell tower of St. Michael's Catholic Church, Lazarus watched it all with detachment. They looked like a bunch of ants running around down there.

But he wasn't worried. They wouldn't find him. After dark he would disappear for real.

Ah, that must be the posse, he thought when a half-dozen men on horseback rode past. The man in the lead wore a star on his chest. One of the riders was the half-breed. Wolf.

Lazarus fingered the scar on the side of his face. "I owe you," he whispered to Wolf's retreating form. "I owe you."

He remained in his hiding place until dark, then made his move.

Brie fell asleep that night on the porch swing waiting for Wolf to come home.

An hour before sunup Booker found her and woke her. "You'll do no one any good this way. Go on to bed. I'll watch for him."

Brie rubbed her eyes and blinked the sleep away, then stared dully into the darkness. Her heart felt like a lump of lead in her chest. Wolf hadn't spoken a word to her, had scarcely looked at her, since leaving Marshall Campbell's office. One question had haunted her since she realized Wolf was riding out with the posse. "Will he come back?"

"He'll come back," Booker said.

Brie spoke the words Booker left unsaid. "But not to stay."

Booker's only answer was silence.

Brie clenched her fingers in the fabric of her skirt. "He can't possibly think his past makes any difference."

"You know better than that, Miss Brie. To him it makes all the difference. Before, he could sometimes forget the past. Now that you know the truth, he'll never let himself forget it. Not when he's around you."

"What truth do I know?" she cried. "I know that you and Charlie Jim are the only family he's ever had. I know he never had a childhood, that he was beaten and abused and . . . and . . . terrible things happened to him."

She paused in hopes her trembling voice would steady. "What did you mean today when you said that Wolf had been too young?"

Booker lowered himself to sit on the top step. "You don't want to hear about any of that. It's not my place to discuss it."

"What did you mean, Booker? Was he . . . abused . . . that way?"

Booker stared up into the night sky. "No, he wasn't. Lazarus preferred . . . older boys. Twelve, thirteen. But he liked to keep a young one around to be sure he had one on hand when the other one grew too old for his tastes."

Brie shuddered and pulled her shawl tighter around her shoulders.

"Wolf was never . . . used that way. But he spent five years being forced to watch what that bastard did to other, older boys. He tried to run off, but he got caught. Every time he got caught, he got a beating. The last time was right before I found him. Wolf and the other boy tried to run off and Lazarus caught them. He beat Wolf first. Whipped him bloody. I imagine he still carries the scars from that one. The other boy . . . Lazarus beat him until he died."

Brie struggled to hold in her tears. She was afraid if she made a sound, Booker would stop talking, and she had to know everything.

"The bastard made Wolf dig the grave and bury the other boy."

Brie shuddered. "And Wolf hit him with the shovel."

"He told you that?"

"He thought he'd killed him."

"Yeah. He said he knew . . . he would have to take the other boy's place then. So he killed him. Or thought he did. They were out on the trail halfway between Cheyenne and nowhere. He was nine years old and terrified that if anyone found him they would hang him for murder, so he took off into the hills. When I found him he was starved half to death and weaker than a kitten from that and loss of blood. If he hadn't been so weak he probably wouldn't have let me near him. I was wintering at a line shack for the Bar B, so I took him to the shack with me.''

Brie hugged herself against the chill of the night. "After what he'd been through I'm surprised he let you touch him.''

"It was a near thing. It took weeks to get him to trust me and finally believe I wasn't like Lazarus. For all he knew, all men were like that.''

"I take it Charlie Jim doesn't know?''

"Wolf never told him, and it wasn't my place. But I think he probably knows. I shouldn't be telling you any of this either.''

Brie cocked her head. "Why did you?''

"Because I've seen the way you look at him. The way he looks at you. I've never seen him as relaxed as he was the day we rode in. He seemed . . . happy. He's never been happy, as far as I know.''

Brie would have spoken, but words failed her. She doubted she would have been able to get anything past the lump of emotion in her throat anyway.

"So if you've a mind to get him to stick around, you need to understand that Wolf thinks his past makes him something less than a whole man.''

"He can't think such a thing,'' she protested.

"He does,'' Booker answered. "When he thinks about his past he feels . . . unclean. Covered in filth that can't be washed away.''

"What do I do, Booker?''

In the darkness she saw him shake his head. "I don't know if there's anything you can do to get through to him. Whatever you did before, it was working. But now . . . I just don't know, Brie.''

* * *

By the time it was light enough to see, the posse was up and moving again, searching the grass and hills, banks and hollows, for any sign of the Reverend Gilbert Lazarus. Wolf didn't believe this second day on the trail would prove any more fruitful than the first. His gut told him they weren't going to find the bastard. They couldn't be that lucky.

In Wolf's mind, Lazarus was still the all-powerful being he'd been years ago. The monster who controlled the world. Who held the power of life and death in his hands.

Wolf told himself it wasn't true, that Lazarus was just a man, an evil one, but a man, nonetheless.

He didn't believe it. If there was a God out there, He surely smiled on Gilbert Lazarus. How else could the bastard get away with his evilness all these years without being found out, without being lynched?

Just thinking of the man made Wolf feel as if a hundred hairy-legged spiders were crawling across his skin. Dirty hairy-legged spiders, for he felt unclean in a way that no soap and water could cure. He was stained clear down to his soul. He knew it.

Now Brie knew it too.

He'd been a fool to get close to her, to let her get close to him. A bigger fool to care, to let her care. To wallow in that caring. To pull it close around him and think maybe, just maybe, it was real, she was real. That maybe . . .

He'd been a fool.

As the day wore on, Wolf kept his eyes trained on the land, looking for any sign of the man. Like the others riding with the marshall, he found nothing. They fanned out, but not too far apart, and swept mile after mile of hill and mesa, valley and canyon. They stopped at every farm and ranch house, every shack. They questioned every traveler, few though they were.

They found nothing. Not that second day, nor the third.

Not a single sign, clue, or word that would indicate Lazarus had ever been anywhere in the area.

And through it all, Wolf fought the vision of Brie that kept looming in his mind. The picture of her when she'd finally realized the truth about the man who had raised him, the truth about the man she'd hired to help save her ranch, the man she'd given herself to.

The look of sheer horror on her face haunted him. The horror that hadn't gone away even when Booker had pointed out that Wolf had not been used the way the other boys had.

She finally had her eyes open. His skin crawled to realize that each time she looked at him now, she would know, and the horror would touch her again.

He couldn't let that happen. He could not let her life be stained by him.

It was after ten that night when Major John Palmer carried a fresh cup of coffee back to his office and closed the door. If Letty caught him drinking coffee this late at night she'd lecture him for an hour about his bad heart. Then she'd start in on him about leaving the Flanigans alone. The woman was a nag, always after him about something. Hellfire, his heart was a lot calmer when she left him alone.

His heart damn near stopped altogether a moment later when he turned toward the room after closing the door and saw the Reverend Gilbert Lazarus sitting on the horse-hide sofa before the empty fireplace. For an instant, Palmer froze. Surprise and anger made his heart pound painfully.

Gone was the fancy white suit. The man before him looked like he'd dressed directly from the poor box at St. Michael's.

Angry with himself for allowing the momentary weakness of fear, Palmer glared at his uninvited guest. "What the hell are you doing here?"

Lazarus smiled. "Such a poor greeting for such an old friend."

"Friend my ass." Palmer walked around his desk and sat down. "I asked you a question."

Lazarus spread his hands out in feigned innocence. "I just wanted to pay my respects to an old . . . business associate, shall we say."

"No, we shall not say," Palmer hissed. "Get out."

"Well, now, I'll be glad to do just that, but I seem to be in a bit of a bind."

"That wouldn't have anything to do with the posse that's after you, would it?"

"How gauche of you to mention it. I could use a little . . . financial assistance. We'll call it a donation to aid in the work of the Lord."

Palmer's eyes narrowed. "The work of the devil, more likely."

"My, my, you weren't so particular the first time we met."

The repeated references to their first meeting made Palmer's blood run cold. The man before him could destroy everything Palmer had worked for his entire adult life. *I won't stand for this.* If Palmer shot the man there in his office, who could blame him? How was he supposed to recognize him, dressed like a rag picker? And he was a wanted man, wasn't he?

As casually as possible, Palmer reached down and slid open his right-hand desk drawer. *Son of a bitch.*

"Looking for this?" Lazarus pulled Palmer's small derringer from behind his back and dangled it, his finger through the trigger guard.

"What do you want?" Palmer demanded, shaking now with rage.

"I told you. Money. Oh, and a horse would be handy, although I'm not overly fond of riding the creatures."

"I don't keep money here at the house."

"Of course you do, my good man. Right there in that

floor safe beneath your chair. If you'd be good enough to open it, I'll be on my way."

Palmer weighed the odds, and didn't like them. Lazarus wasn't pointing the gun at him, but he could, and looked like he would enjoy doing it. "You realize that if you shoot me, you'll never get out of here alive."

"Well, then." The man's smile sent chills down Palmer's spine. "I guess we'll just die together, won't we?"

"You're out of your mind," Palmer breathed.

"Funny you should say that. I thought the same thing about you yesterday in town when I realized you had that half-breed back with you."

Palmer's heart gave a rapid one-two thud, then raced. "What are you talking about?"

"Surely, my good man, you haven't really forgotten that you paid me to take the little waif off your hands all those years ago?"

Suddenly light-headed, Palmer slumped in his chair. "What does that have to do with now?"

Lazarus's mouth dropped open. A moment later he threw his head back and laughed.

"Keep your voice down," Palmer hissed.

"Good God, how priceless. You really don't know, do you?"

"Don't know what?"

The preacher's face hardened. "That half-breed you palmed off on me turned out to be an ungrateful little son of a bitch. I took him in when nobody wanted him and raised him—"

"*Raised* him? You were supposed to *kill* him!"

"—like . . . one of my own," Lazarus continued as though Palmer hadn't spoken. "When he was nine, just about old enough for me to . . . enjoy him, the little fucker got away from me." He fingered the scar along his face. "He almost killed me in the process."

"Jesus H. Christ. He's *alive?*"

Lazarus laughed again. "Oh, this is priceless." He

laughed so hard he pressed a hand to his side as if in pain. Finally his laughter trailed away. "He's alive and well and right here in your own fair town, Major."

If Lazarus said anything after that, Palmer didn't hear him. All he heard was a ringing in his ears. All he saw was a pair of haunting gray eyes. *"Wolf."*

"Yes. He still goes by the name I gave him. You should have seen the way he looked at me. I do believe that a certain young redheaded lady kept him from drawing his gun and shooting me right in the middle of my sermon."

Palmer closed his eyes, then opened them immediately, unable to bear the picture behind his lids. He should have known. Good God, he should have known those gray eyes. Had known them in some part of his mind, he realized now. How could he not? They were his Mary's eyes. His Mary's eyes, on a *half-breed bastard.*

"I'd thought he had forgotten his real name," Lazarus was saying. "But maybe I was wrong."

Palmer turned his head slowly and looked at the man lounging on his sofa as though he didn't have a care in the world. "What do you mean?"

Lazarus shrugged. "It seems a little too great a coincidence that he should turn up here, of all places, don't you think?"

"Are you saying he knows who I am?"

"Now that," Lazarus said, smiling, "is an interesting question, isn't it? Oh, don't look so terrified, Major. Surely if he knew who you were, you would know it by now. Of course, if I don't get out of the state fairly quickly, it would be a simple matter for him to find out, now, wouldn't it?"

Palmer's mind spun in circles. There was another gun in the safe beneath his chair, but he couldn't take the chance of using it now. He couldn't let anyone know Lazarus had been here, and as he'd warned Lazarus, a shot would bring people running.

No, he had to take care of him away from the house. He stared at his desk as a plan formed in his mind. After a moment, he raised his head. "You're right. You need to get away, for your own sake as well as mine. I'll . . . I'll help you all I can."

Palmer not only gave Lazarus the three thousand dollars from his safe, he went personally and saddled two horses in secret, convincing Lazarus that he could show him the quickest route into New Mexico.

Lazarus looked wary, but went along with it. In truth, he never got off into wild country, but he knew he couldn't take the familiar, well-traveled roads this time. Not with a posse after him.

No one heard them leave the Double Diamond headquarters. Palmer led Lazarus west across the mesa. It was nearly two in the morning when they reached the banks of the Purgatoire.

"Here you are." Palmer dismounted, knowing he had just enough time to get home before everyone started rising for the day. "Downstream is New Hope. I suggest you head upriver."

"It would seem the better choice," Lazarus muttered sarcastically. Then his white teeth flashed in the moonlight as he patted his saddlebags filled with the major's money. "Major, it's been a pleasure doing business with you—again."

"There's just one more thing, Lazarus."

"And that would be?"

The shot rang across the mesa, but there was no one to hear it save the creatures of the night.

Chapter Twenty

It was nearly sundown the third day after the revival before Wolf returned to the Rocking F. He hadn't wanted to come back at all, but he'd made promises and people were counting on him.

People. Brie.

He was going to have to face her. He thought he was ready for that, until she came running out of the house as he rode toward the barn. His heart hurt just looking at her, with her flame-red hair loose for once and streaming out behind her. Her face was creased in lines of worry.

He'd done that to her, put lines on her face. Surely no one expected him to be able to live with himself for that.

In hopes of postponing the inevitable, he rode directly into the barn before dismounting. It didn't do any good. Charlie Jim and Booker were there and Brie dashed in before his boots hit the ground.

"Did you find him?" Booker demanded.

Wolf grunted. "You ever try finding a snake in tall grass?"

Charlie Jim nudged Wolf aside and started unsaddling his horse for him. "Even a snake leaves a trail."

"Not this snake, goddammit." Frustration ate at him. Frustration, and dread. He had his back to Brie but he knew she was there. Even if he hadn't been aware of her, he would have known by the way Charlie Jim left off unsaddling Wolf's horse at a nudge from Booker. The two men high-tailed it out of the barn fast enough to raise dust.

Wolf kept his back to Brie and finished unsaddling his horse. When he ran out of excuses, he finally forced himself to turn and face her. But he couldn't make himself look her in the eye. Deep inside, he cringed at what she might see if he let her look too closely at him.

"Supper's almost ready."

It was the last thing he'd expected her to say. Without intending to, he looked at her. The distance, the horror, the disgust he'd expected weren't there. Only a welcome so soft and warm that it stunned him.

"If you've been out with the posse all this time you must be starving," Brie added breathlessly. When all he did was stand there and stare at her, she did her best not to fidget. "I'm sorry you didn't catch him."

"Not half as sorry as I am," he said grimly.

"What will you do now?"

"Eat supper."

"I mean . . . about Lazarus. Will you go after him?"

"Eventually."

Brie clenched her hands in her skirt so he wouldn't see how badly they were shaking. "I know how important finding him must be. If you wanted to go after him, I'm sure Booker and Charlie Jim could take over here for you."

"Are you firing me?"

"No!" He couldn't believe that! "That's not what I meant at all."

"Maybe it should have been."

"Why?"

"It's not like you to be deliberately thick-headed," he said.

Brie stiffened. "No, but it's typical of you," she shot back. "If you think anything I've learned about you in the last few days makes any difference to me—"

"It makes a difference. A hell of a difference."

"Not to me."

"It should!"

"Why?"

"*Why?*" Wolf stared at her, dumfounded. "*Why?* You saw that boy, Stevie. You heard how he's lived, what that bastard did to him."

"Yes, I heard, and it's terrible. Horrible. But what does that have to do with you, with now?"

Wolf turned with jerky movements and started brushing down his horse.

"Answer me," Brie pleaded.

"I should have stopped it!" He whirled on her, his eyes blazing. "I lived with it day in and day out for five years! I saw everything, watched everything. I should have *done* something!"

Brie stared at him in horror. "You were a child! A baby! You can't possibly blame yourself for the vile things that man did." But he did blame himself. The torment of it filled his eyes. "It wasn't your fault, you have to know that. God above, Wolf, none of it was your fault."

"Wasn't it?" His chest heaved as he glared and ground his teeth. "What about all the ones who came after me? What about Stevie? I'm directly responsible for them and I know it. That bastard shouldn't have been alive to get near another boy. He should have *died.*"

"Yes," she hissed, her eyes narrowed. "He should have died. A bolt of lightning should have struck him dead a thousand times."

"He should have died by my hand. I tried to kill him, and I *failed.*"

"Maybe because it wasn't your right to kill him. Did you

ever think of that? What were you, some nine-year-old judge, jury, and executioner? 'Vengeance is mine; I will repay.' Those are God's words."

"Don't you dare quote Scripture to me. I had a bellyful of Bible thumping from that bastard all the years I was with him. God had plenty of chances—years of chances to wipe him off the face of the earth, but He didn't do it. He let him go on and on and on."

"So you decided it was up to you."

"You're goddamn right I did. And you don't much like that, do you?"

"I don't fault you for it, Wolf. I don't," she said earnestly. "Who's to say I wouldn't have done the same thing in your place? All I'm saying is that just because he didn't die doesn't mean you failed. You got away. You survived. That's what matters. His death is between him and God."

"How does your God justify the last seventeen years? How many boys has Lazarus tormented, killed, in the last seventeen years? Where was your God when they needed help?"

"I don't know!" she cried in frustration. "I don't know. I was taught not to play God myself by trying to guess why bad things happen to good people. It's not my place to say, or to judge. Neither is it yours. And none of what's happened is your fault. It's not God's fault either. It's Lazarus's fault."

"Don't forget the man who gave me to Lazarus. I suppose you think I should leave him up to God too."

Brie hissed in a sharp breath. She'd all but forgotten. How could she have forgotten the very reason that had brought Wolf to her? But she couldn't let that stop her from trying to get through to him.

With a toss of her head, she met his glare. "And when Lazarus is dead and you find this other man and kill him, what excuse will you use then?"

"Excuse for what? I'm not making any excuses."

"Aren't you? You've used Lazarus, what he did to you,

the even worse things he did to others, as an excuse to
hunt down this other man. You use both of them as an
excuse to keep everyone around you at arm's length, to
keep yourself from letting anyone get close, to keep yourself from caring."

"They're not excuses," he ground out. "They're facts.
What makes you think I'm even capable of caring?"

"You care, Wolf. You're just afraid to admit it."

"That's ridiculous."

"What excuse will you use when Lazarus is dead and
you find the other man and kill him? When it's all over
and done with, when your past is truly dead and buried,
what excuse will you use then to leave me?"

"I won't need an excuse. Surely by then even you will
have your eyes open wide enough to see what kind of man
I am."

"I know what kind of man you are, probably better than
you do. Let it go, Wolf. Just let the past go and get on with
the rest of your life. That's all you have to do, just let it
go."

"Oh, well, hell, why didn't I think of that? I'll sleep like
a baby now that you've got it all figured out."

Brie crossed her arms and gave him a sharp nod. "Good.
I'm sure you could use the rest. You look tired."

"Dammit." He threw down the brush so hard that it
bounced. "How the hell's a man supposed to get through
to you?"

"What is it, exactly, that you think I don't understand?
That you're to blame for things Lazarus has done? That
you're somehow stained because of him? That you're not
good enough for me?"

"Right on all three," he bit out. "So there's nothing
else to say between us. I'll get your cattle to market like I
promised, and I'll get Palmer off your back. Then I'll get
out of your life."

"Is that what you think I want? For you to get out of my
life?"

"It's what you should want. It's what's best for you."

"Oh, so now you're doing my thinking for me, making my decisions for me, is that it?" Brie took a slow, deep breath to calm her racing heart. It didn't help. She plunged on. "Last week I told you I loved you. You're the same man you were then, and I'm the same woman. My feelings haven't changed."

Wolf closed his eyes and swallowed hard, wondering if he would survive this encounter. "Don't do this, Brie."

"Don't what?" she asked quietly, coming closer. "Don't love you? Don't yearn for the feel of your arms around me again?"

She was close enough now that he could smell the sunshine in her hair. And apples. She'd baked a pie today.

"Don't ache for your kiss? Don't feel so incredibly alive, as if I owned the world, every time I look at you?" She took another step closer.

The hem of her skirt brushed his pants leg. Desperate, Wolf did the only thing he could do. He turned and made for the back door of the barn as if his life depended on it, because he thought just maybe it did. If he fouled her with his touch, surely the God who watched over her would send a bolt of lightning from the clear blue sky and strike him dead.

"She's right, you know."

Wolf stiffened at the sound of Booker's voice, then forced himself to continue rubbing down his horse. He'd left the poor beast standing in the barn all dirty and sweaty. It wasn't like him to ignore his horse, especially because of a woman. Just because this one particular woman scared the bejesus out of him was no excuse to neglect his horse. As soon as he'd seen Brie head back for the house, he'd returned to the barn to tend to the animal.

"You takin' up eavesdropping?" he asked tersely of Booker.

"No need," Booker said calmly. "Most of the time your voices were raised sufficiently to carry to Montana and back."

Wolf fought the urge to cringe. He wasn't used to being embarrassed, wasn't used to shouting at women. But then, he wasn't used to women like Brianna Flanigan, either. A man ought to be able to cut himself some slack, trying to talk sense to a thick-headed Irishwoman out to save him from himself.

"I don't mean you shouldn't kill Lazarus and the other one," Booker said. "They deserve killing, and if you want to see to it yourself, I find no fault in that."

"Glad you approve."

"But like she says, you've got no right to make her decisions for her. I've never seen you like you were the day we rode in. You were laughing, boy. You were happy. Probably for the first time in your life. That woman out there can give you that again if you'll let her. She wants to."

"Butt out of it, Booker."

"I suppose I will," Booker said matter-of-factly. "Just use your head for once and don't throw away your happiness and hers out of some foolish notion that she's better off without you. That's her decision to make, not yours. A man who'll walk away from a woman like that is a fool, pure and simple. Especially when walking away is the last thing he really wants to do." He paused for a moment. "Supper's ready. I'm going to the house."

Wolf stroked the brush down the horse's back again. Then again. And again. Staring blindly at the rich brown hide beneath his hands.

What was a man supposed to do when he knew deep inside that he was right, and he didn't want to be right?

From the dining room window Brie watched Booker leave the barn and head for the house. His steps were slow and heavy, his face somber. Whatever he and Wolf had said to each other obviously left Booker dissatisfied.

He wasn't the only one. She hadn't meant to argue with Wolf, she'd only meant to see for herself that he was all right. To make certain he understood that she was glad he was back.

But he didn't understand, and he wasn't all right. He was blaming himself for things he had no control over. He was leaving her even while he stayed. Soon enough— *too soon*—he would leave for real. As badly as she wanted him to stay forever, she knew she would have to let him go. She only wanted what little time they had left, before the cattle were sold. She wanted that time, needed it, to store up memories to last her through the winter, through the rest of her life.

But she couldn't cause him more pain, and being around her now seemed to hurt him more than anything else.

Yet Brie knew in her heart that she could not give up. Wolf was eating himself alive since realizing Lazarus was not dead. She had to find a way to get through to him, to convince him that his past was not his fault, that he was a victim, and there was no shame in that.

Dear God, show me the way to ease his heart.

When everyone gathered for supper and Wolf did not come, Brie knew she had to do something. She was not above using any method she could to get through to Wolf and make him understand that his past made no difference to her.

"Katy?" she called.

"I'm here." Katy came skipping into the dining room, red ringlets bouncing.

"It's time for supper, but I think Wolf is still out in the barn. Why don't you go get him?"

When Katy bounded out the door, Booker beamed. "You play dirty, girl."

Brie squared her jaw. "I'm not playing."

But then, neither was Wolf. He followed Katy to the house, washed up at the back porch, and sat down at the supper table with the family. He spoke when spoken to, but would not look anyone in the eye. As soon as it was polite, he took himself outside.

"Elly." Brie rose from the table. "Keep everyone in the house tonight, please."

Elly pushed her chair back and stood. "Are you going after him?"

Brie met the eyes of the adults in the room and read no censure in their return gazes, only encouragement. "I am," she said.

Elly rounded the table and stood before her. "I don't understand what's wrong, and I know you said you couldn't talk about it. But whatever it is," she said, reaching out and unfastening the top three buttons on Brie's bodice, "this might help."

Brie's eyes widened. "Elly!"

The younger children watched in confusion, while Charlie Jim turned strawberry red. Booker had the good grace to look away while he grinned.

Rosa looked at Brie's buttons and gave a slow nod. "One more, at least."

Brie felt heat rise in her cheeks.

Elly gave her a quick hug and managed to open two more buttons. "Good luck," she whispered.

With shoulders braced, Brie left the house and followed Wolf as he disappeared down the bank toward the stream.

Wolf knew she was there behind him. He stood at the edge of the stream and ignored her, hoping she would leave. He should have known better.

She didn't hem and haw a bit. She just started right in. "What am I supposed to tell the kids when they ask me what's wrong with you?"

"Tell them you don't know." He stared fixedly at the water rushing past his feet. "Because you don't."

"They think you're mad at them."

"You can tell them I'm not. Tell them now, Brie."

"What?"

Wolf curled his hands into fists. "Go back to the house right now and tell them whatever you want. Just . . . go back to the house."

"And leave you alone, is that it? For how long, Wolf?"

"How long what?"

"How long do you want me to leave you alone?"

"Dammit, Brie."

"For tonight? Another day? A week? A month? How long, Wolf? How long are you going to keep feeling sorry for yourself?"

Wolf whipped his head around and gaped at her. "Is that what you think? That I'm just feeling sorry for myself and this will all go away if I listen to you?"

"Aye, and what else could it be?" she taunted with a deliberate brogue.

Wolf narrowed his eyes. "It wasn't too long ago that you were feeling sorry for me."

"I never!"

"You stood on that porch—" He gestured toward the house, hidden from view by the high, grassy bank. "—and cried because I grew up without a mother."

"Sure and you've got a high opinion of yourself, Just Wolf. I was cryin' because *I* no longer have a mother." The brogue slipped from her voice. "Is that what I have to do this time?" she asked softly, earnestly. "Cry?"

"What do you mean, this time?" he asked despite his determination not to get drawn deeper into this pointless conversation.

"The last time I cried, you kissed me. Is that what I have to do to get you to kiss me again? Or should I just throw myself at you like I did the night we made love?"

Wolf inhaled sharply. Tilting his head back, he squeezed his eyes shut.

Brie couldn't bear the pain she saw carved in his face,

but she could not give in to it or she would crumble. With a hand that wasn't quite steady, she reached up and cupped his jaw.

He jerked as though she'd slapped him.

"Shh, shh." With the tips of her fingers she stroked his cheek. "Let it go, Wolf. Let go of the past. It can only hurt you now if you let it."

Wolf clenched his fists at his sides and tried to pull away from her touch. He ended up leaning into it. He'd always known she held more strength in her delicate hand than he had in his entire body.

She leaned closer until her breath brushed his lips. "We have so little time left together before you leave me," she whispered with a catch in her voice.

"Brie, I—"

"No." She pressed her fingertips against his lips. "I know you'll leave me. I'd rather let you go and wish you well than try to trap you here and have you tear yourself apart trying to get free. You're too much like your namesake, the wolf." Her fingers no longer pressed him to silence. Instead, they caressed his lips. "Don't throw away what little time we have left together on a past that can't be changed."

Wolf knew he should bolt, like he had earlier. If she kissed him, he'd be lost.

She kissed him. Her parted lips pressed to his, so soft, so sweet. He didn't have the strength to pull away. She was so much stronger than he was. He stood there, rock still except for the runaway thundering in his chest, and fought the need to pull her into his arms. Fought it until he shook with the effort.

Still her mouth tormented his. Her tongue traced his lower lip. Her other hand touched his face, trapping him between her soft palms. He'd been right—he was lost. But through the darkness that covered his soul, Brie was there, with her sweet mouth and her gentle hands, like a bright streak of light cutting through the darkness.

With a low moan of defeat, Wolf opened his mouth to hers and wrapped his arms around her. He took everything she offered and begged for more. His mouth was greedy, his hands were greedy. When he cupped her breast in his palm and teased the nipple to hardness, she made a sound of pleasure in her throat that shot straight to his loins.

It was the salty taste of her tears that brought him to his senses. "Don't," he whispered. Shaken by feelings he refused to name, Wolf sipped the tears from her cheeks. "Please don't. God, I never wanted to make you cry."

Brie leaned back slightly in his embrace so she could see his eyes. "These are tears of gratitude."

Bewildered, he searched her face. "Gratitude? For hurting you?"

"For loving me."

Wolf's throat closed, keeping him from uttering the denial screaming through his mind.

"You do, you know." Her smile trembled. "But it's all right if you don't believe it yet." She pressed her head against his chest and wrapped her arms around him. "I'll settle for this."

"No!" The word tore from him in agony. He grasped her shoulders and held her away. "Goddammit, no. Don't *settle,* Brie. Never settle. This isn't good enough for you. *I'm* not good enough for you. *Let me go.*"

"Oh, Wolf." She looked up at him with so much aching love in her eyes that his vision blurred. "I'm not holding you," she whispered.

"Not with your arms," he said roughly. "But you hold me with your eyes, with the way you look at me, with—" Christ, he needed her. It shook him how much he needed her, and sex was the least of it, although it was there, and it was strong. He stared down into her eyes in the growing twilight and read the invitation in those bright green depths. "Brie . . ."

She slid her hands around his neck and pulled his mouth toward hers. "Love me, Wolf." Her lips brushed his. "Just for a little while, just for now. Love me." And with her soft lips, gentle arms, and much greater strength, she brought him, literally, to his knees.

Weak. How could a grown man be so weak as to give in to something he knew was wrong? Not for him. Not wrong for him. She was *right* in his arms, the only woman he would ever need. But for her, this was wrong. He was no good for her. He would hurt her in the end.

But not now, not this minute. Right now he would rather be struck dead than hurt her. She wanted him. Her lips, her hands fisted now in his hair, the way her heart pounded against his lips, all told him how much she wanted him.

He would do this for her, and for himself, and if it felt incredibly selfish, so be it. He wasn't strong enough to turn away. As her hands worked their way beneath his shirt to bare skin, he thought he might never be strong enough.

Her touch was magic. It eased the ache inside him even as it caused a new one. But the new ache was a good one, not one of pain and torment and ugliness, but the clean, honest ache of yearning.

And Wolf knew, as their clothes fell away and he took her down to the small patch of grass beside the stream, that this woman could heal him, if he was only strong enough to let her.

Then he knew nothing, thought nothing, as he feasted on pale, tender flesh and heard the soft sighs of pleasure he brought to her lips. He could do this for her, give her pleasure. And so he did. And in pleasuring her, he found that center of peace, the feeling of home, that he found nowhere else on earth but with Brie.

Taking one precious nipple into his mouth, he found sustenance for his needy soul. Sliding a hand between her legs, he found heat enough to match the inferno building inside him. Joining his flesh with hers, he found an acceptance so complete that it made his eyes sting. And for the second time in his life, his mind whispered a genuine prayer of thanks.

There on the sweet-smelling grass of late summer, they took each other slowly, neither of them in a hurry to reach the end. The sky darkened, but neither paid it any mind. The air cooled, but bodies heated. The stream murmured, but Brie's name on Wolf's lips was softer, his name on hers more musical.

They went up and over the edge together, gently, so achingly gently.

When hearts slowed and skin cooled, they started over. No words, no questions. This time need and fear quickened the pace. Her fear that she would still lose him. His that she would remember his past and be consumed by the horror he'd seen on her face in the marshall's office. His fear that he would never get enough of her to satisfy the hunger, the need.

He took her fiercely this time, hard and fast. She was with him thrust for thrust, urging him on with her hands at his hips, her mouth on every inch of his skin she could reach. She drove him wild. She drove him all the way to the stars, where lights exploded, blinding him to everything but her.

Chapter Twenty-One

Brie woke up in her own bed just before dawn the next morning. Alone. That was her first thought as sleep freed her mind. She was alone.

But last night beside the stream she hadn't been. Last night Wolf had loved her. She held the knowledge close to her heart to stave off the fear that threatened. They had made love four times beside the stream, then he had helped her dress and walked her to the house. He'd kissed her good-night so tenderly that tears threatened at the memory. Yet he'd said not a word and neither had she. She understood all too clearly that she could still lose him. Even in the dark she had been able to see the ghosts and pain of his past in his eyes.

Had those ghosts been what spurred him to saddle his horse and ride out in the middle of the night? She'd lain awake, unable to sleep until she'd heard him return. He'd been gone nearly three hours. The thought of him riding alone in the dark of night made her ache.

Dear Lord, show me the way to bring him peace. Must I let him go? Is that the answer? Please, God, not that.

* * *

Something in the air kept Wolf near the house the next day. He couldn't put his finger on it, but there was . . . expectancy, or something, hanging as hot and heavy as late summer. If he rode out to the cattle, at least one of the men would ride with him whether he wanted them to or not, and he didn't want to leave Brie and the others so vulnerable. Not with Lazarus on the loose.

The string of ranch horses provided the perfect excuse to stick around. While Wolf had ridden each of the animals at least once, there were a dozen or so he'd never ridden out of the corral. Some were still too rank to be trustworthy, and needed work.

Settling fractious mustangs was a hell of a lot easier than walking into that house had been an hour ago, but skipping breakfast with the family, after last night, would have been like slapping Brie in the face. Still, it had taken more courage than he'd expected to look her in the eye.

He'd been afraid. Hell, no woman had ever made him sweat with fear before. But if he'd looked into her eyes and seen shame or horror or any of the dozen other things he'd expected, he wasn't sure he would have lived through it.

Pulling the saddle off the little roan mare he'd just ridden, Wolf shook his head. He would never be able to second-guess Brie. When their eyes had met down the length of the breakfast table, with the boys making feints at each other with their forks on one side of him and Katy dribbling oatmeal into her lap on the other, Brie had smiled at him. A warm, secret smile filled with promise.

How was a man supposed to listen to his head when a woman smiled like that?

He slapped the mare on the rump to send her into the other corral. Out in the yard, Saint Pat started barking. Not his "Hey, kids, can I play, too?" bark, or his "Oh-my-Gawd, it's a squirrel!" bark. This was different. A warning.

And Wolf didn't take the time to wonder when it was he'd learned to tell the difference in the way the dog barked.

With one hand on the top rail, Wolf sprang over the corral fence just as Brie stepped out onto the front porch and Booker called, "Rider coming," from in front of the barn.

Wolf's first instinct was to shout at Brie to get back inside the house where it was safe. He hadn't forgotten the three riders from the Double Diamond, nor that Lazarus was still on the loose. But there was no need for alarm. The rider was Ben Campbell.

"Marshall." Brie stepped down from the porch to greet the man. "This is a surprise."

"Morning." Campbell reined in his horse but did not dismount. "Thought you folks would like to know we found the reverend."

Wolf stiffened. "Where is he?"

"Mac's got him."

"Mac?"

"The undertaker."

Everything inside Wolf stilled. "Lazarus is dead?"

"As dead as they come. Found him floating face down in the Purgatoire. Had a neat little bullet hole right between his eyes."

There was relief, but not as much as Wolf had expected to feel at hearing that finally, once and for all, the man who had beaten and tormented him for five years was dead. Really dead this time.

There was something Campbell wasn't saying. "What?"

Campbell shifted uneasily in his saddle. He glanced once at Brie, then held Wolf's gaze. "I don't suppose you'd care to tell me where you've been lately."

Wolf gave a harsh laugh. "You think I killed him?"

"No!" Brie cried.

Campbell ignored her. "You mentioned that you'd tried before."

The words sliced through Wolf like a blade. Not the

accusation implied—Campbell would be a fool not to suspect Wolf, and Campbell was no fool. What cut was Wolf's sense of failure. If he had succeeded in killing the bastard all those years ago, how many boys would have been spared? How many lives would have remained untainted by that bastard's filth?

"Yeah, I tried. I would have made sure of it this time if I'd found the bastard. And I wouldn't be trying to hide the fact. You're barking up the wrong tree, Marshall."

"Maybe I am," Campbell allowed. "But I wouldn't be doing my job if I didn't ask where you've been since you left the posse."

"Fair enough," Wolf said. "I've been here at the ranch."

"I suppose somebody was with you all the time?"

Wolf snorted.

"I can answer that." Brie crossed the yard and stood next to Wolf.

"I'd rather he did," Campbell said.

"I'm sure you would." Brie gave him a half-hearted smile. "But he won't. Either Booker, Charlie Jim, or one of the kids has been with Wolf every minute since he got back yesterday."

"Fair enough." Campbell nodded, then looked at Wolf. "Haven't been doing any night riding alone, have you?"

Wolf might have taunted Campbell with the truth—he had ridden out last night for a few hours. The barn had closed in on him, and Charlie Jim snored like one of those newfangled buzz saws they used in lumber camps up in the mountains. Brie's scent, sunshine and woman, had been on his skin, teasing him, keeping him awake. He'd tried to outride it, but it hadn't worked.

He shifted his weight, prepared to speak. Before he could open his mouth, Brie sidled so close to him that her skirt covered one of his legs. Beneath the skirt, her dainty little foot stomped down on his instep hard enough to make him wince.

"I promise you, Marshall," she said archly. "I can personally account for his whereabouts last night."

Campbell's eyes widened. "Miss Brie!"

Both Booker and Charlie Jim suddenly found the toes of their boots fascinating.

Wolf would have protested the alibi Brie was providing him, but to do so meant calling her a liar. Damn her. What the hell did she think she was doing?

"If you're going to ask a man how he spends his nights," Brie told Campbell, "you should be prepared for the answer." The smile she turned on Wolf was both teasing and challenging.

Damn her. He was only grateful that none of the kids was around to hear what she'd just done.

Campbell looked like he didn't know whether to laugh, choke, or protest.

Wolf waited until the man rode out, then he turned on Brie. "You little fool! What the hell were you thinking to say something like that to him? You deliberately let him think . . ."

"Yes." Her smile widened. "I did, didn't I?"

"Why?"

Brie sighed dramatically. "I suppose because it was the truth. At least, for most of the night."

Behind them, Booker couldn't take it anymore. He burst out laughing.

Wolf whirled on him, a snarl on his face for Booker and Charlie Jim. "Get lost."

Booker raised his hands as if in surrender. "We're going, we're going. But you might as well give in to her. You appear to be fighting a losing battle, boy."

With a low growl, Wolf grabbed Brie by the arm and started back toward the stream, the only place he could think of where they might have some privacy.

There on the bank, near the spot where they'd made love the night before, he dropped her arm and turned on her. "What the hell did you think you were doing?"

"Giving you an alibi."

"Brie, you lied to the marshall about a murder, for God's sake."

"No, for your sake. You didn't kill that man."

He shook with fury at her blind, stubborn allegiance. "How do you know?" he demanded. "How do you know I didn't ride out after you went in the house and put a bullet right between his eyes?"

Her smile was so poignant it made him ache. "Because I know you."

"You don't know me at all if you think I wouldn't have killed him the minute I laid eyes on him."

Brie shook her head. "I know you rode out last night, and I know you would have killed him, just as I know you didn't."

"What kind of crap is that?" Her rock-solid belief in his innocence shook him. He'd done nothing to deserve such blind faith. Nothing. That she gave it anyway sliced at his pride, humbled him. Yet at the same time, it healed something inside of him that he hadn't known was raw.

"It's not crap," she said defiantly. "It's common sense. If you had killed him, you wouldn't still have such rage in your eyes."

"Goddammit! What do I have to do to convince you to keep your distance from me? Give it up, Brie. Just give it up and let me go."

"Oh, Wolf." Her voice broke and her eyes filled. "I told you before, I'm not holding you. Don't you see? It's what you feel for me that keeps you here."

As the spotted gelding—another ranch horse that needed work—carried Wolf up onto the mesa, he gave the mount its head and let it run. They both needed it. Needed the speed, the exertion, the wind in their faces.

Wolf felt a certain lightness of spirit that he'd never felt before. Was it because Lazarus was finally, after all this time, really dead?

Or was the lightness he felt due to the night he'd spent with Brie?

It could be either one, or both. He didn't care just then. He only wanted to run, to race across the mesa with the sun beating down on him. He didn't want to think, didn't want to face the decisions he knew lay ahead of him. He only wanted to race headlong into the wind.

It didn't help. No matter how fast the horse carried him, Wolf was unable to outrun Brie's words.

You care, Wolf. You're just afraid to admit it . . . It's what you feel for me that keeps you here.

The mustang's hide turned dark with sweat, but still they ran, the horse and the man on his back. Ran until white splotches of foam flecked the scrubby hide. Only then did Wolf slow the animal.

The horse had heart, Wolf acknowledged. And the son of a bitch did like to run. Probably would have run until his heart burst, just for the sheer joy of it.

Wolf wished he could attribute his own need to run to something like joy, but he knew better. Brie was right, on several counts. He was afraid to care. Admitting that, even with no one around but a winded mustang and a circling hawk, was hard. Damn hard. Love was scary business.

But he couldn't deny it any longer, at least not to himself. For weeks, he'd tried to tell himself she would be better off with another man. She deserved better than him. A hell of a lot better.

She deserved a man who wasn't haunted by the ugliness of his past. A man whole of heart and mind and soul. A strong man who would stand beside her, marry her, give her children.

If such a man came along . . . *I'd want to kill him.*

Shit. The thought of another man touching her drove him wild.

She didn't seem to want another man. Said she didn't

care about Wolf's past. Last night, on the banks of the stream . . .

No, he couldn't let himself dwell on last night.

But this morning . . . She'd made a public declaration to the marshall that could ruin her reputation forever, and she'd done it for him. He had to suppose that she really did love him.

Goddamn, he was scared. Nothing in his life had prepared him for the feelings Brianna Flanigan stirred in him. The need to hear her voice, see her smile. The greed for her touch. The wonder, the peace, the rightness of being with her.

All he had to do was give up his revenge, and he could stay with Brie and wallow in her love. Stay and watch Elly marry Letty's son someday, watch Tessa, and then Katy, grow into beautiful women. Watch Sully and Rory reach for manhood and conquer it the way Flanigans conquered everything. The way Brie had conquered a lone warrior wolf.

He could have it all. All he had to do was give up the very thing that had kept him going for most of his life. All he had to do was let go of the past that still haunted him, give up his need for vengeance.

How did a man do that? How could he change his way of thinking, of living, of needing?

You need Brie, whispered a voice in his head.

Yes, he needed Brie, wanted her. She could be his.

Could he let go of his quest for vengeance?

One thing was certain. He would not go back to Brie until he had his answer.

"Come on, boy." He nudged the mustang into a trot. "Let's ride." Maybe if he rode far enough, long enough, hard enough, he could outride his past and face a future free of shadows. Maybe then he would know what he should do. Stay, or go.

* * *

Hank Jennings stood in his boss's office that evening and glared at the man behind the desk. "I can't believe you let me sit in jail for four days."

Palmer eyed his foreman with open contempt. "I can't believe you were stupid enough to get caught doing something that would harm little kids."

"I thought you wanted to get rid of the Flanigans."

"I don't pay you to *think*. I pay you to take orders. Good God, man, I never meant for you to kill children! I just want them off that damn ranch, not dead. I thought you understood that after those three idiots you hired pulled a gun on the youngest boy."

"You never said not to kill anybody," Jennings grumbled.

"Good God, you are as stupid as you look. From now on, you don't do *anything* unless I specifically tell you to. You got that?"

"Yes, *sir,*" Jennings said with a sneer.

Palmer relaxed. "Now, if something terrible was to happen to the half-breed, I wouldn't lose any sleep. Once he's gone, the Flanigans won't be able to hold on."

"You want me to—"

"I want you to do nothing. When I was in town getting you out of jail this morning, I heard the marshall was riding out to bring the half-breed in. Heard they found that traveling preacher with a bullet between his eyes and that Campbell's convinced Wolf did it. The marshall is taking care of our problem for us."

"Huh uh." Jennings shook his head. "You left town too soon. Marshall came back alone."

Palmer stiffened. "What do you mean, alone?"

Jennings smirked. "According to the deputy, Wolf has an alibi for every minute." The leer on Jennings's face was disgusting. "I wonder how he accounted for the nights."

"Are you saying," Palmer asked carefully, tension tightening his chest, "that Marshall Campbell is not going to arrest the half-breed for murdering that preacher?"

"That's right."

Palmer lowered his gaze to stare at the top of his desk. Since the night Lazarus had sat in this very room and told him who Wolf was, Palmer had been trying to figure out just what the half-breed was doing in the county.

Does he know who I am? Who he is?

It didn't seem likely, otherwise Wolf would surely have confronted him by now.

But the only other explanation for why Wolf was so near to Palmer was sheer coincidence. That didn't make Palmer feel a damn bit better. He didn't like coincidence, didn't trust it.

Whatever Wolf's reasons for being here, he was in the way, and he could be dangerous. In more ways than one. That half-breed could ruin everything. He had to be gotten rid of.

"Kill him."

Jennings reared his head back. "Who, the marshall?"

"By God, you are stupid. *Wolf.*"

Slowly, Jennings smiled. "You want me to kill Wolf?"

"I want you to kill Wolf."

"Are you *telling* me to kill him?"

"Yes, goddammit, I'm telling you to kill him!"

"Major Palmer," Jennings said, settling his hat back on his head. "It'll be a pure pleasure."

Chapter Twenty-Two

It was only habit that brought Brie to the breakfast table. She had no desire for food. Wolf was gone. She'd said too much, pushed too hard after the marshall's visit yesterday morning, and Wolf was gone. He'd left her standing beside the stream yesterday and had ridden out without a word. No one had seen him since.

Dear God, how was she to stand the pain?

She'd thought she would be able to survive his leaving, but she hadn't been prepared for him to go this soon, or in this manner. No word. No good-bye.

"He'll come back, Brie."

Katy's assurance from down the table made Brie's eyes sting. She couldn't bring herself to dash the child's hopes that the empty chair beside her would once again be filled by the knight, the warrior they had claimed as their champion.

"I know he'll come back," Katy added.

Brie forced a smile for Katy's benefit. "Maybe," she managed. If her smile wobbled, she couldn't help it.

Her stomach rebelled at the thought of food, but everyone was watching her, so she made an effort to eat. The ham tasted like old leather, the scrambled eggs like sawdust.

Outside, under the front porch, Saint Pat whined. Even the dog missed Wolf, Brie thought. The thumps and thuds told her Saint Pat was wriggling his way out from beneath the porch. It was such a tight fit, she wondered why he kept crawling under there. Surely there were other cool spots that were easier to get to.

The dog let out a trio of yaps.

"It's Wolf!" Sully cried.

Her heart in her throat, Brie sprang from her chair and dashed to the window. It was a full moment before she could turn and face the others. "It was a crow, that's all. Saint Pat was just barking at a crow." She returned to her seat, fighting the urge to run back upstairs and cry into her pillow.

She wouldn't allow herself that luxury. She had a family to care for and a ranch to run. Responsibilities.

Saint Pat yelped again, but no one paid him any mind this time. Until they heard the hoofbeats.

Brie's hope was so strong that it weakened her knees. She couldn't garner the strength to leave her chair again.

"It's him!" Rory cried.

Brie's heart raced. He was back!

Katy merely nodded and broke open her biscuit. "I told you he'd come back."

It was several minutes before they heard Wolf's boot steps on the back porch. The splash of water from the bucket to the basin. The creak of the back door as he entered the kitchen. When he stepped into the dining room, all eyes were on him.

He paused in the doorway.

Brie ate him alive with her eyes. He looked tired, his clothes were dusty and wrinkled, as though he'd slept in them. She'd never seen anything better in her life.

But she wouldn't fool herself into thinking he was back

to stay. This was a lesson for her, one she knew she must heed. He came back this time. But not for long. One day soon, he would leave for good.

Charlie Jim clanked his fork against his plate. "You get lost, boy?"

"No." Wolf tore his gaze from Brie and took his usual place between Katy and Sully.

"People worried," Booker said.

"I didn't." Katy beamed up at Wolf. "I told 'em you'd come back. You want part of my biscuit?"

Wolf cleared his throat and accepted her offer. "Thanks."

Rosa got up and filled his coffee cup from the pot keeping hot on the back of the stove.

"Well?" Charlie Jim demanded as Wolf thanked Rosa. "Where the blazes have you been?"

"I had some thinking to do." He helped himself to a large slice of ham.

"Was it painful?" Booker asked. "You don't seem to have been doing a great deal of it lately."

"Real funny, old man." Wolf took the bowl Sully offered him and scooped the last of the scrambled eggs onto his plate. "I'll be riding into town today."

Brie stared at her plate through blurred eyes. Was this it, then? Had he only come back to say good-bye?

"We need more men to round up the herd, sort it, and get it to market," Wolf said.

Brie swallowed past the lump in her throat. A reprieve. He wasn't leaving yet.

"Of course, we won't be able to keep them on all winter. There'll be plenty of work for the three of us." He motioned toward Booker and Charlie Jim. "But no more than that. If you're staying, that is."

"Are you saying that you're stayin'?" Charlie Jim asked.

Brie held her breath. *Please God, please God, please God.*

"We'll have to hire again next spring."

Brie's head came up with a snap. "We? Does that mean . . . you're staying?"

Slowly, finally, he looked at her. She couldn't read anything in his eyes. Nothing at all. Suddenly she wanted to snatch back her question.

"I thought I would," he said quietly.

Sully and Rory went wild, whooping, cheering, and bouncing in their chairs.

Wolf kept his eyes on Brie's. "Do you have a problem with that?"

Afraid her voice would break, Brie mashed her lips together and shook her head.

Booker looked from Brie to Wolf. "You're staying on as foreman, then?"

His eyes still locked with Brie's, Wolf said, "Foreman. For now."

"For now?" Charlie Jim scratched his head. "What the devil does that mean?"

Wolf tore his gaze from Brie's and looked at Charlie Jim. "It means that for now, I'm going to eat my breakfast."

"In other words, mind my own business."

"You always were a smart man, Charlie Jim."

Brie swallowed back all the uncertainties threatening to choke her and concentrated on the most important thing right then. Wolf was staying. For now. *He's staying.*

Relief brought tears to her eyes. Before anyone could notice, she quickly excused herself and ran through the kitchen and out the back door.

Wolf stared fixedly at his plate for a long moment, silently cursing himself. Then he got up and followed her. He found her with her face pressed against the rough wood of a porch post, the knuckles of one hand stuffed into her mouth while she cried.

"I'm sorry," he said stiffly. "If you don't want me to stay, just say the word."

Brie let go of the porch post and whirled on him. "Not want you to stay? I was afraid you were already gone!"

Never had a question been so hard to voice. "Does that mean you want me to go, or you want me to stay?" Never had an answer meant so much.

"Stay. Stay as long as you like. Stay . . . forever."

The tension that had ridden Wolf since yesterday disappeared with her words and left him weak. To steady himself, and because he just couldn't wait another minute, he wrapped his arms around her and pulled her tight against his chest.

"Stay," she whispered again.

"I'm staying."

When Wolf caught himself whistling on the way into town, he threw his head back and laughed. He'd never felt so good, so free, so at peace in his life. He had Brie to thank for that.

They hadn't settled anything. It was enough, for now, for both of them, that he was staying with her. They hadn't talked about a future. He hadn't told her he loved her.

Marriage. The word used to mean less than nothing to him. Now, with Brie . . . Marriage. Him. *Marriage?*

Yeah, he thought. Marriage. Him and Brie. The idea both terrified and eased him. He'd never thought to marry. But he wanted a life with Brie. Wanted red-haired, green-eyed babies with Brie. Wanted to make sure she was beside him, where she belonged.

Yeah. Marriage.

But first, he had to hire enough men to help them get the cattle to market.

He took up the tune again, and Brie's voice accompanied him in his head. *If that little pink swine won't root, Mama's gonna buy you a brand new boot.*

* * *

Hank Jennings stepped out of the Red Garter Saloon as Wolf dismounted in front of Horace Winslow's mercantile. Hank grinned. This was his chance.

The major had explained things carefully. If at all possible, Hank was to kill Wolf either in a fair fight—or one that would look fair—or in such a way so that folks would think it was an accident.

Accident, hell. Hank much preferred a fight. Right out in the open, where the whole damn town could see that Hank Jennings was the toughest man around.

He settled his hat more securely on his head and crossed the street, catching Wolf tying his horse to the hitching rail. "I wondered what that foul smell was," Hank said, his voice deliberately loud.

Wolf stepped toward the door of the mercantile, trying to ignore Jennings.

Jennings stepped in his path. "Smelled like the north end of a southbound skunk. Now I see it was just a lousy half-breed."

Wolf sighed. A crowd was already gathering. "Would you mind stepping aside?" Wolf asked.

Jennings cackled with laughter. "Whooee! Would you listen to that? *Would you mind stepping aside?*" he mimicked. Then he sneered. "I don't step aside for nobody, much less half-breed trash."

"Let me guess." Wolf propped his hands on his hips. "You wanna fight."

Jennings jeered. "Might as well take on a snot-nosed kid as a stinkin' half-breed who hides behind a woman's skirt. Damn fine skirt, though. You gonna tell us all about what's under it, 'breed?"

"Guess I was right." Wolf took off his hat and stepped back to hook it on his saddle horn. "You're after a fight."

"Is there a problem here?" Marshall Campbell stepped

through the half-circle of men that had formed behind Wolf in the street.

"No problem," Wolf told him.

"Naw," Jennings said, tossing his own hat to the man nearest him. "Hold that, will ya? No problem at all, Marshall."

Campbell pursed his lips and nodded. "Fine. Then you won't mind unstrapping those side arms, will you?"

Wolf waited until Jennings gave in and took off his gun and holster before doing likewise. He lifted his hat from the saddle horn, hooked his gunbelt there, then replaced the hat.

Before he could turn back toward Jennings, the man rammed him in the ribs with his head. Unprepared, Wolf lost his balance and took Jennings with him into the dirt of the street.

Men yelled. Money exchanged hands.

Wolf shoved Jennings away and rose to his feet. "Eager son of a bitch, aren't you?"

"Eager to wipe the street with your ass." Jennings swung at Wolf's head.

Wolf dodged and caught him in the gut with a hard right. The fight was on. Jennings had bigger fists, longer arms. Wolf was ten years younger and moved faster. The bets were running even.

Wolf felt his lip split beneath a left jab, then bloodied Jennings's nose with a left of his own. He wasn't fooled into thinking Jennings would be easy to put down. The man might be older and slower, but he was mean, and he was angry. Wolf used that anger to his own advantage, taunting the man into being careless.

Still, he couldn't avoid those big fists altogether. A two-by-four would do less damage.

* * *

Letty Stockwell, with her son and daughter behind her, stepped out of the mercantile and almost into the melee on the street. James pulled her back. "Watch out, Mother."

In the way of all men, young and old, James watched the fight eagerly. Margery winced as her grandfather's foreman plowed his fist into Wolf's stomach.

Letty ground her teeth. She didn't care for Jennings at all and never had. These days, if truth be told, she didn't care much for her father, either. Now his right-hand man was brawling in the street. This was the last straw. She had told her father countless times to leave the Flanigans alone. Now his foreman was trading punches with their foreman, and people were placing bets. It was just too much.

"Come along, children."

"Aw, come on, Ma," James complained. "Can't we watch?"

"I'll bet Wolf takes him," Margery said before she caught herself.

Letty started to issue a sharp reprimand, but something about the fight suddenly caught her attention. Wolf's shirt was torn, revealing the bronze flesh of his left shoulder blade. At first she thought the dark mark there was a large bruise and wondered how many fights Brie's foreman had been in lately.

But Wolf turned just so, giving her a better view of the mark, and she realized it was not a bruise, but a birthmark in the shape of . . . *Dear God in heaven.*

In shock, Letty extended one hand toward Wolf. "Ten," she whispered. Her vision grayed, then blackened as she crumpled to the boardwalk.

"Mother!" James and Margery scrambled to their mother's side. She lay in a dead faint.

When Letty came to, she found herself on the small sofa in the front room of Dr. Gunter's office. "What . . . what happened?"

"Gosh, Ma." James's face was pale. "You fainted, right there on the boardwalk."

"I . . ." Letty struggled to sit up.

"Easy, young lady." Dr. Gunter's hand, gnarled with age and sprouting long gray hairs along his knuckles, steadied her. "Just sit there a spell and catch your breath."

As Letty straightened, her mind cleared. Memory rushed in. "Wolf! I have to—"

"Now, now, you have to take it easy."

Letty waved the doctor away. "I'm fine. Really. I just had . . . a shock, that's all." She pushed herself from the couch, then had to wait until the room stopped spinning. "I have to find Wolf."

Ignoring the doctor's protest, she rushed out the door and nearly crashed into the four men who were carrying an unconscious Hank Jennings into the doctor's office.

"Gosh," James said. "Looks like Wolf cleaned his clock."

"Where's Wolf?" Letty asked one of the men.

The man, struggling to hold a limp, groaning body, grunted and nodded back down the street in the direction of the mercantile. Letty rushed down the street, her children right behind her.

"What's wrong, Mother?" James lengthened his strides to keep up with her. "Are you really okay? What do you need with Wolf?"

Without slowing her pace, Letty fished into her handbag and handed James some change. "You and Margery go on and have lunch at the café like we planned, then find the major to take you home. He should be through at the bank by then."

James shared a look with his sister, then said, "We'll go with you."

Frantic to find Wolf, Letty wasn't listening. Dozens of questions raced through her mind, taunting her, stabbing her like sharp steel blades. Who was this man called Wolf? Where had he come from?

The birthmark in the shape of a howling wolf's head taunted her. Took her breath away.

Who is he?

In the mercantile, Horace Winslow told her that Wolf had finished his business and said he was heading back to the Rocking F. Letty dashed out of the store and headed toward the livery, where she had left the buggy. The major would just have to find another way to get home.

Chapter Twenty-Three

It was hard to whistle with a split lip, so Wolf settled for humming. *If that brand new boot's not brown, Mama's gonna buy you a golden crown.* The memory of how they'd had to haul Jennings off to the doctor was immensely gratifying. There was also satisfaction in the number of men suddenly willing and eager to work for the Rocking F after the fight.

The best part of the day, however, was returning to the ranch in the early afternoon and having Brie rush out to greet him. Something tightened in his chest at the sight of her smile.

He loved her. It was easy to admit that to himself now. Someday he would tell her. Just as soon as he battled back the fear that everything would go wrong, that something would happen to ruin what they could have together. That she would remember his past and grow disgusted with it. With him.

But all of that was for later. Right now she was glad to see him. Until he reined in and she got a good look at him.

"Wolf! What happened?" As he dismounted, she rushed to his side and gingerly touched his swollen eye.

"Golly, Wolf, you been in a fight?" Sully asked, excited. Rory was with him, eager-eyed.

Booker strolled out of the corral and approached. "I hope the other gentleman fared worse?"

Wolf grinned, then winced at the pain. "Much worse."

"Who'd ya fight?" Rory asked.

"Was there lots of blood?" Sully wanted to know.

"Well, boys, I'll tell you." Wolf reached into his saddlebag. "You wouldn't believe what a man has to go through these days just to buy a little candy."

"Licorice!"

"Golly! Thanks, Wolf."

"You have to share," he cautioned, handing over the treat. "There's enough for everybody."

Only slightly crestfallen, the boys scampered off to distribute the treats.

Booker grunted. "You went to town to hire men. What did you have to do, beat them into submission before they would agree to work for you?"

"The way you nag," Wolf said, passing Booker the reins to his horse, "you're starting to sound like an old woman. Four good hands will be out tomorrow to start work. You can take care of my horse while I figure out where they're all going to sleep."

Booker grunted again, shook his head, then took the horse to the barn.

Only then did Wolf allow himself to focus on Brie. The way she was staring at him with a mixture of caring and concern, he was hard-pressed to keep from kissing her. He stopped fighting the urge and pulled her close for a brief, hard taste.

When he ended the kiss, Brie grinned at him. "You taste suspiciously like licorice."

He shrugged. "I couldn't wait. Already had mine."

"Oh, Wolf." She touched his eye again, his lip. "What happened? You—"

"Hush." He kissed her again. "It was just a little disagreement, that's all."

"A little disagreement? You've been bleeding. Your shirt's torn. You're probably bruised all over."

"Yep, all over." He wiggled his eyebrows. "Wanna see?"

"For shame." She laughed, then sobered again. "Was it someone from the Double Diamond?"

"Jennings."

"What happened?"

Before he could answer, Saint Pat dashed past them toward the road and set up a ruckus. A moment later, trailing a boiling cloud of dust, Letty Stockwell's buggy thundered into the yard. Letty pulled back on the reins so hard, the horse nearly sat on its hocks trying to stop.

"Something's wrong," Brie murmured. She left Wolf's side and rushed to the buggy. "Letty?"

But Letty wasn't looking at Brie. She was staring at Wolf.

"Letty," Brie repeated. "What's wrong?"

"She won't tell us, Brie," Margery said, worried.

"All she's said since she woke up in the doctor's office is that she had to find Wolf," James said.

"The doctor's office!" Brie placed a hand on Letty's arm. "Letty, what is it?"

"She fainted," Margery said, her eyes big. "Right there on the boardwalk, while Wolf and Mr. Jennings were fighting."

Still staring at Wolf, Letty swallowed. "I . . . have to talk to Wolf."

"If it's about the fight—" Brie started.

"I have to talk to Wolf." Frantic now, Letty pushed Brie aside and climbed down from the buggy.

Wolf watched, apprehensive, as Letty rushed toward him. Halfway there, she slowed and came the rest of the way slowly, warily.

"I apologize if the fight offended you or caused you distress," he said stiffly.

Letty stood before him and stared intently. "Who are you?" she whispered.

Surprised, Wolf frowned. "I don't—"

"What's your full name? Your real name? Where do you come from?"

A streak of fire raced up Wolf's spine. She knew something. About him. It was in her eyes.

"Why?" he asked Letty. "Why do you ask?"

"I saw . . . I thought I saw . . . a birthmark."

Yesterday and all last night, Wolf had ridden alone across the mesa wrestling with his past, his future. All his life he had vowed to find out where he was from, why he had been given to Lazarus. The need to know had burned in him from his earliest memories, consuming everything else he might have done with his life. For years he had been searching for the person who could give him answers.

But out there on that vast mesa that stretched from the mountains into forever, he had realized that if he let it, that need to know would cost him the one thing that had become more important to him than anything else in his life—Brie.

So he had let it go. And in letting go, he had been freed.

Now a woman he barely knew stood before him asking the very questions that had haunted him all his life. The need for answers, a need newly buried, rose up again.

Feeling the air stir against his bare shoulder where his shirt was torn, he turned his back to her. "This birthmark?"

Letty emitted a small cry and pressed her fingers over her lips.

Wolf turned to face her. "What about it?"

Letty swallowed hard. Her face was ashen. "Is it . . . a family mark? Did your father have one like it?"

"I don't know who my father was, Mrs. Stockwell. Nor my mother, for that matter. I don't know if either had a birthmark."

As he spoke, Letty's face crumpled into lines of distress.

"You've seen a mark like this before," Wolf stated.

She nodded. "Yes."

"Where?"

Tears filled her eyes as she shook her head. "What is your name, your real name?"

"Letty?" Brie asked, coming to stand beside her.

"Mother?" James took his mother's hand. "What's going on?"

Again she shook her head and stared at Wolf. "Tell me your name. *Please.*"

Wolf took in a long breath, then let it out. She wasn't going to give him anything until he told her the truth. That, too, was in her eyes.

"I don't know my real name," he confessed. "All I know is that when I was four years old, a man who lived in Denver, a man who went by the title of Major—"

Letty cried out again and pressed both hands over her mouth.

"—gave me to a traveling preacher named Gilbert Lazarus."

For the second time that day, Letty's eyes rolled back in her head and she fainted.

"Mother!" both of her children cried.

"Letty!" Brie reached for her, but couldn't hold her. Wolf leaped forward and caught the woman before she hit the ground.

"Inside, quickly," Brie ordered. Breathless with concern, she led the way to the house and into the parlor, where she had Wolf lay Letty on the sofa.

Elly, Tessa, and Rosa rushed in to see what the commotion was about.

"Hurry," Brie urged. "Get me a cool, damp cloth."

"This is just what she did in town," Margery said, eyes wide with fear. "What's wrong with her?"

"I don't know, honey," Brie said. "Stand back and give her some air."

Letty came around before Rosa made it back with the damp cloth. When her eyes cleared, they lit on Wolf and instantly filled with tears. Her face contorted into a mask of anguish. "He lied!" she cried. "All these years! Damn him, damn him, damn him!"

"Letty?" Brie placed a hand on her friend's shoulder. "Letty, tell us what's wrong. Why would you think Wolf lied?"

"Not Wolf," she managed, slowly sitting up. "Dear God . . ." Her voice trailed away as her gaze lit on her children. "What I'm about to say," she told them, "is going to shock you."

Wolf stiffened at her words. His heart pounded. He wanted to shout at her to get on with it, spit out whatever it was she had to say. But he bit back the words and let her go at her own pace. Because he thought he knew what she was going to say.

"No matter what you learn here today," she told James and Margery, "remember that I love you. I love you both so very much, and I loved your father."

"Mama," Margery cried, "you're scaring me."

"I'm sorry. It's not scary. I do love you, I will always love you." Then slowly she turned to Wolf, who squatted beside the sofa. "Sit here, please." She patted the cushion beside her.

With his gaze locked on her steady blue eyes, Wolf sat beside her.

Another tear rolled down Letty's cheek and her lips trembled. She struggled visibly for composure. "Your name," she said, her voice hitching with emotion, "is Bridger Ten Wolves Palmer."

Deep inside Wolf, waves of ice and fire fought for supremacy and left him trembling.

"I called you . . . Ten. You're . . . that is, I . . . I'm your mother."

Blood roared in Wolf's ears, drowning out the gasps and cries of shock from Letty's children, Brie, the others gathered in the room. He heard none of it, saw none of them. He saw only the woman before him, heard only her words echoing over and over. *I'm your mother. I'm your mother. I'm your mother.*

After a long, stunned silence, James spoke. "He's our brother?"

"Your half brother." With effort, Letty tore her gaze from Wolf and looked at James and Margery. "Before I met your father, I met . . . and loved . . . another man. He was a Shoshone scout for the army at Fort Bridger, where the major—he was a captain then—was stationed."

"Wolf's father was a Shoshone army scout?" Brie breathed.

The trembling inside Wolf spread to every muscle. *Shoshone.*

"His name," Letty said, turning back to Wolf, "was Nine Wolves. The first son of every first son in his family bears the mark of the howling wolf."

As if stretching muscles long unused, the wolf on Wolf's shoulder flinched and prickled.

"When my father found out about us, he sent me away to Denver with my mother. He . . . knew I was expecting you. I was sixteen. He ordered me to . . ." She swallowed and closed her eyes, unable to go on.

"To get rid of me," Wolf finished for her.

"Yes."

"Why didn't you?" he asked stiffly. "A white woman carrying a half-breed bastard?"

"Don't call yourself that!" Letty gripped his arm with desperate strength. "Don't call yourself that."

"No one would have blamed you," Wolf went on. "No one would ever have needed to know."

"I would have known," she cried. "How could I rid myself of a child I desperately wanted? Nine Wolves was . . . I loved him. No one will ever know how much I loved him. He was good and kind and strong. I see much of him in you. You have his birthmark, his hair, his mouth. My

God, I can't believe I didn't recognize you on sight. When you look at me, I see my mother's eyes."

Wolf's throat closed with emotion. He had his father's mouth, his grandmother's eyes. He wasn't a nobody, sprung from nothing. The woman before him was his mother. His *mother*.

"My . . . father. What happened to him?" Wolf asked.

With her eyes still closed, Letty took a deep breath, then looked at Wolf. "He was killed during a scouting mission for the army the day after Mother and I left for Denver. That's one reason I wanted you so desperately. You were all I had left of him. When the War started and Father was sent east, Mother and I stayed in Denver and I told her I intended to have you, keep you. I have to suppose she never told Father in any of her letters during the War."

She looked at Wolf and smiled sadly. "You were the most adorable child, so sweet and loving, so beautiful. I used to sing to you."

Wolf swallowed. *If that golden crown falls down, then you'll be the sweetest little baby in town.*

"What—" He had to stop and clear his throat before going on. "What did you sing?"

Letty closed her eyes and smiled. "Hush little baby, don't be sayin' a word. Mama's gonna buy you a pretty red bird."

Wolf's vision blurred. A lump the size of a cantaloupe rose in his throat. *The song. No wonder . . .* Here, then, was a memory that hadn't been totally denied him.

"I loved you so much." Letty's voice broke with emotion.

Wolf flushed beneath her words. No one but Brie had ever told him he was loved. No one. Not ever. The ache in his chest nearly took his breath away. God, how he hurt. "Then why," he asked, his voice cracking, "did you give me away?"

"I didn't!" Letty cried. "Great God in heaven, I would have killed to keep you with me! He told me you were dead." She folded her arms across her stomach and rocked back and forth. "He told me you were dead."

Outside the dog barked, but no one paid any mind.

"Who?" Wolf demanded, knowing the answer. "Who told you I was dead?"

"My father! Oh, God, it was my father. There was a fever. Mother died less than a week before he came home at the end of the War. I'd been trying to fight it off, but when he arrived and I knew there was someone to take care of you, I . . . I gave in, I guess. I was delirious for days. When the fever broke and my mind cleared—" Letty's jaw tightened and her eyes hardened to blue glass. "—he told me you had come down with the fever, too. That because you were so young, just four, you didn't stand a chance. *He told me you died.*"

Letty tilted her head back and squeezed her eyes shut, sending more tears to streak her damp cheeks. "May God forgive him, for I cannot. I knew you were a surprise to him, but he was my father. You were his grandson. I trusted him. And *he told me you died.*"

Overtaken by anguish, Letty fell forward into Wolf's arms and sobbed.

Wolf closed his eyes against the rage inside him at what had been done to this woman, and to him, by the one man on earth they both should have been able to trust. There was time later for hate, for vengeance. For now, he held a weeping woman to his chest, praying he wasn't squeezing her too tight.

Mother. She is my mother!

His heart cracked in two with a pain so sharp it stole his breath. *She's my mother.* Something inside him shifted, righted. Soared.

"You stinking half-breed bastard, take your hands off my daughter."

At the sound of Major Palmer's voice from the doorway, everyone froze.

"Whatever he's been telling you," Palmer claimed, his face flushed with fury, "is a goddamned lie."

With a shriek of pure rage, Letty sprang from Wolf's

arms. "He's told me nothing! The lies are yours, all yours. All these years you made me think he was dead. All these years!"

The major's face turned ashen and sweat beaded his upper lip. He read the bitter anguish on his daughter's face, the confusion stalking his grandchildren. The hatred from Brie. From the half-breed radiated a white-hot rage from those gray eyes that haunted his dreams, his nightmares. Mary's eyes.

"You gave him away!" Letty nearly choked on the words. "You lied to me and gave my son to a stranger. My *son!* Your own grandson." Slowly Letty steadied. Her voice cracked with ice. "May God forgive you, for I never will."

"I did it for you!" Palmer burst out, frantic to regain his daughter's affection. "Don't you see, Letty? I got rid of him for you, so you could have a good life. A fine man like Lamar Stockwell never would have looked twice at you with a half-breed bastard hanging on your skirts. I did it for you!"

"A fine man like Lamar," Letty said coldly, "would have understood that I'd loved another man before him."

"Not a goddamn stinking *Indian.*"

"In fact, he did understand. I told him all about Nine Wolves. You didn't know that, did you? I told him about the son I'd lost. Do you know what Lamar did, Major? He held me while I cried, and he cried with me. He cried for the son I'd lost."

"It's a miracle he didn't leave you when he found out," Palmer thundered.

"Leave me? No, he didn't leave me. He asked me to marry him." The cold disdain in her voice gave way to the heat of rage. "It was for nothing, do you hear me? You tore apart two lives for *nothing,* except your own need to control everything and everyone around you."

"He was supposed to die!" Palmer shouted. "If Lazarus had done like he'd promised, it wouldn't have been a lie. The little bastard should have died!"

Every ounce of color drained from Letty's face. "What are you saying?" Her eyes turned black with horror. "You gave him to someone you thought would kill him?"

This was Wolf's fault. If the son of a bitch had died like he should have, none of this would be happening. Palmer wondered what his daughter would think of her long lost bastard if she knew the kind of pervert Lazarus had been. Maybe all was not lost. Maybe if Letty knew the full truth . . . "He wasn't supposed to be killed right off," Palmer said with a smirk for Wolf.

"That's enough, Palmer." Wolf clenched his fists against the urge to draw his gun and put a bullet right between the man's eyes. "You've hurt her enough already."

"You stay out of this, you son of a bitch," Palmer said with a growl, his face flushing red again.

"I take back my wish for God to forgive you." Letty stepped closer to her father, eyes narrowed with hatred. "I hope you rot in hell for what you've done."

"Don't you dare talk to me like that!" He raised his arm in the air.

"Touch her," Wolf said coldly, flexing his fingers, "and you die. Right here, right now."

Palmer lowered his arm and glared his hatred at Wolf. "By God, Jennings should have finished you off in town today like I ordered. Nobody threatens me. Nobody." He reached for his gun.

Wolf had his gun out and aimed before Palmer cleared leather. The only thing that kept him from pulling the trigger then and there was that he didn't want to shoot the man in front of James and Margery. They were the innocents in all that had happened. Wolf did not want to be responsible for forcing them to watch their grandfather die before their eyes.

Letty and Brie didn't see Wolf's draw, but they saw Palmer's. With a shrill cry, Letty lunged at the major. Her fingers, like long, sharp claws, raked furrows down his face.

In reflex, maybe in shock, Palmer batted at her hands, then shoved her away.

Letty stumbled backward and fell.

Wolf roared in rage.

Palmer raised his gun and aimed at him.

Brie saw the gun pointed at Wolf and screamed. Without thought, she threw herself in front of him. As she landed against his chest, two bullets fired.

It seemed, for a moment, that both men had missed. They stared at each other in hatred. Until Brie slumped and Wolf put his arm around her to steady her. It was then that he felt her blood seep between his fingers.

Wolf's rage turned to ice. His mother lay in a heap on the floor; Brie was shot. *Jesus, God, she can't be dead.* Without thought, Wolf pulled the trigger again. And again. And again.

Palmer staggered with the impact of each bullet. Four slugs in his chest, and the bastard didn't fall.

Grimly, purposefully, Wolf put his last two shots directly between his grandfather's eyes.

Chapter Twenty-Four

Wolf was certain that his heart did not beat even once from the instant he realized Brie had been shot until he placed her on her parents' bed down the hall and she moaned, letting him know she was, for now, still alive.

From the hall Rosa shouted orders. "Hot water! Scissors. I need scissors. Stop that crying. There is no time to cry. I need bandages."

Through the commotion, Wolf heard Booker and Charlie Jim burst into the house, brought, he knew, by the gunfire.

Where was Rosa? What was taking her so damn long?

Oh, God, Wolf thought, looking down at Brie. She was so pale, with not a drop of color left in her ashen cheeks. With a flick of his fingers he whipped off his bandanna, folded it, and pressed it against the wound near her shoulder blade to stem the flow of blood. His hands were shaking. Hell, he was shaking all over.

Rosa and Letty rushed in carrying towels, scissors, bottles, and jars. "Step aside," Rosa ordered. "We will tend her."

Wolf narrowed his eyes. "I'm not leaving."

A few moments later, he almost wished he had left, when Rosa turned Brie onto her stomach and used a small knife to dig the slug from her back. Wolf held Brie down throughout the ordeal to keep her from moving and doing further damage to herself. The pain of the knife probing for the bullet roused her momentarily—just long enough for her to cry out, whimper, then pass out.

Wolf was shaking from head to toe and couldn't stop. She could have been killed. Because of him. Trying to save him.

Sweat coated his face and made his hands slick against her skin. Finally, the slug was removed and Rosa motioned him out of the way. She padded the wound and bound it tightly. The three of them, Rosa, Letty, and Wolf, watched as the pad turned red with blood. Rosa hissed and changed pads, applying more pressure, until finally, the flow slowed, then stopped.

"Thank God," he muttered.

"Sí gracias á Díos, Wolf. He has surely answered our prayers this day. With plenty of rest, she will be fine."

"You're sure?" he asked, afraid to take his eyes off the slight rise and fall of Brie's back with each shallow breath she took.

"I am sure."

"Come away," Letty said softly, pulling Wolf toward the door. "Let us make her more comfortable, then you can sit with her."

Reluctantly, Wolf went. At the door, he paused and turned back to Letty. "I'm . . . sorry."

"For what?"

Would the mother he'd just found hate him now? "I killed your father."

Letty's mouth trembled. "Please don't apologize. He gave you no choice. In truth, I'm not certain that I wouldn't have killed him myself if I'd had a gun."

* * *

It was Wolf's fault that Brie had been shot. He'd killed his own grandfather. She wouldn't want him now. That was the thing that kept circling in Wolf's mind as he sat beside her bed and prayed for her to wake up and assure him that she was going to be all right. Other thoughts crowded in as well. The knowledge that he had a mother. A half brother and half sister. The identity of his father. A name, a real name.

And a birthday, he thought with irony. Before she had left to take the major's body home for burial, Letty had informed Wolf that next week, September 17, to be exact, was his twenty-seventh birthday. She was coming to the Rocking F that day to celebrate.

Who would have thought he would even know when his birthday was, let alone that anyone would want to celebrate it?

But overriding everything was the knowledge that Wolf had shot and killed his own grandfather. Killed him without regret.

To expect Brie to react the way Letty had was, to Wolf's mind, like expecting the sun to rise in the west.

It was nearly dawn the day after the shooting—with the sun rising in the east, he noted grimly—before Brie stirred. She had been moaning in pain off and on most of the night, nearly driving Wolf to his knees with his helplessness to ease her suffering. But this time, she opened her eyes.

Wolf slid from the chair to his knees beside the bed, afraid to touch her for fear of accidentally causing her more pain. But he ached to touch her.

"Wolf?"

"I'm here. No, don't move," he said as she shifted her shoulders and cried out. "Don't move, honey."

"What . . ." Her eyes widened. 'The major'.

"It's all right. Don't worry about him now. You're going to be fine, but you have to take it easy."

"I was so scared. He was going to shoot you."

"He was going to try. Dammit, Brie." He leaned his forehead down and pressed it to hers. "What were you thinking to step in front of me that way? You could have been killed. You almost were."

"I couldn't let him shoot you."

"I thought I knew how much you meant to me until that moment when I realized you'd been shot and I thought . . ." His voice shook. "God, I thought I'd lost you."

Brie swallowed and closed her eyes. "I thought I was going to lose you."

"So you stepped in front of me and took the bullet yourself." A shudder of remembered terror shook him.

"What happened after that?"

Wolf raised his head. "Are you thirsty? Here." From the pitcher beside the bed, he poured her a cup of water and helped her sip. "Are you warm enough? Too warm?"

"What happened, Wolf?" Her eyes searched his for answers. "What aren't you telling me?"

Wolf bit back a sigh and pulled his chair closer to the bed. There were some things a man couldn't say while on his knees. He braced his forearms on his thighs and stared down at his hands rather than look at her. "This should wait until you're feeling better, but you have a right to know, since it's going to change how you . . . feel about me."

"I love you," she said softly.

In the glow of the lamp on the dresser, Wolf met her gaze. "And I love you. You have a right to know that, too. I've never said those words to another living soul. I love you."

Brie's eyes filled and spilled over.

"Don't," he whispered achingly. With an unsteady hand,

he wiped the tears away. "It'll never work for us, Brie. I'm not the kind of man you need."

"You're exactly the kind of man I need. You're the *only* man I need."

"I killed him, Brie."

"The major?"

"The major. My own grandfather. I didn't just shoot him. You need to know that. I emptied my gun into him. Deliberately."

Brie's eyes slid shut. "I'm glad he's dead."

"Brie . . ."

"Am I supposed to be shocked that you shot him?"

"Shouldn't you be? Maybe you don't believe me."

"I believe you. He got what he deserved. Now it's your turn."

"To get what I deserve? There's a scary thought."

"Does it scare you to realize that you suddenly have a family?"

"No. I'm not sure that's sunk in yet. What scares me is that one day you'll look around and realize that I'm a man who's capable of murder, who has committed murder, and you'll grow to hate me."

"It wasn't murder," Brie protested.

Wolf rubbed his face with both hands. "I think we should pick this up later, when you're more rested."

"It was self-defense, not murder. Either way," she said before he could interrupt, "he's dead. Now you have no more excuses."

Wary, he asked, "Excuses for what?"

"To try to convince me I shouldn't love you. Nothing you can say, nothing you can do, can change how much I love you, Wolf. If you're going to leave me, you're going to have to do it because you want to, not because I don't love you."

"You think I want to leave you?" he cried hoarsely.

"Don't you? Isn't that why you've just spent the last ten

minutes trying to convince me what a terrible man you are because you killed a man?''

"I don't want to leave you."

"Well let me tell you something, Bridger Ten Wolves Palmer." Her voice rose, her eyes narrowed. Her brogue thickened. "If you hadn't killed the bleedin' bugger, sure as Saint Paddy drove the snakes from Ireland, either Letty or meself would have done it. For what that man did to you and Letty, I would gladly have killed him meself. So now who's the terrible person here, I'm askin'.''

If he laughed, she would think he was laughing at her, and she'd probably hurt herself when she tried to clobber him. "Are ya sayin', then, lassie, that ya be wantin' me to stay?''

She blinked in surprise at his perfect brogue. "Are ya makin' fun 'o me, Just Wolf, or have ya been hangin' around that Irishman Mahoney too long?''

Wolf slid from his chair again and pressed his face against her neck, all urge to laugh and tease gone as quickly as it had come. "I love you."

With her uninjured arm, Brie held him close. "Then stay with me," she whispered.

"I want to." He raised his head and looked into her eyes that spoke of exhaustion and pain. "But—" Fresh fear cut off his voice.

"But?" she asked, her voice filled with trepidation.

Wolf took a deep breath for courage. "You mentioned once that I was too much like my namesake."

"I remember. I didn't want you to feel trapped."

"There's another thing about wolves you need to know."

Slightly wary, Brie frowned. "What's that?"

It was now or never. With another deep breath, Wolf held out his heart with both hands. "Wolves mate for life."

Brie gasped.

"Will you marry me?"

Her eyes filled with tears. "Oh, yes, I'll marry you."

Relief, and something he'd never felt before that was

called joy, left Wolf limp, yet stronger than he'd ever felt. A slow smile spread across his face.

The man without a name, a past, or a home, suddenly had all three. He was Bridger Ten Wolves Palmer, and his mother used to sing to him.

The most beautiful, courageous, loving woman in the world was in love with him. In her family and his, plus the children Wolf and Brie would bring into the world, the warrior had his tribe.

The wolf had found his mate.

Epilogue

On the date of his twenty-seventh birthday, Wolf experienced his first birthday party in twenty-three years. The first party he remembered ever being thrown in his honor. Letty fussed over him, and he let her. Brie got tears in her eyes watching the two of them get to know each other.

Margery accepted her new half brother into her life and heart and made no bones about it. When James was a little slow to come around to accepting Wolf, Margery bloodied his nose. She considered the act an extra birthday gift to Wolf.

A few weeks later, before Wolf and the crew drove the cattle to market, Wolf and Brie were married by Reverend Benton, who had finally returned to the Methodist Church in New Hope. Booker stood as best man, and Charlie Jim gave the bride away.

It was the first time Wolf had ever stepped inside a church, and he went willingly, for Brie. And maybe a little for himself, too. Surely his new family, his bride, and all the happiness they brought him were blessings. Maybe there was a God after all.

During the next two years, the Rocking F and the Double Diamond underwent many changes. Hank Jennings was, quite naturally, out of a job. After a little arm-twisting— very little, Booker liked to joke—Charlie Jim took over the running of the Double Diamond as the new foreman. Under his guidance, James learned to read the land and cattle, to judge men for their character. And under Charlie Jim's management, the grass on the east mesa and in the south valley was coming back.

James was nineteen now, and Elly Flanigan was leading him a merry chase. He'd changed his mind about going to college, deciding that he could learn more from Charlie Jim than from any textbook.

The rest of both families and the hands of both ranches were laying bets on who would make it to the alter first, James and Elly, or Charlie Jim and Letty.

Wolf stood on the front porch at the Rocking F and grinned, remembering how his mother had blossomed in the glow of Charlie Jim's hesitant courtship.

Booker and Rosa spent their summers on the Rocking F, but Booker claimed Colorado winters were too cold for his aging, island soul. Before the first snow flew each year, he and Rosa headed south to the warmer climes of Mexico where Rosa had family.

In New Hope, Marshall Campbell had retired last year and opened up the gun shop he'd always wanted. He was teaching the trade to Stevie, who had stayed with Ben and Mavis. No one who wasn't in Campbell's office that day Wolf, Booker, and Brie had brought Stevie in had ever learned of Stevie's past. Wolf sometimes wondered if even Mavis knew all of it.

But word had gotten around that the kind-hearted marshall and his wife had taken in an orphan. Now they had three other orphaned children in their home. Mavis finally had the children she'd always wanted.

As Wolf gazed out across the yard toward the new corrals

they'd added last year, Sully shot out of the barn with Rory and Saint Pat hot on his heels.

"What are you smiling about?"

Wolf turned toward the door as Brie stepped out onto the porch. "The boys," he said, laughing. "They're at it again."

"Well, so is your daughter. She told me she simply would not go to sleep until you held her."

It still amazed Wolf that something so beautiful and perfect as the bundle he took from Brie could have come from any part of him. Three-month-old Caroline, named for Brie's mother, was a daddy's girl through and through.

He shouldn't be amazed at Caroline's beauty. She was a miniature replica of her mother, with fiery red hair and milk-white skin. Her eyes were blue, but Brie and Letty assured him they would soon turn green. He was going to hold them to that.

He'd been right the day he and Brie had married. Surely no man had ever been more blessed. Without a single hesitation, he humbly whispered a prayer of thanks.

WATCH FOR THESE ZEBRA REGENCIES

LADY STEPHANIE   (0-8217-5341-X, $4.50)
by Jeanne Savery
Lady Stephanie Morris has only one true love: the family estate she has managed ever since her mother died. But then Lord Anthony Rider arrives on her estate, claiming he has plans for both the land and the woman. Stephanie soon realizes she's fallen in love with a man whose sensual caresses will plunge her into a world of peril and intrigue . . . a man as dangerous as he is irresistible.

BRIGHTON BEAUTY   (0-8217-5340-1, $4.50)
by Marilyn Clay
Chelsea Grant, pretty and poor, naively takes school friend Alayna Marchmont's place and spends a month in the country. The devastating man had sailed from Honduras to claim his promised bride, Miss Marchmont. An affair of the heart may lead to disaster . . . unless a resourceful Brighton beauty finds a way to stop a masquerade and keep a lord's love.

LORD DIABLO'S DEMISE   (0-8217-5338-X, $4.50)
by Meg-Lynn Roberts
The sinfully handsome Lord Harry Glendower was a gambler and the black sheep of his family. About to be forced into a marriage of convenience, the devilish fellow engineered his own demise, never having dreamed that faking his death would lead him to the heavenly refuge of spirited heiress Gwyn Morgan, the daughter of a physician.

A PERILOUS ATTRACTION   (0-8217-5339-8, $4.50)
by Dawn Aldridge Poore
Alissa Morgan is stunned when a frantic passenger thrusts her baby into Alissa's arms and flees, having heard rumors that a notorious highwayman posed a threat to their coach. Handsome stranger Hugh Sebastian secretly possesses the treasured necklace the highwayman seeks and volunteers to pose as Alissa's husband to save her reputation. With a lost baby and missing necklace in their care, the couple embarks on a journey into peril—and passion.

Available wherever paperbacks are sold, or order direct from the Publisher. Send cover price plus 50¢ per copy for mailing and handling to Penguin USA, P.O. Box 999, c/o Dept. 17109, Bergenfield, NJ 07621. Residents of New York and Tennessee must include sales tax. DO NOT SEND CASH.